OPERATION DARKSAIL

By K.P. Hayden

Text copyright © 2013 K.P. Hayden

Second Edition

All Rights Reserved

ISBN 978-0-9857915-8-2

Edited by: Rebecca Stroud

Editorial Assistance: Kimberly G. Hayden

Cover Design: Ott & Associates

Richmond, VA

OPERATION DARKSAIL

Dedicated to all who gathered sea legs upon her decks:

USS Raymond A. Spruance DD-963

The Silent Warrior

11/27/1972-12/8/2006

The stalwart men and women of the United States Navy

OPERATION DARKSAIL

Prologue

November 22, 1718

Ocracoke Inlet, North Carolina

"Damn this excruciating wait. If there is truly a merciful God in heaven, let this day come and be done with."

The British Naval lieutenant adjusted his cutlass and repositioned a pair of pistols tucked behind the thick leather belt strapped to his midsection.

Mine hands must possess sight of their own, he thought to himself. *The slightest hesitation shall be tallied in shreds of bloodied flesh.*

He drew his next breaths in slow, careful lengths, determined to remain in control of his waxing anxieties. The darkness borne of a moonless night had proved a most formidable adversary, an orgy for the sword-wielding demons of one's imagination. He sensed tension growing amongst his men as well; each likewise grappling phantoms crafted of their own inner workings.

Perhaps this is an omen. The harbinger of a pending slaughter. My fellow officers had warned me not to command this exercise.

"Death is a sea sailed in quest of self-glory," one proclaimed.

"Only an idiot would proffer the devil-maker his own neck on such a foolish lark," remarked another.

The lieutenant ripped those thoughts from his mind. "I shall not grant defeat a victory whilst I have unspent powder at arm's reach," he said out loud.

He stepped to *Rochelle's* railing, the larger of two sloops Governor Spotswood of Virginia had provided for the assault, and peered seaward toward the spot where lecherous pirate Captain Edward Teach was anchored the evening prior.

A tepid fog held at bay the flint to morning's torch. The quality of the breeze, rising from the northeast and then rapidly retreating, was no less unsettling. Reliable winds would surely be required to navigate the shallow waters of Pamlico Sound during battle. His confidence in his pilot, a Proclamation freebooter himself no less, was a month's wage short of nil. Yet the rogue had delivered both sloops through the narrow inlet and to secure anchor. He should be thankful for that much.

"He's still out there, Captain," said a reassuring voice behind him. "Wager the Queen's bustle on it. I can smell the bastard's rum."

"Yes, but where?" the lieutenant asked. "Teach knows these waters the way a harlot knows the stains of her bed linens. Must we just sit and wait for him to slithers up and dash us to splinters?"

The lieutenant and his first officer had been through many close scrapes together. Though a subordinate, he was a most valuable confidant; reliable as the tides, yet as nimble as a man twenty years less.

"It matters not what roost he has chosen, my Captain. He shan't strike before the cock crows for one and all."

Hearing such confidence helped calm his own nerves a

2

little. "I shall infer from that, my friend, that your soul harbors little fear of this battle?"

"Fear makes way upon a sea of ignorance," came his answer. "Death has been upon me more occasion than I've patience to recall. If it claims no retreat this day, so be it."

"Well spoken," replied the lieutenant. "Yet there resides immense power in fear. Leveraged by ambition, it can forge a most formidable alliance. Are the marines prepared?"

"Only those topside required to hoist anchor and make sail. The rest are positioned below as instructed."

"Very well, then," said the lieutenant. "Do what you must to keep them stable."

Rochelle boasted a contingent of thirty-five elite sailors and marines. The lieutenant could not see *Ranger*, the second of Governor Spottswood's sloops, but knew she and her crew of twenty-four men were just a stone's throw to starboard, waiting dawn just as they.

Edward Teach and his men had already destroyed one of Her Majesties swiftest frigates during a ship-to-ship engagement on open sea. Never before had pirate gunnery been so overwhelming; never before had a pirate crew sailed away, at will, in victory against a vessel of the Royal Navy. With no cannons at his disposal now and precious little water to maneuver in, what chance did these two small sloops truly possess?

To the east, over the narrow rise of harrowed sand and scrub juniper known as Ocracoke Island, the darkness slowly began to recede.

"SHIP HO!" shouted the topman. "Two points to starboard. SHIP HO! Two points to starboard."

"Hoist anchor and unfurl the tops," the lieutenant commanded. He turned to his first officer. "Marksmen to their posts. Three shots to summon *Ranger*."

True to his reputation, Teach had devised a scheme to provide his gunners a clear line of fire to both *Rochelle* and *Ranger*. *Adventure*, the smallest vessel in Edward Teach's five-ship pirate fleet, was less than a quarter-league seaward with nine cannons run out through the ports on her top deck.

As *Ranger* made for *Adventure's* port side, the lieutenant piloted *Rochelle* toward her starboard. The plan was to draw *Adventure* into a crossfire of muskets, forcing Teach's men to take cover rather than work their cannon. Once they had achieved the advantage both sloops could close for the kill. But the attack had to be swift for any chance of success.

"The pirate's windlass is still at anchor, sir," reported the first officer. "With so much at stake, surely he'd not forget to lift the hook."

The lieutenant raised his spyglass. Indeed, *Adventure's* anchor was still out. It was difficult to believe such unprecedented good fortune. *Rochelle* and *Ranger* continued to close. Yet Teach made no attempt to sail. Something was critically amiss.

Suddenly *Rochelle* skidded to a stop. It was as though the hand of Neptune had reached out and grasped her keel. The lieutenant hooked his arm around the mast to keep from tumbling to the deck. He cast an eye toward *Ranger*; she had also ceased making way.

Teach had repositioned his ship in the darkness to place an expansive shoal between *Adventure* and both British sloops, cutting off any possibility of advance against him. A brilliant maneuver.

The lieutenant helped his first officer to his feet. "It appears my earlier question has secured its own resolve. When this is done, remind me to separate our pilot from his head."

A booming laugh resounded across the water. "Ahoy! 'Tis a beautiful morning for a stroll of the beach, is it not? Though, from where I stand, it seems your compass has led you astray. What foul luck."

The infamous pirate captain Edward Teach waved a hand toward his starboard cannons. "Perhaps the breath of my black angels shall grant the freedom you desire. It would seem most inhospitable of me not to assist. Prepare to be boarded by HELL." He hoisted his massive cutlass into the air and shouted. "FIRE!"

Blackbeard's port cannons thundered; smoke vaulted from the line of black muzzles. *Ranger* absorbed the brunt of the first crushing broadside. The lieutenant raised his glass again to assess the damage. *Ranger's* single mast had been pruned even with the gunwales; two gaping holes now filled her port hull.

The lieutenant recognized *Ranger's* captain. His voice was labored, suggesting injury, but still clearly in command of his vessel. The synchronous crackle of musket fire from his snipers split the air. Grounded and broken, *Ranger* and her crew were not ready to give up the fight, but now they would be of no use during the assault.

Adventure's starboard cannons erupted next; a spinning bar shot hit the center of *Rochelle's* jib, tearing a gaping hole but sparing the yard and riggings. Two balls crashed through the gunnels. With so few men on deck, there were no injuries. A fourth and a fifth shot both splashed harmlessly into the sea.

"Six anything not needed for battle," shouted the lieutenant. Lessening *Rochelle's* weight may lift her from the sand and spare her *Ranger's* fate.

The men brought up water barrels and other nonessential ballast and tossed it over the side.

Wishing no further delay, Teach cut loose his anchor and fired a second starboard salvo at *Rochelle*. This time his gunner's aim was not so expertly placed. Only one shot struck solid timber; three of *Rochelle's* seamen were bloodied, but her hull and mast were spared again.

Assisted by a surging tide and another measure of breeze, *Rochelle* inched forward. Possessing no cannons, *Rochelle* had to close quickly and take the fight to *Adventure* hand-to-hand.

But the breeze flushed from the sails once again, leaving *Rochelle* drifting to starboard. The lieutenant ordered all sweeps to their locks. As his men positioned and then lay back on the oars, Teach's starboard cannons intermittently spat flames again. Three balls burst through *Rochelle's* port freeboard, propelling a shower of splinters skyward, maiming another half-dozen men.

A report came from below that *Rochelle* was taking water. The lieutenant realized another battery of Teach's cannon would likely dispatch his efforts to the bottom of Pamlico Sound. "Man the siphons!" he shouted. The pumps would extract the water and buy a little more time.

Rochelle had to get moving. The lieutenant grabbed one of the sweeps himself. Gritting his teeth, he threw all his strength behind it; it felt as though the whole sea were pushing back against him.

"*Adventure* has halted," yelled the first officer.

The lieutenant ceased rowing and spun around; a string of profanities rose above the distant musket fire. Sure enough, *Adventure* was not moving. *Could it be?*

Another fusillade of curses delivered his answer. Eager to advance the battle, Teach ran afoul the exact shoal he'd used earlier in his defense. Perhaps *Rochelle* was not dead yet.

The breeze kissed *Rochelle's* sheets once again, coaxing her forward. The lieutenant ordered the sweeps idled and resumed his attack under sail. If the winds held this time, he might reach *Adventure* before Teach could reposition his cannons.

He ordered the bodies of the mutilated seaman to be left on deck and gave extra pistols to those still capable, instructing each to appear dead, too. The element of surprise could yet be his. Only the helmsmen and an able midshipman accompanied him topside. The rest were directed below once again.

As *Rochelle* crossed *Adventure's* bow, the pirates launched a salvo of bottles with strips of burning cloth trailing behind them. The lieutenant dove for the deck and covered his head with both arms. Teach's grenades exploded, filling the air with a pulpy smoke and a tempest of twisted metal shards. The helmsman, doing likewise, leapt back to his feet and crisply maneuvered *Rochelle* alongside. The young midshipman, not recognizing the pirate's ploy, failed to seek cover. He now lay on his back writhing in agony from a multitude of gashing wounds. There was no time to provide medical assistance.

The wind whisked away the smoke. Teach surveyed *Rochelle's* deck and saw the array of dead seamen. Proclaiming victory close at hand, he ordered his men to cross over. The lecher himself was first atop the gunwales.

The lieutenant waited until approximately twenty pirates were aboard then sounded the charge. *Rochelle's* hold flushed open and a wave of whooping and shouting marines flooded on deck.

Undaunted, Teach rallied his men. Cutlasses clashed and pistols blazed. The numbers of wounded quickly mounted.

Wielding his massive cutlass before him like a windmill, Teach slashed everything in his path. He paused only to pull cocked pistols from a brace slung loosely across his burly chest, firing and then hurling the spent weapons into the melee; shouting insults behind them.

A stocky, round-faced pirate gashed the lieutenant's left arm with a dagger; a burning pain rocketed up to his shoulder. The lieutenant jerked a pistol from his belt and shot the culprit in the chest at point blank range, pitching the pirate backward over the rail into the waters of the sound.

With sweat rolling down the sides of his face and blood

7

dripping from his left fingertips, the lieutenant paused to wrap his wound with a strip of linen he'd tucked inside his shirt. He evaluated the battle: his marines were fighting with dirks and cutlasses in pockets all across *Adventure's* deck. Most, if not all, bloodied; stepping over and around the dead and wounded as they struggled. It appeared the scales of victory could tip either way.

There was no cause for delay. The lieutenant sought out his first officer and seized him by the arm. "Circle around Teach's flank and wait for me to gather his attention. When pistols are drawn, lay to him with your sword from the opposing side."

The lieutenant stripped from his jacket, threw down his battle helmet, gripped a cutlass in both hands and forged ahead. He clashed steel with that of a lesser foe. With eyes firmly affixed on the pirate master, he disposed of the other with a single stroke of his blade.

The gap between him and Edward Teach quickly closed. Each drew a pistol. At the precise moment, the lieutenant's first officer laid into Teach, as instructed, with a dirk, sinking the stubby blade deep into the pirate's side. Teach reared back and roared like a wounded beast, recklessly discharging his weapon. With all his weight on the heels of his boots, the bullet sailed harmlessly over the lieutenant's head.

The lieutenant's aim however held true. His bullet struck Teach directly in the center of the chest. Teach roared again. Wavering only slightly, he switched his cutlass to his right hand and lunged forward.

The lieutenant could not believe the pirate's incredible resolve. Everything the stories had foretold of his physical prowess was true, if not understated. The lieutenant threw aside his pistol and hoisted his cutlass athwart his body in an act of sheer defense. With one powerful stroke, Teach severed the blade in half.

Both pistols spent, his cutlass destroyed, and no available

shelter or means of escape, the lieutenant watched Teach raise his heavy steel once more, certain to inflict upon him a finishing blow. But as Teach slammed the blade downward, a British seaman leapt onto his back and raked a dagger across his throat.

Gasping for air, blood spewing from this newest and many other wounds, Teach faltered one more time. A gang of marines set upon him, stabbing his body from all angles. Those of *Adventure's* crew still standing dropped their weapons. They could do nothing but watch in amazement.

Weakened, but still spouting vulgarities, Teach windmilled his cutlass, managing to separate his attackers once again. He pulled the last pistol from his brace and was lugging the hammer to a ready position when a long, frothy breath gurgled outward from his lungs. He tilted his head to the side, dropped to his knees, and toppled face first onto the deck.

The British sailors rang out in cheer. The lieutenant knelt to examine the remains of his powerful adversary. It had taken no less than five pistol shots and twenty cutlass wounds to chart Captain Edward Teach's final course.

The lieutenant grabbed a cutlass from the deck and hacked the pirate's head from his neck. Then hoisted the bloody mass into the air by its hair and shouted, "VICTORY!!"

OPERATION DARKSAIL

Chapter 1
0530: 21 August 2008
Southern Atlantic Ocean

Six hours had passed since patrol aircraft made initial contact. Commander Robert Maynard knew there was no telling how long a disabled submarine, as was now the general consensus had been drifting amid undersea currents before that. Twenty-four hours—maybe more—submerged and helpless; a bauble in the hands of a great, indifferent child. One hundred-twenty lives at stake, maybe more. Typically the optimist, Maynard had a very uneasy feeling.

The thirty-six-year-old officer straddled the threshold to the starboard bridge wing of the United States Navy destroyer, *Spruance;* his athletic, six-foot frame nearly filling the width of the opening, and searched eastward into the small rift forming between darkness and light: A breeze tugged at the sleeve of his khaki uniform: Daybreak posed a host of new problems.

He removed the *Spruance* baseball cap and ran his hand across a mat of cropped black hair; then checked his watch: *Spruance* had been trailing the mysterious light for thirty minutes.

The helicopter pilot's voice broke in over the air communication radio frequency. Maynard stepped back inside the bridge.

"*USS Spruance,* this is *Wind Devil.* We're at hover, twenty yards behind the light source. Altitude 100 feet. No visible surface structure. Speed has slowed to five knots, heading due south. Impossible to make a positive identification. Awaiting orders."

"Captain," said Maynard. "I suggest conducting an active sonar search while *Wind Devil* has a firm visual. The moment the sun breeches that horizon there's going to be a thousand new reflections to sort through."

"You make the call, XO," answered Captain Lawrence, *Spruance's* Commanding Officer, as he was reaching for the radio handset. "*Wind Devil*, this is *Spruance.* Keep all eyes focused on that light. If it's being towed by a submerged vehicle, the cable should create a visible trail of cavitation. *Spruance* out." Lawrence returned the radio transmitter and stepped over to the bridge radar repeater.

Maynard punched the button on the 1JS phone circuit call box located on the bulkhead behind the chart table. "Bridge, Sonar Control."

"Sonar, aye," replied the Sonar Watch Supervisor.

"Sonar, go active. Search window ten-thousand yards. Center your sweeps around bearing two-zero-zero."

"Sonar, aye. Going active."

Within seconds, the fluted tones of a two-hundred-fifty-thousand watt sonar transmission resonated through the bridge. If a submarine had ruptured a nuclear reactor, the pressure hull would have likely been compromised as well, driving the whole superheated mass steaming to the floor of the Atlantic Ocean. So there must have been some other type of propulsion failure.

But why didn't the captain blow ballast and surface? Maynard asked himself. *And how can a disabled submarine drift at speeds which exceeded the velocity of the prevailing currents?*

The first report came back from Sonar—no echoes—as did the second and third. After five complete sweeps, there were still no contacts.

No echoes meant there was no solid object to bounce the transmitted sound energy back to *Spruance's* sonar transducer. Sonar had confirmed what Maynard already suspected: The light they were following was not a submarine distress beacon.

A flash of white lightning suddenly streaked diagonally across the starlit sky, engorging the tender shoulders of dawn into the full light of day. The focal spur speared the water in the same general vicinity as *Wind Devil* and a deafening clap of thunder broke directly overhead.

Maynard recoiled from the boom and a wave of pressure rolled through his skull, exacerbating the discomforts of a night deprived of sleep. He rushed over and snatched the radio handset. "*Wind Devil*, this is *Spruance*. Still with me?"

The radio speaker crackled. "That heater damn near boiled my eggs, Commander," the pilot exclaimed. "It scored a direct hit on our patch of light. Stopped it dead in the water."

A strange cool sensation washed across the back of Maynard's neck and the hair on his forearms stood straight up. Experience had taught him well when to trust his instincts. "*Wind Devil*, increase your altitude and back away from that contact," he ordered.

"*Spruance*, there's some kind of new movement. The glow is increasing." The pilot's words were rushed and with elevated pitch. "It's dividing into three separate lights...they're rising out of the water like they're attached to something. A larger structure's becoming visible beneath them."

"Sweet Mother of Jesus. *Spruance,* it's a ship! A whole damn brigantine! Just raised up out of the water right in front of me under full sail...there's not so much as a blemish on her canvas!"

"Whose ship?" demanded Lawrence.

"*Wind Devil.* Confirm your last transmission."

The heavens off *Spruance's* port bow exploded in a massive display of twisted blue and white tridents of lightning. Flash after flash hurtled toward the sea and *Wind Devil*; thunder fists battered *Spruance's* weather decks and superstructure. Maynard shielded his eyes with his forearms to prevent the harsh light from destroying his night vision.

The forward lookout called down to the bridge. "SURFACE CONTACT. Three bright lights, forty degrees off the port bow."

"*Wind Devil*, this is *Spruance*. Do you copy?"

Maynard held his breath awaiting a response. He keyed the radio transmitter again, nearly crushing the handset in his grip. "*Wind Devil.* Do you copy?"

An excited voice sang out over the Combat Information Center communication circuit. "Bridge, Combat. We've lost radar contact with *Wind Devil!* I repeat. We have lost radar contact with *Wind Devil.*"

Maynard caught the Officer of the Deck by the arm and slapped the radio handset into her hand. "Keep trying."

He grabbed a pair of binoculars from the chart table and raced onto the port bridge wing, joining Captain Lawrence.

The torrent of lightning slowed and a bank of thick, swirling clouds materialized above the three lights. The sea surrounding the lights swelled with towering walls of water, knifing left and right like a herd of frightened stallions. Yet, where *Spruance* was, the sea remained perfectly still.

Maynard listened as the OOD made another attempt to contact *Wind Devil.* He lowered his binoculars and looked into the bridge, hopeful of some kind of response. There was none.

Maynard returned his gaze seaward...to his amazement, the

storm had disappeared. He stared in shocked disbelief.

Before he could fully process that development, the forward lookout shouted over the sound power phones again. "New surface contact, forty degrees off the port bow."

Maynard rotated forty degrees; a little farther to the east the sun was now racing over the horizon like a huge ball of fire. "I've got it," he exclaimed.

"Where in the HELL did that come from?" He tracked the vessel through his binoculars for several more seconds. "It's a large sailing vessel, Captain, closing at a high rate of speed."

Maynard lowered his binoculars and looked Lawrence square in the eyes. "Three masts, all sails fully intact. There's no way a heavy sailer could cut that blow in one piece."

Lawrence shouted into the bridge. "Officer of the Deck. Get me a fix on that new contact. Reveille the crew and post men on the O2 and O3 levels to search for debris from *Wind Devil*. Petty Officer of the Watch, muster boat crews for rescue detail. Helm, steer a course of two-zero-zero and make turns for thirty-five knots."

He turned to Maynard. "Lay to Radio and get a message to Commodore Perkins at Destroyer Squadron Twenty-four Headquarters. Tell him our helicopter is down and to get us some help out here."

"Captain, Combat reports no radar contacts off the port bow," exclaimed the OOD.

Reveille was passed over the 1MC general announcing circuit. Maynard ducked back inside the bridge, rushed to the radar console and dialed-up the surface contact tracking display himself; Captain Lawrence came around on the other side. Just as the OOD had reported, there wasn't another surface contact within thirty nautical miles.

"That's impossible." Maynard searched out the port bridge

wing hatch again. The sailing vessel was now within plain sight.

"What in the hell's going on around here?" griped Lawrence. "Officer of the Deck. Belay those orders. Sound General Quarters!" He pointed at Maynard. "Get back here as fast as possible."

A series of loud gongs rang throughout the ship. The Petty Officer of the Watch shouted into the 1MC microphone. "This is not a drill, this is not a drill! GENERAL QUARTERS! GENERAL QUARTERS! All hands man their battle stations!"

Maynard sprinted from the bridge and angled down the ladder toward the deck below. He was met by a line of sailors headed up, buttoning shirts and zipping dungaree trousers.

"Make a hole!" he shouted.

The men squeezed to one side far enough to let him pass. He hit the deck in full stride and ran aft to the radio shack, punched in his security code and threw the hatch open. Senior Chief Radiomen Charles Balf was barking radio console assignments to his men.

"Get me Commodore Perkins at DESRON Twenty-four," Maynard ordered. "On the double."

Balf grabbed a pair of headphones and put through the call himself to Destroyer Squadron Twenty-four Headquarters in Mayport, Florida. When he reached Commodore Perkins, he handed Maynard the headset.

Maynard summarized the downing of *Wind Devil* and requested assistance. "No, sir, the ship was not on radar before the storm ensued," he said. "And we're still not picking it up. Closing at a high rate of speed...yes, sir, the same spot where *Wind Devil* went down. Thank you, sir, we'll take every precaution." He handed the headset back to the chief. "DESRON Twenty-four's staying on the line."

"Yes, sir," Balf replied.

Maynard bolted from radio and raced toward the bridge, his mind clicking through every reasonable scenario he could formulate to explain what was happening. Not one made any sense.

Spruance's engines reversed and Maynard felt her shudder toward a stop. He broke into a full canter and scaled the ladder back up to the bridge. When he arrived, he found Captain Lawrence staring through one of the port windscreens, his eyes pinched down to mere slits. Maynard retrieved his binoculars from the radar console; the port bridge wing fifty-caliber machine gunner locked and loaded her weapon.

"DESRON Twenty-four is staying on the line," Maynard said. "What have I missed?"

"I don't know where in the hell this thing came from," said Lawrence. "But I intend to hold my ground."

Maynard raised his binoculars and swept the ship from stem to stern. What he discovered made his throat go dry. "They're packing cannons, for Christ's sakes."

"I count twenty topside on the spar, and another ten gun hatches, starboard side, main gun deck below," Lawrence replied. "I'll bet a week's pay they're fully stocked and ready for business. No flags, no antennae and only that Grim Reaper-looking character topside at the helm."

Maynard zeroed in on the helmsman. Its lanky body was shrouded from top to bottom in a brown robe; the skin on his hands was the color of ivory. More like bone than flesh.

The icy sensation on the back of Maynard's neck migrated to his stomach. "Should we muster the security force?"

"I've got M-60 and M-14's gunners positioned on the signal bridge and helo hanger, and the fifty-caliber machine guns on both bridge wings. All shooters have orders to return fire."

The wind flushed from the ship's flack sails and it coasted to within forty yards of *Spruance's* port beam. The water between

17

the two flattened to a sheet of glass.

Maynard examined every inch of the ship. It was approximately one hundred-ten feet long and of either French or Italian architecture, early eighteenth-century. Each of her three towering masts was hewn from three lengths of timber, only slightly tapered on the rise, stout and true—virtually impossible to fabricate from white pine stock commercially available today.

Every detail was immaculate, right down to the sculptured billet head of a buxom island maiden attached below the bowsprit and expanse of carved scrollwork adorning the freeboard and bulwarks. She had obviously been detailed by master shipbuilders.

The timbers on the after-decking and taffrail were a lighter shade of brown, indicating that section may be newer than the rest of the ship—streamlining deck houses and poop decks was a common practice in the days when merchant vessels were pressed into naval service.

Spruance's helmsman maintained perfect separation between the two ships; nothing moved topside on either vessel.

Finally, a man perhaps four-inches taller than Maynard, and forty pounds heavier, appeared at the base of an amidships ladder just forward of the helmsman and proceeded up on deck. He was dressed entirely in black, with a profuse beard and shoulder-length black hair. His shirt was opened to the waist exposing an oxen-like chest; a wide-bladed cutlass with a solid gold handle and knuckle cage was loosely belted to his left side. The wind swirled the thatch of hair about his head obscuring most of his facial features except for the eyes which were vigilant and piercing.

He strode to the railing and glared up to where Maynard and Lawrence were standing. "Who are you?" he shouted. "And from whence have you come?" His speech was coarse and defiant, with a definite British accent.

The Boatswain's Mate of the Watch handed Captain

Lawrence the 1MC microphone and switched on all topside loudspeakers.

"This is the Commanding Officer of the United States Ship *Spruance*. State your intentions or give way."

"Give way?" roared the dark figure. "Why, we've just arrived." He pointed a finger at Lawrence. "No man dispenses of me as though I were a child. Show your face so I may know the coward that you are."

Maynard grabbed a bullhorn and stepped toward the hatch.

"Stand fast, Commander," Lawrence ordered. He pulled the bullhorn from Maynard's hands. "I'll handle this."

"Captain, I don't think..."

Lawrence stepped through the hatch onto the port bridge wing. Maynard followed him that far.

Lawrence raised the bullhorn to his mouth. "Who are you? And what do you want?"

The dark figure stared at him for several moments and then broke into laughter. "What a magnificent vessel for such a pathetic stature of a man. Why, yours should easily make three of mine. But on this day size is of no consequence." He raised his powerful arms from his sides, palms out, as if welcoming an old friend.

"I'd be nothing more than a humble planter, Captain of the *Queen Anne's Revenge*, following the trades to northern markets. And I wish but to have a word with that delightful young lad lurking in the shadows behind you."

QUEEN ANNE'S REVENGE! Maynard raised his binoculars and zoomed in on the man's face again; the dark figure was staring straight back at him.

Maynard's pulse doubled. He twirled the binocular strap around his neck and stepped onto the bridge wing.

Lawrence reached back and stopped him. "You know these people?"

19

"Not exactly," Maynard replied. He and the other captain locked eyes. The face was all too familiar, similar to one his mind's eye had attempted to create thousands of times.

Queen Anne's captain flashed a wry grin.

Lawrence shoved Maynard toward the hatch. "Then get back inside the bridge. That's an order."

Maynard didn't move. The muscles in his legs would not respond.

"That's an order, Commander! Go back inside the ship."

Maynard stepped into the bridge, leaving the hatch open behind him.

Lawrence lifted the bullhorn to his mouth again. "This is my ship and you will address me alone."

"How charming," the dark figure said. "One coward protecting the whelp of another. Well, since you're unwilling to produce your lad, permit me to introduce mine."

He raised a clinched fist above his head. A column of seamen armed with muskets filed up on deck and formed a line to his left and right. Maynard counted fifteen in all, dressed as if they had just walked off the set of a Disney film.

Maynard glanced at the young sailor on the bridge wing, white-knuckling *Spruance's* port fifty-caliber machine gun. Her eyes were racked with fear, yet she faithfully manned her post. He wasn't at all comfortable having her exposed like that but, if weapons fire erupted, he would need that fifty-caliber gun.

"Relax and breathe deeply, Gartside," he said to her in a calm, controlled voice. "But be prepared to take cover."

In one fluid motion, the dark figure drew his cutlass and severed a line attached to the mainmast pinrail. A flag bolted up to the top of the mast. Maynard immediately recognized the imagery: a skeleton holding an hour glass in one hand and a bloodied spear in the other. It was the standard of the infamous pirate Blackbeard.

Identical to a souvenir his father had purchased him at a gift shop in Cape Hatteras twenty-five years ago.

Queen Anne's starboard gun ports slung inward and the working ends of ten cannons thrust out. Her captain pointed his cutlass at Lawrence. "I shall make my request but once more and once more only. Permit me to speak with the son of Maynard. I intend him no harm. At least for now."

All of Maynard's internal alarms sounded. *How does he know my name?*

"Mister, you are making a colossal mistake," Lawrence shouted. "You are perpetrating an act of aggression against a vessel of the United States government. I am authorized to defend this property with every means at my disposal."

"I sense the advantage is mine, dear Captain. Hence you are the one making a mistake. So be it, you leave me no choice." The bearded figure hoisted his cutlass into the air and slashed it down onto the railing. "FIRE!" he shouted.

Maynard leaped through the hatch and hauled Lawrence to the deck. *Queen Anne's* cannons responded with a series of deafening blasts and she disappeared behind a vaulting wave of smoke. Cannon balls smashed into *Spruance's* hull; bullets splattered against the thick windscreen glass above him; Gartside's lithe body slammed against the bulkhead and slid downward, leaving a smear of blood; the M-60 machine guns on the signal bridge and helicopter hanger clattered into action.

Maynard sprang to his feet, lifted Gartside and shuttled her through the hatch into the bridge. He next grabbed the handles of the powerful fifty-caliber gun and spun its muzzle seaward. He aimed at the spot where *Queen Anne's* captain was last standing and cut loose a hail of lead, pinning the firing mechanism until the barrel burned cherry-red.

As the smoke cleared, Maynard saw his last tracer and two

21

bullets pierce the center of the dark figure's chest. The big man didn't as much as rock backward onto his heels.

Maynard's lungs cramped as though every cell in his body sucked in a slug of oxygen at the same instant.

The shooting came to an abrupt halt; separation between the two ships was now less than twenty yards.

Queen Anne's deck was deserted again except for her helmsman and captain. The big man looked down at his chest and laughed. "Good show, young mate. But not good enough."

Maynard felt a hand clasp his shoulder.

Queen Anne's captain reached inside the opening of his shirt, producing a cocked pistol. He pointed the weapon and fired.

The hand on Maynard's shoulder recoiled sharply. Maynard whirled around and saw Lawrence stagger backwards and clutch his chest, blood gushed from between his fingers.

Maynard intercepted Lawrence as he stumbled forward and dragged him toward the bridge. The Officer of the Deck and the chief quartermaster rushed over and took Lawrence from his arms.

The hole in Lawrence's chest was making wet, gurgling sounds. The quartermaster tore open the captain's shirt and placed the palm of his hand directly over the wound.

"Get us out of here," Lawrence commanded.

"Ninety degrees to starboard and full bells," Maynard shouted to the helmsman. Lawrence's blood had leaked down the front of Maynard's khaki uniform. He wiped his hands on his pants and rushed back onto the bridge wing.

The dark figure was pointing his cutlass at him. "Run, you cowardly bastard. Run!" he shouted. "We shall make our acquaintance soon enough. Even your planks of iron are no match for me."

Spruance's engines screamed into high-fire. Maynard stepped back into the bridge and steadied himself against the chart table as the ship made a steep roll to starboard. "Fire control solution," he demanded.

"Still nothing on radar, sir," answered the OOD.

Why wasn't that ship showing on radar?

Maynard's first instinct was to circle back and blast every splinter of *Queen Anne's Revenge* from the sea. But without radar guidance his five-inch guns and missile systems were useless. He couldn't battle cannons with machine guns and wasn't certain yet how badly *Spruance* had been damaged. He glanced down at his injured captain. First thing he had to do was get out of range of *Queen Anne's* guns.

A medical team rushed onto the bridge. Master Chief Hospital Corpsman Nita Brown applied a battle dressing to Captain Lawrence's chest as the others loaded him onto a stretcher. Maynard caught a glimpse of Lawrence's face as they rushed him away: his jaws and cheeks were clinching against the pain, but his eyes could not contain the extent of his terror.

Maynard bolted back onto the bridge wing; blood was everywhere. He leaned over the railing and searched aft for *Queen Anne's Revenge*. Her sails were full once again and the dark figure was standing at the taffrail, waving his cutlass above his head.

Chapter 2
0745: 21 August 2008

Maynard toured *Spruance* to assess the damages. Seven projectiles from *Queen Anne's* cannons had breached her hull leaving a row of jagged, half-moon tears; two were dangerously close to the waterline. Captain Lawrence and Seaman Gartside were the only crewmembers seriously wounded; Maynard realized *Spruance* had been extremely fortunate.

Chief Hull Technician Ray Hatton and two damage control specialists were alongside in the motor whaleboat sizing up the repairs from the water. Once certain the cleanup and restorations were progressing properly, Maynard hurried aft to sick bay to check on Captain Lawrence.

Master Chief Brown met him as he eased through the door. The worry clouding her azure eyes confirmed everything Maynard feared he may find.

Captain Lawrence lay on a stainless steel examination table; globs of blood had soaked through the weave of the sterile gauze wrapped around his chest. He was wearing inflatable devises of some type on his lower extremities and a rack filled with digital instruments and IV bags was positioned next to his head. Lawrence's chest was barely moving. The audio on the heart monitor sounded like an old automobile engine that sputters and knocks after the ignition is switched off.

Brown removed her latex gloves and ushered Maynard to the rear of the compartment. Her shoulder-length blond hair was pulled back with a banana clip, and her smooth skin was ashen.

"He's lost a lot of blood, sir," she said in a voice just a few decibels above a whisper. "We're giving him volume expanders to help maintain his blood pressure. The compression dressings on his legs will direct what blood he has left to the vital organs. I've clamped off the heaviest bleeders but can't get his left lung to inflate. We're getting set to take x-rays to locate the bullet but we've got to get him to a trauma center, and fast."

"Will he survive the flight to Jacksonville?" Maynard asked.

"He has to," Brown replied. "I'll give him another dose of morphine before liftoff. At least he won't know he's in pain."

Maynard nodded. "I know you will do what you can, Doc. What about Seamen Gartside?"

Brown pulled the curtain to a darkened room behind them. A black body bag lay on a bunk with a sheet draped over it. Gartside couldn't have been more than nineteen years old.

Maynard's jaw clenched. The people responsible for this were going to pay dearly.

"Commodore Perkins' helicopter is ten minutes out," Maynard said. "Have Seaman Gartside's body ready to transport with the captain."

"Bob," said Lawrence in a slow, strained voice. Maynard stepped over and bent down next to him. Lawrence pulled his oxygen mask aside. "Damages?"

"Nothing we can't put a Band-Aid on, Captain."

Lawrence pursed his lips and dipped his head. "Any trace of *Wind Devil*?"

"Nothing yet, sir. Aerial units are en route to help."

Lawrence reached out and clasped Maynard's hand. His grip was weak, his skin clammy.

"Exterminate those bastards," Lawrence groaned, forcing the words. Tentacles of bloody spittle shot from the corner of his mouth. "Every last one of them."

Maynard blinked back a tear. "You have my word, Captain."

Brown placed her hand lightly on Maynard's shoulder and replaced Lawrence's oxygen mask. "We have to get the films ready, sir."

Maynard stood, still holding Lawrence's hand. *This can't be happening.*

Lawrence nodded again and released his grip. "Take care of my ship, Bob," he said from behind his mask. "That's an order."

There was a tacit undertone in the captain's message, almost acceptance. Hopefully, it was just the morphine.

"Yes, sir." Maynard snapped his captain a salute.

Brown stuck a needle into the shunt on the IV line and injected more antibiotics.

Maynard left sick bay and lingered in the passageway outside. *What could anyone possibly have to gain from this?* The image of the dark figure blazed into his thoughts again; the callous look in his eyes, the two fifty-caliber rounds piercing the center of his chest.

"It couldn't possibly be Blackbeard," he cursed. He glanced around to ensure no one had overheard his spoken thoughts.

The beating sound of helicopter rotor blades filtered down from above, and six bells sounded over the 1MC. "Commander, Destroyer Squadron Twenty-four arriving."

Maynard swung onto a ladder and headed for the flight deck.

* * *

Commodore Perkins' portly torso emerged from the helicopter bay door before the rotors had stopped turning. A cardiac surgeon and two CCU technicians from the Mayport Naval Hospital were a half-step behind him. Maynard ducked his head and hurried out to greet them.

"Welcome aboard, sir," said Maynard, saluting first and then extending a hand.

"How are the repairs going?" Perkins inquired.

"The hull technicians are fitting patches now. They should begin welding them shortly."

Maynard followed Perkins to Captain Lawrence's stretcher. Perkins grasped Lawrence's hand but the captain didn't seem to recognize him. Perkins motioned to Brown. "Load him up and get going."

Maynard led Perkins on a survey of the damages and then escorted him to the captain's in-port cabin located just forward of the amidships quarterdeck.

"I had the Master-at-Arms bring your gear in here," Maynard said. "Captain Lawrence's things are still up in his sea cabin."

Perkins walked over to the desk and picked up a framed picture of Captain Lawrence and his family. "I've known Jack for nearly twenty years. Six months from now, he'd be retired and dickin' around on that ranch of his in Montana. Busting broncos and tossing cow chips. The hard-headed bastard."

Perkins replaced the picture. "My people will contact us the moment he's out of surgery. Now, what have you recovered from *Wind Devil*?"

"Nothing," Maynard replied. "We're directly over the spot where she went down now."

27

"The frigging ocean doesn't just swallow a whole damn helicopter," Perkins fumed. "There's got to be a piece of the rotor or a flight manual or something. How about *Queen Anne's Revenge*?"

"She turned north. I decided not to pursue. We needed to evaluate our damage first. The lookouts tracked her visually for a little over twenty minutes. They estimated her speed between eighteen and twenty-one knots."

"Twenty-one knots? That's preposterous." Perkins' typically pink complexion turned crimson all the way to the top of his round, balding head. "Heavy sailers like the one you described can't do twenty-one knots."

Perkins looked Maynard in the eyes, exhaled, and made a feeble attempt at relaxing. "Dammit, Bob. I'm sorry. This thing's got me wired hotter than a three-legged Kentucky virgin. Without radar, I assume your big guns were of no value."

"Correct, sir," Maynard replied. "We didn't even attempt to fire."

The door opened and Lieutenant Commander Felix Wright entered.

"When my helicopter returns from Mayport, it will take over *Spruance's* flight operations." Perkins said. "We'll need to make space for the additional crew."

"I'll take care of it, sir," Wright answered.

"So what provoked the attack, Commander?" asked Perkins.

Maynard took a deep breath to organize his thoughts; this was not going to be easy. "I believe *Queen Anne's* captain was looking for a fight. When we maneuvered alongside, Captain Lawrence told him to state his intentions or give way. That's really all it took."

"And you returned fire?"

28

"With M-60s, M-14s and the port fifty-caliber machine gun."

"Any casualties?"

"Nothing we can confirm," Maynard replied. "*Queen Anne's* deck was obscured by the smoke from her cannons. When it cleared, everyone was gone."

"Signalman First Class Olson claims he saw a tracer from the fifty-caliber pass right through *Queen Anne's* captain," Wright added.

Perkins' eyes searched Maynard's face. Maynard just knew the commodore was going to ask him about the shooting. He would have to admit that his bullets hit *Queen Anne's* captain center mass, just as Olson had described.

"Were his guts splattered all over the deck?" Perkins asked Wright.

"Not that I can confirm, sir," answered Wright.

"Then the commander must have missed. Let's neuter that scuttlebutt here and now. The United States Navy doesn't go around shooting ghosts. Is that understood?"

Wright nodded his head and Maynard felt a short burst of relief.

"We can give the repairs two more hours and then must join the search for *Queen Anne*." Perkins said. "Put as many hands as you can spare on deck with binoculars. If we don't find debris from *Wind Devil*, we'll leave it to the aerial boys. The *McCracken* is leaving Mayport within the hour. Her side-scan sonar will locate the wreckage." Perkins ran his eyes to Wright and then back to Maynard. "Now, gentlemen, why didn't that ship paint on your radar displays?"

"At first we believed it was electromagnetic disturbance from all the lightning," Maynard answered. "But radar maintained all other contacts to the north and east. The satellite network didn't

29

detect her either. We ran a quick diagnostic on all interface and display systems as a precaution. Everything checked out. We can go cold and put a man aloft to inspect the hardware but I don't think we'll find anything."

"Do it anyway." Perkins checked his watch. "But be quick about it. It's going to get crowded out here and we'll need radar to keep everyone straight. You're convinced that ship wasn't present before the squall?"

"If she was, I'm certain *Wind Devil* would have reported it sooner."

"Could it be jamming our equipment?" Perkins asked.

"I don't think so," answered Maynard. "There were no antennae or other outward sign of advanced electronics."

"They downed a friggin' helicopter, didn't they?"

"That was probably caused by the lightning," Maynard replied, perhaps a little too quickly. "The static electricity in the air alone was enough to cook *Sea Hawk's* electrical system."

Perkins' face turned red again. "Old pirate ships don't just jump out of the water and attack Navy destroyers with muskets and cannons." He deposited himself in the chair behind the desk. "Anything else?"

Maynard looked at Wright. "That's about it."

"Blackbeard the pirate my aching ass," spat Perkins. "The bastard's been dead for three hundred years, for crying out loud."

The commodore's reference to Blackbeard caught Maynard by surprise. He wasn't prepared to hear that name spoken so openly just yet.

"The vessel's captain didn't actually identify himself as Blackbeard," Maynard interjected. "I merely stated he was flying Blackbeard's flag."

"He called his ship *Queen Anne's Revenge*, didn't he? *Queen Anne's Revenge*, Blackbeard, they're all the same damn thing. If the media weasels get wind of this, they'll make the O.J. Simpson murder fiasco look like a pygmy circus."

"*Spruance's* upcoming port visit to Boston has been placed on hold. Commander, you're to assume duties as *Spruance's* CO. Wright, you'll be filling in as Executive Officer. For now, I'm just along for the ride."

Maynard had almost forgotten the reason *Spruance* had put to sea in the first place was to participate in the change of command ceremony in Boston. Maynard was assuming command of the USS Constitution, the oldest active duty warship in the world.

Perkins studied Maynard's face again. "You look like hell. Why don't you head to your cabin and get some shuteye?"

Maynard cleared his throat. "I'll sleep when the captain of the *Queen Anne's Revenge* has a rope around his neck."

"Negative. I need all your edges fully honed. Wright can tend to things for a while."

"I'd best check on Chief Hatton first," Maynard said. "Can we get you anything?"

"Yeah, how about a couple cheese sandwiches and a bottle of Maalox. I've got a case of acid reflux so bad I can taste my Fruit of the Looms. And by the way. What ever happened to that light you were following?"

* * *

Before Hands finished pouring rum from a stone jug, Blackbeard snatched his cup and gulped it down in a single swallow.

"How dare they play such foolish games with me? Did you not hear how that captain spoke to me? Be on my way, said he." Blackbeard stood and started pacing, slapping his cup back and forth between his hands. "As though I were begging crumbs from his table."

He tossed the cup at Hands for another filling. "I'm Blackbeard the Pirate, by thunder, and I'll not tolerate such insolence! I shall crush them all as though they're cockroaches beneath my boots." He scooped up his cup again, drained it second time and slammed it back on the table.

"Could it be so much time has passed that the mere whisper of my name no longer makes the bravest sully his backsides like a fevered child? Governors have bowed before me. I take what I want and request from no man."

He paced the deck again.

"I'll not be so unjustly treated. These seas shall be mine once more, lest I draggle the tide with the blood of ten thousand souls!" He grabbed his cup and slugged down another mouthful of rum.

"To what place have we come, Captain," asked Hands in a deep voice flavored with a melodic Jamaican accent. "Where ships of iron make way with no sail?"

"'Tis the place of our grandchildren's grandchildren, I'd surmise," Blackbeard answered. "But such is none of our concern," he snapped. "It is only that we are here which matters. Delivered by the twisted generosity of Old Scratch to avenge my untimely departure from this world."

He placed his right his hand to his throat, walked to the rear of his cabin and glared out a gallery window.

"Oh, young Maynard, I can smell thy gut churning; the bile of the day's unfolding burning your every thought. Am I Blackbeard reincarnate? Or an imposter? Tormented by the destruction of your command as though it were the incompetence of your own hand that caused it.

"The conflict within you shall fester to a boil. I shall see to that; months to thee are but moments to me. To me, you shall come. And when the moment is right, you shall learn how it feels to have a blade of steel drawn across your throat."

He turned to Hands again and stroked his beard. "All in due time. First, we must tend to matters of a more delicate nature. Aye, more delicate, indeed."

Placing his cup gingerly on the table this time, strolled over to his wardrobe, opened the door and examined his reflection in a small mirror affixed to the inside. "Perhaps we may soon encounter the fairer confluence of human composition. How I have longed to experience the female arts once more. The affections of one so lovely for the blood of one such the coward. A meager price to pay for my redemption, I should think. Yet a craving so powerful as to compel the cursed one to summon me from my eternal unrest."

Blackbeard slammed the wardrobe door, lunged forward and thrust his fists down upon the solid mahogany table. "Should this ship fail me in my quest for revenge upon the son of Maynard, with these hands I shall return each one of you to the fires of hell. One scrap of flesh at a time."

He twirled a thick lock of beard around his right index finger. "But we mustn't act in haste. No, indeed. That may create opportunity for irresistible temptation." He cocked his head toward Hands and grinned. "Certainly, I'd not be so unappreciative as to question the Prince of Lies' sincerity when presented such a splendid opportunity. No, certainly not. That would appear most ungrateful of me."

The cabin door burst open and *Queen Anne's Revenge's* Boatswain, Garrat Gibbons, rushed in as fast as his spindly legs could carry him. His typically haggard facial features were stretched with excitement. "Ship, oh, Captain! A second iron maiden, three points to port."

"Ready the cannons fore and aft!" Blackbeard shouted.

33

"Stand by to fire a shot for range. A pint of ale to the first gunner to strike a blow." He pointed at Hands. "Fetch my glass."

Hands hobbled over to the sideboard and returned with Blackbeard's spyglass.

Blackbeard snatched it and hurried topside via the rear ammunition scuttle. He marched over to the port railing and raised the periscope. "Aye, another iron bucket from which to dipper a king's ransom."

He pulled off his bandana and held it over his head, allowing his long black hair to weave freely upon the wind. The sun glittered off the gold inlay of a ring he wore on the little finger of his right hand. A gift Captain Benjamin Hornigold, his former mentor, had given him the day he re-commissioned *Queen Anne's Revenge*.

"Old Hornigold's bones would be nothing more than the rotted husks of whale droppings," he sneered. "But not me," he shouted in a rising voice. "Blackbeard lives again!"

Queen Anne quickly closed to within effective range of her cannons. "Hoist the Roger, and bring up the lads," Blackbeard ordered.

He watched as his black banner ascended to the top of the mainmast: a flag bearing a skeleton clutching an hourglass in one hand and plunging a spear into a human heart with the other. He gazed back across the water at the other ship. "Sorry, mates. Your time has expired indeed."

The boarding party assembled on deck. Blackbeard shouted to his master gunner. "Mister Morton, you may issue the appropriate greeting when ready."

Morton began timing the rhythm of the swells. At the precise moment, he touched a slow match to the fuse of one of *Queen Anne's* eight-pound bow chaser cannons. A column of smoke leaped from the muzzle and the cannon wheeled backward into the restraining tackle.

Blackbeard raised his periscope and watched the projectile splash into the sea half a length off the vessel's starboard side. His gunners' skills were rusty. "Recover, and fire again. And be quick of it."

The men quickly reloaded the cannon. Morton pushed the quoin inward to provide more elevation on the barrel and started timing the next shot. This iteration he scored a direct hit, a meter or so above the waterline. The ship slowed.

Blackbeard ordered the *Queen* to starboard and then commanded a full broadside of his port twelve-pound guns. Cannon balls rained down upon the ship's deck and superstructure. The vessel answered with a flurry of small fire.

"Helmsman, come to port and follow her bow!" The helmsman dipped his head. Blackbeard turned to Morton. "All gunners to fire at will!"

The new target rolled to port in an attempt to flee. Blackbeard's helmsman circled astern and brought the *Queen's* starboard battery to bear. Blackbeard directed another salvo of cannon fire. With no avenue for escape, the vessel drifted to a stop. *Queen Anne's* gunners reloaded and fired again.

"Stand-by the grapples!" Blackbeard roared.

The helmsman squeezed *Queen Anne* close in for boarding. Grappling hooks were heaved over and clanked across the vessel's rusted decks, latching onto her railings and bulwarks and pulling tight. Two ships bumped together. The crew tied off the lines and hoisted over boarding ladders.

Blackbeard barked the order to board. Amidst the whoops and battle cries, he shouted, "Shred all those who may resist!"

Hatches flew open and the vessel's crew met Blackbeard's men with a barrage of pistol fire, bringing the entire boarding party to an abrupt halt. Blackbeard jumped onto one of the ladders, thrust his cutlass into the air and shouted, "Satan's malice shall mend thy wounds. Lay forth to restore your master's glory!"

Bullets from quick pistols stung Blackbeard's flesh. He paid them no attention and slammed his cutlass down onto the shoulder of the first seaman he came upon. With a flick of the wrist, he dislodged the blade and shouted to his men again. "Tis but lambs to a slaughter! Rush forth lads, lest I'd have them all for myself."

The boarding party renewed their charge.

One of the ship's crew leapt from behind a hatch. Planting his feet wide apart and shouting unintelligible words in Spanish, he swept a quick-pistol across the advancing horde until it made an empty clicking sound. He then threw the pistol to the deck and dove over the railing.

Blackbeard heard the crack of a musket behind him and watched a seaman's body twist helplessly into the waves. The other crewmembers dropped their weapons and raised their hands skyward.

Blackbeard herded the crew of his new prize amidships. He gazed around at the strange iron structure and stomped his foot on the deck. "Such a heap of rusting scrap. Which of you cowards dares claim to be captain of this scow?"

One of the seamen cut his eyes to an older man wearing a white shirt with a brown stain down the front of it. Blackbeard walked over and laid the tip of his cutlass against the man's throat. "Aye, has been many an idle breath since I last drank the blood of a Spaniard. Grant me the bounty of yer hold lest I rip out yer heart and quench my thirst here and now."

The other captain tried to answer, but the weight of the cutlass against his throat was interfering with his speech. Blackbeard eased the pressure.

"Si, mucho cocaine, in hold." The captain swallowed hard.

"Si, mucho gold, mucho gold."

"Now that's more hospitable." Blackbeard lowered his cutlass and pushed him forward. "Lead me."

The captain took a step toward a hatch; Blackbeard yanked him back. "Miller, come with me. Hands, you and Garrat watch over the prisoners. The rest of you scour the deckhouse and quarters. Appropriate anything of value." He jabbed the cutlass into the captain's back again. "Get on with it."

The captain led Blackbeard down two steep metal ladders into the belly of the ship's hold. The lighting was poor and the air was layered with the stench of oil. The Spaniard pulled a lever on the bulkhead and a series of lamps in the overhead snapped a couple times. Then a faint light illuminated the chamber.

Blackbeard was intrigued by the instant light. He toyed with the lever, turning the lamps off and on, and shot a glance at Miller. "We shall need to fetch some of these to the *Queen*."

Blackbeard and Miller followed the Spanish captain over to a stack of long wooden crates. The captain motioned to them and grinned. "Cocaine. Mucho gold."

Blackbeard splintered the top of one with the butt of his cutlass. The Spaniard quickly removed a white bundle and passed it to Miller. Blackbeard speared the bundle with a knife and the contents funneled out onto the deck.

"Si, cocaine," said the Spanish captain. "Very good. Mucho dinero."

"'Tis nothing but a lot of bloody pulp meal," Blackbeard bellowed. "I'll tolerate no more of this foolishness, damn yer soul." He bent over and met the captain nose to nose. "Show me the real goodies or, with your God as my witness, I shall peel the hide from yer skull with my teeth."

The captain motioned to the crates again.

"Blast you!" Blackbeard grabbed the captain around the

neck, thrust the tip of his cutlass into his stomach and gradually increased the pressure. The Spaniard's mouth gaped open and a gaseous groan slithered outward.

"Perhaps the nature of this treasure is unknown to us," interjected Miller.

Blackbeard lowered his cutlass and pushed the captain face first into the spilled powder. "Perhaps then, if he feasts upon it, he shall fill his knickers with pieces of gold."

Miller laughed.

"Bind his hands and feet and lash 'im to his beloved crates. Should he resist, gut 'im and cast his carcass over the rail." Blackbeard pushed Miller aside and stormed back to the ladder.

The men had returned from their plundering with only a gold cross, a couple rings and a handful of silver coins. Blackbeard gathered the loot in his hand.

"Nothing but meal pulp and trinkets," he spat. "Is there nothing of worth in this new world?" He cut his eyes to the Spanish sailors. "Bind them all so the gulls can pick out their eyes!" he shouted and tossed the spoils over his shoulder into the sea.

As he headed for a boarding ladder, he pointed back at Hands. "Be certain to leave behind a proper spectacle of it."

Chapter 3
1900: 21 August 2008

Angela Killian stretched across the foot of the bunk in *Deja Vu's* master stateroom. It had taken most of the first day to get accustomed to the incessant rocking of the forty-six-foot sloop. But the seasickness finally passed and her stomach was settled to the point where she could afford to relax a little.

She tucked her arms behind her head and watched as her boyfriend, Marc Vane, prepared supper. Marc had tended to her all day, trying to anticipate her needs and make sure she was as comfortable as possible. It had been a month since he'd given her that kind of attention.

"This is the life," Angela sighed. "No schedules, no billable hours, no depositions and no oppressive courtrooms. Now that I'm feeling human again, you may never get me back to Charleston."

"If you think this is great, wait until you see what else I've got planned," Marc replied.

Angela cocked her head to the side. "Give me a hint and I'll make it worth your while."

"Nope. That would ruin the surprise."

She smiled. "Okay, but I intend to file a complaint if it doesn't include floor pillows and Swedish truffles."

Angela glanced around *Deja Vu's* cabin. The ceiling and bulkheads were lined with a reddish tongue-and-grove teak, rubbed to a satin finish. The galley was decked in light sandalwood that filled the interior with the sweet smell of cedar. Every nook and cranny of available cabin space had a purpose—map storage, first-aid kit, and additional cans of food. Yet the recessed lighting in the overhead and under the pantry cabinets gave it all a cozy glow.

Angela rolled onto her stomach and propped her head in her hands. "What would you say if I told you I didn't want to practice law anymore?"

Marc stopped slicing a loaf of Italian bread and stared back at her with a look of tolerant disbelief. "I'd say you would break your father's heart. A law firm named Killian, Barnhart and Killian, implies there are at least two Killians."

He lay the knife aside and wiped his hands on a towel. "What would you do?"

"Something with disadvantaged kids. Try to make a difference before they turn out like their parents."

"Courts help children every day," quipped Marc.

"Yeah, like in divorce settlements."

Marc winced.

"I didn't mean it like that," Angela recanted. "You're an excellent divorce attorney. But the kids always pay the price for their parent's stupidity. I can't bear to look into their faces anymore."

"You want happy?" asked Mark. "Rescue a three-year-old with cigarette burns on his butt because he wouldn't potty train fast enough. Or better yet, get a child out of a crack house."

Marc picked up the knife and began attacking the bread again. "An experienced attorney can accomplish more for mismanaged children than any number of underfunded social programs. Give it a chance."

Angela remained silent for a moment. "Maybe I just want to be a mom," she said softly.

Marc didn't reply.

Thinking it best to change the subject, Angela eyed a brass statue attached to the jamb above the main parlor door. She had seen it earlier and thought it was a sculpture of an iris blossom. A closer examination revealed the petals were actually horns and a long, narrow chin; the center of it was a small skull. She'd intended to ask Marc about it, but then started puking her guts out and totally forgot about it.

"What's that figure above the main hatch?" she asked. "I've never noticed it before."

Marc glanced over his shoulder to the place she we referring to. "It's a ram's head. I found it at an antique shop in Savannah during the McConnaster divorce case last month. The shopkeeper claims it once belonged to pirate Captain Stede Bonnet. When I mentioned our vacation plans, he insisted I buy it."

"Probably sells twenty a day with that exact same story," Angela replied.

"The original price tag was eight-hundred bucks. He said if I placed it over the main cabin door that it would ward off evil spirits. So I gave him a hundred."

"It certainly doesn't do anything for seasickness."

Marc grinned and flipped a light switch on the bulkhead; the bottom of it illuminated. "Captain Bonnet was obviously a man ahead of his time," he said smiling. "I thought it would make a fun conversation piece."

"I think it's creepy." Angela looked away, but her eyes were drawn back to it. She got up and threw a dishtowel over it.

Marc switched off the light. "Whatever floats your boat."

Within minutes, Marc had assembled a seafood feast, confessing most of it had been prepared by a chef in Charleston.

With the range of sensations Angela had experienced throughout the day, food was the last thing she needed. She picked her way through the appetizer and main dish, evidently eating enough to keep from hurting Marc's feelings.

After dinner, she cleared the dishes and tidied up the galley. Marc pulled out the chart table and examined the global positioning system, then walked the points of a protractor across a nautical chart.

"One hundred twelve point three miles," he exclaimed. "Right on schedule." He checked the autopilot and stepped toward the parlor doors. "I need to check the trim before we turn in."

Angela returned to the stateroom. She changed into a sheer, white negligee cut with scrumptiously plunging neckline and stepped in front of the mirror. The silky fabric hugged the contours of her breasts and flat stomach like a thin layer of crushed pearls.

She retrieved a tube of mascara from her cosmetic bag and applied it, giving her forest green eyes that seductively vulnerable look men so craved. She wanted to provide Marc's animal instincts every incentive to exorcise whatever sexual demons had been haunting him.

She propped herself on the pillows in her bunk, arranged her dark hair about her head and shoulders, and moistened her lips with her tongue.

Marc telephoned her the night he returned from Savannah after the McConnaster case. It was late and he hadn't eaten supper. So she grabbed some Chinese food and drove the short distance to his townhouse. When she arrived, she promptly deposited the bag of food on the kitchen table and steered him straight to the bedroom; undressing both of them along the way, and nudged him backward onto the bed.

As the anticipation of their lovemaking spiraled toward critical mass, a focal element of Marc's anatomy unexpectedly plummeted from its position of relevance. Despite her efforts, it could not be revived. Understanding he had been under incredible pressure in Savannah, she wrote the whole thing off to stress.

It happened a second time the next night and then a half a dozen times over the next three weeks. Marc began avoiding intimate situations all together, which only fueled her frustrations. She hoped this vacation would turn things around. If not, it could quite possibly signal the demise of their relationship.

Marc knocked at her door. "Is everything okay in there?"

"I've got something in my eye," Angela said, doing her best to sound convincing. "Would you mind taking a look?"

Marc opened the door and entered. When he saw her perched on the bed, he stopped so fast it looked like he collided with an invisible wall.

"This looks to be a cleverly conceived trap, counselor. I'd best proceed with caution." Marc knelt next to the bunk.

Angela threw her arms around his neck and drew his lips toward hers. "Thank you for everything." She kissed him firmly.

Marc tensed and then cut the kiss short. "The pleasure is all mine." He peered into her eye. "Looks good to me."

"That's not the part of me that craves your attention." Angela tried pulling him onto the bed with her.

Marc resisted again. "Sorry, sweetheart, but I'm bushed. Let's get a good night's sleep and start fresh in the morning?"

He gave her a dry smooch on the forehead and rose to his feet. "I'll leave a light on in the galley in case you need anything."

"Where are you going?" Angela asked.

"I'll be right next door."

"We're not even going to sleep in the same bed?"

"I thought separate bunks tonight would be more comfortable. If *Deja Vu* catches quartering swells, we'll just be banging into each other all night."

More rejection; Angela was exasperated. "I thought banging into one other is what lovers are supposed to do."

"It's just for one night," Marc responded. "Tying up my caseload and getting ready for sea has really knocked the wind out of me."

Angela slowly passed the fingers of her right hand across her breast. "It would be a shame to waste such a perfect evening. I promise to take it easy on you."

Marc grinned and reached for the door. "Tomorrow. Gives me something to look forward to. I'll have breakfast waiting for you in the morning."

Angela struggled not to show her disappointment. "Whatever floats your boat." She hated to repeat Marc's dreadful cliché but under the circumstances, it seemed appropriate.

She rolled onto her left side and clutched a pillow to her chest. "You can leave the door open in case you change your mind."

After Marc left, Angela peered into the parlor, catching the light emanating from the ram's head...figures that would be the light he left on for her.

The shadows of the ram's horns crawled up the bulkhead and fanned out across the overhead, its eyes glowed like two tiny, orbs. It was staring at her again.

"Marvelous nightlight." She reached out and kicked the door shut. "If you're Stephen King."

* * *

Maynard found himself in a peculiar semiconscious state; asleep, mostly, yet still fully aware of his immediate surroundings—so much so he could feel beads of sweat collecting at his temples and rolling down the sides of his face.

44

The dream descended upon him in biblical fashion, images as vivid as any he'd ever witnessed with eyes wide open. Similar to a dream he'd experienced just two nights earlier.

He was totally naked and alone, at night, floating on his back upon a motionless sea. One moment stars were twinkling across the sky above him, the next they were bleached away by crackling bolts of lightning. Thunder pounded his eardrums; torrents of rain pelted his body like salvos of liquid bullets. The mass of clouds and rain and lightning swirled above him, hurling twisted sea spouts from its outer edges like flimsy arrows.

In the middle of it all a mouth-like void opened between cheeks of billowing strata, encircled by fangs of shredded cloud. Behind, a throaty cavern spiraled deep into the heavens. The mouth grew wider and wider as if intending to engulf Maynard and the sea surrounding him. A thin sliver of lightning shot outward from it, striking the sea beside him like a flaming javelin; boiling the water and sending a surge electrical energy careening through his body.

Other shapes appeared. Three spires ascended skyward, impaling the paunches of the swirling clouds. Each beset with a full complement of sail, straining against the might of the powerful wind and thunder. The next flash exposed a hull, the frameworks towering back into the sky and canting inward like the bones of a great foundered beast, bulwarked by subsequent strokes of lightning in planks of smoke and fire. Lightning continued to plummet earthward until the entire vessel had amassed.

Another strike, more powerful than those before it, slammed the top deck and lingered before the main mast for several seconds, leaving behind a perfect ring of fire. From behind the flames, a hulking figure angled forward. He stepped into the ring like an actor taking center stage, tossed back a shroud of rain-soaked hair and belted a laugh that pierced the tempest like honed steel.

"Avast ye mortal bastards, hear me roar. I've held firm onto my claim. No righteous soul shall be spared my wrath, damnation is my game.

I've Satan's breath upon my sails. Hell's flames have forged my steel. This Queen is crewed to sail once more, revenge has struck a deal.

Behold, I am Blackbeard! Loins of silk shall welcome mine to fester foul and greed; and the nest I grout with blood and guts shall nurture Luci's seed.

Revenge upon the last of his, 'tis the spoils which waits for me. These retched bones have weighed their time, now fate has set them free!"

The dream instantly changed. Maynard found himself standing, the ground around him was littered with broken bodies. Panic gripped him, and the pungent odor of fresh blood flooded his nostrils.

There came a plea for help somewhere behind him. He turned and searched; the ground no longer looked like ground at all. It had a grain to it like the deck of an old ship. Maynard's mind eddied. He spotted a life ring inscribed with the words *USS Constitution.*

It couldn't possibly be the USS Constitution. Not my Constitution!

He next sensed he was falling. A wedge of pain swelled through his back and buttocks when he landed; the white T-shirt he wore was smeared with a frothy red blood.

Voices were shouting at him. A rash of gunfire cut through the darkness to his right, girdled by peals of clashing metal.

The dark figure appeared at the edge of the dream again, looming before him like a demon in a child's nightmare. The shouts around him grew louder and louder. Maynard shuddered; beads of sweat skipped down his forehead like rocks upon a frozen pond, sliding into his eye sockets and burning like drops of acid. His heart pounded so hard he thought it may explode through his ribs.

Blackbeard moved closer until he was standing directly above him. He placed his heavy right boot in the center of Maynard's chest, pinning him to the deck. Blackbeard rolled a deep, throaty laugh; the smell of him was asphyxiating—the stench of a butchered animal left to rot in the sweltering sun.

Blackbeard raised his thick cutlass into the air; his hair and beard swept about his head like an executioner's hood, his eyes glowing with hatred. Somewhere behind him came five or six rapid flashes of light.

Maynard could no longer tell if this was still a dream or actually happening. Blackbeard lunged downward with his cutlass...

Maynard bolted upright in his bunk panting. It took several moments to realize where he was and several more to catch his breath. His throat was dry and throbbing.

A ringing sound to his right made him leap out of bed...it was only the telephone in his stateroom. Maynard gulped down several liters of air, gathered his composure, and reached over to answer it.

"Commander Maynard...Yes, sir. I'm just fine...I'll be right up."

Perkins needed him in radio. Maynard cradled the phone, switched on the overhead lights and quickly got dressed. His typically nimble fingers fumbled to mate the buttons with the holes on his khaki uniform shirt.

The refection of his face he saw in the mirror next to his wardrobe looked like a negative of an old photograph: pallid skin, eyes besieged by dark circles.

Blackbeard's words roared back into his consciousness.

"We shall make our acquaintance later."

Maynard collected his thoughts, retrieving the threads of an idea he was working on before falling to sleep. He stepped over to his sink and splashed cold water onto his face, toweled off and set out for radio.

The passageway aft through officer's country was abandoned. The blue night lighting from the overhead fixtures cast ghostly hue across the deck and bulkheads. Maynard quickened his pace.

He arrived at radio, punched in the security code and pushed open the hatch. The look on Perkins' face told him there was more trouble. His thoughts jumped to Captain Lawrence.

Perkins handed him a message:

'Search teams have boarded a drifting trawler, thirty miles north of Grand Bahamas Island. The ship, *Columbian Star*, of Panamanian registry. Heavy weapons damage. Four crewmen dead, three wounded, one missing. DEATH and MAYNARD painted on outer bulkhead in blood. Illegal substances involved. Proceed with Extreme Caution!

 Vice Admiral Hays
 COMMANDER, SURFACE FORCES ATLANTIC'

"Is there something you're not telling me, Commander?" said Perkins.

Maynard glanced around. Every ear in the compartment was tuned to their conversation. "Let's step outside, sir."

Perkins followed Maynard out of radio and down the passageway about ten feet.

Maynard selected his words carefully. "Commodore, on November 22, 1718, British Naval Lieutenant Robert Maynard killed and beheaded the pirate Edward Teach at Ocracoke Inlet, North Carolina. Lieutenant Maynard was my ancestral grandfather." Maynard mentally braced himself for Perkins' initial reaction.

The commodore's breathing increased but he managed to restrain his ire. "I'm listening. By Edward Teach, I suppose you mean Blackbeard. What's that got to do with this?"

"You mentioned the news media earlier. Consider this. I'll be the third member of the Maynard family to take command of the *USS Constitution*. My return to Boston has been the subject of commentary in newspapers from Miami to Portland. It even made the national evening news. What if someone is using my connection to Edward Teach as a tool to embarrass the United States government?"

"And assemble a ship full of lunatics, with cannons, to attack a United States Navy destroyer," Perkins replied. "That's totally asinine, Robert. Who could possibly have the savvy to pull off a stunt like that?"

"It wouldn't be that hard to put together. *Spruance* has to sail from Mayport to Boston. Knowing the general time frame and the direction we would be traveling, it wouldn't be that hard to locate us. I can't explain the storm, or how the ship just appeared out of thin air. Maybe it was bad luck and stellar seamanship."

"What you're suggesting would cost millions," Perkins protested.

"There's bound to be a hundred Bin Laden wannabes lurking around the Middle East. With all that oil money the finance piece would be a spit in the bucket. Why not beat up on the United States Navy with an old pirate ship? Modern combatants aren't really equipped to defend serious a close-quarters assault. It's either a scenario like that, or you must consider the alternative."

Perkins's jaw muscles flexed. "Which is what?"

Here come the fireworks, Maynard thought. "Blackbeard has returned."

Perkins craned his head to the side. "I knew that's what you

49

were going to say. Jesus Christ, Commander, if I told Admiral Hays something like that he'd have my balls run up the jack staff. And rightfully so."

Maynard said what needed to be said and there was no taking it back. "At this point, I don't think we can rule out anything."

"Except phantom ships and goddamned dead pirates."

Perkins turned and stomped back toward radio. "Go back to your stateroom and get some more sleep. I'll have the corpsman bring you a handful of sleeping pills and a case of medicinal brandy. What you don't use, send back to me."

Perkins paused at the hatch. "Blackbeard the Pirate, my flaming ass!" He punched in his security code and shot Maynard another hard look. "Maybe he's got the ghost of Saddam Hussein posing as his Executive Officer."

Chapter 4
0745: 21 August 2008

Angela awoke; something felt different. She pulled on a pair of white cotton shorts and a skimpy aqua-colored bikini top and set out to find Marc. She found him in the galley fixing breakfast as promised.

"Why aren't we moving?" she asked.

"Take a look topside," Marc replied.

She poked her head through the galley doors and looked around. The sails were flat and lifeless; the wind turbine used to charge the emergency batteries was not spinning. She ducked back inside and Marc handed her a cup of coffee.

"Are we stranded?"

"It's nothing to get excited about. Slack winds happen all the time. The GPS alarm lit up a couple hours ago. We're only a few degrees off course."

Angela followed him over to the chart table.

"It happened sometime during the night. The current has pulled us roughly thirty miles south." Marc pointed to a pair of lines that angled off in slightly different directions. "The black line is where we're supposed to be, and the red one is where we actually are. I was waiting until you got up to start the engine and get us back on course."

"Will it throw off our schedule?"

"Not much. When the wind returns, we'll wet the sails and make up for any lost time." Marc stepped over to the galley. "So, how about breakfast?"

OK, Angela thought. *If Marc wasn't going to worry, that's good enough for me.*

Marc brought her a plate of cheese eggs, toast and bacon, and gave her a peck on the cheek. "The glass of juice on the table is for you. I need to check the engine. Be back in a minute."

* * *

Maynard was summoned to Perkin's cabin; he knocked on the door twice before entering. Perkins was sitting in the outer chamber. His eyes were puffy and his face was all red again.

"Captain Lawrence is dead," he said flatly. "Complications from a blood infection."

Maynard deposited himself in a chair just inside the door. He reflected upon their final conversation. Lawrence already knew he was dead; both of them did, really.

Maynard understood what lay ahead of him. "I promised Captain Lawrence I'd punish the bastards behind this. And I intend to keep that promise."

Perkins stood and wiped his eyes. "Then let's organize a posse find and lynch these shitheads."

"I need to inform the crew," Maynard said.

"I suggest holding a second morning muster," said Perkins. "Maybe have a memorial ceremony in the helo hangar later this afternoon. I'll see if I can arrange to have a chaplain flown out."

"Certainly," Maynard replied, his sadness now morphing to anger.

"Admiral Hays has postponed the change of command ceremony in Boston until you can get there. *Constitution's* acting skipper has agreed to remain aboard until a new schedule gets worked out."

Perkins snagged a piece of paper that was lying on the desk behind him. "We have something else to deal with. It appears that rogue storm front of yours is back. It cropped up last night about a hundred miles south of Nassau and has been growing stronger by the hour. The National Weather Service has named it Tropical Depression Drummond. Aircraft out of Pensacola are patrolling to the south just in case *Queen Anne's* skipper tries to navigate through it again."

Perkins sat on the corner of the desk and his eyes sought Maynard's. "Robert, I suggest you pack your bags and head to Boston. Leave this mess to me."

"I can't do that, Commodore. It's me *Queen Anne's* after."

"You don't know that," Perkins snapped. "We don't know anything right now other than the fact that Captain Lawrence and Seaman Gartside are dead. But I'll tell you this. If you intend to remain aboard *Spruance*, you better have your head in the game. And by that I mean *my* game, Commander. Not some ghost of Blackbeard horseshit. We can't afford any mistakes. Got that?"

"Yes, sir," replied Maynard as he rose to his feet. "If you'll excuse me, I'll pass the word for Officer's Call."

"Hold on," Perkins said. "There's one more thing."

He reached behind him and grabbed a second sheet of paper. "I found this on Captain Lawrence's desk. I don't believe he had a chance to discuss it with you."

Maynard took the paper and examined it. It was a message to Captain Lawrence, date stamped: 0500: 21 August 2008.

'Your request to have Commander Robert Maynard

succeed you as Commanding Officer of the *USS Spruance*
DD-963 has received final approval. We will require a
response from Commander Maynard within thirty days.'

Regards,
Rear Admiral, Basil L. Sterns
Commander, Second Fleet

Maynard sat down again. His guts had been pulled in so
many directions the past forty-eight hours he needed a map to keep
track of it all. This must have been what the captain wanted to talk
to him about yesterday; why he was in such high spirits just before
the attack. "When did he put in for this?"

"Just before you were awarded command of *Constitution*.
I'll see that you get a copy of his recommendation letter. You'd
have thought he was nominating his own son. I know you and the
missis have other plans. But if you chose to accept this, your tour
aboard *Constitution* will be shortened to eight months. At which
you will return to Mayport and assume formal command of
Spruance."

Perkins' brow furrowed. He looked Maynard directly in the
eyes. "I know for a fact Lawrence called-in several favors to
arrange this. It's one hell of a compliment. You'd be wise to
consider your options carefully."

* * *

By evening, the winds had not returned and Marc was keeping a close eye on the fuel gauge. Angela could see signs of concern playing at the corners of his mouth.

She volunteered to prepare supper; Marc used the opportunity to study his charts.

They slept in separate cabins again.

Chapter 5
0630: 22 August 2008

A piercing alarm wrenched Angela from a deep sleep; there were heavy footsteps running across the deck. She flung open her stateroom door and found Marc hovering over the engine console flipping switches. She hurried over to him.

He managed to silence the alarm and then tried to restart the engine. Three dull, metallic clanking sounds resonated from the engine compartment behind them followed by total silence.

"Shit," Marc exclaimed.

"What's happened?" Angela asked.

Marc pushed by her, his eyes not even grazing her face. "We lost oil pressure. This is bad...really f'ing bad."

Angela followed him on deck and aft to the engine compartment. A cloud of greasy, blue smoke billowed out when he lifted the hatch and a dismal expression unfolded down his face.

The engine and walls of the compartment were covered with a viscid film of oil; a pool of it was collecting in the bilge.

Marc grabbed a rag, extracted the dipstick, and examined it. There wasn't the slightest trace of oil on it.

"Christ," spat Mark. "What's next? First the winds abandon us and now we don't have an engine. Without either, the

Bitch of the Blue drives us anywhere she damn well pleases."

Angela forced herself to remain calm. "Can we fix it?"

He flung the dipstick down in disgust. "Not unless you packed an extra set of pistons."

"I've got a hair dryer."

Marc stared at her as though she'd sprouted a second head. "A hair dryer? Great, maybe you can blow us to Nassau."

Angela winked at him.

"What's that for?"

"I don't need a hair dryer to do that. Just the stamina."

Marc's face turned red, and Angela braced herself.

He stopped and took a deep breath. "Let me get this straight. Our engine just melted, we're adrift in the middle of the Atlantic Ocean, and all you're worried about is my penis."

"Hey, you said blow, not me." Angela had never seen Marc this distraught.

"Who needs an engine?" she asked. "We're on a sailboat, for crying out loud. Columbus didn't have an extra set of pistons and discovered America, didn't he?"

Marc slunk to the deck and folded his head in his arms. "I think you mean Vespucci, not Columbus."

After several moments, he looked up and managed a tenuous smile. "You're right. What's thirty grand for a new engine? It will probably only cost twice that much in Nassau."

Angela was encouraged. "That's more like it. And if the radio doesn't work, we'll just open and close the engine hatch and send smoke signals."

"We can always radio for help," Marc said. "And we have the emergency generator if we need it."

Angela hoped she knew what she was doing. It made sense to establish contact with somebody before they actually needed help. But Marc's confidence had already taken enough of a beating.

* * *

A shout rang out from the top of *Queen Anne's* main mast. "Sail ho, Captain! Port quarter."

Blackbeard squinted into the distance. "What is it, boy?"

"It's a might small, Captain. A single-masted sloop, slack at sail. Perhaps a craft of sport."

"Sport indeed," Blackbeard sneered. "Well, 'tis a grand day for sport, lads. Helmsman, thirty degrees to port. Let's go take a look."

Chapter 6
1130: 23 August 2008

Angela was sunning on the cabin roof and flipping the pages of a yachting magazine. "This article claims the three leading causes of boating fatalities off the coast of Florida last year were accidental drowning, drowning caused by prolonged exposure, and attacks by giant, man-eating squid. At least we won't starve to death."

Marc climbed out of the engine compartment. "I'm an attorney, not a grease monkey." He slammed the engine hatch and sulked over to her. "Are we having fun yet?"

"Yeah. And getting a killer tan."

"Great. That'll help conceal the fact we're Americans when we wash ashore in Cuba. I'm going below and get cleaned up. Need anything?"

"I'm good. Thanks."

Angela set the magazine aside; the sun was straight overhead and scorching hot. She checked her watch and decided to give herself another ten minutes. She rolled onto her back... and felt a slight breeze cross her face.

A breeze? She sat up and looked at the wind chimes she'd made out of vegetable cans and spoons; it didn't move. She felt it

59

again, this time strong enough to blow her hair around to the side of her face. She scanned the horizon and spotted a small white dot off to the west and bounced to her feet.

"Ship ho!"

Marc stuck his head through the parlor doors. "What?"

She pointed to the white dot "It's a ship, I think. We're rescued."

Marc came up a moment later with a pair of binoculars. "It's a ship all right, and under full sail. They must have a bigger blow dryer."

Angela peered through the binoculars. "Do you suppose they have a shower?"

Marc went below again and returned with a flare gun. He stretched his arm above his head and shot an orange fireball two-hundred feet into the sky.

"I don't know about a shower," said Marc. "But maybe they can give us a tow." He put his hand on her arm. "You'd better hide from sight. At least until we know who they are." He rolled his eyes across her partially exposed breasts. "And you may want to put a shirt on."

Angela started to protest, but realized Marc was right. She swaggered in the direction of the cabin.

"There's a zippered black case in the bottom of the sail chest with a pistol in it."

"What for? You don't think..."

"Just a precaution. You should at least know where it is."

* * *

"You men get below," ordered Blackbeard. "Hands, pick five gents an' remain with me. We needn't frighten our little friends with so many ornery faces."

When they were within hailing distance, he stepped over to the railing. "Ahoy there. Lost yer blow, have ya?"

A young man wearing canvas-colored short britches and darkened spectacles stood amid the sloop starring back at him.

"Have you no tongue?" asked Blackbeard. "Your sails, man," he said, pointing to the sloop's canvas. "Appears they've lost their way."

"They've been slack for over a day now," the man replied. "You don't seem to be having any trouble, though."

"Aye, so you speak the King's word." Blackbeard squinted up at *Queen Anne's* sails. "Indeed, the winds of August have always been my friend. Sir Edward Teach is the name, from the crystal shores of New Providence. 'Tis a smart little cutter ya got there. Can't even make out 'er planking."

"The name's Vane. Marc Vane. Thanks for coming over. I lost power early this morning and have been drifting ever since. You wouldn't have a mechanic on board, would ya?"

"Oh, what foul luck." Blackbeard put an arm around Hand's shoulders. "But Mister Hands here is quite adept with fixin' things. He'd be delighted to assist."

Teach caught Vane glance back at the parlor doors.

"By all means," Vane said.

"Splendid. Garrat, lower me pinnace." Blackbeard pointed to the men standing behind Garrat. "You lads lend yer backs to the oars."

He climbed aboard the small boat. Garrat mustered a working party at the boat davit and lowered it to the water.

Once alongside, Hands tied a rope to the sloop's starboard cleat. Marc leaned over and helped him aboard; two oarsman remained with the boat. Blackbeard instructed the third one to stay by the sloop's rail, and followed Vane aft to a hatch in the deck.

Marc opened the hatch. "Here it is, gentlemen. Deader than

hell."

Blackbeard raised a woolly eyebrow. "Indeed. Hands, be a bright lad and jump down there and see what you can do."

Hands peered into the engine compartment, scratched his chin and stepped down.

"Edward Teach and Israel Hands are quite a legend in these parts," Vane said. "You guys on some kind of nostalgia voyage?"

"Well, now," Blackbeard said with a grin. "I was beginning to think no one remembered."

"You wouldn't be heading for Nassau by any chance? Or Charleston? We could sure use a tow if you can't get it running. I'd gladly pay you for your troubles."

That was the opening Blackbeard had been hoping for. "Shall I assume by *we* that you'd not be alone on such a splendid day as this?"

Marc eyed him cautiously but Hands chimed in before he could reply.

"Captain, it's a painful dead fer sure." He ran his finger across the hunk of metal and scraped up a thick glob of oil. "Whatever it 'tis, Captain, appears she's lost all 'er blood."

Blackbeard cut his eyes at Hands and grinned. "What a pity. Charleston says ya? Aye, I knew it well once. Haven't soiled me boots there in more than a cat's nine." He fixed his gaze on Vane. "Sorry, lad, but Charleston ain't in me charts."

He reached inside his shirt, whipped out a dagger and thrust the point under Vane's nose. "This little folly bores me. Now, kindly escort me to yer valuables and I'll be on me way."

Vane took a step backward and nearly stumbled over the open engine hatch.

The seaman standing by the railing eased over to the cabin and slammed his foot down on the coach roof. A sharp crash and a thud resounded inside.

"Captain. There's a body below," he exclaimed.

"Angela, get the gun!" Vane shouted.

"Angela," Blackbeard repeated. He narrowed his eyes. "What might we be hiding down there? Perhaps I'd best see for myself."

With a flick of his powerful forearm, he slashed the dagger across Vane's neck and a shower of blood rained upon the deck; Vane clutched his throat and folded to his knees.

Blackbeard bent down and wiped the dagger on the back of Vane's shirt, then kicked his writhing body through the lifelines and into the sea. It floundered for a couple seconds, bubbled, and then sank from sight.

Blackbeard set his sights on the cabin door. "Angela. What a delightful name. It flows from the tongue like silk." He pointed to a bucket and growled to Hands. "Cleanse that blood."

* * *

Angela was watching through a crack in the cabin doors; the big man with the beard and wide-brimmed hat looked as if he belonged on a wanted poster. The other two were unshaven and sweaty; so much for a refreshing shower.

Why would Marc allow such unsavory characters aboard *Deja Vu*? She tried to listen in on the conversation but couldn't make out much of it.

The sight of the dagger caused Angela's heart to leap into her throat. Her muscles recoiled at the loud thump on the overhead, landing her on her backside on the galley floor, dragging a collection of pots and pans down with her. She rushed to the sea chest, pulled out the pistol and retreated to her stateroom.

Perched on the foot of her bunk, she eyed the microphone hanging from the ship-to-shore radio. She ran over and grabbed it.

"Mayday! Mayday! We've been boarded by pirates..."

At that very moment, the burly man came bursting through the parlor doors. Angela retreated backward and fell half-seated on the bunk; the microphone cord snapped tight and wrenched the transmitter from her hand. Without thinking, she cupped both hands around the butt of the revolver, leveled it at his chest and fired.

The pistol jerked in her hands but the giant didn't as much as flinch. She squeezed off two more shots, center chest. Again, nothing. Angela froze.

The giant filled the cabin; he had to bend at the waist to keep from raking his head on the overhead. Two other pirates peered down through the remains of the cabin doors.

"Well, well. What do I have here?" he asked. He pointed to the gun cradled in her hands. "That little toy you're holding shall grant you no comfort from me, my dear."

"Keep away from me," Angela warned. "Marc?" she called. No answer. "What have you done to Marc?"

"Marc? Oh, you'd be referring to that fine, young Buccaneer above," he replied. "I'm afraid since such dire circumstances have befallen you, he thought it best to discharge your care onto me." He held the palms of his large hands out in front of him. "You'll be as safe in these as if they were your mum's."

"I demand to see Marc this instant," Angela said.

He took a step toward her. "Lower your pistol, darlin'. It will do you no good to resist. I assure you Captain Edward Teach t'would never harm a lady."

"Keep away from me, or I'll..."

"Blast my parts to hell?" asked Teach. The other pirates chuckled. "Hell hath no need of that which it already possesses." The laughter increased.

Angela pulled the trigger again. Splinters flew from the door jamb beside the big man's shoulder. The laughter abruptly ended.

Angela couldn't believe her eyes. She had just shot the guy three times and there wasn't even the slightest trace of blood on his clothing. Her head grew light and she thought she might pass out.

"Kindly cease with that annoyance," said Teach. He looked down across his chest. "You're burning holes in my finest linens."

He reached over and peeled the gun from Angela's hand and tossed it on the bunk. "There. That's much better now, isn't it?"

Angela attempted to distance herself from him by crab-walking toward the head of the bunk. "What are you going to do to me?"

He put his index finger to his lip. "We hadn't the mind to find such priceless treasure so soon. But it wouldn't be proper to leave a lady alone on the mighty blue. There may be ruffians about."

The radio receiver crackled. "This is the United States Navy destroyer *Spruance*. We have received your distress call. What is your situation?"

Teach turned his attention to the radio, and Angela made a break for the door. Without looking, he reached out and grabbed her by the arm, stopping her dead in her tracks.

"What's your hurry, Angel?" he asked, guiding her by the arm over to the radio. "Who's the little mate inside this box?"

"That's the United States Navy," Angela spat. "They heard every word you just said and are coming to rescue me."

"Indeed. I believe we exchanged pleasantries with these gentlemen just yesterday. And fully grown men, they were. This scallion could hardly possess the breadth of a mouse."

He released her arm. "No matter. 'Tis time we were on our

way. You are welcome to join us aboard the *Queen;* I can assure you, you shall find us most delightful company. Mister Hands!"

A dark-skinned pirate climbed down into the cabin.

"Kindly escort my little angel aboard and see she's made comfortable in my cabin."

Hands reached for Angela.

"I'm not going anywhere!" she shouted and jerked away.

"Ah, the spirits of the kinder fare. It's like the beauty of a violin to my soul. But judging from the tender hide on those lovely hands of yourn, you'd not be a sailing lass. Without a mate ta strike yer bow, how do you plan on making Charleston?"

Angela cut her eyes at him. "How did you know I'm from Charleston? I didn't hear Marc tell you that."

"Edward Teach is a man of many talents," he replied.

"Better do as yer told, milady," Hands said. "The Captain ain't known for 'is patience."

Angela glared at Teach; he was at least three times her size. What if they had killed Marc? And how could he just stand there grinning like that? Of course, they could easily do the same to her.

Hands reached for her again.

Angela slapped his hand away. "I know the way out."

Teach moved aside to let her pass; she could feel his eyes canvassing every inch of her body.

He quickly stepped in front of her again. "How careless of me." Teach ripped what was left of the parlor doors from their hinges and threw them up on deck. "You might 'ave been injured."

He glanced at the figure of the ram's head above the door jamb and gave it a shallow bow. His smile broadened. "By your leave, O' Gracious One," he said, and offered Angela his hand. "If you please."

Angela pushed his hand aside, too.

As one of the seamen was lowering Angela into the boat,

Teach called out. "Garrat. Fetch another launch and four fresh pair of hands. If any scoundrel disturbs so much as a lock of the ladies hair, I'll render the *Queen's* barnacles to the lot of ya."

Angela looked for any sign of Marc and found nothing: There was not any blood or evidence of a struggle.

Her eyes briefly met Captain Teach's, and he flashed another grin.

CHAPTER 7
1248: 23 August 2008

Maynard was seated at the table in the wardroom next to Commodore Perkins, taking a lunch of lemon-crusted halibut and scalloped potatoes, when the Boatswain Mate of the watch's voice boomed over the 1MC. "Commanding officer, your presence is respectfully requested in radio."

Maynard jumped up, rushed over to the telephone. "This is the Captain...did you get it on tape? Outstanding. I'll be right up." He cradled the phone and turned to Perkins. "Radio just received a distress call."

Perkins wiped his mouth with a napkin, rose and followed Maynard out the door.

Maynard entered radio and Lieutenant Yeatts shouted, "Captain in radio!" Three sailors manning the stacks sat up at attention.

"As you were," Maynard said. "Let's roll the tape, Lieutenant."

Senior Chief Balf switched on the digital recorder. "Mayday! Mayday! We've been boarded by pirates!" It was followed by a loud crash, part of a woman's scream, then complete silence.

"That's all we got, sir," Yeatts said.

"Did you answer?" Perkins asked.

"Yes, sir. Several times. There's been no reply. The transmission was too short to get a solid fix."

"How about the satellite network?" Maynard asked.

"No help, sir", Yeatts replied. "That's all they got, too. She could be a hundred miles in any direction."

"Contact the other search units," Perkins said. "Have them concentrate on a 100-mile radius around *Spruance*. Put a call through to Admiral Hays. Tell him what we've got and forward our coordinates. In the meantime, keep trying to raise that caller."

Maynard picked up the telephone and dialed the bridge. "Give me the Officer of the Deck." As he waited, he contemplated the logistical problems of having a woman aboard *Queen Anne's Revenge*.

"Fallis, pass the word for Lieutenant Commander Fox to lay to Combat. Then pass to flight quarters. I want the LAMPS crew dressed and ready to launch in five minutes."

"Who's got the watch in Combat? Tell Buchanan to bring his track up to date and have the quartermaster meet me at the plotter with current charts of the area. After you've secured from flight quarters, come down and I'll fill you in." He hung up before waiting for a reply and headed out the door.

"Lieutenant Commander Fox, your presence is requested in Combat," sounded the 1MC. Followed by, "Flight Quarters, all hands man their flight quarter stations..."

When everyone was assembled in Combat, Maynard began the briefing. "Gentlemen, listen closely. A few minutes ago, radio received a brief distress call. All attempts to establish communications with the caller have failed so now we must find where it came from. Lieutenant, play the recording."

Yeatts played the message again.

"That's all we have. The message originated from a low frequency, commercial-band radio. We currently have thirty confirmed contacts within that range."

Maynard circled the 100-mile search radius with a grease pencil on a six-by-four-foot sheet of thick glass called the vertical plotter. "Our current heading is one-eight-zero degrees. We will continue on this bearing, post additional lookouts, slow to launch *Sea Hawk*, then come back to speed and continue south.

"Fox, once airborne, fly out fifty miles due north and conduct an east-west search back toward *Spruance*. Pack as many eyes aboard your bird as possible. Look for smoke and debris." Maynard pointed to the symbols on the plotter. "As you locate each of these contacts, radio back to Lt. Buchanan and confirm. If you come across a heavy sailer, contact me immediately. Keep her visual, but do not approach. Got that?"

Fox nodded his head.

"We don't know exactly what we're looking for. It could be anything from a pleasure craft to a merchant. Commodore Perkins has radioed Surface Forces Atlantic for support. When the other units arrive, they'll start searching the south, east, and western perimeters. Lieutenant Buchanan, keep me informed of all new sightings."

Maynard turned to Yeatts. "Contact all merchants in the area. Find out if they have seen anything unusual, and tell them to keep their eyes open. One of them may have intercepted the call and already be attempting a rescue."

Maynard looked at each man. "Any questions?"

No one answered. "Then let's roll."

* * *

Angela had been alone in Blackbeard's cabin for several

hours. She had tried to watch through the gallery windows as *Queen Anne* placed *Deja Vu* in the distance behind them but the glass was too encrusted with salt to see much.

Marc was dead. She was nearly certain of that, and she was being kidnapped by a ship full of cutthroats. They were probably going to kill her, too, or worse. She wondered if she would ever see her parents again; her death would devastate them. That thought made her cry again.

Angela allowed herself one more flurry of tears, then composed herself and tried to figure out what to do.

When one of her court cases seemed hopeless, her father would always tell her, "Strike a deal or file an appeal." She wiped away the tears.

"There's just one of me and probably a hundred of them. The last thing I can do is let them know I'm scared."

A knock at the door jarred her from her thoughts.

"Young lady, this is your captain. I'd have a word with you now."

In her most defiant voice, she said, "Unless you're taking me home to Charleston, the answer is 'No!'"

The door opened slowly. The captain, Hands, and a third man entered; the latter two were holding her suitcase and cosmetic bag. The captain removed his hat.

"I hope the lady's rested a bit from our earlier meeting. I would so prefer it to have been under more cordial circumstances."

"I demand you take me to Charleston," Angela said. "My father is a very influential attorney and will expect my safe return."

"Ahh," Teach exhaled. "Charleston, 'tis a lovely place this time of year. A might on the humid side, as I recall." He looked at his comrades who nodded in agreement. "I should hope to return some day. But where are our manners? Allow me to introduce my friends."

Waving his arm to the right, he said, "This is my Lieutenant, Mister Richards, second in command of the *Queen Anne*." He turned to his left. "And this fine, black-skinned gentleman on me port, with whom you've already been acquainted, is one Israel Hands. The *Queen's* faithful Sailing Master. Hands and Richards will be seeing to your comfort during yer stay with us. And I, of course, am your Captain. The honorable Edward Teach. Graciously at your service." He finished his introduction of himself with a bow.

"I don't care who you are," Angela said. "Just take me home. Now!"

The captain righted himself. "Why, you'd not find our company to your liking, my dear?"

"No. Being held hostage by a gang of murderers always make me snarky. That and the fact this place smells gorilla farm"

Captain Teach smiled a wry grin. "Well now, me angel, you needn't be so peevish. You're no more a hostage here than I. We've even brought about a few of your possessions so's ya'd feel at home."

Richards and Hands stepped forward and set the bags on the deck.

"I hope you'll find all the things you'd need. Soon as ya become accustomed to the *Queen's* ways, you'll have full reign of her. Mister Hands here shall be your personal guide and servant."

Angela shot a look at Hands; he was not as frightful looking as she had first thought. She had also failed to notice that he walked with such a pronounced limp.

"Forgive me, Captain Teach, or whoever you are. I don't recall being asked to join you. Nor did I hear you extend my friend a similar offer."

"Well," he said with a toothy grin. "I always say, 'tis more honorable to beg forgiveness than to seek permission."

He quickly changed the subject. "I ask that you'd kindly accompany me to the mess and lend a hand identifying a couple trinkets we appropriated from yer sloop. I hope you'll forgive our indulgence, but we found a few wee items most irresistible."

Angela was accustomed to manipulation. She searched each of their faces for any indication they might have something else in store for her. The captain's face was set in his perpetual smile; the other two were practically expressionless. She needed to find a way back to the main deck so decided to go along with them, at least that far.

"Why, by all means," she said and motioned toward the hatch. "I'd be happy to identify your stolen property."

The captain led the way; Richards and Hands brought up the rear. From the captain's cabin, they entered a larger chamber with tables and chairs—the wardroom perhaps—then passed through another hatch that emptied into a space the entire width of the ship.

When she first came aboard, the passageways were dark and her eyes hadn't had a chance to adjust. The gun ports had since been opened allowing the last of the day's light to filter in.

Along the outer bulkheads on both sides, was a line of long black cannons with a squatty pyramid of cannon balls stacked neatly in a brass box next to each one.

The smell of something cooking began to overwhelm her, and there was talking and laughter. Whatever was on the menu smelled better suited for a swarm of flies.

She followed Captain Teach down another ladder that landed in a compartment with a couple tables; she guessed it to be the crew's dining area. When she and the captain entered, everyone went quiet. Seated there must have been thirty of the roughest-looking humans she had ever seen, all of them dressed like pirates. It was as though she had been sucked back two hundred years in time.

Sixty dirty eyeballs glided around every curve of her body. A wave of male musk enveloped her and, for some bizarre reason, released a surge of adrenaline; she felt her nipples harden against the thin fabric of her red tank-top. A dozen or so sleazy grins let her know that her reaction hadn't gone unnoticed. She crossed her arms against her chest.

A stocky, round-faced man with a large pink scar on his left cheek was standing next to a table littered with objects taken from *Déjà Vu,* including some cans of food. Angela's eyes zeroed in on the radio.

"What're ya gawkin' at, ya bunch of sows?" shouted the captain. He scoured the room with his eyes. "Finish yer grub and be off with ya." The men quickly returned to their eating.

Angela followed the captain over to the man with the scar.

"This is me Quartermaster, Thomas Miller," he said. "He's been examining some goodies of your'n and has a couple questions regarding their function."

The second Miller began to speak, Angela felt a sharp pain in her right buttocks. She shrieked and jumped forward. When she searched behind her, she saw the captain grope forward with his arms, seizing nothing but air.

A little man ran out of the compartment waving both hands above his head and shouting, "I pinched the lovely mermaid's bottom! I pinched the lovely mermaid's bottom!"

The crew burst into laughter.

Captain Teach whirled around and eyed one of the seamen standing across the compartment. "Garrat! Harpoon that little varmint and haul him before the mast. I shall throttle his hide ta ribbons for this. Fetch my ray's tail and a bucket of brine."

"You will do no such thing!" Angela shouted. The crew's mess fell as silent as a tomb again. "Please. Just let him go."

The Captain whirled around and faced her; the whites of his eyes were glowing like hot coals. He exchanged several breaths before speaking. "As you wish, my dear."

His attempt to control his anger only made his eyes redder. "For you, this time, he shall be set free."

The crew began to cheer. The captain whirled around again and held out his fist. Angela couldn't see his face but, from the reaction of the crewmen, his expression must have been something frightful.

"As I warned ya before," he boomed. "A mere brush with our guest here shall cost ya your blood. You have my word on that. There shall be no more forgiveness." Captain Teach glared at Angela to emphasize his point then scanned the mess a second time, looking every man directly in the face.

Angela's first stand had been successful. But, in front of the crew and all, she hoped it hadn't been too costly.

Miller was fighting a smile. "That wee lump of troublesome flesh, milady, is one Jeremiah Ratliff. The *Queen's* most trusted rat."

His Porky Pig-like features finally gave way to a grin. "And he thinks you'd be a mermaid." His comment drew another round of hushed laughter from the crew.

"You should be honored he's taken such a fancy to ya. 'Tis not often the Rat ventures so far from 'is hole. Why, he usually don't make his presence known 'til weeks after sail. That is, lessen we find him sooner, a swingin' from a yard with a snoot full of the captain's rum."

Miller glanced at Teach as if to seek approval, and then continued. "Aye, many a lucky man owes 'is skin to the Rat, you might say. Myself included." As he took a step toward her and started to put his arm around her shoulders, he eyed the Captain and immediately halted himself.

"One day, we was a haulin' in this nice, fat Spanish galleon, just off'n the coast of Barbados. I had me three ornery Spaniards a looking ta see how many pennants they could snatch from me hide." He put his hand to his face and touched the scar. "Still carry the stichin's ta prove it."

He flung his hands out at Angela and startled her. "When, in the blink of an eye, roustin' from 'is hole comes ole' Rat; pistols in both hands just a blazing. Dropped two of 'em dead in their tracks and pinned the third through the heart with a dagger. Oh, that were a thing of beauty, it was. Rescued me ragged old carcass that time, for sure. Yes, many a man owes an immense debt to the ole' Rat there. Excepting the captain, that is."

"That's enough of that little annoyance," the captain warned, his temper now partially contained. "You'd be wise not to bore our guest with so many of your foolish tales, Mister Miller. You might be telling more than was beneficial for you."

Miller cast his eyes at the floor to avoid the captain's stare.

"Now, where were we?" Captain Teach asked. "Ah, yes. The trinkets."

Miller proceeded to ask Angela a series of questions about the equipment; both he and the captain were particularly interested in the radio.

Miller's affable nature had a calming effect on her. She willingly explained the operation of the radio. She felt foolish instructing sailors how to use a radio but did it anyway. Yet she didn't dare touch the transmitter key. Seeing the Captain's fury once was more than enough.

Angela also showed them how to use the binoculars, flare gun, and a can opener...intending to use the latter to open a can of fruit cocktail she planned to eat for supper.

With their curiosities satisfied, Captain Teach grabbed the binoculars and slung the strap around his neck, then slipped a brass clock shaped like a ship's wheel into his pocket. He instructed Miller to establish an accounting of everything else, place it in a canvas bag and stow it in the hold. On his way out, he told the cook to bring two trays of grub to his cabin. Angela declined hers.

"Oh, before I forget." The captain reached into his coat and pulled out a small gold box. "One of your new mates found these. Nothing's more comforting to a lovely lady than the sparkle of her own jewels."

Angela inspected the contents; every piece of jewelry she had brought was still there.

The captain and Hands escorted her back to the cabin. It had since grown dark. Hands walked in front of them carrying a lantern. Once inside, he lit several brass oil lamps hanging from pegs in the overhead and closed the door as he left.

Angela sat at the large mahogany table. Teach went over to the wardrobe and took out a jug and two cups. He pulled the cork from the jug with his teeth, placed the cups on the table and commenced filling them with a fragrant, amber liquid. Angela instantly recognized the sweet aroma of rum.

He handed her a cup and held his up in a cheer. "To smooth seas, following winds, and many a fond leave in old Charleston." He threw his head back and gulped his rum down in one swallow.

Angela took a small sip; the rum had a robust flavor. Then it began to sear the lining of her mouth. She spat it back into the cup.

The captain laughed. "'Tis a delightful brew, is it not?" He poured himself another cup.

"For stripping the deck," Angela choked.

There was a knock at the door. Hands brought in a large tray and placed it on the table in front of the captain and hurried out again.

"Are ya certain you'll not be joining me?" asked the

captain.

Angela shook her head and looked down at the can of fruit cocktail. He took a spoon from his tray, dipped it in his rum, wiped it on the sleeve of his topcoat and held it out for her. She stared at it for a moment, took it, and began to dig in.

She scrutinized the captain's every bite and was surprised how mannerly he handled himself at the table. She half expected him to slurp his food off his plate like a dog. Instead, he took normal-sized bites and chewed each one thoroughly before swallowing.

When he was finished, he got up, removed his tray from the table and poured himself another drink.

Not having eaten since breakfast, Angela was starving and ate the whole can of fruit cocktail. She spooned the last drops of syrup from the bottom and washed it down with a mouthful of rum, grimacing only slightly, and set her cup on the table.

"Looks like somebody found themselves an appetite," said the captain. "So tell me, little lady, where was ya heading before I rescued you?"

Angela contemplated his use of the word *rescued*, and decided to drop it. "Nassau. We were sailing to Nassau."

"Nassau, aye. 'Tis a dangerous place for my kind in Nassau. What with all the King's men stirring about."

"Kings men?" Angela questioned. "There hasn't been a king in this half of the world in over a hundred years."

"Why, the authorities of course," he replied. "The last time I harbored Nassau they held a ransom on my head."

"And just when was that?" The captain got an impish smirk on his face. Angela knew she had found a soft spot.

"Oh, must of been about April or so, as I recall."

"April of what year?" Angela demanded.

He looked at her out of the corner of his eye and carefully

contemplated his response. "It would've been in the year 1718, of course."

Angela leaned back in her chair. "Oh, you guys are good. Cut the crap, mister. This is 2008. That would make you what, about three-hundred years old?"

He raised a bushy eyebrow. "Aye, you're quite right, my dear. Three-hundred-twenty-seven, to be precise." He beat his fist against his chest. "But I'd not feel a day past thirty-two."

"You expect me to believe that I'm floating around in the middle of the Atlantic Ocean with a bunch of three-hundred-twenty-seven-year-old pirates."

"No, of course you wouldn't, my dear. I said I'd be but twenty-seven and five. A mere babe compared to some of them." Teach chuckled, finding humor in his own comment.

Angela got up from the table and walked around the cabin.

"So you claim to be the infamous Edward Teach, or would you rather I call you Blackbeard? There have been hundreds of stories written about you. For example, being killed in the early 1700's during a raid by the British."

"Aye. A nasty scrap it was, too. Lost nearly all my men in that one."

"But now you're here. So let me guess. You've returned to apologize for all the terrible things you did when you were alive. Well, let me save you clowns the embarrassment, Captain Blackbeard. People don't believe in that kind of tripe anymore. It's been played a million times. So why don't you just take me home and go back to where you came from?"

"I have come to reclaim that which is mine." His tone was becoming less temperate.

Angela thought for a moment. "What would the infamous Blackbeard want to reclaim? But, of course. His treasure. That's it. Blackbeard had a treasure, didn't he? You've come back to find it.

Well, you can save that bull crap for the tourists. I suppose along the way you plan to pillage, kidnap and murder innocent people, too."

Blackbeard leapt from the table. "Hold your tongue with me, young woman! I am no common thief. I am Edward Teach, a man of honor. I'd throttle the likes of any man who speaks such lies."

He took a step to his right. "I was a noble servant to the crown during the warring with Spain. I fought through blood and sweat while the Blue Bloods gorged their pockets with the fruit of my conquests. I brought harm to no women or babes as they so claimed, and I spilled the blood of nary an innocent man. My years have taught me there's no such creature as an innocent man! I slayed only those who sought to slay me first."

Blackbeard grabbed the front of his shirt and ripped it from his body, exposing a grossly blemished and hash-marked chest. In the center of it was a purple scar the size of Angela's fist. She took notice there was no evidence of fresh bullet wounds. Wounds that would have been left behind by her shots from Marc's pistol.

"Look at me," he said slapping his hands upon his chest. "These are the badges I received from my struggles. This is how they showered upon me their gratitude."

He dropped the shredded shirt to the deck. "For ten long years, I mired amid their battles. Colored the sea red with the blood of the King's enemies, we did. It was me and mine that bore the crown to victory; it was the strength of our cannons and the bounty wrought from the vessels we plundered.

"It was us," he shouted. "We delivered our spoils to the King's coffers so he could sell it to provision his armies and fleet. But when the battles were over, when they had no further need of us, they called us murderers and cutthroats and enlisted sums upon our heads."

He righted the chair he had knocked over and slammed it to the deck. "So we struck back where the sword could plunge the deepest. Taking each and every ten penny due us, one vessel at a time. It mattered not what color was put to their mast, for they all were the same. To those who offered resistance, we taught a painful lesson; those who surrendered, we set free; those who begged to join us, we welcomed." He looked her in the eyes. "Those who sought to stop us, we slaughtered for the sheep that they were.

"At last a king's pardon was offered. The Royal Proclamation. Any scoundrel who volunteered to lay down his cutlass was promised clemency. Proclaimed to be a free man. Only to be dragged from his sleep and hanged like a traitor for any purpose, by any man who sought to acquire a name for himself in the King's eye.

"Clemency his royal posterior," Blackbeard said, pointing at her. "The King could not be responsible for loosing ill will back into the likes of gentle folk. So, my men and I took to sea aboard the *Adventure*. To defend ourselves in the only way we knew how. Our time was at hand, indeed, but I'd not lie down and be taken like a whore.

"As you say, that morning's light at Ocracoke, in the face of the king's two small sloops, was to be my last. I chose to make my stand. And I'd have gutted them all, the cowards. But they'd not face me like a man. Cowards!" he roared. "Cowards, all of them! Instead, they lanced and blasted me from behind."

He removed the scarf from around his neck and uncovered a jagged scar that spanned the breadth of his throat and disappeared over each shoulder.

"I'd fought until every drop of my blood had forsaken my flesh, until I could muster the strength to fight no more. Then, and only then, would I surrender my cutlass. In the end, their captain, the most grandiose coward of them all, cut off the head of a defenseless man to proclaim his victory."

Angela sat down at the table. Naked from the chest up, Blackbeard walked around to the other side and kicked the chair out of his way. He placed his hands upon the table and leaned toward her. She could see every detail of his butchered chest; felt the waves of heat that radiated off his body.

So powerful were his emotions that she couldn't decide whether to cover her eyes and cry, or reach out and take hold of his hands. This was not the outcome she had expected from her interrogation.

At last, she summoned the courage to speak. "But the world today is civilized. Men find practical ways to resolve their differences."

"Speak not to me of civility in the same tongue as man." His anger was retreating now, and his tone returned with some of its earlier pleasantries.

"Tell me, Lady Angela. Is your precious world so different? Is there no substance to greed? No lust for power? No injustice? Are all men free to go about life as they please, fearing no persecution from failure to conform?

"You mentioned your father is a servant of the law. Yet does he not profit from the crimes of the wretched? Is there no longer wealth to be gained from misdoings? Do your kinsmen not contrive to take that which is the property, the very sovereignty of their neighbor? Tell me, do your ruling voices truly protect the free will of all men, regardless of lineage or position? Do they not associate themselves with men of wealth and circumstance? Not whose wealth could better serve the needs of the many, but those whose wealth could best serve them in return?"

He waited for an answer. Angela could offer none.

"No, I thought not. You see, our worlds are not so different, my dear. The ledgers of history are besieged by men who seek to preserve perspective, but 'tis their own perspectives that get set to word. The higher truths are often buried among the bones of the less desirable.

"I have returned, as you say. Though they will seek to destroy me once more, things shall be different this time. I have made my pact, and you, my dear, are as much a part of it as I. It is destiny that brings us together. Your destiny and mine."

He reached over and gently lifted her face until their eyes met. "No, milady. I am not the ruffian as has been told. I am not the villain slandered by the scratchings of the King's chroniclers. Yea, I am but a spirit. A spirit returned to claim the rights it so deserves; rights which no longer shall be defiled by the whispers of injustice."

Chapter 8
1530: 23 August 2008

The search for the distressed continued into the afternoon. When *Sea Hawk* had worked in from one hundred miles to sixty, she returned to refuel. Maynard sent her back out again.

At 1623 hours, Fox radioed his next report. Maynard was standing at the quartermaster's table examining charts of the Bahamas Islands.

"*Spruance*, this is *Sea Hawk*. Do you copy?"

The Officer of the Deck handled the call. "Go ahead, *Sea Hawk*."

"We have located smoke bearing one-one-zero, range about fifty-two miles from your mark. Proceeding east to investigate. We'll report back if we find something. *Sea Hawk* out."

"Officer of the Deck. Come around to one-one-zero, and make turns for thirty-two knots," Maynard ordered.

The quartermaster drew a line on his chart from *Spruance's* current position along a bearing of one-one zero and measured off fifty-two miles. It placed the sighting approximately 200 nautical miles north of Grand Bahama Island.

Thirty minutes passed.

"*Spruance*, this is *Sea Hawk*, over."

"Go ahead, *Sea Hawk*," answered the Officer of the Deck.

"We have located wreckage. There is debris strung out over a mile or more. Awaiting orders."

Maynard took the headset. "*Sea Hawk*, what is your fuel situation?"

"We've got about another hour, sir."

"Lower a raft and recover anything that might identify the vessel. When your time's up, mark the spot and hightail it back to the barn. We'll come to full speed and rendezvous with you."

* * *

Fox made a slow pass over the debris site. The surface of the sea was littered with nautical charts, clothing, food wrappers and a variety of other buoyant articles.

The vessel had not totally burned. What appeared to be a large section of the stern was smoldering but still relatively intact. He positioned the helicopter above it and the aircrew threw out a bundled raft which sprang into shape when it hit the water. Two crewmen rappelled down and began sifting through the wreckage.

Fox had a strong distaste for salvage operations. Over the years, he had found helmets with heads, boots with feet, and various other chunks of flesh cannibalized beyond recognition. Perhaps the gods would show compassion today.

Within twenty minutes, his crew had recovered a lady's handbag, a wedge of charred transom and a man's shirt. The crew attached a radar transponder to the stern of the raft, and moored the raft to the remains of the hull. When the last man was dry, Fox powered up and headed for home.

* * *

Maynard was standing next to Commodore Perkins in the helo hanger when *Sea Hawk* touched down. The helo recovery team quickly unloaded the salvaged items.

The piece of transom was badly burned but the words 'Deja' and 'Charleston' were clearly discernible. Maynard examined the contents of the handbag. Most of it had spilled out but inside a zippered compartment he found a case of birth control pills with the name *Angela Killian* printed on the label. There was no address. The shirt had the initials MWV monogramed on the left pocket. It wasn't much, but more than enough to determine ownership.

Sea Hawk was refueled and sent back out. Thirty minutes later, *Spruance* arrived at the wreckage. The motor whale boat and captain's gig were lowered and guys hauled up more debris.

The gig crew located a narrow, blue waterproof box containing the ship's log and registration papers. The documents identified the vessel as the *Deja Vu* out of Charleston, South Carolina. Her skipper was Marc Vane. Vane had carefully documented the slack wind conditions and the sloop's engine troubles. The manifest also listed a passenger: Angela Killian.

Maynard read the last entry. It was date-stamped eleven-fifty hours, August 24, 2008 and read: 'We have been sighted by a large sailing ship and it is headed our way. Perhaps they will be gracious enough to share their wind.'

Maynard handed Perkins the log book. "I imagine the captain of the large sailing vessel had more in mind than just sharing his wind."

Perkins examined the entry. "One more victim or two?"

Maynard knew the answer to that question.

The boat crews retrieved everything worth salvaging and

86

were hoisted back aboard. Maynard directed the supply officer to catalog the items, place them in plastic bags and store them in the forward boatswain's locker.

It was dusk when *Spruance* put the remains of the *Deja Vu* behind them. Technically, the fate of her crew was still a mystery.

Spruance secured from flight quarters, and *Sea Hawk* was rolled into the hanger for the night. Maynard stood alone on the fantail and watched the final traces of the sunlight wash back into the ocean. The woman in the distress call, Angela Killian, had specifically used the word 'pirates'. Maynard was certain she was still alive; it was well-documented that Blackbeard had an insatiable thirst for women. Marc Vane, on the other hand, would not have been so fortunate. Death may have been the kinder misfortune.

Chapter 9
0800: 24 August 2008

Angela was seated at the mahogany table in Blackbeard's cabin wearing a ruffled white shirt he had given her to sleep in. It wasn't nearly as flattering as the negligee but a lot more comfortable.

She leaned forward and propped her head in her hands. Despite all the creaking and popping noises the ship had made throughout the night, she felt incredibly rested. In fact, when she awoke, she had nearly forgotten where she was.

For some reason, she no longer possessed the overwhelming desire to escape her predicament either. Rather, she was curious—if not excited—about what might happen next.

She started thinking about Captain Teach's speech yesterday. Had it been a scene from a movie it would have been an Oscar winning performance.

What did he mean when he said he'd made a pact? That destiny had brought them together? *A pact with whom*?

He obviously had a short fuse, but never actually said Marc was dead. Maybe he was holding Marc in another part of the ship. Who knows, maybe Marc was even a participant in all of this.

She looked around the cabin again. It was precisely twelve-paces wide and six-paces deep—having stepped it off nearly a hundred times the day before. The bulkheads were covered in an exquisite dark wood; mahogany perhaps, or walnut. Several hand-drawn nautical charts were tacked to the bulkheads; cabinets and drawers were built into the forward bulkhead around both sides of the door. Her eyes fell upon the bed.

Blackbeard. She couldn't get her mind off him. He commanded such a powerful presence, say nothing of being one of the largest men she'd ever stood next to. Yet his movements were agile like a gymnast.

He obviously ruled his ship with an iron fist--the reactions of the men in the galley was testament to that. Overall, he had been remarkably gentle with her, almost compassionate. Certainly not like someone planning a murder.

Angela slid her hand up her arm and touched the place where he'd grabbed her on *Déjà Vu* when she tried to get away. She could still feel the warmth of his skin.

Everything about him exuded passion. As though he knew exactly what he was doing...and that nobody could stop him.

But what about the wounds from her gunshots?

"Oh listen to me," she said out loud. "I'm fantasizing about Blackbeard the pirate. He's nothing but a thief and a cutthroat."

She looked at the door again. Something new caught her eye...a carving in the jamb just above the hatch. She went over for a closer look. It was a ram's head very similar to the sculpture Marc had purchased at the antique shop in Savannah. She traced the outline of the horns with her fingernail.

Evil spirits. Strength and determination. 'If you think this is great, wait until you see what else I've got planned.' Those were all things Marc had said to her. All these things were somehow connected.

Angela went back to the table and sat down. "This has got

to be a dream."

Dream or not, she was starving. A nice, hot shower wouldn't hurt either.

She threw the bag of clothes Hands had brought on the bed and started rummaging through it. Her hand struck a large, solid object. She pulled out Marc's shaving mug.

"Why would they include this?" she asked herself.

She placed it aside and continued searching the bag. There was nothing else of Marc's in it. She glanced at the ram's head and then back at the mug again. "Protection from evil spirits." Maybe Marc intended for her to find it.

Her father had taught her to move forward with her eyes open and never jump to conclusions; the world was seldom what it seemed. Yet, Angela couldn't suppress the feelings of anticipation brewing inside her. She pulled out her favorite jeans and a light green crew neck and got dressed.

She heard noises outside her cabin; doors were closing, there were some scrubbing sounds, and the slurred words of a pair of men singing...badly.

There was a loud knock at the door, followed by a rattling of keys at the lock.

"Wake up in there," said a commanding voice. It was Captain Teach.

"'Tis a beautiful morning and I'll have no goldbrickin' while there's chores that need tending."

Angela put her ear to the door. The other sounds stopped.

"Come along now, I can't be larking about all morning. A captain's moments are of immense value."

She pulled open the door just wide enough to peek out. There he stood, dressed in a black shirt and pants, smiling down at her through a forest of whiskers. He was carrying a tray containing several dishes, one of which was a crystal bud vase with two daisies.

Where on a pirate ship would he keep flowers?

Angela let him in.

"Thought these fixins' here might take the edge off," he said. "Never heard so much snoring from one small parcel in all my years. I'm pleased you found my cabin such to yer liking." He placed the tray on the table.

"I don't snore," Angela protested. "Besides, how could anyone sleep with all that noise out there?"

"Aye, I see yer still got a twinge of that ole' snarky attitude. Thought you had gotten beyond that."

He pulled a chair from the table and offered it to her. "Have a seat and eat up while it's still warm. You must forgive old Parsons there. He ain't accustomed to cooking for a lady. Though it beats retching from the scurvy."

Angela sat down, and he scooted her up to the table. Breakfast consisted of some kind of greasy fish, a bowl of lumpy yellow stuff, two untoasted English muffins and a cup of warm orange juice. Her cutthroat friends had obviously done a shoddy job raiding *Deja Vu's* galley. She nibbled on one of the muffins and took a sip of juice.

"All that racket, my dear, is the makings of a little housekeeping. Seems someone amongst us finds the *Queen* a tad on the ripened side. So, to keep from seeming inhospitable, we decided to air her out a bit. When yer finished here, you'll be tasked with spiffing up my quarters. Mister Hands will provide ya with all the essentials. When she's clean, there'll be a fresh tub of water fetched up for yourself."

"I'm not your maid," Angela said. "You look quite capable of cleaning up your own mess."

"T'wern't my idea. Ah well, suit yourself," he said and started toward the door. "I'll check back on ya later. Perhaps you'll be a little more cordial." He departed and closed the door behind him.

Angela studied her tray again and pushed it away.

There was a soft tapping noise behind her. She turned and found Jeremiah Ratliff standing next to the captain's wardrobe.

"Rat!" she shrieked. "Where did you...stay away from me, you little rodent!"

"Shush, missy. If old Hands hears us, he'll skin me bones fer sure."

"Get out of here or I'll scream!"

"I'd come to bring ya a little present." He held out a box of Mrs, Freshly's Oatmeal Cream cookies. "Thought yer might have a penchant for these." Ratliff inched toward the table, sat the box down, and quickly backed away.

One end of the box was opened and a couple were missing.

"Found them aboard that scowl we hauled in yesterday." He glanced at his feet. "I owed ya that much for saving me from the captain's lashing. He'd 'ave a walloped me a big one, he would 'ave. An' I beg yer forgiveness for pinching ya on your private side, too. I ain't never been sophisticated with me manners. But I had ta make certain ya wasn't a sea hag sent to bring our bones back to the fires."

He smiled, exposing what remained of his front teeth—two upper and two lower—and he actually did resemble a rat. "You're fer real, alright."

"How did you get in here?" Angela asked.

"Found me a passage up from the powder hold, only the captain's 'spose ta know of it. But I'd not be a bothering ya from it. Promise ya that from top to bottom of me heart."

Angela guessed him to be fifty or so years old. He was a tiny man; not a dwarf, just small. And in his ragged clothes and floppy hat, he looked like a turn-of-the-century London street urchin. Certainly not the sort to pose a threat to the likes of Captain Teach.

She recalled the comment Miller made. "Jeremiah, why is the captain afraid of you?"

"You may call me Jeremy, if ya like." He cast his eyes at the floor again and took a step backward. "Mercy, milady. Ya shouldn't have gone and asked that. Those are the kind a things that can earn a mate the sting of the ray's tail."

"You can trust me," said Angela. "Haven't I already proved worthy of that?"

Ratliff looked around and sniffed the air as though to ensure no one else was there.

"I shall tell it if you must know. But just this once. And ya mustn't ever speak of it again." He took a seat at the table and placed his hands in front of him. "'Tis not fear, Lady Angela. The captain fears nary heaven nor hell. I suppose it all goes back ta that wretched day of Ocracoke, an' our tussle with the Royals."

Angela sat across from him.

"When the sun come up that morn, we was all set for battle. I knowed it was gonna' be a rough one, too. The wings of death were stretched upon the wind, that day they were. As the Royals sloop came about, we tossed over bottles of sulfa' and nails ta blast 'im to pieces. When the smoke parted, there weren't a body standin'. We figured we'd got most of 'em, an' hoisted over the ladders ta finish off those what was left.

"Once across, it were my job ta find a hidin' spot and help as I could when one of me mates got in trouble. Cept', when I started over, I got a foot tangled in the riggings and were pitched over the side. I ain't no match for the water, ya see. But the Lord saw fit to fashion me with hollow bones so's I can float. Like a cork, I am." He grinned.

"After all me mates was aboard, up from the holds come the

93

Royals, a whoopin' and a hollerin.' Then all of 'em took ta fightin'. We was a gettin' the best of 'em too, we was. Until the captain got blasted by the British skipper and was laid-to by a pack of swordsmen.

"I should a been there ta protect 'im. It were my responsibility. Then when all the fightin' was over, there 'eh was, sprawled face down upon the deck. I could barely place an eye on 'im, but knew he'd not be a layin' there lessen the powers of life had departed his bones."

Jeremy got solemn. "Some of me mates leaped over the side but were shot dead to the water by the Royal's marksmen. Them who surrendered was later taken up ta Virginia an' hanged. I couldn't bare the thought of lettin' me mates down again. So I made my way to Williamsburg for the trial, if ya have a mind ta call it such. From my hidin' spot across to the gallows, I said a prayer as each of 'em took the devil's walk".

"A ghastly life that was," said Ratliff. "With all the guilt, an' the hangings an' all. Ya see, I was the only member of *Adventure's* crew to draw a breath beyond Williamsburg that day and I don't think the captain 'as forgave me for it."

"Oh, Jeremy, how horrible," Angela said. "But none of that was your fault."

"Aye, we all have our crosses ta bare, milady. And mine's the death of Blackbeard."

"But if everyone was either killed or hanged, why are you here now?"

"I don't know, missy," Ratliff answered. "We just is." He stood and shuffled his feet. "I'd best be gettin' lest I be nabbed for trespassin'. But, if ya ever need anything, just give a call for yer ole' mate Rat. I've got nigh everything you could ever want." He smiled and showed his teeth again.

"Be warned of this before I go." His smile immediately fell

away. "There'd be danger aboard the *Queen*. 'Tis the devil's hand that brung her here and 'tis the devil's hand which sails her. You'd not be safe as long as you're aboard."

Jeremy put his hands in his pants pockets and rocked onto the balls of his feet. "I'll be watchin' over ya, though. Jeremy Ratliff always repays his debts. You'd best turn yourself around now so's I can get." He waited for her to turn her back.

"Hey, Jeremy," Angela said over her shoulder. "Thanks for the Mrs. Freshly's. They're my favorite."

Angela sneaked a peek just as Jeremy was about to climb into the wardrobe. He stopped and reached over and yanked a brass nameplate off her suitcase and stuffed it into his pocket. When she looked a second time, he was gone.

* * *

Sea Hawk's rotor blades were churning the skies again just after first light. Morning quickly progressed into afternoon. Over twenty aircraft and surface vessels were now involved in the search. So far, there was no trace of *Queen Anne's Revenge*.

Maynard was getting impatient. At least they had not encountered any more plundered vessels. He suspected Blackbeard had already found most of what he was searching for.

At 1530-hours, Maynard was discussing several new contacts with the Combat Information Watch Officer, Lt. Buchanan, when Fox's voice resonated over the air net.

"*Spruance,* this is *Sea Hawk*. Do you copy?"

"Roger, *Sea Hawk*. This is *Spruance,*" Buchanan answered. "What's the verdict?"

"OK, ROTCY BOY. I've got your bad guys dead to rights. Bearing one-six-five, fifty-six miles from your location. Over."

"Roger that, *Sea Hawk*. Wait one while I inform the

captain." Maynard walked up behind Buchanan, switched on the external speaker and increased the range on the CIC Watch Officer's radar display to one hundred miles. The display showed a symbol indicating the position of the helicopter, but no sign of a surface ship.

Buchanan examined the display. *"Sea Hawk*, I show no other echoes in the vicinity. Over."

"Well the damn things right here in front of me, Lieutenant. Clear as the pimples on your sister's face; a three-masted sailer under full canvas."

"Confirm *Sea Hawk's* position," Maynard said.

"Sea Hawk, confirm your position."

The helicopter's symbol on the radar display grew from a light yellow to a bright orange, indicating Fox had pushed the identification button on his radio transmitter.

"That's a copy, *Sea Hawk*. I have your position confirmed. There are no other contacts on that mark."

"Then you've got a couple maverick electrons somewhere, ROTCY boy. She's right in front of me. If it was your girlfriend, I could read the tag on her training bra."

Maynard took the headset from Buchanan. *"Sea Hawk*, maintain separation, I repeat, do not approach. We'll run a system check and get back to you shortly. Do you copy *Sea Hawk*?"

"Roger, *Spruance*. Holding position. Be advised, this cork's making tracks. You'd better pick up the pace if you want to catch her before nightfall."

"I copy *Sea Hawk*. Coming up to speed now. *Spruance*, out." Maynard turned to Buchanan. "Double check your displays again. I'm going to radio. Let me know as soon as you're done."

* * *

Data System Technician Second Class Wolf disconnected his oscilloscope and was closing the Combat Watch Officer's radar console when Maynard and Commodore Perkins returned.

"Everything's fine here, sir," Wolf said. "The power supply is stable, the display voltages and sweep frequencies are within specs. Target presentation is good, and all the controls respond like normal. I can't find anything wrong."

Lieutenant Commander Fox's voice resonated over the air link again. "*Spruance,* this is *Sea Hawk.* Over."

"Go ahead, *Sea Hawk,*" replied Maynard.

"The target has stopped dead in the water, sir. I don't think they have spotted us though."

"We can't wait any longer," said Perkins. "Order *Sea Hawk* in for a closer look. But we don't want to provoke anything just yet."

Maynard relayed the orders to Fox and then called up to the bridge. "Officer of the Deck, increase turns to thirty-two knots. Heading one-six-five degrees."

"Bridge, aye."

Several minutes passed before Fox reported back in. "*Spruance,* I don't see any radio antennas or any form of navigational radar. Only a lookout atop each mast."

Maynard took the headset. "*Sea Hawk,* what's your position?"

"Eight hundred feet, and about two hundred yards off her port bow. I'm circling around her port side to get a look at her markings."

Thirty seconds later, he called in again. "Captain, she's got cannons strapped to both her port and starboard gunwales, with more gun ports below the main deck. This is undoubtedly our guy, sir. There is a bunch of men in the water. Appear they're having swim call."

"What was that?" Fox exclaimed. "Are you sure?" There was another brief pause. "*Spruance*, big eyes just confirmed the markings. It's the *Queen Anne's Revenge*, all right. And be advised, we're running low on fuel. If we stick around much longer, we may need to surf our way home. It will be dark by the time we get refueled and back out. Unless this cork's got running lights, we won't find her again today."

Perkins spoke up, "Bring *Sea Hawk* in. Get her refueled and send her back out. We've got nothing to lose."

"We could commit another asset," said Maynard.

"The fewer the better. It's going to be hard enough to keep a lid on all of this as it is."

"*Sea Hawk*, return to the farm as quickly as possible," Maynard ordered. "We'll get you refueled and send you back out."

"Roger, *Spruance*. I'll make one more pass and bring her home. *Sea Hawk,* out."

Maynard called the bridge and ordered flank speed. With all four of her LM-2500A marine gas turbines rolling into high fire, *Spruance* sounded like a 747 powering up for takeoff.

"Whoa! Shit!" shouted Fox. "Those bastards just took a shot at us! That's affirmative, *Spruance*. We're losing pressure in the starboard fuel tank."

"*Sea Hawk*, disengage immediately," Maynard responded

"I'm way ahead of ya, Captain."

It was a full sixty seconds before Fox checked back. Maynard held his breath.

"*Spruance,* this is *Sea Hawk*. Everything is A-OK. The starboard tank was about empty and I'm transferring the remaining fuel over now. No signs of fire.

Maynard, Perkins, and Buchanan breathed a unanimous

sigh of relief.

"Fuel transfer complete and we're heading in. Have a fire party on standby. *Sea Hawk* out."

"Sir, what are the odds of us experiencing that same radar glitch again?" asked Buchanan.

"Slim and none," Perkins replied. "Nor is there any such thing as a stealth sailboat." He looked at Maynard. "We've got to figure out a way to track this damn thing. Commander, lay to outboard and see if they can pull anything out of those billion-dollar spy satellites of theirs." He turned to Buchanan. "Lieutenant, let me know when *Sea Hawk* is two miles out. I'm going to radio and fire off a rocket to Admiral Hays."

Perkins stomped out of Combat.

Maynard turned to DS2 Wolf, who was still standing off to the side. "Wolf, you come with me. I need your help with something. Lieutenant Buchanan, let me know when *Sea Hawk* is five minutes out. Contact the bridge and have the helo recovery team in full fire gear, hoses charged."

* * *

Blackbeard strolled around topside as the men were pulling up buckets of water to rinse the decks. "Garrat!"

"Aye, Captain," answered Garrat, climbing down from the riggings.

"Once the *Queen's* properly scoured, rig some lines and heave these scoundrels over the side. I'll have every single rotted carcass bristled pink as a baby's bum. Ensure Rat participates in the festivities as well."

After the chores were finished, Garrat ordered the men into the water. A couple of the older seamen grumbled but, for most, it was an opportunity to play.

Garrat threw out wooden scrub brushes and cakes of lye soap. "I'll have nary one of ya foul bastards boardin' 'til he's fit ta straddle the Queen Mother herself."

It took Hands, Garrat and two others to corner Jeremy and wrestle him to the deck. Once under control, they picked him up and carried him to the railing.

"Unhand me, ya bunch a thievin' shit pinchers!" Rat shouted. "I'll hack the whorein' seeds from the lot of ya. You'll rue the day you ran afoul of Jeremy Ratliff."

Hands grabbed him around the neck. "Hold yer trap, ya little imp, a'forn I tie a rock around ya." Jeremy tried to kick him in the groin, but Garrat intercepted his foot.

The men hoisted Ratliff over their heads and tossed him into the water. Hands lingered beside the rail to make certain he resurfaced. Garrat and the others walked away cackling amongst themselves.

When Jeremy bobbed up, he sculled the water with a stream of profanities.

A strange beating noise filtered down from the sky and all festivities came to an abrupt halt. The men in the water splashed for the ropes and climbed back aboard. Blackbeard tramped over to the railing, joined by Hands and a group of six or seven other sailors. Together they watched a black dot in the sky grow toward them.

Garrat came running up from behind. "What in the name of Satan's fire's that?"

Blackbeard grinned. "Why, lads, 'tis nothing more than a partridge with a snarky attitude. I'd have me a rightly-powdered blunderbuss, if you may, Mister Garrat. I think I shall test my hand at fowling."

Garrat gave Blackbeard a puzzled look and set out as ordered.

Queen Anne's deck was swarming with wet sailors, gawking and mumbling amongst themselves. The flying contraption made several wide circles around the ship and then stopped directly overhead, nearly scraping the tops of the masts. Ratliff was still in the water.

Garrat returned. He removed the musket's tamper and shoved it down the barrel to pack the shot, then dusted powder from a powder horn into the frizzen pan and handed it to Blackbeard.

Blackbeard raised the musket and took careful aim. "I'll be needin' a hound to fetch me quarry," he said and squeezed the trigger.

The powerful musket jolted his shoulder. "Any volunteers?" He lowered the musket and let go a thundering laugh.

The contraption responded with a furious rushing sound, followed by a steep climb skyward.

"Oh now. I think I've gone and hurt its feelings," Blackbeard quipped.

The deck erupted in nervous whoops and cheers. The flying machine leveled off and made a beeline for the horizon.

"Mister Hands, make all canvas to the wind," Blackbeard ordered. "And waste no time of it."

Hands looked out at Jeremy Ratliff still struggling to swim back to the ship. "What about the little one?"

"Little one, Mister Hands?" Blackbeard replied. He looked at Ratliff. "I see no little one. Now do as I command and make us off."

* * *

Angela listened as the helicopter approached. She pounded her fists against the thick glass of the gallery windows. "Help! I'm down here! I'm down here," she shouted.

She continued trying to signal until the roar of the helicopter engines was lost in the slap of the water against *Queen Anne's* hull.

Chapter 10
0500: 25 August 2008

The flight crew worked through the night repairing the damaged helicopter fuel tank. By 4:00 AM, the job was complete; *Sea Hawk* was ready to fly again.

The tactical team in Combat had inserted a phantom contact into the radar display that corresponded with *Queen Anne's* last known position. Assuming Teach would try to escape, Maynard estimated she would be within a 150-mile radius of her point of contact with *Sea Hawk*.

Commodore Perkins convened a briefing in the wardroom. Maynard positioned himself at the rear of the compartment.

"Gentlemen, the Joint Chiefs of Staff held an emergency briefing last night with the President and the Secretaries of the Navy and Defense. Capturing *Queen Anne's Revenge* has become a top national security priority. Additional resources have been placed at our disposal should we need them."

Perkins pulled a laser pointer from his breast pocket and aimed it at a nautical chart attached to the wardroom movie screen. "This is how things are going to shake out. At midnight last night, the *USS Fitch* got underway from Mayport and is currently steaming east toward the Bahama Islands. She and her LAMPS II will take up station off the western coast of Great Abaco and conduct a search southward through the lower Eleuthera Island chain.

"At zero-four-forty-five this morning, Admiral Hays scrambled two fresh squadrons of S-4's from Pensacola Naval Air Station." Perkins pointed to an area from Andros Island east to San Salvador and south to Guantanamo Bay, Cuba. "They will be searching the two southern most quadrants.

"The Coast Guard has dispatched two heavy cutters and two Sea King helicopters from Miami. They will concentrate their search from the tip of Florida, east to Grand Bahamas Island and south to Andros where they will link up with *Fitch.*

"A squadron of F-18's has been combing the entire area since the *Sea Hawk* incident yesterday. Thus far, there have been no sightings and the Pentagon is starting to get anxious. And the President is demanding to know why a hundred-billion-dollar's worth of high-tech military hardware can't locate a single friggin' wooden sail boat." The corner of Perkins's mouth toyed with a smile.

"Finally, another wing of F-18's from Oceana is patrolling the areas north to make sure *Queen Anne* doesn't slip away behind us.

"As I stated earlier, *Spruance* will be coordinating the search. All sightings will be reported to Combat and plotted on the two vertical plotters. Both boards will be updated every three to five minutes. Lieutenant Buchanan has instructions to keep a running list of all active contacts in these sectors, including ship type and nationality. At this point, we are assuming the incidents involving *Spruance, Deja Vu, Columbian Star*, and *Sea Hawk* are all related. That means that there are a bunch of civilians involved."

Perkins shot a look at Commander Fox. "Judging from

everything else these guys have been up to, *Sea Hawk* may have gotten off lucky."

He returned to his movie screen. "When one of our assets locates the *Queen Anne*, my orders are to forward the positioning to *Spruance* and then lay back. *Spruance* and *Spruance* alone will intercept her. Under no circumstances, is any element of this task force to approach *Queen Anne* without my personal authorization.

"Mister Buchanan, your air track supervisors are to make sure all aircraft maintain adequate separation. There's going to be a lot of traffic out there and we don't want any slip ups."

Buchanan nodded his head.

"We're not certain if the pirates are holding any prisoners. So far, everybody has been accounted for except one person from the *Star* and the two crewmembers of *Deja Vu*. Commander Maynard has reason to believe the Killian girl may still be alive."

Maynard and Perkins' eyes met; Maynard wondered if Perkins was going to let the name Blackbeard slip. He hoped not.

Perkins put down the pointer. "Our friends out there have already killed twenty people. Judging from the distance between the various attacks, it is possible there may be more than one aggressor involved.

"Once *Queen Anne* has been sighted, we will sound General Quarters and make a run at flank-speed to her location. All hands are to muster at their battle stations in full gear, dress down, and hold. When we are within twenty-five miles, we will return to full battle preparedness. At that time, designated members of the Security Alert Force, back-up Alert Force and Augmentation Forces will be positioned at strategic points along the ship's weather decks. They will be armed with M-14's, M-60's and side arms. All weapons will be locked and loaded. Snipers will be positioned on the signal bridge, 02 level amidships and on top of the helo hanger, we will have two gunners manning each bridge wing 50-caliber gun. At no time is any other member of this crew permitted outside the skin of the ship.

"Topside forces will be under the direction of Lieutenant Commander Wright. They are not to fire until he, Commander Maynard, or I give the command. And only, let me emphasize this, and only if we take fire first. We want *Queen Anne* to surrender peacefully. Chances are it's going to get messy. *Fitch* and the Coast Guard cutters will close in from the other sides and surround her. If she starts shooting, *Spruance* has been instructed to return fire with all means available. If something happens to us, *Fitch* will achieve effective range and blow the shit out of *Queen Anne's Revenge* with her surface to surface missiles."

Perkins paused and looked around the room. "Once *Queen Anne* is overtaken, she will be boarded by a landing force, and what's left of her crew will be placed under arrest. Hopefully, we can take her captain alive. If not, at the very least, we will provide the US taxpayers a new floating tourist attraction.

"Lastly, the landing force will rig a ten-inch hawser to her bow, and *Spruance* will tow *Queen Anne* to Guantanamo Bay for safekeeping. At that point, our job will be complete.

"So far, *Queen Anne* has managed to elude our radar and satellites. Once we have her, we can't afford to lose her again. Commander Maynard and Petty Officer Wolf have devised a small radar transponder that we will secure to her hull. The HT's have attached it to the end of a marlin spike and packaged it so it can be fired from a shot line canister. We can rule out planting it from the air. So, regardless of what happens, we've got to get close enough to get a clean shot. I'll turn things over to Commander Maynard now to brief you on the workings of the transponder."

Maynard rose from his chair and walked to the front of the compartment. "We only have one shot at this so we have to make it work." He looked at his gunnery officer. "Ensign Shanaberger, we will need your best marksman."

"That would be Gunners Mate Second Class Mottley, sir," Shanaberger replied without hesitation.

"Good. Get him to the fantail as soon as possible to get in some practice. If he hits the mark, I'll buy him a case of beer when we return to Mayport."

"Right away, sir," Shanaberger replied.

"Gentlemen, each time our radar sweeps the transponder, it will transmit back an echo that will appear on our displays. We've given the echo a distinctive symbol which will enable us to identify it quickly from the other contacts. The transponder has an effective range of roughly thirty miles and a battery life of six to seven days. Once activated, I don't see any way *Queen Anne's Revenge* can get away from us.

"Now, there's a nasty storm cell approximately 150 nautical miles north of New Providence. If it behaves, it shouldn't affect our operation. It is stationary for now and, if the National Hurricane Center's guidance is correct, it will make a turn east and stay out to sea. But we may run into some strong winds and rather heavy seas. So be prepared. Conduct a walk down of all spaces and secure any loose articles.

"Our port visit to Boston has been delayed indefinitely. Radio will be contacting the chairman of the *Spruance* Family Club at twenty-two hundred hours. If any of your men need to get word to their wives, have them post their messages on the message board outside Radio by twenty-one thirty. Obviously, all Internet communications are secured until further notice. This is real-time stuff, guys. If you have any questions, ask them now."

Maynard looked around the wardroom. No one responded.

"We will be launching *Sea Hawk* at zero-six-hundred. Flight quarters will be set at zero-five-thirty."

Fox jumped up and bounded for the door.

"Not so fast, Lieutenant Commander Fox. Make room for two machine gunners aboard your bird. I don't want you out there naked again. Got that?"

Fox gave a nod and returned to his seat.

"Alright, grab yourselves some breakfast and get ready to roll. Let's get this mess cleaned up and put these guys behind bars." He looked at Fox. "Dismissed."

* * *

Blackbeard had taken up residence in Mister Richards' stateroom ever since Angela had come aboard. Richards' quarters were cramped and lacked the exquisite furnishings of the captain's cabin. He and Richards were seated at a small chart table attached to the rear bulkhead.

"We shall hold course and skirt the gale," said Blackbeard. "Our little friend is certain to return home to tattle on wee nasty pirates for burnin' a hole in 'is feathers. They'll be coming to fetch us. But first, let them chase our shadow for a while. When they think they have us, we'll come about and blast them from the sea."

"Aye, Captain," Richards said. "But don't think it wise to risk the treasure over a lark with a man-o-war."

"Mind me not of my obligations, Mister Richards. 'Tis my purpose for which we sail and 'tis my scheme by which we sail it."

"Aye," Richards replied. "But you'd not forgotten that each of us was promised a share of the treasure for helping you retrieve it. We've already bested the Royals once. With Ocracoke only a few days sail, the men will wonder why they need risk a second peril."

Blackbeard pointed a finger in Richard's face. "Because it is they who have what it is we seek. If I could just stroll ashore and make claim to it, I wouldn't have need for any of you, now would

I? We must fight for what we've come for, Mister Richards. The lot of you had best serve as I command and not give me any dissonance, if you have thoughts ta ever hold a penny of it." Blackbeard pointed to the door. "Now be gone from my sight and see to the preparations yourself. Check the riggings on the talking box like the lady showed us. I may have need of it soon."

Richards got up to leave.

"Fetch Morton to his cannons. I'll have each primed and ready for my command. And strike the lookouts and keep an eye for that sky contraption. I must know the instant it returns."

Chapter 11
0610: 25 August 2008

"*Spruance,* this is *Sea Hawk*. Over."

"Go ahead, *Sea Hawk*," replied Buchanan.

"Up and clear, ROTCY boy. All systems go. Commencing a sweep north to make sure you boys didn't let these punks slip away. When I find them, you can read about it in the headlines."

"Keep your eyes peeled, Commander, or that headline could be an epitaph. *Spruance* out."

Fox had barely finished speaking when one of his aircrew reported something floating in the water. He banked his helicopter to the left and dropped down to investigate.

"*Spruance,* this is *Sea Hawk*. You folks had better hold muster and count heads again because we've got a man in the water. Lowering a hero team to fish him out."

Fox hovered close to the surface and the crew dropped a rubber raft; two sailors rappelled down and rowed over. When they reached the floater and the forward seaman grasped him around the shoulders and pulled him in.

Fox positioned the helicopter over the raft again. After a brief struggle, the hero team got the man strapped into a harness and Fox winched him aboard.

110

"*Spruance*, it appears your pirate friends needed to make a little extra room. This old boy definitely ain't one of ours. Muster a medical team on the flight deck. *Sea Hawk* out."

* * *

Spruance came to a full stop to facilitate *Sea Hawk's* recovery. Maynard was surprised to his new guest hog-tied and lying face down on the helicopter's deck. The little man was immediately taken into custody by the Chief Master at Arms, and escorted to the Master at Arms shack. *Sea Hawk* returned to the sky.

Maynard and Perkins were waiting in the crew's recreation room for the prisoner to be delivered. Master Chief Radiomen Balf brought Maynard the latest weather forecast. The hurricane had started moving again, taking a brisk track north. The outer fringes were beginning to engulf the southern Bahamian provinces of Long and Great Exuma Islands. Winds around the eye were close to 100 miles per hour; storm surges were being felt as far north as Andros Island. Maynard handed the message to Perkins.

The movement of the hurricane was actually positive news. It set a lower search boundary and cut off the *Queen Anne's* southern escape routes. Maynard felt the noose was tightening.

There was another knock at the door. The Chief Master at Arms pushed the prisoner into the compartment and closed the door.

The funny little man stood before Maynard in a pair of coveralls that were twice his size; his hands were cuffed behind his back. His eyes immediately fixed on Maynard.

"Here he is, Captain," said the Master at Arms. "And he's a feisty little bastard."

The MAA put a black cloth bag and a long, crooked dagger

on the table in front of Commodore Perkins. The contents of the cloth bag had been placed in a clear plastic, evidence bags.

"He used that hog sticker to put a five-inch gash in one of the hero crew when they hauled him from the drink," said the MAA. "It took Doc Brown thirteen stitches to sew it up. The boys and I wrestled him out of his clothes and got him into these coveralls. I apologize for the way he looks but this is the closest thing we had that fit. He hasn't spoken a word since coming aboard."

The little man took a step toward Maynard. The Master at Arms jerked him backward.

"It's alright, Chief," Maynard said. "Let him go."

"You'd be him," the little man said softly.

"He'd be who?" Perkins demanded.

"You'd be the one. I knowed it the moment I laid eyes on ya. You'd be the son of Maynard."

"How in the hell could you possibly know that?" Perkins demanded again.

"With the Commodore's permission," Maynard said. "I'd like the Chief Master at Arms to step outside."

Perkins glanced at Maynard, then back at the prisoner. "You're dismissed, Chief," he said. "But hang close."

The little man fiddled with his handcuffs, and they fell to the deck. He kicked them toward the door. "Don't forget yer lovely bracelets, mate."

The Master at Arms jumped for him but Maynard interceded again.

"Just wait outside, Chief," Maynard said calmly.

"You two know each other?" Perkins asked.

"No, sir," Maynard replied.

Perkins glared at the little man. "Alright, mister. Just who are you, and what in the hell are you guys doing out here?"

The little man did not respond.

"It's okay," said Maynard, in a reassuring voice. "Just answer the question."

The prisoner looked at Perkins. "I'd be Mister Jeremy Ratliff, your Lordship. But me mates call me Rat. Crewman of the *Queen Anne's Revenge*."

Perkins looked poised to choke him. "Why did the crew of the *Queen Anne* make an unprovoked attack against a vessel of the United States Navy? And why did you murder the crew of the *Columbian Star*?"

"I suppose it's 'cause they made a spectacle of 'im. The captain ain't got no patience ta be made a fool. But I'd not murdered anybody, me Lord, and I have no say in the doings of the *Queen*."

"Commanding Officer to the bridge," boomed the 1MC.

Maynard quick-stepped to the phone. "This is the Captain...Lay a course immediately and make preparations for general quarters. Have radio forward the coordinates to Admiral Hays. I'll be up in a few minutes."

Maynard cradled the phone and turned to Commodore Perkins. "The F-18's have located *Queen Anne's Revenge*. She's sixty miles southwest of our current position. *Sea Hawk* is en route to intercept."

"It's about friggin' time." Perkins turned his attention to Ratliff again. "I want answers, mister, and I want them now. You can start by telling me what in God's name you people think you're doing out here?"

"You mustn't go an' attack the *Queen Anne*, Governor," warned Ratliff. "T'would be a foolish man's choice. The captain wants but to lure the son of Maynard into a fight, but will best whoever stands against 'im."

"Who wants to lure the son of Maynard to a fight?" asked

Perkins.

"Why, Blackbeard, Governor. Captain of *Queen Anne's Revenge*."

"I've heard all the Blackbeard bullshit I'm going to take!" Perkins shouted. "Blackbeard is dead, by thunder. So cut to the chase, little man, and tell me what's going on before any more people get killed."

"Aye, and dead he was, too," said Ratliff. "Saw it with me own eyes, I did. But now he's come back and he's brung the rest of us along with 'im."

Maynard listened intently. This man standing in front of him was quite possibly a breathing volume of maritime history; an original member of Blackbeard's crew. There were a thousand questions Maynard could like to ask. But only one mattered right now. "Why has Blackbeard come back?" he asked.

"'Tis 'cuz he's found 'is head, I'd wager."

That wasn't exactly the answer Maynard was expecting.

"Surely, you being men 'o the sea 'ave heard of Teach's lantern," Ratliff continued.

Maynard shook his head.

"Why don't you enlighten us?" Perkins replied.

"I just might, Governor." Ratliff gripped the front of his shirt with both hands like he was holding the lapels of a topcoat. "When the captain was slayed that fateful mornin' in Ocracoke, you see, 'is head were hacked clean from 'is neck and lashed to the bowsprit of the Royal's sloop. What remained of 'is body was pitched over the side. But when 'is hide touched the sea that day, 'is bones sprung back to life and started splashin' around like they possessed a power of their own. A searchin' for its missing head parts it was. And, for the next twenty-one days, he was spotted by fishermen, jest a splashin' around atop the waves, still a searchin'. After that, he disappeared. Except at night, when the moon is full,

114

and his spot in the water takes a yellow glow ta it. Ya'd not see 'is body though, but ya knowed the glow were the light from Teach's lantern, searchin' through the darkness ta find 'is missin' head.

"They say the day he found it, the light would take to the sea and he'd return to the living, sailing atop a gale as though he'd never departed. And now, here he is. With 'is head a sittin' atop his shoulders like it never got took."

Perkins drummed his fingers on the table. "What good is a lantern if you don't have a head?" He looked at Maynard. "Guess that solves the mystery of your submarine distress beacon. I'll let you explain it to Admiral Hays."

Maynard's attention was focused on Ratliff.

"So, I am to assume you're a ghost, too," Perkins said. "Is that your story? What kind of ghost gets his butt stranded out in the middle of the ocean? Why don't you just fly back to land and go haunt an old graveyard somewhere?"

"A ghost I might be, Governor. And if you had any sense about ya, which from the way yer a talkin' I'd 'ave my doubts, ya'd not go a messin' with the *Queen*. The captain will not permit you lay a finger on 'er. Them others tried, and ya seen what good it done 'em. Only the son of Maynard can have a go at her. And if you'd commence ta treatin' me a little more cordial like, I might show ya how to make a fight of it."

"Why would you help us?" Maynard asked.

"The captain must be stopped before it's too late. An' I must protect the kind lady, asI promised."

"What lady?" Maynard demanded.

"The lady Angela."

Perkins picked up the evidence bag and examined the suitcase tag engraved with Killian's name. "What does he want with her?"

A series of loud gongs rang out over the 1MC. "This is not

115

a drill! This is not a drill! General Quarters, General Quarters. All hands man their battle stations!"

Perkins jumped to his feet. "Chief!"

The Master at Arms charged back into the compartment. "Take the prisoner and lock him up. Put him in a straightjacket if you have to and post a watch. Just make sure he stays put."

Ratliff lunged at Perkins, grabbed his leg, and bit him on the thigh.

Perkins cursed and backhanded Ratliff across the face. Ratliff tumbled into the bulkhead and crumpled to the deck. The Chief Master at Arms pinned him, cuffed his hands again, and jerked him to his feet.

Ratliff's lower lip was split open by Perkins' blow and a stream of thick, bloody droplets formed along the tip of his chin. As each droplet engorged and released it vanished before landing on the deck.

Maynard watched in disbelief. The blood on Ratliff's chin faded and the cut disappeared right before his eyes.

Perkins's eyes were pasted on Ratliff, too. "Well, kiss my flaming ass."

* * *

"Captain," reported the Officer of the Deck. "Battle stations manned and ready. The quartermaster has plotted a course to intercept the target. ETA, one hour and thirteen minutes."

"Very well, Mister Fallis," Maynard replied. "Make turns for flank speed. Lock down battle condition Zebra."

"Condition Zebra and flank speed. Aye, sir," Fallis repeated.

Maynard walked over to the bridge intercom box. "Combat, Bridge."

"Combat, aye."

"Instruct Commander Fox to give us five minute updates on the target's movement so we can adjust our course as needed."

"Combat, aye. Getting that information for you now, Captain."

Spruance's LM-2500 marine gas turbines were given the throttle once again. In less than ninety seconds, the ship's speed indicator passed forty knots.

Condition Zebra was set, and all watertight doors and hatches were closed and dogged-down tight. *Spruance* was now fully prepared for battle.

Maynard could not peel his thoughts away from Ratliff—how that blood and cut just disappeared. Every time he tried to establish eye contact with Perkins since, the commodore turned away. Who could blame him? It was a lot to digest.

In less than thirty minutes, *Spruance* reached the first turn point. Maynard ordered the helm to zero-nine-zero, due east.

"Mister Fallis," Maynard said. "Pass the word for relaxed battle stations. All hands are to remain on station. In twenty minutes, we come back up to Condition 1 and position the security forces."

After relaxed stations was passed, Maynard stepped over to the Boatswain's Mate of the Watch. "I'd like to have a word with the crew now."

The boatswain's mate keyed the microphone and gave two long blasts on his pipe, signaling that the ship's commanding officer was about to address the crew. He handed Maynard the microphone.

"This is the captain speaking. We have relaxed from general quarters for about twenty minutes or so as we continue east toward our objective. I'd like to take a moment to fill everyone in on what's taking place. As you all are aware, we have been in pursuit of *Queen Anne's Revenge* these past few days. Minutes ago our LAMPS team located her again and now *Spruance* is making a full-speed run to overtake it. Our goal is to force her captain to surrender.

"Let's be honest. I don't expect them to just surrender to our boarding party. So we have to be ready for anything, including another exchange of fire. I want to reassure each of you that we are not in this alone. The *USS Fitch* and two Coast Guard cutters are in transit along with *Spruance*, and we have fighter support from Pensacola and Oceana. I have been given strict orders from the Joint Chiefs of Staff to defend ourselves with all available means should the need arise. If weapons fire ensues, all hands are to remain on station and listen up for directions. When orders are passed, I want each one of you to act quickly and responsibly.

"We are all men and women of the United States Navy, and this is what we have been trained to do. I am one-hundred-and-fifty-percent confident team *Spruance* will prevail. As I told your division officers during Officer's Call this morning, let's get this mess cleaned up and sail to Boston for a little well-deserved R&R. So stay loose and be prepared for when we resume Condition 1 steaming. That is all."

* * *

"Captain, the flappin' albatross is back," shouted *Queen Anne's* main top lookout. "To the horizon, off the starboard beam."

Blackbeard stalked over to the starboard railing, raised his binoculars, and peered across the water.

"Aye. So there it is. Come back for a second helping, have ya? Well, ole' Blackbeard has prepared a little welcoming present for ya."

"Garrat, break out the muskets and batten down the gun

ports. Main gunners, man yer cannons to the main and light yer torches. I'll have every hand in position and my *Queen* fully trimmed for battle. Morton, muster yer spar cannon crews at the hatches an' await my orders." He turned to Hands. "Fetch my cutlass and brace."

Hands disappeared below. He returned carrying Blackbeard's heavy cutlass and a brace of seven pistols. Blackbeard hoisted his cutlass into place, cinched the belt down tight, and concealed the pistols under his shirt.

"Once set, all hands 'er to stand fast and not twitch so much as an eyelash." Blackbeard shouted, "Helmsman!"

The hooded figure dipped its head.

"Hold course and be prepared to seize the wind south upon my command." He turned to a group of seamen on deck. "'Tis another glorious day, me lads. A jug of rum to the first to foul the deck with a Royal's blood."

Satisfied the preparations were progressing properly, he scanned the horizon. "Come to papa, you little whelp, so you may know the feral beast that breathes within."

* * *

Angela was curious what all the commotion was about. Finally, Hands opened the door and looked in on her.

"You'd best stay low, missy, and remain clear of them portholes there," he said pointing to the gallery windows. "Storm's a coming." As he closed the hatch, a grin flashed across his face. "He who masters the howls of darkness shall protect ye."

Angela ran over and beat against the door with her fists. "What's going on out there?!" she shouted. "Let me out of here!"

Chapter 12
1300: 25 August 2008

"*Spruance*, this is *Sea Hawk*, over."

"Go ahead, *Sea Hawk*."

"Buchanan, I have you fifteen nautical miles due west of the objective," responded Fox. "Be advised, it's getting pretty rough up here."

"Roger that, Commander. We're showing wind gusts up to thirty-four knots. I'll bring you home as soon as we have *Queen Anne's Revenge* in sight."

"You'd better make it quick, Buchanan," Fox said. "This bird ain't no showroom model."

"We won't let anything happen to you. *Spruance* out."

* * *

Maynard scanned the latest weather information and handed it to the Officer of the Deck. The quartermaster was maintaining a continuous plot of the storm and *Queen Anne's Revenge*. *Spruance* was closing on both...dangerously close. Blackbeard had not only returned atop a gale, he was using it as a shield.

120

Next to the hurricane symbol on the quartermaster's chart was the name *Drummond*, so anointed by the National Weather Service. Ironically, that was one of the many aliases Blackbeard used during his glory days as a pirate.

After *Sea Hawk* located *Queen Anne*, Perkins ordered the Coast Guard Sea Kings back to Miami. There was no need placing any more men or equipment at risk than necessary. The two cutters and *Fitch* were going to ride it out with *Spruance*.

When *Spruance* had closed within visual range, a white flag flew to the top of the pirate's main mast.

Maynard paid it no attention. He slowed to ten knots to make his approach, and eased alongside *Queen Anne's* starboard quarter. The two ships sailed side by side not more than forty feet apart. The wind and growing swells made it extremely difficult for the helm to maintain even separation. Every sensor in Maynard's body was on full alert.

Lieutenant Commander Wright had the ship's security force in position on the topside weather decks. Petty Officer Mottley reported in from the forward port break, prepared to plant the transponder.

Seamen were lined shoulder to shoulder on *Queen Anne's* top deck, but their captain was not among them.

The Petty Officer of the Watch handed Maynard the 1MC microphone and switched on all topside circuits. Maynard walked over to the port windscreen and looked out. This was all a formality; Blackbeard would never surrender.

"Aboard *Queen Anne's Revenge!* This is the Commanding Officer of the United States Navy destroyer *Spruance.* Acting upon orders from the government of the United States of America, we are placing the captain and the crew of *Queen Anne's Revenge* under arrest for the crimes of murder and high-seas piracy. Standby to receive your boarding instructions."

Not one of *Queen Anne's* crewmen moved. Blackbeard was watching from some place somewhere, calculating his strategy, searching for an advantage.

Four minutes had passed.

"I repeat. This is the Commanding Officer of the United States Navy destroyer *Spruance*. We are placing you under arrest for the crimes of murder and high-seas piracy. Surrender, and stand by for boarding."

Growing swells slapped the ship, kicking up a spray which was caught by the wind and whipped around the outer superstructure. Droplets pelted the windscreens and rolled back toward the sea in crooked streams. Maynard switched on a wiper.

Five more minutes, and still no reply. Maynard quelled a wave of anxiety; Blackbeard was making him sweat it out. He keyed the microphone again. "This is your final warning!"

At last, *Queen Anne's* captain showed himself, pushing his way through a wall of sailors. Dressed in black from head to toe, he defiantly strode into clear view; his long black hair and beard witching upon the wind behind him. The heavy cutlass was strapped to his left hip.

"Surrender your ship and prepare to be boarded," Maynard ordered.

"Whaaat?!" Blackbeard shouted. He pointed to the top of his mast. "I appear before you under the white flag of truce yet you demand I surrender my *Queen*. Damn you for villains! Stand before me now, son of Maynard, so we may become better acquainted."

Maynard placed the 1-MC microphone on the chart table and headed toward the hatch.

"Stand fast, Commander," Perkins ordered.

"Not this time, sir," Maynard replied. He undogged the hatch and stepped out onto the port bridge wing, reminding himself to remain calm; emotion only worked to Blackbeard's advantage. The first strike would be quick and deadly. There was no other way to do this.

"I have orders from the government of the United States of America to seize your ship and all its properties. Stand by and prepare to be boarded."

"Damnation seize my soul if I shall receive your quarters or grant you same!" Blackbeard shouted.

"If you won't surrender, I have no choice but to take your ship by force." Maynard held the index finger of his right hand into the air and twirled it a circular motion. Gunnery alarms sounded on *Spruance's* forecastle and fantail. Both 5-inch 54-caliber gun mounts rotated and the barrels angled downward until they were pointed directly at *Queen Anne's* bow and stern.

Blackbeard smiled. "A rather lovely tune. 'Tis a shame I can't recall the words. Though surely you jest. You've but two lonely cannons and I have so many."

He gestured to the row of steely black cannons tackled to the *Queen's* deck. "I'm afraid I must test your word, young Maynard. For on this day, I'll not be bested by a measly two cannons." He drew his cutlass, pointed it at Maynard, and shouted, "FIRE ALL GUNS!!"

Queen Anne's starboard gun ports opened. Her cannons breached the freeboard and thundered a series of reverberating booms. The seamen standing around Blackbeard reached for the deck and then stood up with muskets locked and ready.

Cannon balls impacted *Spruance's* superstructure below Maynard's feet; musket shot splattered against the bridge windows behind him. Maynard did not flinch. Blackbeard intended for him to die but would wait for the opportunity to do it personally.

From above on the signal bridge, the security force's M-60 machine guns cut loose with a clatter of full metal jacket fury.

Spent shell casings cascaded down from above in a river of brass; splinters of wood exploded from *Queen Anne's* deck. Blackbeard's marksmen were blown back like a chorus line of rag dolls.

Blackbeard roared at his men, "Get up you cowards and fight! You'd not be dead until I say yer dead!"

One by one, his men pulled themselves from the deck.

"Fight you bastards, fight!" the pirate ordered. "Lest I turn my cutlass and slay you myself."

His marksmen jumped for their muskets, reloaded and fired again.

Blackbeard ordered up his topside cannon crews. The guns below were rolled out the gun ports and set to resume firing.

Maynard shouted into the bridge. "Away the transponder!" He glanced down at the forward hatch leading from the port break. Petty Officer Mottley crawled out on his stomach, shouldered his M-14, and waited until both ships were in the trough of a wave. When they were at their closest point, fire spat from the end of the shotline canister. The transponder struck *Queen Anne* just below the bowsprit and held firm. It was a perfect shot.

He heard Mottley's voice over the bridge radio circuit. "Bridge, that will be one case of Foster's lager, served large and at room temperature."

Spruance's security force continued to pour on the small arms fire, but the bullets weren't stopping anyone. Lieutenant Commander Wright reported his topside forces had suffered multiple casualties. Maynard ordered the security force back inside the skin of the ship.

Blackbeard commanded his marksmen to cease fire, too. He pointed his cutlass at Maynard. "Be you the blood of Lieutenant Robert Maynard, the King's coward and murderer of innocent seamen?"

Maynard knew he could not fire *Spruance's* big guns at

Queen Anne at point blank range, especially with the Killian girl aboard. He called into the bridge. "Ninety degrees to starboard and full bells. On my command."

The transponder was in place. There was no need to risk further damage to *Spruance* or her crew. But a force deep inside Maynard made him step back to the bridge wing railing; a sense of complete calm enveloped him.

He shouted back at Blackbeard. "I am Maynard. You are the murderer of innocent seamen, dammed to hell by the will of God."

Blackbeard pointed to bloody water washing through the signal bridge scuppers and down *Spruance's* outer bulkheads. "I see no God here. Only the blood of his sheep." He pounded on the shank of his sword against his chest. "Through all these years, I have held fast to my word and shall force thee Maynard to fight me as a man. Fight, or know my wrath in a sea of thy kindred's blood."

Maynard did not skip a beat. "From the looks of things, your death at Ocracoke has suited you well. One must wonder why you wish to do it again."

The words escaped Maynard's mouth before he had time to contemplate what he was actually saying. "Should I kill you now, or would you rather surrender and save the embarrassment?"

"Embarrassment, indeed," Blackbeard replied. He turned to his men. "This one speaks as though I've invited him over for a pot of tea."

He turned back around. "Tell me, young Maynard, how does the living slay one who is already dead?" He threw open his shirt and slapped a ragged scar in the center of his chest. "Does he cower at the backs his men and fire a pistol, or does he draw cold steel across one's neck from behind? Your favored methods shall grant you no triumph this time, dear Maynard. A fight to your death it shall be, and the battleground shall again be of my

125

choosing!"

Maynard was impressed by Blackbeard's display of discretion: there was absolutely no evidence of malice in his tone.

"First, hand over Angela Killian," Maynard replied. "I will fight anywhere you want, but I will not risk her safety."

A toothy smile filled the lower reach of Blackbeard's face. "Aye, the sweeter the spoils, the more succulent the victory. Defeat me, and the girl shall be yours with not so much as a single hair out of place. Until then, I will see she's made comfortable in my quarters."

Blackbeard hoisted his sword into the air and continued. "So be it. The son of a coward has spoken. Ocracoke it shall be! Ship-to-ship and man-to-man." He leveled his sword on Maynard. "But at the end of it all, it shall just be you and I."

Maynard looked into the bridge and gave the helm a nod.

"It will take steel honed upon the breasts of angels to belay our deeds," Blackbeard shouted. "As for you, young Maynard, there is but one that may champion mine. I shall give you five days to prepare."

Spruance's engines screamed into high-fire, and she pitched hard to starboard. But Blackbeard was ready. He issued a command and *Queen Anne's* guns responded again. One topside cannon misfired, two missed wide as *Spruance* angled away. The fourth was perfectly aimed, sending a projectile crashing through the windscreen right next to where Maynard was standing. Pellets of thick glass showered in upon the bridge crew. The cannon ball ricocheted off the overhead and came to rest against the starboard bulkhead.

Blackbeard's lower guns hammered *Spruance's* port side one more time. Maynard felt a large explosion behind him in the vicinity of the helo hanger. He rushed inside the bridge; Perkins was picking himself off the deck.

126

"Captain!" shouted the Officer of the Deck. "*Fitch* reports a lock on the transponder. She's requesting permission to fire."

"Fire as soon as we're clear, goddammit!" Perkins shouted.

"Class Bravo! Fire in the helo hanger," yelled the Petty Officer of the Watch.

"Bridge, Combat," shouted the Combat Watch Officer. "Two direct hits in Sonar Control, with casualties. Emergency assistance responding from Combat."

"Damage control party to the hanger!" Maynard shouted. "Medical team to sonar."

The ship's bell clanged a rapid sequence of gongs. "THIS IS NOT A DRILL! THIS IS NOT A DRILL! Fire! Fire! Class Bravo, fire in compartment..."

Maynard's brain was tending twenty details at once; he should have disengaged cleanly from *Queen Anne's Revenge* while he had the opportunity.

"Damage in the Number Two starboard passageway," reported the Officer of the Deck. "Injuries in the galley."

"Ten casualties topside," reported the Messenger of the Watch.

⚓ ⚓ ⚓

"Helmsman, come about," Blackbeard ordered. "Make all canvas to the wind. Let us sail into the might of the devil's fury and celebrate our victory."

The lower sails were run out and *Queen Anne* pushed forward. Ten windblown cannon blasts echoed in the distance but all ten projectiles plummeted harmlessly into the sea.

The rain fell in buckets and Blackbeard watched the runoff funnel into the bullet holes left in *Queen Anne's* decking. The splintery edges softened, and the holes faded away. Satan's hand would make *Queen Anne* whole once again.

He smiled and looked back at Maynard's ship. Soon, he would have the son of Maynard completely at his mercy.

Chapter 13
1600: 25 August 2008

The Coast Guard cutters turned west and sailed for Miami. They would be of little use against the increasing winds of Hurricane Drummond. *Fitch* continued to skirt the outer edges of the storm, attempting to maintain a fix on the transponder. But disturbance caused by the lightning was making it extremely difficult. In less than an hour, they lost the signal completely.

Maynard pointed *Spruance* due north to give the crew a chance to bandage her wounds before returning to Mayport.

Blackbeard's gunners had inflicted considerable damage. The thin steel plating of *Spruance's* hull and aluminum superstructure were designed for anti-submarine warfare—fast and quite. She was not constructed for a direct pounding by cannons.

Maynard and Perkins examined the damage in Sonar Control. A repair team struggled to preserve the remains of several sailors, being thrown from side to side by the wind and waves.

Jagged holes in the outer bulkhead allowed the wind to swirl the stench of scorched flesh from Sonar into Combat. Maynard smelled the carnage well before he entered the space.

Twelve sailors were packed into Sonar Control at the time of the battle. The Antisubmarine Warfare Division Officer and chief technician were dead. They and two console operators were butchered by cannon balls which burst through the outer bulkhead behind them. A third was electrocuted when his console exploded in his face; others were shredded by a hail of shrapnel. Two others, also mortally wounded, lay face down on in a pool of body fluids. Most of it their own, some of it the blood of their shipmates. The rest stood shocked and pale, masked like Apache warriors in streaks of blood.

The damage to the galley was not significant. A steam line to a large jacketed cooking kettle had been severed and was hissing a cloud of powdery mist. The after-damage control team was working to secure the leak, clear debris, and cover the holes in the exterior bulkheads. The third damage control party was cleaning up from a fuel explosion in helo hanger. The fire completely destroyed *Sea Hawk*.

The topside security forces fared the worst. Ten were dead, their final faces twisted in primeval expressions of terror and disbelief. Another group was lined up against the bulkhead; some sullen, others wrestling the ghosts of misery, awaiting triage in a makeshift battle dressing station.

A bloody stew washed back and forth across the 02-level weather deck, clinging to the boots of medical personnel. A bagging detail was loading the dead into large black body bags, the zippers flashed like angry teeth. Maynard directed the casualties be taken to the refrigeration deck for temporary storage.

Perkins radioed SURFLANT to brief Admiral Hays on the situation. Three helicopters were dispatched to transport the wounded back to Mayport. Hays offered his condolences, and ordered him and Maynard to return with the last of the wounded.

Spruance would be piloted back to Mayport by Lieutenant Commander Wright. Wright's orders were to enter port after sunset so the darkness would conceal the damage. Only authorized personnel would know of *Spruance's* return. A controlled statement would be issued later.

Maynard finished surveying the damage, and set out for radio. He punched in his security code and pulled at the hatch. The door felt heavy, but he refused to give into fatigue now. There were only five days to prepare...five days or what?

"Lieutenant Yeatts," Maynard said. "Put through a secure call to Captain Richard Maynard in Boston." He wrote the telephone number on a piece of paper. "Once you've reached him, patch it through to the commodore's cabin."

Maynard departed radio. When he arrived at Perkins' stateroom, he found the Master at Arms and Jeremy Ratliff already there. He placed Jeremy in a chair next to Perkins and crouched down to address him face to face.

"Mr. Ratliff. How do I kill Blackbeard?"

* * *

Queen Anne was tossed around as she sailed deeper into the swirling storm, slicing into massive waves and propelling frothing towers of water over her bow and railings. Crewmen dangled by hand and toe amid the riggings, taking in the mainsails and lashing them to the yards.

Blackbeard stood alone on the quarterdeck with his face tilted skyward, water dripping from his beard and clothing. His feet were planted firm and wide. A bolt of lightning rifled downward, striking the deck in front of him.

"I am not thy fool!" he shouted. "I have left thy markings upon the faces of the godly and shall strike again whence the moment's right. These seas once again are yours, and the fates of the many bow to thy whim. Soon, they and you shall draw breath as one. To this we agreed. Thy will shall be wrought, but the methods I employ shall be mine." He pounded his fists upon his chest.

There was another flash of lightning.

"'Twas you that commissioned my marrows for this task, one from which I shall not fail. But my thirst shall be quenched as well. Your desires and mine are two grapes upon a vine that must ripen as one."

He clenched his fists and raised them into the air. "From this course I shall waver not. Not while the skies above my head are blue. 'Tis yours to decide, and decide this moment you shall lest I take one step more."

There was no sign.

"I speak with resolve. Return my soul this moment to rot in hell once again, or honor thy covenant and permit my hands revenge upon the blood of the one who defiled mine!"

The clouds exploded and another stroke of lightning sliced down from above. Sailors plummeted down the riggings and scurried for cover below decks. Then, suddenly, the winds let up.

Blackbeard lowered his arms and peered back into the clouds. "I shan't forsake thy generosity. Guide me now, so we may both embrace our destiny."

He turned and pointed to Garrat, now pensively reemerging from the hold. "Garrat, fetch about some kegs of rum. Each man shall drink his fill. The eye of the tempest is upon us. Let us relax our brows and revel in victory."

* * *

Angela sought shelter under Blackbeard's bed for protection from objects flying around the cabin. The storm muffled the sounds of gunfire but she had unmistakably heard—and felt— the roar of *Queen Anne's* starboard cannons.

There was a hard knock at her door.

"Are you decent, my lady? The gale has passed and we are freed to roam about."

Angela crawled out from under the bed, brushed off, and hurried over.

Blackbeard strolled into the cabin, obviously in high spirits. "Well now, you appear to have come through it all unfettered."

"What's going on?" Angela demanded. "Ships are supposed to navigate around storms, not charge through the middle of them."

She looked around the cabin. The drawers in the cupboards were hanging open; charts, cups and articles of clothing were strewn all across the deck. The large mahogany table had scooted against the deck and was resting against the opposite wall, the chairs askew and broken. "Who's going to fix my cabin?"

"Ah, 'tis nothing carpenter's mallets cannot restore."

"What was all that shooting about?" Angela asked.

"A celebration, my dear. We've bested the devil's wind and have sailed into the shallows of his eye. Few seamen can champion such a blow once it's got them firmly in its grip. So we celebrate. 'Tis tradition to spit in the eye of the enemy, is it not?"

"Next time, I'd appreciate a little warning."

"Aye, so we shall. But, now, allow me to change from these wet things, then let us share a drink to the occasion."

"I need Valium," Angela replied.

Blackbeard stepped to his wardrobe and started to unbutton his shirt. "You may turn and face the bulkhead if you like." He gestured with his hand to the wall. "Needn't privy you to all my secrets." He started humming a tune.

Angela turned away. "When are you taking me home?"

"Home?" Blackbeard echoed. "I thought you were enjoying yourself."

"Getting thrown around by a hurricane is not my idea of

enjoyment."

"And that, my lady, we must remedy with most haste."

Angela couldn't resist the urge to sneak a peek. She cut her eyes and slowly turned her head until his backside came into view. His shoulders and haunches were thick with fibrous muscle, and his back formed a perfect V from the top of his shoulders down through his hips.

A sheet of muscles rippled as he bent over to remove his pants. But there was something odd about the texture of his skin. She craned her head a little more to get a better angle.

There were numerous purple lines drawn in random patterns across his back. It dawned on her that they weren't lines...they were scars, every bit as gruesome as the ones on his chest. There must have been thirty of them, like someone had used his body for a grotesque game of tick-tack-toe.

How could anyone do such a thing to another human being? He must have endured unimaginable pain.

Blackbeard finished, backed away from the wardrobe and closed the doors. "Now, that's much better."

Angela quickly turned around.

"All dressed an' fit for a lady." He rubbed his hands together. "How about that drink?"

"Make mine a double," Angela said.

"Now, there's the spirit. Allow me to summon a couple mates to join us. 'Tis time you gained comfort with my crew, and they with you."

Blackbeard nodded his head and bounded for the door. He paused at Hands, who was manning his post right outside, and whispered something in his ear. Hands grinned and followed him down the passageway.

Angela heaved a sigh of relief. She walked over to the mirror and straightened her hair. *Just what in the hell is going on around here? Who are these people? And why am I here?*

Blackbeard returned carrying three stone jugs and a fist full of cups. "This should satisfy your thirst."

He pushed the table back to the center of the cabin, righted the usable chairs, offered her one—which she accepted—and sat down across from her. There was another knock at the door.

"Come in, lads," boomed Blackbeard. "The festivities are just beginning."

Hands, Richards, Miller, and Garrat entered. Judging from the smell of liquor, the latter two had already engaged in festivities of their own. Miller and Garrat plopped down at the table. Hands, ever vigilant, remained standing.

"You, too, Mister Richards, Mister Hands. Have a seat. You needn't gander about like spectators."

Richards and Hands each pulled up a stool.

Blackbeard looked around the table and raised his cup. "Just like the good ole' days, eh lads?"

They all returned the toast.

"Aye, but I'd not recall the pleasure of such charming company back then," Miller said, raising his cup to Angela.

"Mind yer manners now, Miller," Blackbeard warned. "The lady here is our guest. We must make 'er feel at home."

The men all threw back their drinks. Blackbeard filled the cups again. Angela, at first, only sipped at hers.

"Just like the captain here," Miller continued. "Always mindful of the ladies. Why, in our day, the maidens would 'ave trampled the rest of us just for a chance to catch his eye. He always quartered the finest among them too, I might add." He lifted his cup to the captain again. "Let's see now. Believe t'was twelve, no thirteen maidens he toiled before the mast. Wedded most of them myself. Eternally devoted to each, was he. And they to him. Aye. Was a well-known fact the mighty Blackbeard could not resist the charms of a lady."

"That'll be enough of that nonsense," said Blackbeard.

Thirteen wives," Angela said. "I'm impressed. Sounds like you were easier to catch than you were to hold."

"Fourteen to be correct, my dear," Blackbeard replied. "Your friend, Miller here, always forgets the Governor's niece, out from Charleston. Wedded her in the spring of 1718. And a thing of beauty she was, too. All of sixteen years, and delicate as a peach blossom."

"Sixteen?" Angela's outburst brought a round nervous laughter. Blackbeard didn't look too bothered by it.

"I'll have you know my Mum was married for three years an' with two little ones by the time she was sixteen. T'was nothing to scoff about." Blackbeard rapped his fist against his chest. "And look what a magnificent steed made I."

"Sorry," Angela replied. Tell me more about your blossoming Charleston love."

"'Tis not much to tell. I had a mind to settle down an' become a respectable citizen. I'd made fast with the King's Proclamation and built a sturdy, white house atop a hill in Bath Town. Had it fancied up with all the finest comforts known to the world. Aye, a lovely home it was. Then one day, the old itch came calling. Found myself putting back to sea aboard *Adventure*. A true man of the sea has no appetite for the soil. He must wash back into the ocean like the tides. So, off I went. Sailing up the coast to New Philadelphia. From there, things got a tad busy, ya might say, and I lost track o' the little darlin'. Was just as well, though. Her pappy never held favor to my company."

"That's sad," Angela said. "She might have been the one to make an honest man out of you."

"Now there's a novel thought," Miller said. "Edward Teach, the honest captain of thieves." The men joined in another round of nervous laughter.

"Had me a wife one night," Garrat interjected. "Took pert near two bottles o' rum and a month's spoils to carry 'er back ta' me cabin. T'were worth every halfpenny, though. Could barely steady me legs for nigh a fortnight."

"Sounds like he holds his maidens like 'eh holds his rum," Hands said.

"I hear tell he'd dampened his knickers before she'd even hoisted the pins from her bonnet," Blackbeard added. The men cackled with laughter again.

"Now, that's not so," Garrat squawked. "Nearly twice the size of me, she was. And very honored to quarter the interest of such an upstanding gentleman."

"After two bottles of rum, she probably passed out and fell on you," Angela said. "That's what broke your legs."

Garrat frowned. "Come on now, not you too. I thought we was chums."

The men had another good laugh, even Garrat. Angela poured another round of drinks, filling Garrat's cup first.

The drinking and storytelling continued for another forty minutes or so. Hands fetched two more jugs. Angela was beginning to get lightheaded and tapered back. Sensing the mood had sufficiently loosened, she decided to initiate a subtle interrogation.

"So, what are you guys really up to? You don't expect me to believe you just sail around out here all day shooting your cannons. Something has to be pay for all this."

"Aye," Miller answered. "We'd be searching for treasure. The sea's rich with goodies spoiled from countless Spanish galleons."

"So this is an expedition? But why the costumes?"

"These is not costumes, my lady," Garrat said. "'Tis the way men of the sea dress."

"Yeah, yeah, I've seen those movies, too. I suppose you have an old treasure map or something. Is the pirate gag just for publicity?"

"Pirates is what we is, dear lady," Hands said. "For sure, you'd heard of Blackbeard and the crew of *Queen Anne's Revenge*. We'd be known sand from the sands of the Canary Islands to the folds of the Queen's knickers. We sail once more to collect our dues."

"Okay, let's see if I've got the gist of this," exclaimed Angela. "Somebody came across one of Blackbeard's old maps and has hired you guys to search for his treasure as pirates. So this is a documentary."

"Our map walks within the captain himself," Garrat said. "'Tis nary a pinnacle of these waters that's not known to Blackbeard, the most courageous captain to navigate the mighty blue."

They each held up their cups in another toast. Angela gazed at her host as he sat rolling his cup between his massive hands. His eyes had that twinkle that she was becoming fond of. He certainly fit his part.

She and Marc had actually stumbled into the filming of a documentary. That's why they kept her stuffed away in this musty old cabin. The producer, or whatever, needed to work her into the story without spoiling the rogue atmosphere of a pirate ship. At some point, they would have to offer her a contract. No sense risking a venture like this with a liability suit.

Maybe her father's law firm had already taken care of that. Perhaps her father and Marc had arranged the whole thing.

"Alright, gents," Blackbeard said. "'Tis time to test yer resolve. Let's engage in play to see who's best. I'll wager five pieces of gold to the winner. Any takers?"

"Here, here," Garrat slurred.

"And I," added Miller.

Hands—who, next to Richards, was the least intoxicated—replied, "Not I." He looked at Angela and started to rub his left knee. "Last time I gamed, I nearly got me leg blowed off."

Richards likewise declined the invitation.

"Then fetch me five of the bravest amongst the lads," Blackbeard said to Hands. "And a game we shall have."

"What are you going to do?" Angela asked.

"A mere show of strength. 'Tis harmless play I create to reminded the crew who's in command. Say now, would ya care to wager a kiss to the victor?"

Angela flashed him a suspicious smile. "I'm not getting involved in this."

"Aye, where's your sense of adventure? You could boast to all of Charleston how you were once an official member of Blackbeard's crew."

That was the first time Blackbeard had mentioned taking her home. Maybe she was right; this was all just a big stage. "Alright, Captain Blackbeard," she said smiling. "You're on."

"Then prepare yer pucker, milady, and off to the hold we shall go!"

Once all the players were assembled Blackbeard led the way. Angela followed him down two sets of ladders into the bottom of *Queen Anne's* hold. He carried a lantern with a smoky globe that cast a shadowy amber illumination across the deck and bulkheads. There was barely enough light to keep from tripping over obstacles littering the deck.

Blackbeard halted at a hatch. He lifted the latch, pulled it open and directed the others to file in. It was musty and cramped inside.

"I call this little game, HELL," he said and hung the lantern from a peg in the overhead. "Mister Hands, if you will kindly furnish me the combustibles."

Hands stepped outside and returned with two smudge pots and passed them to his captain.

"Splendid. Now, the rules are this. I shall ignite these two little flower pots and place them upon the deck. I shall then close the hatch and see who can brave the vapors longest. He who does shall win the five pieces of gold." He jangled the coins in his pocket. "And a kiss from the lovely Angela."

Garrat whooped his delight at the prospect of that.

"Now, strip to your trousers and toss yer blouses to the lady. Can't have you stifling the fumes with the sleeves." The captain took a sulfur match from his pocket, struck it on the seat of his pants and lit the contents of the two pots.

He turned to Hands and Angela. "If the two of you will kindly excuse us, the lads and I have a little business to tend to."

Angela followed Hands out of the compartment. Blackbeard slammed the hatch closed behind them.

Angela wafted her hand in front of her face. "That stuff smells horrible."

Hands struck a match then reached into the darkness for a second lantern. "The scent of Devil's Lilac."

The lamp produced a bright light which illuminated the center of the compartment. Angela spotted several sets of eye peering back at them. "Don't even tell me those are rats."

"Aye, so they are," Hand said. "Thought you was partial to the wee varmints." The lantern light sparkled off his white teeth as he spoke.

Angela leaned against the bulkhead and put a hand to her forehead. "I think I drank too much."

"Ya'd sleep well tonight, I'd think. But ya best step aside that hatch lest you be pummeled when they break."

* * *

Inside Blackbeard's hell, several minutes passed. The smoke from the pots was thickening.

"Aye, reminds me of a fragrant spring morning in Hell," Blackbeard said. "For certain, you mates recall the pleasantries of Hell now, do you not?" He leaned against the bulkhead and reached into his pants pocket again. "It brings out a person's appetite."

Blackbeard produced a bloodstained napkin and unfolded a strip of raw meat. He dangled the meat across his tongue, then gnawed off a large chunk and chewed it so that all of them could see the juices squeezing through his teeth.

"Nothing better than a chaw of spotted dog ta get the 'ole guts churning. Yet it gives one the vapors something fierce." He rapped his fist on his chest, belched the meat back up, and began chewing it again.

Miller grabbed his stomach.

The smoke from the pots had all but obscured the light from the lantern. Blackbeard positioned himself in front of the hatch to ensure nobody could escape before he had finished his fun. He observed Miller eyeing the latch, slowly edging himself toward it.

"You gents were having such a jolly time of it above. Where is the humor of it all now?"

Blackbeard kicked the crewmen standing next to Miller in the stomach and he fell to his knees gasping.

"That's it, lad. Suck in deep. Let your rotted self take stock of it as a reminder of where you'll be returning should ya lose sight of the task before us. When we next battle the Royals, victory shall not be so easy." He raised his voice to emphasize that point, but not so loud that Angela might hear it outside.

"When I command you to fight, you fight. When I

command you to kill, you kill. Only then, shall we earn the victory we seek. And with victory, you shall enjoy a life of riches beyond imagination. Just as I promised. You gents would be wise to remind your shipmates as well. Failure will not be tolerated."

The smoke was beginning to burn Blackbeard's lungs, too, but he forced a smile. "'Tis so peaceful down here, don't you agree?" He reached into his pocket again and extracted his whale-bone pipe. Passing it under his nose, he drew in a big snort. "Ahh," he exhaled. "Care to join me for a smoke?" He leaned forward to light his pipe off the lantern.

Miller made his move for the hatch. He dropped his shoulder and hit it with every scrap of strength he possessed. The hatch ripped from its hinges and flew across the hold. The others tumbled out behind him and fought their way to the ladder.

Up on the quarterdeck Blackbeard had arranged a reception by a band of drunken shipmates armed with buckets of water.

Blackbeard sauntered from the chamber, toking on his pipe and cackling to himself. Hands and Angela came over for a closer examination. Blackbeard tried his best to appear unaffected.

"Why, Captain," Hands said. "You'd look as though you be coming straight from the gallows."

Blackbeard rocked back onto his heels. "Mister Hands, that's a brilliant idea. Next time, we shall play at gallows and see who can dance upon the breeze longest without being throttled." He leaned over and glared his sailing master in the eye. "Perhaps the option to decline may not be entertained for that one."

Hands turned and hobbled for the ladder to join the others.

Blackbeard led Angela by the hand up to the main deck where he gave himself a rinse of clean water, scrubbing vigorously to remove the stench left upon his skin by the smoke. He escorted Angela back to her cabin and poured the last two shots of rum from the crocks. Angela took a seat at the table and slugged hers down without even wincing.

"What did you mean yesterday when you said you had made a pact?" Angela asked. "That fate had brought you and me together."

Blackbeard emptied the rum from the other cups into his own and gulped it down. "I was wondering when you'd come back to that." He sat in his chair at the head of the table.

"You see, my dear, my purpose for sail is twofold. One is to lay claim to my treasure, as you have so cleverly perceived. The other is for redemption; redemption for my untimely departure from this miserable world. In order to obtain either, I must first render the devil's tax. The price I must pay is to select a bride and father a child in his most unholy name. For this purpose, you have been chosen."

Angela stared back at him. Moments passed. "Oh, swell. I'm supposed to have sex with Blackbeard the Pirate and give birth to Satan's baby. *Pirates of the Caribbean* and *Rosemary's Baby* all rolled into one. Is that what this is all about? You pay the tax, and I get stuck with the stretch marks. And I thought this was going to be just your average romantic sail to the Bahamas."

Angela leaned across the table toward him. "Suppose I choose not to be selected? What will you do then? Make me walk the plank?"

"Walk the plank," he answered. "Whatever do you mean?"

"You know, toss me to the sharks. Take a long walk off a short pier."

"Why, no, my dear. I would never do such things to a creature so lovely as you. The choice, of course, is yours. As it must be. But enough of that talk for now. I should have never broached the subject. 'Tis late and a lady must have her rest."

"You drop a bomb like that and then just send me off to bed. Don't you think I might want to discuss it?

143

He rose from the table. "We can speak of it again tomorrow, if you like." To his surprise, Angela didn't protest.

"I hope Parsons can find me some decent food somewhere." Angela yawned. "I'm getting tired of Oatmeal cookies."

Blackbeard raised an eyebrow. "Say, how's about that kiss for yer champion?"

Angela shuffled over to the edge of the bed and eased into a sitting position. "You'll have to come over here to get it." She fell back onto the pillows. "I'm done."

Blackbeard placed her legs on the bunk, covered her with a sheet and knelt on the deck beside her.

She grabbed him by the front of his shirt. "How about we just go ahead and get it over with? Take me now before I realize what I'm doing."

"How would thou be taken?" he replied softly, not quite understanding the question.

She massaged the thick, bristly hair on his chest. Her eyes went half-kilt. "Any way you want."

"Aye." Blackbeard felt himself blush.

He watched her eyes slowly draw close. "Though it is your flesh I desire, my love, your heart is that which perplexes me most."

Angela nestled her head into the pillow. "Whatever."

He pushed the hair to the side of her face. "The ageless one has chosen wisely that our paths should cross. Your charms are truly a rare brew of spirit and humanity. Indeed, charms that shall serve his purposes well."

He took a deep breath and slowly released it. "So strong and so alive, yet so soft and so innocent. My doings have brought you to this foul place. Through my lust for redemption, you must bear the light of the unholy. To foster it in your womb as your own, only to have it snatched away at some point for objectives far beyond the structure of your heart. I have spoken this evening of my own mother. My endeavors, no doubt, did much the same to her; ripped the very soul from her flesh, they must. This, too, I did for my own contrivances."

"Over the years, how many other mothers' hearts have I so disheveled? Aye. Though from my featured course, I cannot depart. The likes of Maynard shall grant me nary a moment's rest. Indeed, they shall haunt 'til the end of time."

He stroked Angela's hair again. "Perhaps, when our union is at hand, I may summon the strength to resist. Perhaps that one just act may sway the balance from so many wretched doings. Aye, 'tis much to consider. But the decision to accept my seed must be yours and yours alone. There can be no other way."

He paused for a moment. "Choices. Perhaps somewhere therein resides a solution. But for now, my lovely Angela, sleep soundly and rest those emerald tides of your'n. There is yet so much in life for them to behold."

He leaned over and pressed his lips to her forehead and turned down the lantern. Then walked to the door, pausing once— only briefly—to look back at her.

Chapter 14
2200: 25 August 2008

Maynard sat on a jump seat in the rear of the helicopter, holding a flashlight in his left hand and scribbling notes on a small spiral notepad with his right.

It was imperative he organized his thoughts before meeting with Admiral Hays, but the steady pounding of the helicopter rotor blades overhead was making it almost impossible to concentrate. He tried to stay focused.

He glanced at Perkins sitting next to Jeremy Ratliff; both of them were staring back at him. Blackbeard's words echoed through his brain again: "Be you from the blood of Robert Maynard...the same of that cowardly Maynard that murders innocent seamen...I have held fast to my word...I shall force thee to face me as a man...fight or know my vengeance in a sea of thy kindred's blood."

Ocracoke, Ocracoke, Ocracoke! The words bounced around his head like a tape recorder stuck in endless replay.

It couldn't possibly be Blackbeard...Blackbeard was dead, dead, dead! Maynard slammed his foot on the helicopter's deck and the jolt shot a wave of pain up his leg. If nothing else, it reassured him that he wasn't dreaming again.

He looked at the charred body of Lieutenant Commander

146

Fox; clutched in his bloody hand was a small copy of a Gideon's Bible that Lieutenant Buchanan had placed there before they lifted off. Blood had filtered through the fibers of Fox's bandages and was drying in rust-colored patches. It was doubtful he'd survive.

Blood. Just like in the dream. Everywhere there was blood. The faceless bodies and piercing shouts were merely a preview of his impending battle with Blackbeard. Maynard was convinced of that now. A battle that would culminate with him lying on his back surrendered to the mercies of Blackbeard's sword.

The helicopter plodded on through the darkness. Maynard leaned forward holding his notepad between the flats of his hands. He looked at Ratliff again; Ratliff had to be the key to all of this. Suddenly, an idea returned to him. He waved the notepad in the air to get Commodore Perkins' attention. Perkins unbuckled his seat belt and squatted next to him.

"When we land in Mayport, I need to get to the Exchange."

"What the hell for?" Perkins asked.

"There are a couple things I need before the briefing."

Perkins motioned to one of the air crew and the petty officer came over. Perkins snatched his headset and put it on.

"This is Commodore Perkins. Put through a call to Lieutenant Commander Curtis Jenkins with DESRON Twenty-four. Be quick about it." He waited for the pilot to make the call.

"Jenkins, this is Perkins. We'll be on the tarmac in about ninety minutes. Have a car waiting to escort Commander Maynard to the Navy Exchange...that's right, the Exchange. Get a hold of Caruso at Special Services and tell him to have it open in thirty minutes...I don't give a damn if he's watering the little woman's mattress flower! Orders from Vice Admiral Hays. Tell Caruso if he's not open by the time Commander Maynard gets there, I'll have his reassigned to a supply desk on a tug boat in Cleveland before sun up...Perkins out."

Chapter 15
2335: 25 August 2008

At 2335-hours, the helicopter touched down at the Mayport Naval Air Station. A medical team loaded Lieutenant Commander Fox into an ambulance and sped off for the hospital. A stocky young man rushed over and saluted Maynard as a third car pulled up.

"Commander Maynard, I'm Lieutenant Junior Grade Harry Clements. Lieutenant Commander Jenkins has instructed me to accompany you to the Navy Exchange, sir."

"Very well," Maynard replied.

The lieutenant walked him to a black sedan with a pennant on the hood bearing a commodore's star. Perkins, practically dragging Jeremy Ratliff by the shirt sleeve, headed for the other vehicle.

"Captain Caruso from Special Services will be meeting you there," Clements said. "But, be prepared, sir. Commander Jenkins had to get him out of bed."

Maynard got in the car and Clements drove off. A light drizzle began to fall and he switched on the windshield wipers.

"Sir, if you don't mind my asking, what do you need at the Exchange this time of night?"

148

"Reading materials," replied Maynard.

Clements smiled and shook his head. "Yes, sir."

In less than five minutes, they pulled up in front of the Exchange; the place was lit up like a Macy's grand opening. Captain Caruso was waiting alone outside.

The lieutenant looked at Caruso. "Glad it's you and not me, sir. Should I go ahead and break the ice?"

"Stay here and keep the car running," Maynard said.

Maynard got out and hurried over to Caruso, extending his hand. The captain reluctantly accepted.

"Thanks for meeting me, Captain," Maynard said.

Caruso looked down at the silver oak leaves pinned to the collar flaps of Maynard's khaki shirt. "Where's Admiral Hays?"

"He sent me in his place." Maynard pushed the door open and went inside. Caruso followed.

"Looking for anything in particular, Commander? Maybe I could interest you in a nightgown for your wife. That is, if you ever let her to sleep."

The Exchange was the Navy's equivalent of Super Wal-Mart. It was place where active and retired military personnel could purchase anything from standard issue Fruit of the Looms to scuba tanks. Maynard ignored Caruso's sarcasm.

He threaded his way through the aisles over to a section containing books and periodicals. He picked up several hunting magazines and fanned the pages until he found what he was searching for. He tucked the magazine under his arm and moved on.

Caruso watched with tempered curiosity but didn't say a word.

Next, Maynard headed toward a display of books on naval history. He knew the book he wanted was still in print because he'd seen it at the Cape Hatteras Lighthouse gift shop just a few months earlier.

He stopped and scanned the bookshelf and spotted the red book with bold lettering and a black-and-white picture on the cover. He grabbed a copy, studied the picture, and took the remaining two copies.

Caruso was standing so close behind him that Maynard could smell the minty aroma of his toothpaste. "Put these on the admiral's tab," Maynard said and made a dash for the front of the building.

"You bet I will, Commander," Caruso yelled. "And thanks for shopping the frigging United States Navy!"

Maynard hit the front doors in full stride and hustled out to the car. He jumped in, stuffing the magazine and two copies of the book into his briefcase, keeping the third copy out for himself.

"DESRON Twenty-four?" Clements asked.

"Go. And turn the interior light on."

Maynard opened the book and began flipping pages. He stopped, skimmed several paragraphs, then took a pen from his pocket and underlined a couple key passages. Clements adjusted the rearview mirror so he could better view Maynard's activities.

A few minutes later, Clements pulled into the parking lot at DESRON Twenty-four. Half a dozen spaces were occupied by large black sedans; two of them bearing pennants with white stars attached to the front of the hood. A group of the enlisted men, drivers most likely, were gathered next to one of the cars smoking cigarettes. They saluted Maynard as he walked up the sidewalk.

Lieutenant Commander Jenkins waited for him at the front door.

"Good evening, Commander," Jenkins said. "I hope you found everything you needed at the Exchange."

Maynard gave him a nod. "Thanks for arranging it. After Captain Caruso has a chance to cool down, you might give him a

150

call and express my appreciation."

"I'll see to it first thing in the morning." Jenkins opened the door and followed Maynard in.

DESRON Twenty-four was as quiet as a morgue. Judging from all the vehicles outside, it should have been crawling with people. Jeremy Ratliff was seated in a chair next to the door.

Maynard heard footsteps charging up the hallway from the conference room. Perkins stepped around the corner, his face red. "Lieutenant Commander Fox passed in the ambulance on the way to the hospital. They could not revive him."

Maynard sat his briefcase on the floor. That placed the death toll near forty. Perkins had reminded him on several occasions that none of this was his fault but that no longer mattered; Maynard felt the weight of each departed soul as though they all were heaped upon his shoulders.

"I know how ya feels, me Lord," Jeremy said. "I've lost a bundle of me mates, too. All too many I might 'ave saved."

A wave of anger welled up in Maynard. Ratliff and his ilk were responsible for this. But when he looked in the little man's face, he saw two ragged old eyes that spoke of a life of hardship and injustice.

Jeremy was not the one to blame for this. Maynard's anger subsided.

"Secretary Turnbul, Admiral Hays, and a cluster of Pentagon brass are waiting in the conference room," Perkins said. "They haven't met our little friend here yet. I thought it best if you and I talk to them first. Your father's flight arrives at the Naval Air Station in about twenty minutes. Jenkins will meet him on the tarmac and brief him during the drive over."

The front door opened and Lieutenant J.G. Clements walked in.

"Clements, keep an eye on Mr. Ratliff here until I call for

him. See to it that he doesn't float off." Perkins looked at Maynard again. "We'd better not keep the Secretary waiting."

Maynard picked up his briefcase and followed Perkins down the hall to the conference room. After a flurry of quick introductions, everyone was seated.

Admiral Hays looked at Perkins. "Alright, Commodore, what went wrong?"

Perkins recounted the events leading up to the battle. When he finished, Hays turned his full attention to Maynard.

"And, at that point, I assume you returned fire, Commander?" Admiral Hays asked.

"Yes, sir," Maynard replied. "With M-14s and M-60s."

"What were the casualties aboard *Queen Anne's Revenge*?"

Maynard was not sure how to phrase his reply. Finally, he answered flatly, "zero, sir."

"Zero," Hays repeated.

Secretary Turnbul threw himself back in his chair. "You mean to say your people returned fire with automatic weapons and didn't hit a damn thing, Commander?"

"Begging the Secretary's pardon, I didn't say we didn't hit them. I just don't think we killed any of them. The members of our security force are excellent marksmen. When we opened fire, we knocked *Queen Anne's* men to the deck as you would expect. They just got back up." Maynard directed his next comment to Admiral Hays. "Every time we shot one, sir, he got back on his feet and continued to fight."

"Could they have been wearing vests?" asked one of the admiral's staff officers.

Maynard shook his head. "Some of them were barely wearing shirts." He looked at Hays again. "The first time we encountered *Queen Anne*, I shot their captain twice in the chest with a 50-caliber machine gun. Those rounds should have blown holes through him the size of grapefruit yet there wasn't even the slightest drop of blood."

Hays remained calm. "I get the picture, Commander. What happened next?"

"After we planted the transponder, *Queen Anne's* captain demanded to talk to me. His men had lowered their weapons so I decided to chance it."

"What compelled you to do that, Commander?" Hays asked.

"We need to know why he's doing this."

"What did he say?"

Maynard stopped to gather his thoughts, and rubbed his hands across his chin. The pirate's words populated his thoughts once more.

"Take your time, Commander. I know it's difficult."

Maynard cleared his throat. "He demanded to know if I was related to Lieutenant Robert Maynard of the British Royal Navy."

"Why would he want to know that?" asked Hays.

There was a knock at the door. Perkins sprang up and opened it. Jenkins and Mr. Maynard filed in. When the commander saw his father, he released a sigh of relief. He got up from his chair and clasped hands; his father had a stern look on his face.

Admiral Hays walked over. "Captain Maynard, it's indeed a pleasure to see you again. He extended his hand. "Sorry we had to bring you out like this but, under the circumstances, I'm sure you understand."

"That's alright, Admiral. I'm still on the muster."

Hays introduced Secretary Turnbul and then turned to Perkins. "I believe you already know Commodore Perkins here."

"It's been a long time, Perky," said Mr. Maynard.

"Damn near fifteen years, Dick, if my memory serves me. How's retirement?"

"Making an old man older."

The admiral finished the introductions and the group was seated again. Hays remained standing, his mood was all business again. "I was just about to ask the commander why the captain of the *Queen Anne's Revenge* would be interested to know if he was related to a historic British Naval officer."

Maynard exchanged a quick look with his father before he spoke. "Admiral. In November of 1718, Lieutenant Robert Maynard, acting on orders from Governor Spottswood of Virginia, engaged and killed the pirate Blackbeard at Ocracoke Inlet, North Carolina. It was one of the bloodiest naval battles to ever take place in the waters of North America."

Hays stood silent for a moment. "I'm familiar with the history, Commander."

"Lieutenant Maynard was my great-great-great grandfather," continued Maynard. "My father and I are the last two descendants of his bloodline."

Hays returned to his chair. His eyes were laser-focused on Maynard's face. "I know, Commander. I just needed to hear it from you. Your father and I go back a long way. I don't know if he remembers, but your family history came up during a conversation he and I got into one night in the wardroom aboard the *USS Sherman*. A man doesn't forget a conversation like that."

Hays leaned forward and put his hands on the table in front of him. "What happened next, Commander?"

Secretary Turnbul looked as though he was ready to hit the ceiling.

"He said he would force me to meet him man to man, sir," Maynard replied.

"Meaning?"

"Meaning, he wants me to fight him."

"He has already battled *Spruance* twice. Why would he

154

want to fight you again?"

"It's not a battle of ships he's looking for, sir."

"So you're telling me you believe Blackbeard, or someone posing as Blackbeard, is trying to enact some kind of revenge against you and your family?" asked Hays. "Is that what this is all about?"

"Yes, sir. That is what I believe." Maynard glanced over at Commodore Perkins, who was squirming in his chair again. "There's no other explanation that fits."

"You're out of your mind, Commander," spat Turnbul. "What a ridiculous conclusion. Do you take us for fools?"

Maynard's father spoke up. "Admiral, I've brought something I'd like to share with you. It may shed some light on what Robert is trying to explain."

"By all means, Captain," said Hays.

Mr. Maynard rose, looked around the room and cleared his throat. "At the end of the battle at Ocracoke, after Lieutenant Maynard's men had finally taken Blackbeard to the deck, lying there with blood seeping from his many wounds, history claims that he simply expired. The truth is he didn't just die. He spoke and what he said was heard only by Lieutenant Maynard. His words had such a significant impact on the lieutenant that he wrote them in his diary, just as Blackbeard had said them, and left instructions for the journal to be passed down through each generation of Maynards. He also insisted there always be a Maynard son on active naval service in whatever navy occupied the continent of North America. That legacy should not be hard to verify. Frankly, it has actually been more of a curse.

"Shortly after Ocracoke, a scandal broke out. It was generally assumed Blackbeard had amassed an immense fortune he had secretly buried at some remote spot along the Outer Banks of North Carolina. Since it was never officially recovered,

155

Spottswood assumed Lieutenant Maynard had managed to pilfer it. The allegations were never proved, of course, but the lieutenant was dismissed from the British Navy in disgrace."

Mr. Maynard reached into the inner left pocket of his sports jacket and produced a vacuum-sealed plastic bag. Inside the bag was a ledger about the size of a checkbook. He unsealed the bag, removed the ledger, opened the black leather cover, and carefully thumbed through the stiff, wheat-colored pages.

"This is Lieutenant Maynard's personal diary, painstakingly preserved by my grandfathers. On the night before Robert left to attend Annapolis, I sat him down and read this passage:

'November 22, 1718. As the murderous scoundrel, forever to be known as Blackbeard the Pirate, deposited himself upon the spar amidst an expanding pool of his own vitality, he positioned his head such that only our eyes could meet, and spoke to me with the full firmness of his deviled resolve. In a voice that only I should detect, he said..."You shall know mine kind once more. Vengeance upon you. And the fires of Hell to any who stand in my way."

It is my most utmost conviction and deepest of fears that one day—either I or one of mine—shall know his company once more. May the eternal mercies of our Almighty God protect us all.'

Mr. Maynard looked at all the faces around the room. "You see, gentlemen, that's why all your attempts to defeat *Queen Anne's Revenge* have failed. Let me add one more thing. As I alluded earlier, our grandfather's request has been more of a curse. Because of it, Maynard sons have died in every America military conflict since. Through it all, our numbers have dwindled; in my generation, there were only two male children. The other, my cousin, was shot down over Vietnam. That left just me. Robert is my only son. He and his wife have been blessed with two beautiful daughters. Robert is the last son of British Lieutenant Robert Maynard. Blackbeard has come back to eradicate the last of the

Maynard bloodline. And the Navy, with all its conventional firepower, cannot not stop him."

The conference room had become cold and silent. Robert could see disbelief growing upon the faces of the others. But not a one of them, including Secretary Turnbul, offered any kind of objection.

"Admiral," said Maynard. "My father and I would like an opportunity to speak with you in private."

The admiral leaned forward again. He appeared to be reading something in Maynard's face, and then sat back. "Gentlemen, I believe it's time for a break. Take ten and give the commander and me a chance to talk."

The other officers got up and slowly exited the room, each stared at Commander Maynard as they passed. Secretary Turnbul appeared irritated by the dismissal but followed the others into the hallway.

Perkins was the last to leave. Hays pointed to him. "Get Ratliff outside before the Secretary sees him."

* * *

Perkins rushed down the hallway. When he reached the foyer, he found Jeremy sitting at the front desk clicking a ball-point pen in his left hand. He and Clements were playing tic-tac-toe.

"Clements, take that little squirt for a walk."

"Sir, where did you find this guy? He just hustled me out of twenty bucks." Jeremy looked up and started clicking his pen again.

"I said, take him and go. Now move!"

Clements grasped Jeremy by the shoulder and stepped out the door just as Secretary Turnbul turned the corner from the hall.

157

* * *

In the conference room, Admiral Hays' brown eyes had become dark and piercing again. He stood and walked around, stopping at the window and gazing out.

He turned to Maynard and said in a low but fully lucid voice. "The two of you feel certain about this Blackbeard notion, don't you?"

"Sir, at this point, I'm not really certain what to believe," said Maynard. "But I do know two civilian vessels have been attacked, and one of the US Navy's finest warships has been battered twice. A lot of good men won't be going home to their wives and families. I also believe in God, sir. If good can work through mediums, then so can evil."

"And you just told the Secretary of the Navy, who works for the Secretary of Defense, who is chief counsel to the President of the United States, that the United States Navy—supported by hundreds of billions of taxpayer dollars—is trying to track down and capture the ghost of Blackbeard the Pirate. That his ghost has somehow been resurrected and is currently hiding in a hurricane off the coast of Florida. Those are not the kind of explanations they want to hear coming from the mouth of the senior ranking officer of the United States Navy's entire Atlantic Fleet, the most powerful and destructive military force in the modern world, Commander."

Hays walked back and stood before Maynard. "So just what makes you think he would go to all this trouble just to kill to you?"

"I can't answer that, Admiral. But I know our radar cannot locate Blackbeard's ship, and that our weapon systems can't stop him if it could."

"I've got five Hawkeyes combing the edges of that hurricane and a squadron of F-18s on full alert in Pensacola," Hays responded. "When our friend out there—whoever or whatever he is—pops out of that storm, the F-18s will lock onto your radar transponder and commence strafing runs. And, by God, we will pound *Queen Anne's Revenge* until every trace of her has been erased from the face of this Earth!"

Hays relaxed, walked around the table, and sat back down in his chair. "I assume you have a plan."

"Yes, sir," Maynard replied. "There is also a female hostage aboard *Queen Anne*."

"I can't help that now," snapped Hays. "First thing tomorrow morning, the Secretary and I will fly out to *Spruance* to inspect the damages. When I get back, we'll talk. He looked Maynard in the eyes again. "Do we have an understanding about the Killian girl?"

"Yes, sir."

"Anything else before we call the others back in?"

"Just this." Maynard opened his briefcase and pulled out two copies of the red book titled *Blackbeard the Pirate*. He slid them across the table. "I've highlighted a couple paragraphs."

Hays picked up the book and examined the cover, then cut his eyes at Maynard. "Commander, I've followed your career with considerable interest ever since your graduation from Annapolis. I've watched you mature into a strong and competent leader. I hope to God you know what you're doing. If not, you just laid waste to a brilliant career. Personally, I'm banking on the F-18s."

Hays stuffed the books into his briefcase.

Maynard went to the door and asked the other officers to rejoin them.

"Gentlemen, that is all for tonight," said Hays. He turned to Secretary Turnbul. "Sir, we'll head out for *Spruance* first thing tomorrow morning as planned. Captain Lee will have a helicopter waiting for us at 0600 sharp." He glanced around the room at the others. "I need the rest of you back here at 1300-hours."

Chapter 16
0745: 26 August 2008

The rotor downwash swirled up layers of thin mist as the helicopter slowly circled *Spruance*. The damage to the ship's exterior was not as severe as Hays had expected. Most of it was already concealed under sheets of aluminum.

After touchdown, Lieutenant Commander Wright hurried out to greet Admiral Hays; he escorted him and Secretary Turnbul to the wardroom where he attached a diagram of the ship to a movie screen and began the briefing.

"Admiral, Mr. Secretary, as you can see by the X's on the diagram here, we took a total of twenty-five hits from hostile cannon fire. The sixteen red X's mark where the projectiles penetrated the hull and superstructure. The nine green X's indicate where they bounced off areas supported by internal framework. Only nine of those that actually penetrated managed to detonate.

"As Commodore Perkins stated in his message to you yesterday evening, we suffered our heaviest damage in Sonar Control. Both of the pirate's rounds that impacted that space exploded inside the skin of the ship. Five of the twelve personnel manning their General Quarters stations in Sonar at the time were killed, including Lieutenant Junior Grade Jack Seglem and Senior

Chief Petty Officer Jeff Morton. Five additional personnel were seriously wounded. Other than some ancillary gear, most of the equipment in sonar is a total loss."

Wright's use of the word pirates made Hays uncomfortable.

"Only one shell penetrated near the water line, here in the weapons berthing compartment." Wright pointed to a spot on the starboard side of the ship, just forward of the amidships quarterdeck. "This projectile also exploded. Fortunately, we were at General Quarters and no one was in the space. There was no serious damage. The forward Damage Control Team did an excellent job shoring up the hole and preventing a more serious problem.

"We took four hits along the second-deck passageway between the ship's office and the galley. No serious damage resulted from any of these either, and only minor injuries. We took three hits in the galley and crew's mess passageway; two men were killed and three more wounded. The damage has already been repaired and the galley is fully functional again.

"Two rounds struck the helo hanger, one detonated and one did not. Six members of the helo detachment were killed. Another eight were wounded, mostly by flying debris and burns after the helicopter's fuel tank exploded. Fortunately, *Spruance's* bulk fuel JP-5 storage tank was not affected, but the helo was totally destroyed.

"The last shell which exploded struck the after-paint locker. The fantail phone talker was quick to respond and reported the hit to the bridge. Once the weapons fire had ceased, HT Chief Hatton and a fire crew hustled out and foamed the space. He probably saved us from another rather nasty chemical explosion. Finally, the last shell to strike us was the one which hit the bridge but this one failed to detonate."

"How about the security forces?" Hays asked.

161

"Ten dead and seven seriously wounded. We received word just before you landed that all the wounded have made it through surgery. So far, so good. And you probably noticed from the air, all the holes along the main weather decks have been temporarily repaired. I suspect it will require time in the yards to affect anything permanent. As for Sonar Control, the area has been sealed off and a watch posted to ensure no one disturbs it. If you'd like, I can remove the barrier so you can see it firsthand. But I must warn you, it is not pretty."

"That's okay, Commander," Hays said. "It can wait."

"How about damage to the ship from small arms fire?" asked Captain Lee, Admiral Hays' senior aid.

"Sir, I've asked Gunners Mate Chief Dunbar to come up and answer any questions you may have regarding the hostile's ordinance. But to answer your question, sir, small arms damage appears to have been minimal."

Wright set his pointer on the table and looked at the admiral. "That's all I have. Before I bring in Chief Dunbar, I'd be happy to answer any other questions."

"Mister Wright, were you able to get any photographs of the damage before you commenced repairs?" Lee asked.

"Yes, sir. Pictures were taken by the helo detachment photographer's mate and individual members of the crew."

"I think it would be wise if you held quarters and confiscated all film, camera and cell-phone cards," said Hays. "Bring them to me along with the shots taken by the helo crew. Search all the berthing compartments if necessary. Information regarding this matter hasn't been released to the public and we need to keep it bottled as long as possible."

"I'll see to it personally, sir." Wright looked around the room again. "If there are no further questions, I'd like Chief Dunbar to talk to you for a few minutes."

Wright walked to the door and returned with Chief Dunbar, the latter carried a gym bag that made a metallic, clanking sound when he sat it on the table.

Dunbar cleared his throat. "Mister Secretary, Admiral Hays, and fellow sirs. I'm from the mountains of Tennessee and have been a hunter ever since I was six years old. My father preferred using black powder rifles. So until I was sixteen, they we all I ever had. Dad also dressed for Civil War re-enactments as part of the First Knoxville Artillery Division of the Tennessee Volunteers. I'd tag along and help with the chores, and was usually responsible for cleaning and polishing the cannons at the end of the day. I suppose that's why I became a gunner's mate in the United States Navy."

He opened his gym bag and lifted out one of the objects. "What I have here is what is referred to as a twelve-pounder, except it weighs closer to twelve-and-a-half. This is the one the bad guys shot through the bridge." He turned it around so Hays could see the large hole drilled into the core.

"When the XO called me to the bridge, I found it lying against the starboard bulkhead. I couldn't determine what type it was from a distance but, since it didn't explode, I figured it was either a blockbuster or a dud. When I got close enough to see the fuse assembly here, I about dropped my teeth. After I was fairly certain it wasn't live we put it in a bucket of water and took down to the HT shop. Later we drilled the fuse and emptied the charge.

"Exploding rounds have been around for a couple hundred years. This one's not as robust as the ones they used during the Civil War. It is not perfectly round and there's no rifling marks cut in it, which tells me it was fired from a smooth-bore cannon. So what you actually have is an extremely unstable piece of ordinance. The shooters don't even know if it's going to work. If you asked me, they're lucky it didn't blow up in their faces.

"The way I see it, either the powder got wet, the fuse wasn't primed correctly, or it's just so damn old that the powder wouldn't burn. Some of these are filled with nails, like a Claymore mine. Others, like these, fragment the casing. Either way, they mess up whatever's near it."

Dunbar sat the cannonball on the table and reached into the bag a second time. "This is the other projectile type they used." He lifted out a second cannonball. "It's called a blockbuster. It's a solid chunk of steel with no charge inside; this one's a sixteen-pounder. They require a different powder charge to shoot, were cheaper to produce and didn't explode if they were accidentally dropped. Fire one at a wooden ship with a light powder charge and it's like driving a bus through the side of a barn. Most of what they shot were blockbusters. My guess is, they were trying to conserve powder or these babies would have probably gone clear through us."

Dunbar set the second ball down. "Lieutenant Commander Wright asked me to brief you on the pirate's small arms. I was at my G.Q. station in Mount 51 so I didn't see any of the shooting. But from what I gather, it sounds like they used old flintlock muskets. And judging from the way their rounds splattered on the bulkheads, they didn't know much about modern ballistics."

"Why's that?" Hays asked.

"Lead, sir. All they used was lead bullets. If a shooter truly meant business, he'd use hollow points and sabots. Hell, if I was them, I'd use a nine-millimeter Uzi. Flintlocks are too slow and, if you get your frizzen pans or flints wet, they are totally useless. It would also be difficult to find a supply of flintlocks to outfit that many men. I don't know of but a few companies that still make them. Most are for decoration."

There was a knock at the wardroom door. Lieutenant Commander Wright stepped over to answer it and came back with a grim look on his face.

"Thanks, Chief," Hays said. "We'll probably want to talk again later."

"Yes, sir." Dunbar gathered his stuff and quickly exited.

Wright handed Hays a closed metal clipboard. "Radio just received this."

Hays silently read the message. He gritted his teeth, and slammed the binder closed. "DAMN!" He got up and walked to the front of the room.

"Mr. Secretary, this is a message from Commodore Perkins. Minutes ago, six F-18s and the *USS Fitch* launched an attack on the *Queen Anne's Revenge*. She had just pulled away from a cruise liner that was skirting the southern edge of the hurricane. The Hawkeyes failed to pick up on the transponder signal; instead they intercepted a distress call from the cruise liner. Gentlemen, the attack failed, and *Queen Anne* has disappeared back into the storm. Perkins indicates there are casualties."

"Ours or theirs?" Turnbul asked.

"Passengers on the cruise liner."

"Captain Lee, hustle to radio and contact Commodore Perkins. Instruct him to organize a rescue with whatever resources he can muster. I want that cruise ship escorted to Guantanamo Bay as quickly as possible and sat on. Alert Admiral Klaus in Gitmo and instruct him to make preparations to receive and moor a commercial cruise liner. Send helicopters out with medical personnel and have *Fitch* put as many of their people on that ship as she can spare. Keep the passengers calm and give them anything they want. Let them know the Navy is doing everything humanly possible to assist them. Under no circumstances is anyone allowed contact with the outside.

"Commander Wright, get my bird ready. I'll be returning to Mayport immediately. Mister Secretary, you're welcome to come with me or stay here and complete your tour of the ship. The rest of you question every man that witnessed what happened yesterday, and do it fast. When I reach Mayport, I'll turn the helo around to come get you. Report back at DESRON Twenty-four no later than 1300-hours."

* * *

Blackbeard had his entire crew wedged into the mess and adjacent passageway. He pounded his fist on a table. "I said there was to be no lootin' and no killin'! You were to take only what I said was needed, then make us off: Morsels for a lady's palate. Nothing more! If any one of you buckets of pus wish to challenge my command of this ship, let him step forward now and be out with it."

Each man looked away as Blackbeard's eyes fell upon them.

"I thought not. From this moment forward, all of you shall do exactly as I say. If so much as one of you dares to take exception, I'll keel haul the whole lot. There will be no more insubordination." He glared around the mess again. "Now get yer filth from my sight."

Men started climbing over one another trying to get up the ladder.

"Get on with ya now," shouted Blackbeard. "Before I change my mind and lash your hides just for sport!"

Blackbeard ducked into the galley to get a tray of food for Angela, then headed down the passageway. He pushed open the door to his cabin and kicked it closed behind him. Angela lay face down in her bunk, out cold. He set the tray on the table.

"Rise and shine."

The sprawling mass of hair and pillows didn't stir. He gave her shoulder a brisk nudge. "'Tis a new day, me Angel, and I've a table fit for a princess."

Angela slowly began to move. She pushed herself up with her hands and flopped onto her back. "Oh, God. Just let me die in peace."

"Aye, so there is somebody in there."

"What's left of one. I feel like I've been flattened by a beer truck."

"I suppose I should have cautioned ya about me rum, little darlin'. But you seemed to be having such a good time of it."

"That wasn't rum, it was rat poison. And please stop yelling."

"Aye, you'll feel better once you've got something in yer belly. I had Parsons fix a hefty breakfast. Just like you requested."

"Don't come anywhere near me with that. I never want food in my stomach again."

"Now, that's no way to be. I shall leave it on the table. You can take it when you're ready. You mustn't hurt the Parson's feelings. He went to considerable effort to procure just the perfect fixings."

Angela moaned again and pulled a pillow over her head.

"Perhaps I should return a bit later."

"Bring a pistol and put me out of my misery."

Blackbeard chuckled as he departed.

* * *

Angela didn't have a clue what time it was when she finally pulled herself out of bed. She managed a sitting position and then teetered on the edge of the bunk until she could gather the courage to stand. Shuffling like a hunchback across the deck to the mirror, she stared at her reflection. Her prized bronze skin was the color of army fatigues, and the whites of her eyes looked like Washington,

D.C. street maps.

"Oh, God. That can't be me. I already am the devil's mother." She contemplated what she had just said, and dropped it. Now was not the time for thinking.

She turned from the mirror and wandered over to her suitcase, peeled off her clothes, and sponged off with a basin of water provided on a small table next to the bed. The lukewarm water was only marginally refreshing.

She slowly got dressed. The odor of stale rum mixed with the aroma of Parson's breakfast was more than she could tolerate so she decided to go topside and give that a try.

She angled over to the door and pulled it open, expecting to find Hands sitting there, surprised to find he was not. Angela picked her steps through the outer chamber and down the passageway, located the ladder, and climbed up onto the main deck.

The shock from the light felt like someone jabbed ice picks into her eyes. She ambled over to the railing and drew in a long, deep breath. The damp, salty air was slightly more invigorating than the water in the basin.

This was actually the first time she had been on deck during full daylight. Suffering as she was, the beauty of it all was still spectacular: massive white sails, polished riggings, and an intricate network of ropes and pulleys. She spotted Garrat hauling something out of the water and headed aft. She eased up behind him and tapped him on the shoulder.

"Oh, Jesus!" he yelped and whipped around as if mounting a counterattack. He saw it was Angela and relaxed. "You ought not sneak up on a mate like that."

Angela apologized.

"Aye, you don't look so fit, milady. Appears ya had a wicked time of it with the captain's spirits."

Angela nodded. "Big time. Where did ya get the shades?"

"The what?" he asked.

"The shades. You know, sunglasses." She pointed to the pair resting on the bridge of his bony nose. They were the first normal thing she had seen since coming aboard.

"Oh, me colored spectacles. Found 'em this morning. They make me look quite fetching, I'd say."

"Mind if I borrow them?"

"No, no, here. I'd be honored."

Angela slid the glasses up her nose and looked around. "That's better, thanks. What are you pulling out of the water?"

"Why, I'd be fishin'. The water in these parts is teaming of snappers and prize billfish."

"Any bites?"

"Naw. The storm's a got everything all churned up. But ya never know. There may be a big 'ole chomper eyeballing me trimmin's as we speak."

No sooner had the words left his mouth, his line pulled tight and yanked him forward, almost threading him through the pickets on the railing. Angela grabbed him but he'd already released the line. The line was flying seaward.

"Thar she blows!" Garrat shouted. "Stand back now, Missy. Let 'im take as much of it as he wants."

A handful of crewmen came over to investigate. Garrat's coil of line unraveled for several minutes and then gradually started to slow.

"Aye, this one's a beaut," Garrat said as he bent over to pick up the remainder of the coil. He walked over to the capstan and wrapped the line around it, still allowing the fish to take what it wanted.

When the line stopped feeding out, he looked back at the others. "Let's heave to."

Angela stepped out of the way. Garrat and two other seamen inserted long, wooden bars into the pigeonholes at the top of the capstan and started turning in the line. As they did, it snapped up off the surface of the water like a tightrope.

"Missy," said Garrat, "grab the rope as it comes off the capstan and steady back on it. Don't let no slack come of it."

Angela did as she was directed, and leaned back on the line with all her strength.

"That's it, milady. Hold on fast so's we can turn 'im in."

Fifty yards behind the ship, a giant blue marlin burst from the surface of the water, its long, gleaming bill fenced with the halyard. It was the largest billfish Angela had ever seen.

For over an hour, they labored with the marlin. Garrat kept a steady eye on their slim but steady progress. The creature would relax for a moment, allowing Garrat to take several turns and then, with another burst of energy, it would soar into the air again to resume the fight. If the line got too tight, Garrat stopped the turning and allowed slack to pass out.

"Don't keep letting it out, silly," Angela said. "We'll just have to reel it all back in again."

The onlookers cackled. "Yeah, Garrat. What'chya trying ta do? Catch 'im or hang 'im?"

"Ya got ta give 'im all the line 'eh wants, milady, or he'll toss the hook and dive for Neptune's cellar."

A second group relieved Garrat's crew at the capstan. Angela held on fast; focusing on the fish helped her forget how lousy she was feeling.

"Here, let me help with that," said a voice behind her.

Angela slapped back with her hand. "Get out of my way. I've got it."

"Aye, me Angel. I think they'd be room enough for the two of us. Besides, ya mustn't tatter those lovely little hands of yours."

170

Angela looked around and saw it was Blackbeard. "Oh. Sorry."

The shadows shortened and then began to lengthen again, but the fight continued. Angela was getting fatigued but was determined to stay her post. Men in groups of three took turns at the capstan until the last of the mighty marlin's strength was exhausted. Finally, they drew it alongside and held it in place until a boat davit could be rigged to hoist it from the water. When it was up and clear, everyone cheered.

"He must be nigh five-hundred stones, Garrat," Miller said. "What ya gonna' do with 'im now?"

"We're gonna' skin him, chop 'im up, and have Parsons toss 'im in the pot and cook 'im."

A lump rolled up inside Angela's throat. She looked at the captain.

"Mates, I say we let the lady here decide," Blackbeard said.

"You can't just kill him!" Angela blurted.

One of the men spoke up. "What? An' just let 'im go?"

"Why ya wanna' do a thing like that?" asked another.

"Come on, guys," Angela said. "You've proved your manhood, now let him go. You can eat a can of tuna or something."

Everyone turned to Garrat. "Gents, the lady's heart 'as spoken," he said. "Freedom it shall be."

Garrat pulled a knife from his pocket, jumped up on the davit and slashed the line in two. Everyone crowded the railing to watch the fish splash back into the sea. It floated on its side for a moment, quivered and then—with a powerful thrash of his tail—darted back into the waves.

Blackbeard removed the bandana from around his neck and tied it around Angela's. "For lending to and helping yer mates haul in such a magnificent prize, I hereby pronounce you Master Fisher Maiden of the *Queen Anne's Revenge*."

171

"Here, here!" Garrat said. The others repeated the cheer.

Angela threw her hand in the air. "High five."

Blackbeard gave her a puzzled look.

"Oh, never mind," she said, and put her arms around both him and Garrat.

As the men disbanded, a small group gathered amidships near the starboard railing and began to talk amongst themselves. One of them peered back where Angela and Blackbeard were standing. Blackbeard and Garrat noticed them, too. Blackbeard's body tensed and his brow furrowed.

Angela found it odd that she had not seen Jeremy while pulling in the marlin.

* * *

Admiral Hays arrived at Mayport a little after twelve bells. He set up a command center in the commodore's office and initiated conversations with Admiral Hawthorn at the Pentagon, Rear Admiral Klaus in Guantanamo Bay, and then radioed the captain of the *Fitch*.

Secretary Turnbul commandeered Jenkins' office. He listened in on Hays' telephone conversations and then put through a call of his own to the Secretary of Defense.

Hays buzzed Jenkins. "Jenkins, have the commodore and Commander Maynard finished yet?"

"No, sir. They and Mr. Ratliff have not shown their faces all morning. The commodore ordered they not be disturbed unless Blackbeard has laid siege to Charleston again."

"Tell them to wrap it up," said Hays. "I need the conference room at 1300-hours."

"We'll have it ready. Sir, Captain Lee and the other staff officers have just landed."

"Good. When they arrive, please escort them back."

"Yes, sir."

Ten minutes later, Captain Lee knocked on the admiral's door.

"Alright, Captain," said Hays. "Let's hear it."

Lee sat down; he looked exhausted.

"Admiral, we interviewed twenty-five witnesses from the bridge, the signal bridge, the security force and the after lookout. They all reiterated the same story; dead men who just wouldn't die. One of the M-60 gunners claims he knocked the same pirate on his butt three times. Said it was like shooting ducks on a pond. Each time, the bastard got up and tried to reload his musket. The whole bunch was apparently unstoppable."

"We'll see about that," Hays said.

There was another knock at the door. Jenkins and Secretary Turnbul entered.

"Admiral," said Turnbul. "The President and the Joint Chiefs of Staff have requested your recommendations before they determine our next course of action."

"Yes, sir, Mr. Secretary," said Hays. "Commodore Perkins and Commander Maynard have been working on a plan. I think it's time we find out what it is."

When the brain trust had reconvened around the conference table, Admiral Hays resumed the briefing. "To bring everyone up to date, at zero-eight-fifteen this morning *Queen Anne's Revenge* emerged from the hurricane and attacked a cruise liner trying to beat the winds to Miami. Her sails were torn, and she was pretending to be disabled. The captain of the cruise liner lowered a small boat to render assistance. The pirates seized the launch, boarded the ship and took control of it. Then *Queen Anne* came along side and our friends commenced playing pirate again.

"Six F-18s and *Fitch* converged on *Queen Anne* shortly

173

after she pulled away. They strafed her; *Fitch* shelled her with their 76-mm gun, and fired three Harpoon surface-to-surface missiles. All attempts to destroy *Queen Anne's Revenge* failed. One of the F-18 pilots said they put enough twenty-millimeter rounds into her to air-condition a shopping mall."

The room fell silent again. Secretary Turnbul scribbled on a notepad in front of him.

Captain Lee spoke up. "What do we do now, Admiral?"

"We listen to Commander and Mr. Maynard. That's what." All eyes shifted to Commander Maynard.

Chapter 17
1300: 26 August 2008

Maynard always considered himself a reasonable and circumspect officer; never one to act on a whim or take an uncalculated risk, either with himself or the men who served under him. But what he was about to propose threw all that out the window.

He opened his briefcase and removed a manila folder, the hunting magazine, a copy of the red book and walked to the front of the room.

"Gentlemen, in my mind I have reenacted my great-grandfather's battle with Edward Teach a thousand times, trying to imagine how I would have fought it if I were in his shoes. I figured I'd write it all down in a book someday.

"As most of you know, I will be assuming command of the *USS Constitution* in the coming weeks. I propose we prepare her for sea immediately, pilot her out of Boston Harbor under the cover of night, and set sail to destroy *Queen Anne's Revenge* on the open seas."

Secretary Turnbul let out a groan. "Commander, that's absurd. *Constitution's* two-hundred years old. She couldn't possibly undertake that kind of mission."

"With all due respect, Mr. Secretary, you are wrong," replied Maynard. "I spent the better part of a week aboard *Constitution* back in May. The truth is, only about ten percent of her timbers are original material. Five years ago, she underwent another extensive restoration. When they first got her in dry dock, they discovered there had been remarkably little deterioration since her bicentennial overhaul in 1975. Even so, every inch of her was examined and then either refurbished, repaired or replaced, right down to her turn buckles and bow spar. She was also fitted with new masts and sail."

Maynard turned to Admiral Hays. "Sir, *Constitution* is in better shape now than she was one hundred years ago. Let there be no doubt about it, *Constitution* can hold up her end of the deal. It's the rest of us we need to focus on."

"What about a crew?" demanded Turnbul.

"*Constitution* has a regular complement of forty-nine sailors; two officers and forty-seven enlisted. They don't really have the necessary sailing skills but are comfortable working aloft and are familiar with her riggings. I will drill them from the moment we leave Boston until we arrive off the coast of the Carolinas. By the time we fight, they will be able to shift sail at a moment's notice."

"You expect a bunch of museum keepers to fight pirates who have already sacked a United States Navy destroyer, Commander?" The Secretary tossed a copy of the red book onto the table. "It says here it took five bullets and twenty cutlass wounds to kill Blackbeard the first time. Can a bunch of museum keepers do that?"

Secretary Turnbul is correct," Maynard said. "We can't expect *Constitution's* crew to fight Blackbeard. Not by themselves. *Constitution* is armed with fifty-four cannons. Most of them can be made to fire. We will need a minimum of 150 to 175 gunner mates trained to use them. We'll also require at least seventy-five Marine Corps infantry hand-to-hand combat specialists and as many Navy SEALS as can be spared. A second and much smaller contingency of troops should be positioned in Ocracoke should *Queen Anne* decide to put ashore. We'll also need boatswain's mates, signalmen, cooks, storekeepers and all the usual support personnel. A crew of about four hundred men in all.

"*Constitution's* raised bulwarks make her like a fortress. They will provide maximum protection to our deck forces against level small-arms fire, and provide a firing line for our marksmen. Of course, *Constitution* is primitive. Once we leave Boston, we will be without conventional electrical power. We will require portable power generation, battle lanterns and satellite communication equipment to keep in touch with our command center. We must be completely self-sufficient.

"We are also going to need a lot of weapons." Maynard produced the copy of Southern Sportsmen magazine and flipped to a paper-clipped advertisement for Knight muzzle-loading firearms. "They must be black powder like these. We should have at least two hundred rifles, two-hundred-fifty to three hundred pistols and all the supplies that go with them. Each man will also be issued a cutlass or a dirk, and any other sharp weapon he can carry.

"The SEALS and Marine Corps combat specialists will give the rest of the crew a crash course in hand-to-hand combat on the way down. Each man should at least know the basics. Hopefully, by the time we go man-to-man, we will have sufficiently reduced their numbers so that our marines can handle what's left without putting the rest of the crew at risk.

"As for the black powder weapons, all recruits are trained in the use of firearms during boot camp. All we need is to acclimate them to a new style of weapon and give them as much practice as possible. I suggest we enlist a Knight factory representative to assist with the training."

Maynard looked around the room. "We must begin making preparations aboard *Constitution* immediately. We need to have her underway for Little Creek within twenty-four hours to pick up supplies and the rest of the crew. With a little luck, we can make the sail from Boston in under two days. I estimate it will take a day in Little Creek and then another sixteen hours to Ocracoke. The ground detachment will proceed to Ocracoke ahead of us and prepare a secondary assault from the beach.

"Last spring, the Corps of Engineers dredged a navigation channel from Ocracoke Inlet, across the Pamlico Sound and up the Neuse River to New Bern, North Carolina. The channel was cut to a depth of thirty-five feet; fully loaded, *Constitution* will have a keel of about twenty-one. Finding enough water to sail her should not present a problem but, in order to maneuver outside the shipping channel, we need to find areas that have at least twenty-two feet of depth. I propose, once our landing forces arrive in Ocracoke, they begin mapping the sound to chart the position of hidden sand bars and other obstacles. The map can be airdropped to *Constitution* prior to entering the inlet.

"In addition, Ocracoke Island must be evacuated. There's a small Coast Guard lifesaving station there that should be able to help. The last thing we need are more witnesses. Additional ferries will be required from the North Carolina Department of Transportation. The only way off the island is by ferry. Blackbeard will attempt to get into Ocracoke ahead of us to take his own soundings. Like us, he will need to know where it's safe to maneuver.

"*Constitution* is fast, maneuverable and can deliver a broadside of twenty-six 24-to-32-pound guns. That's more firepower than any other heavy frigate ever built. We will engage *Queen Anne*, keep a safe distance as long as possible, and pound her with our cannons until she's ready to crumble. After which we will come alongside, cross over, and let our marines and SEALS finish the job."

Maynard continued undisturbed for another ten minutes filling in the details. When he had finished, he looked around the room.

All eyes returned to Admiral Hays.

Captain Lee was the first to break the silence. "Hell, Commander, the only thing you left out was a dinner menu and seating arrangements."

"Suppose your cannons can't do the job?" Turnbul asked bluntly. "Do you have a contingency plan? Perhaps a more reasonable alternative."

"No, sir. This is the only way we can stop Blackbeard and *Queen Anne's Revenge.*"

"And you are certain of this?" asked Hays.

"Yes, sir," Maynard replied.

"Suppose *Constitution* becomes disabled or even worse, sinks before you can attack," Turnbul said. "Given her age and the worsening sea conditions, I see that as a distinct possibility. Suppose you manage to engage *Queen Anne* and are the ones defeated. What happens then?

"I understand you are a very capable officer, Commander Maynard but, according to the plan you just outlined, you'll be fighting in a manner that's not exactly in keeping with the current doctrines of naval warfare. I'm also curious as to why you think you are qualified to lead such a mission."

" Step back and listen to yourself. I think we all need to consider the potentially disastrous consequences of risking a national treasure like *Constitution* on a ghost hunt. Not to mention the credibility of the entire United States Navy."

Maynard glanced at his father and received a nod of

179

encouragement. "Mr. Secretary, Blackbeard has already killed over forty people; most of them were members of my crew. I can assure you that I am painfully aware of the consequences. This plan will work. As for experience, sir, I must disagree with you again. We have journals filled with it. In fact, our nation's very heritage is built upon it.

"I've personally studied every document on historic naval warfare I could get my hands on since I was ten. As my father indicated yesterday, naval history is also *my* history. I have studied all the major battles between the British Navy and the Spanish Armada, including every bloody detail of Trafalgar. I've studied the battles of the War of 1812, including Isaac Hull's capture of HMS Guerriere, the Barbary Coast, and the battles between the British and the Caribbean pirates. I'm familiar with the tactics of Captain William Bainbridge, Captain Thomas Truxton, Samuel Nicholson, Mad Jack Percival, John Paul Jones and Admiral Horatio Nelson. And I've dissected every detail of my grandfather's defeat of Blackbeard.

"I do not have Blackbeard's practical experience. That's his advantage. Our advantage is the *USS Constitution's* fifty-four cannons and a twenty-one-inch thick live oak hull. As I see it, the most serious consequence we can encounter will result from our failure to act swiftly and decisively. Once the media gets its hooks into this, each move we make will be plastered across every television screen in the free world. Our tactical solution will include a half-dozen or so imbedded news crews. And, if any of them get killed, every person in this room will become an instant celebrity."

Secretary Turnbul squirmed in his chair and leaned back. He caught sight of Jeremy seated in a far corner of the room. "Where does he fit in?"

Perkins spoke up. "We rescued Mr. Ratliff from the sea the

day after the attack on *Spruance's* helicopter. At first, we believed he was a member of the *Queen Anne's* crew but he turned out to be a stowaway from the *Columbian Star*. When the *Star* was attacked, he managed to cross over to *Queen Anne*. The cook later found him, and Blackbeard made him walk the plank. He's provided us crucial details regarding the location of the *Queen Anne's* main powder holds. He also knows where they're keeping the Killian girl and has volunteered to guide us. I take full responsibility for him."

The light on the commodore's intercom lit up; he punched the button. "What is it?"

"The Chief of Naval Operations is on the phone. He wishes to speak to Admiral Hays."

"Give us two minutes and patch him through to my office."

"Yes, sir. And Rear Admiral Godsey has been waiting in the hallway for fifteen minutes. He said if you make him wait any longer he'll make you pay all your wife's delinquent parking tickets."

"Oh, shit." Perkins checked his watch. "Give him my apologies and escort him right down."

Hays rose from his chair. "Gentlemen, let's take a thirty-minute break. Be back in here at fifteen-forty-five." He pointed to Commander and Mr. Maynard. "You two come with me. Mister Secretary, is there anything I can get for you?"

Secretary Turnbul ignored the offer and headed for the door. He stopped and looked Perkins in the face. "I'll be in my office."

"I'll have Jenkins bring you some fresh coffee." Hays turned to Perkins and his eyes got wide. "For God's sake, Perky. Made him walk the plank?"

"Well, it was just a..." Perkins cleared his throat. "I'd better see to Admiral Godsey."

At fifteen-thirty hours, Hays excused Commander and Mr. Maynard. At seventeen-hundred, he and Secretary Turnbul returned to the conference room. Hays addressed the group.

"Admiral Hawthorne and the Joint Chiefs of Staff have examined all the intelligence we've pieced together over the last thirty-six hours, and have briefed the President. Secretary Turnbul has requested to speak with you before he outlines our next course of action."

Secretary Turnbul stood, buttoned his sport coat, and walked to the front of the room.

"The President has ordered the Navy to put an immediate end to this *Queen Anne's Revenge* situation. He requires it be executed in such a manner that it does not draw attention from the media or the general public. Consequently, a large scale assault is out of the question. Since three conventional attempts have already failed, as did my good-faith effort to convince the President otherwise, you have been ordered to proceed directly with a modified version of Commander Maynard's plan. *Constitution* is to be prepared for battle. You will have all of the resources of the United States government at your disposal."

"What about Mr. Ratliff?" Maynard asked.

"Commander, I don't give a damn if you take the whole freaking Salvation Army. The Navy will not be responsible for civilians that want to commit suicide. And if you manage to locate the Killian girl, I suggest you rescue her. But if you don't, she was never there." He pointed to Ratliff. "Find that man some decent clothing!"

Turnbul walked back to the table, collected his papers, and then focused his full attention on Maynard. "Commander, keep this in mind. Should you fail, whether you're among the casualties or not, you will go down in history as the man who hijacked and destroyed the *USS Constitution.* An interesting footnote to an otherwise illustrious family history."

The Secretary and his aids left the room.

"Alright, Commander," Hays said. "If that didn't blow your posterior out of the H20, we may actually stand a chance. We must have *Constitution* underway by no later than midnight tomorrow. Our code name going forward is Operation Darksail. From this point on, all communications will be over secure networks. As few people as possible are to know what's going on.

"The majority of our supplies will be expedited through the usual Navy channels. If anybody gives you any flack, report them directly to me. As of this moment, our command center is being transferred to Washington. All of you, including Admiral Godsey, will be ready to ship out by nineteen-thirty.

"Commodore Perkins, *Constitution* will be placed under your charge at DESRON Twenty-four. You and Mr. Ratliff shall proceed to Boston and begin making preparations for sea. I've got a jet en route from Pensacola to pick you up. Clements will drive you to the air station. Lieutenant Commander Butch Fallon will be expecting your arrival but won't have the slightest idea why you're there. So take it easy on him. When Commander Maynard reports on board, you are to depart for Little Creek and take charge of things there. On your way to the air station, make a quick stop at the uniform shop and solve Mr. Ratliff's clothing dilemma.

"Captain Maynard, you are to get yourself into a set of regulation khakis. The CNO has just reactivated your commission. You'll be working as his liaison to overcome any obstacles we may encounter in Boston." Hays looked around the room. "Any questions or comments?"

"Admiral," said Commander Maynard. "I just had a thought."

"We're all ears, Commander."

"I need to track down an old classmate of mine named Theodore Huber. We were on the fencing team at Annapolis before he dropped out to join the Marines. Huber could handle a fifty-pound broadsword like a pocket knife. I was told he retired and moved to Minneapolis. We could certainly use his help."

"Captain Lee," Hays said, "you're now officially in charge of personnel. Find Theodore Huber and get him aboard. Try running his name through the Bureau of Naval Personnel or the Fleet Reserves. Anything else, Commander?"

"No, sir. At least, not now."

"Jenkins, put through a call to Captain Stuckey at the Pentagon. He'll be our point man until we relocate. Instruct him to recruit plenty of help and string plenty of phone line. The rest of you have less than two hours to get yourselves organized."

Hays turned to Maynard. "Commander, since you seem to have all the right answers, how do you suggest we get *Constitution* out of Boston?"

"Admiral," Mr. Maynard said. "I think I can help with that." He reached into his coat pocket and removed a neatly folded map.

Chapter 18
1400: 26 August 2008

At two o'clock, Roger Killian called it a day. He thought working would help keep his mind off Angela's disappearance but all it did was cause him to worry about not being home. The authorities were offering little hope for her safe recovery; however, his instincts told him his daughter was still alive.

He left the office, climbed in his car, and started home. At this time of day, traffic was still light and the drive proved somewhat relaxing.

Killian parked along the curb at 20 South Battery with its magnificent white columns and black iron gates woven in jasmine. He walked to the front, got the mail, inserted his key into the lock, gave it a twist, and pushed through the door...just like he had done nearly every day for the past twenty years.

He found himself remembering when Angela was a child, how she would bolt from the house to greet him when he got home in the evenings. "Daddy! Daddy!" she would scream, all big-eyed and smiley-faced; her long, baby-fine hair chasing behind her. He would sweep her off her feet and give her a big hug. She'd plant one of those sticky-lipped baby kisses on his cheek, and they'd laugh and tell each other all about their day. Angela always wanted to know if he'd put away any bad guys, thinking all lawyers fought to put criminals behind bars. Not knowing that many, like he, actually argued to keep them out.

"No, Dammit. This is not over." He slammed the door behind him to expunge the thoughts from his mind.

The house felt empty. He checked the clock on the fireplace mantle; the slim, metallic second-hand glittered in the afternoon sun as it advanced in crisp even increments. Each tick felt like a hammer against his skull. He examined the answering machine; there were no messages.

He walked into the kitchen to fix a drink, then headed into the den. He lay back in his recliner, grabbed the remote, tuned to *Foxtrot News* and slugged down a gulp of bourbon. The last seconds of a Caribbean Ship Lines commercial was airing, the one depicting a handsome young couple embracing against the railing of a ship, a beautiful sunset painted across background. "Thank you very much," he groaned between sips of bourbon.

"Welcome back to Foxtrot *News*, I'm Mary Anne Bonny. The top story this hour is Hurricane Drummond as it continues to grind away at the Bahamas..."

Killian wondered how much Caribbean had paid for that commercial as he listened to the rest of the report.

"Drummond is still sporting sustained winds in excess of one-hundred miles per hour and is tracking north, northwest at a speed of eighteen knots. The winds are expected to strengthen overnight, and the National Weather Service is predicting landfall to occur along the southern portion of North Carolina's Outer Banks within the next seventy-two to ninety-six hours. Authorities have begun a mandatory evacuation of Cape Hatteras and Ocracoke Islands, and expect to have it completed by late tomorrow afternoon. No one is being permitted to stay behind. *Foxtrot News* will begin airing live coverage of the hurricane from

Cape Hatteras to Wilmington, North Carolina at 6PM Eastern Standard Time tonight.

"There have been no new developments in the story *Foxtrot News* broke yesterday concerning the young Charleston, South Carolina couple who is missing after a rupture and subsequent explosion of the fuel tank aboard their small yacht. Debris was found floating across several miles of ocean and, so far, there have been no signs of survivors. A Coast Guard spokesman said search and rescue teams will continue searching throughout the night and as long as weather permits.

"In a related story, Navy and Coast Guard officials have released details of three other maritime disasters that have occurred within the past forty-eight hours. We are told that all twelve crew members of the *Columbian Star*, a small South American freighter, were found murdered and their ship sailing out of control late Monday evening off the coast of the Florida Keys. Sources told *Foxtrot News* authorities found traces of cocaine in several of the ship's cargo holds and that the deck was littered with automatic weapon shell casings. The ship was reportedly en route for Baltimore. The full scope of the incident is still under investigation.

"Also, an explosion occurred yesterday afternoon aboard the United States Navy destroyer, *Spruance,* during a routine weapons handling evolution while the ship was returning to the Mayport Florida Naval Station. *Foxtrot News* has learned that several crew members received minor injuries as a result of the blast. No casualties were reported. The names of the injured seamen are being withheld pending family notification. No other details have been made available.

"In addition, a cruise ship belonging to the Emerald Island Luxury Cruise Line suffered heavy damage early this morning while attempting to skirt the southern winds of Hurricane Drummond. The ship, which was headed for Miami, was damaged by heavy seas and gusting winds. A number of passengers were reportedly injured and a Navy frigate has rendezvoused with the liner to render medical assistance.

"And, finally, the Coast Guard has issued a formal shipping advisory for an area of ocean extending from Massachusetts Bay to the southern tip of Cuba. The advisory went into effect at two o'clock this afternoon and extends some two hundred nautical miles out to sea. The advisory has been upgraded to a warning for smaller vessels and light aircraft. All maritime traffic is expected to remain clear of the restricted area, and updates will be issued as needed.

"And, it's time for a break. Stay tuned to *Foxtrot News* for these commercial messages. We'll have the day's top stories and the closing numbers from Wall Street when we return. Fair and balanced."

Roger Killian switched off the television and stared at the blank screen.

"Coincidence? Why on earth would the Navy be handling weapons on the outer edges of a hurricane?" He said aloud. He placed his glass of bourbon on the coffee table and reached for the telephone.

* * *

Jeremy Ratliff was fitted with three new sets of khakis and provided the rate insignia of Master Chief Petty Officer. Next, Perkins and Jenkins wrestled him aboard a Navy Gulfstream bound for Boston.

Perkins deposited Ratliff in a window seat, buckled him in, and sat down next to him.

"Now, Mister Jeremy, just relax and enjoy the ride. People do this kind of thing every day. In two hours, we'll be in Boston. If you feel like you're going to blow your cookies, do it in one of these." Perkins opened an airsick bag and handed it to him.

The plane powered up and started to roll. Jeremy closed his eyes tightly and began talking rapidly to himself—Perkins couldn't understand a single word he was saying. He reopened them just in time to see the runway fall out from under the plane. He sat as stiff as an ice sculpture, and started talking even faster.

Once fully airborne, the jet leveled off and Jeremy became glued to his window. He bounced up and down and craned his neck from side to side gawking at the landscape that passed beneath them.

"Two hours, says ya? Why, I'd neva' heard such. In my day, it'd take at least five days. With a strong wind at that. Aye, 'tis a wonderful time ya lives in, Governor. Why, you gents got iron ships, carriages that don't need no horses, an' a bloke can fly upon the wind like a bird. Yes, sir, 'tis a wonderful time indeed. I just may have a mind to stick around for a while."

Jeremy reached inside his shirt and pulled out a pen and a small notepad and drew a tic-tac-toe grid. He looked at Perkins and grinned. "How's about a wee game of chance, Governor, ta pass the time?"

At the midway point, the flight crew passed out large Ziploc bags containing a ham sandwich, a bag of chips, and a can of soda.

"And what might we have here, Governor?" Jeremy asked.

Perkins opened his bag and took out the sandwich. "Supper."

Jeremy toyed with the bag trying to open it and, finally, bit off one of the corners.

"Here, like this," Perkins said. He unzipped the bag and dumped the contents on the tray table in front of him. He unwrapped Jeremy's sandwich, handed him the chips, and popped

189

the top on a Pepsi. "Seals freshness in, keeps moisture out. Enjoy."

After landing in Boston, the jet taxied to a special area of the tarmac reserved for military aircraft. A car was waiting to take Perkins, Jenkins and Ratliff to *Constitution*. The driver tossed their gear in the trunk and headed off.

Upon arrival at the museum, Lieutenant Commander Fallon greeted Perkins with full military honors and six bells were sounded.

"DESRON Twenty-four arriving!" shouted the Officer of the Deck. Six side boys popped to attention and rendered a crisp salute.

Perkins returned the salute. "As you were." He pulled Fallon aside. "Let's talk in private."

"There's an office is just down the hall."

Jeremy and Jenkins tagged along behind. Once inside, Fallon closed the door.

"Lieutenant Commander Fallon, *Constitution* is being placed under my command at DESRON Twenty-four. Until further notice, this exhibit is closed and I want the entire area surrounding it secured. Commander Maynard will be arriving in a couple hours to assume duties as your new commanding officer."

"My commanding officer?" repeated Fallon. "With all due respect, Commodore, I have orders to report to NAS, Naples."

"Not just yet." Perkins tossed his khaki combination cap on Fallon's desk. "Commander Maynard has requested that you remain aboard for a couple weeks. He needs your help handling things around here."

Fallon listened with his head half-cocked. "Commodore, did you just say *Constitution* has been placed under the Command of DESRON Twenty-four?"

"That's exactly what I said."

"Sir, DESRON Twenty-four is a combat group. The

Constitution is under the command of the Director of Naval History. Does Captain Barchi know about this?"

"If he doesn't, he soon will." Perkins picked up Fallon's phone and dialed the Pentagon. "This is Commodore Perkins. Put me through to Admiral Hawthorn." Perkins looked at Fallon while he waited and flashed him a smug grin.

"This is Commodore Perkins, sir...Yes, sir, I'm telling him now...No, sir, we'll be ready...Yes, sir. Just a moment." Perkins handed the phone to Fallon. "The Chief of Naval Operations wishes to speak to you."

Fallon's top lip quivered. He cautiously reached out and took the phone from Perkins. "Lieutenant Commander Butch Harry Daniel Fallon, sir...Yes, sir...Yes, sir...Yes, sir, immediately...No, sir...Thank you, sir, good bye."

Perkins jerked the phone from Fallon's hand and hung it up.

Fallon looked at Jeremy and Jenkins. "Would one of you please tell me what's going on?"

"Well, do you want the job or not?" Perkins asked. "If your answer is no, I'll be forced to stuff you in one of these closets until this whole friggin' thing blows over."

"Okay, I'll take the job! You said Commander Maynard needed my help handling the ship. What ship?"

"It's all terribly simple. Commander Maynard is taking the *Constitution* to sea tomorrow night to track down and destroy Blackbeard the Pirate. You just volunteered to be his Executive Officer. Now, how about taking me and my little buddy here on tour? We need to start making modifications to accommodate a full crew."

Perkins turned to Jenkins. "After everything's secure, organize a detail and round up everything we might need in Little Creek. Pile it up near the back doors there." He pointed to the front of the building. "Pull those shades so no one can see in from the parking lot."

Perkins retrieved his cap and placed it on the crown of his head. "We've got about an hour to kill before I need to return to the airport." He looked at Fallon. "Mister Fallon, *Constitution*, if you please."

* * *

Maynard and his father arrived in Boston at 2200-hours. Numerous logistical problems needed to be solved to prepare *Constitution* and move her out to sea.

At 2230, a group of plainclothes DOD security specialists infiltrated Boston. Their task was to ensure *Constitution* departed with as little outside interference as possible; Maynard was not entirely certain exactly what that involved.

At midnight, a boat pulled alongside *Constitution* with a detachment of Coast Guard regulars, midshipmen and two sailing instructors from the three-masted training ship *USS Eagle*. Their job was to assist during the sail to Norfolk. The detail was under the commanded of Coast Guard Lieutenant Chuck Pasarelli.

To disguise movement about *Constitution's* top deck, a dark tent was erected over her brow and amidships quarterdeck. All nonessential lighting was secured and the gun ports were battened tightly. The windows around the Captain's Galley and all skylights were blacked out. From the outside, the ship appeared to be tucked in for the night. Inside, it was teaming with activity.

At 0130, a dark gray Navy bus and short-bed tractor-trailer squeezed up to the brow. A working party of Navy hull technicians unloaded construction materials, berthing supplies and the dry stores needed to sustain the crew during the sail to Virginia. They also brought aboard a secure satellite communication system so Maynard could stay in contact with the Pentagon, along with

192

battery-powered lighting and a portable radio.

After the supplies and equipment were aboard, a small propane-fueled fork lift was rolled out, and all the spare cannons and cannon balls from the museum grounds were loaded for transportation to Logan Airport. The hull technicians began preparing *Constitution's* galley and berthing areas for her complement of officers and crew. By daybreak, the truck was gone, the tarps were removed, and there was no outward sign that anything was out of the ordinary. *Constitution's* regular crew held muster on the pier and commenced their usual daily activities.

In the captain's quarters, Maynard was trying to get some rest. However, sleep wasn't in the cards. He had always dreamed of one day commanding the *USS Constitution*, but the irony of it all was now settling in on him. Tonight would be *Constitution's* first extended voyage in over one hundred years, and quite possibly her last. Ever. If he failed, his family could bear the burden of any disgrace that may befall them.

But if *he* didn't stop Blackbeard, who would?

Chapter 19
0600: 27 August 2008

Commodore Perkins was seated behind the commanding officer's desk at SEAL Team II headquarters at the Naval Amphibious Base in Little Creek, Virginia, leafing through the copy of Southern Sportsman Magazine Commander Maynard had given Admiral Hays.

Jenkins knocked on the door. "Chief Dunbar's here, sir."

"Good. Show him in." Perkins looked up as Dunbar entered. "Good morning, Chief. How was the trip up?"

"Fine, sir, if ya take to all that flying business."

"I've got something here I need your help with." Perkins folded back a page of the magazine and handed it to Dunbar. "Captain Lee tells me you're an expert on this stuff."

Dunbar glanced at the ad. "Yes, sir. Those are Knight muzzle loaders, some of the best black powder firearms on the market. You going hunting?"

"I'm not, but you may be." He pointed to a chair next to his desk. "Have a seat. I need at least two hundred of these and all the supplies that go with them by first thing tomorrow morning. I'll also need about three hundred or so black powder pistols."

Dunbar sat down and folded his hands on his lap. "Five

hundred weapons. Sounds like you're outfitting an invasion force."

"Here's the deal," continued Perkins. "In two days, Commander Maynard will be arriving in Little Creek sailing the *USS Constitution*."

Dunbar's eyes lit up like a pair of Roman candles.

"I don't have time to go into detail but I'll tell you this much. Three conventional attempts to stop *Queen Anne*, including the two by *Spruance,* have failed. So we're going after her with *Constitution's* cannons to blow the living shit out of her. What we need is a gunnery officer who's familiar with cannons and black powder weapons and can teach *Constitution's* crew how to use them."

Perkins sat on the corner of his desk. "The CNO has authorized me to commission you at the rank of Chief Warrant Officer Four if I think that you can handle the assignment. So, what do you think? Can you do it?"

Dunbar looked out through the office door at Jenkins, then back at Perkins. "I don't know, sir. Two days is a mighty short time."

"That's all we've got. We have to stop this Blackbeard son-of-a-bitch before this whole damn thing spirals out of control."

Dunbar nodded his head slightly. "Blackbeard? I figured it was something like that. They busted up *Spruance* something fierce. You thinking *Constitution* can even the score?"

"Yes, I do. And so does Commander Maynard."

"Commander Maynard's a fine officer, sir. So was Captain Lawrence." Dunbar stood and faced Perkins. "I didn't get a chance to shoot those barefoot hooligans with my guns, ya know. Kind of makes a guy feel left out." He thought for a moment. "I'll give it a shot, sir, but I'm gonna need some help."

"Name it."

"There's an old shipmate I deer hunt with every year,

named Jack Ritter. He was my supply petty officer for a while on the *New Jersey*. It took a lot of spare parts to keep those old turrets working but Ritter never let me down. We all figured he was destined to be a used car salesman, that's why we called him Smiling Jack. He 214ed and opened a hunting supply store in Boon, North Carolina. Ritter can clean shave a tom turkey at sixty paces with a 50-cal muzzle blaster. I've seen him do it. Should be able to help track down all the supplies we need, too. Black powder gear is a good chunk of his business."

"Call him and get him out here today," said Perkins. "Jenkins will arrange transportation. Give me a chance to clear this with Admiral Hays first. In the meantime, pull together a list of the equipment we'll need. Some of the *Constitution's* spare cannons are on trucks over at the gunnery range. You need to have them ready for gunnery practice first thing tomorrow morning."

Dunbar stroked the bottom of his chin. "If that's original equipment, sir, we'll need to check them for metal fatigue. If any of them are soft, they're liable to blow apart in our faces."

"Oh, shit. I hadn't thought of that." Perkins picked up the phone. "Give Jenkins a list of everything you'll need to complete the testing. The ones aboard *Constitution* will need to be checked, too."

"How many cannons does the *Constitution* have, sir?"

"Fifty or sixty."

Dunbar leaned back and arched his eyebrows. "We're going to need a lot of bodies to work them. I'd say at least eight or nine men per gun."

"Captain Lee is working on that now." Perkins punched Admiral Hays' phone number. "This Ritter character, can he be trusted?"

"Known him for about fifteen years, sir. Was even in his wedding. You can trust him."

"Don't give him any details. Just get him out here. But first, Maynard has a couple details he wants to discuss with you."

"Jenkins," Perkins shouted. "Get Commander Maynard on line two."

* * *

Barbara Maynard was standing on a ladder painting around a ceiling light fixture in the kitchen of the new home in Boston. Something on the radio caught her attention. She stepped down off her ladder and turned up the volume.

"The Boston Mayor's office announced late this morning that federal highway examiners will be closing the downtown tunnels and the Charles Town Bridge at ten o'clock tonight for structural testing. Officials indicated that a contractor hired for renovation work three years ago has been cited for using substandard building materials at two other locations. The same contractor was involved in the construction of the Catawba River Bridge near Lancaster, South Carolina that collapsed last August, sending six motorists to a watery death. The testing is scheduled to be completed by 4AM tomorrow morning and should not affect rush hour traffic. During the closure, commuters are encouraged to use the John Cross and Longfellow bridges."

Barbara climbed back up her ladder and continued painting.

* * *

Theodore Huber was sitting at his desk in his Minneapolis office going over security details for an upcoming preseason football game when the telephone rang. He tapped the hands-free button, and continued working. "Twin Cities Security, Huber speaking."

"Is this Master Sergeant Theodore Huber?" asked a voice on the other end.

"Well, nobody's called me that in a while," Huber replied. "But this is he."

"Master Sergeant Huber, my name is Captain Stephen Lee. I work for Vice Admiral Hays at Surface Forces Atlantic Headquarters in Washington, DC. If you can spare a few minutes, the admiral would like to speak with you."

"It would be a pleasure, sir." Huber set his work aside as Lee transferred him. "Now, why in the hell would COMSURFLANT want to talk to me?" he asked out loud.

"Huber, this is Admiral Hays."

"Good afternoon, Admiral. This is quite an unexpected honor for an old leatherneck. What can I can I do for you?"

"Something has come up that I need help with. Commander Robert Maynard has recommended you as a prime candidate for the job. Can you make yourself available to me for the next couple weeks?"

Huber hadn't seen Robert Maynard in over ten years. However, he detected the degree of urgency in the admiral's voice and that meant action. Huber loved playing soldier more than anything else in the world; during times of conflict, there was nothing more exhilarating.

The admiral probably couldn't give him any details over the phone so Huber simply said, "Yes, sir."

"Good. Captain Lee has booked you on American Airlines Flight 626, departing Minneapolis-St. Paul at sixteen-ten this afternoon. There will be tickets waiting for you at check-in. You'll change planes in Philly and arrive at Norfolk International Airport at nineteen-fifty hours. A Lieutenant Commander Jenkins will be there to meet you. Pack your bags for the field and travel in civilian clothes. What's your favorite football team, Huber?"

"Minnesota Vikings, sir."

"That's too bad. I'm a Packers man myself. Be wearing a Vikings ball cap so Jenkins can identify you."

"Yes, sir."

"Maynard tells me you were once pretty handy with a broadsword. Can you still operate one?"

"Like a natural extension of my hand."

"Outstanding. Bring one or two with you. In your checked baggage, of course. When you arrive in Norfolk, you will assume the rank of Chief Warrant Officer Four. Jenkins will have everything you need. And one last thing, Sergeant Major. You know the drill...tie up all loose ends. See you in Norfolk."

"Yes, sir. Thank you, sir."

Huber hung up the phone and pushed away from his desk. "Broadswords? What has Maynard gotten himself into?" He checked his watch. "Only one way to find out."

He grabbed the phone again and punched the large red button on the speed dialer.

"Sweetheart, pack my bags. I'm shipping out. Be home in thirty minutes."

Chapter 20
1300: 27 August 2008

The chopper carrying Jack Ritter touched down at Seal Team 2. Dunbar was waiting.

Ritter jumped out and unloaded three sea bags with an array of long, cylindrical bundles protruding out of the top of each. He also had three large, hard-sided suitcases and a pair of overstuffed duffle bags.

Dunbar hurried out to greet him.

Ritter looked at the rank insignias on the collar of Dunbar's uniform shirt. "Whoa, CWO4. Somebody's gotten ambitious."

"Should have stayed with me, kid. I'd have taken you places."

Ritter smiled. "I'm here now, aren't I?"

They shook hands. "Good to see ya again, partner. Let me give ya a hand with your gear." Dunbar shouldered one of the sea bags and grabbed a suitcase and a duffle bag. "Follow me doe killer."

He hustled into the building and over to the commodore's office. Perkins met them at the door.

"Commodore Perkins, this is Smiling Jack Ritter," Dunbar said. "He ain't much to look at but don't let that fool ya."

"It's a pleasure," said Perkins. "What's with all the luggage?"

"Well, from what Dunbar or, should I say, Mister Dunbar, told me on the phone, I figured you could use every piece of artillery you could get your hands on. Practically cleaned out everything I had left."

He unclasped one of the sea bags and extracted three of the cylindrical bundles. He handed one to Perkins, one to Dunbar and started unwrapping the third one himself.

"Gentlemen, this is a Knight Model 93 Wolverine inline muzzle-loading black powder rifle. Six and one-half pound composite stock with a 22" barrel, one in 28 rifling that can target a 50-caliber projectile clean enough to split the hairs on a Budweiser frog at a hundred yards. I've got sixteen of these babies; five in blue, five stainless steel, and another six in cammo. In those bags, we've got about eighty pounds of sabot-jacketed lead and enough Pyrodex to blow a bank vault.

"I also brought along two Kentucky pistols, two dozen straight-line cappers, twenty packages of rapid loaders, shoulder slings and five cleaning kits. Now, Mrs. Ritter's got her eyes on a new minivan, so who's got the checkbook?"

Dunbar shook his head. "Damn boy, you ain't changed a bit."

"That's nearly eight-thousand dollars' worth of product there. With hunting season just around the corner, I need the cash to restock or my customers are gonna shoot *me*."

Perkins pointed his weapon out the door and pulled the trigger, then aimed it directly at the center of Ritter's forehead. "Can you get me one hundred and eighty-four more of these, and another two hundred and ninety-eight pistols by tomorrow morning?"

"Holy shit, Commodore. Who pissed you off?"

"We need them first thing tomorrow so you can start training our men to use them."

Ritter shot a look at Dunbar and ran his hand through his hair. "Would you mind telling me what in the name of bloody hell the United States Navy needs with five hundred black powder weapons."

"Just tell us what it will take to get them here," answered Perkins. "Let me worry about why."

Ritter looked at his feet and remained silent for a second; his moustache started twitching like a rabbit's nose. "Do I get a mark-up or is this one of those for God and country things?"

Perkins took a dislike to Ritter. "You can have any damn thing you want," he huffed. "Just get me what I need."

"For an order that large, I'd say we'd have to go directly to the Knight plant in Centerville, Iowa," said Ritter. "Two months ago, it wouldn't have been a problem. But a month shy of hunting season most of their stock has probably been shipped out. If we're lucky, they'll let us dip into their Christmas stash." Ritter handed his musket to Dunbar. "Point me to a telephone and let me work some magic."

Perkins showed him the phone. Ritter sat down and pulled a note pad from his shirt pocket. He flipped through the pages, grabbed the receiver and started to dial.

Perkins took Dunbar by the sleeve and pulled him outside.

"I know what you're going to say, sir," Dunbar said. "He's a bit on the obnoxious side. Always has been. But if he can't get us those weapons on short notice, then nobody can."

Perkins exhaled and put his hands up. "Alright, Chief, it's your call. But if he tries to rip me off, I'm gonna grab one of those twenty-two inch composite stock frog splitters and make a popsicle out of him. How are you coming with my cannons?"

"I've dye-tested and ultra-sounded all seven of them. One

of the twenty-four pounders has got more cracks than Jack Daniel's liver. The rest are okay. We've got one set and ready to test fire, thought you might want to see the first shot."

Jenkins walked up. "Jenkins, Dunbar and I are going to the artillery range for a few minutes." Perkins motioned at Ritter. "Keep an eye on Gadhafi's little brother while I'm gone."

Jenkins glanced in the window; Ritter was gesturing with his hands above his head. "That must be our friend, Jack Ritter?"

"No. That's Dunbar's friend, Jack Ritter," Perkins answered.

Jenkins smiled. "I just got word from Captain Lee. He's rounded up another seventy-eight gunner's mates from San Diego. He also commandeered a dozen gunnery instructors from NTC Great Lakes. That gives us almost two hundred sixty men so far; three hundred twenty counting what's aboard *Constitution*. Admiral Godsey's making similar progress with the stores and berthing supplies, too."

"Outstanding. When will the crew start arriving?" Perkins asked.

"The Norfolk and Oceana contentions are arriving now. The others won't be in until later tonight. Ten SEALs and a detachment of Sea Bees checked in from Ocracoke. They've begun working on the charts of Pamlico Sound. The rest will report here at 0400 tomorrow morning."

"Good, start making berthing arrangements. And see that the trucks are on the tarmac by 2200 to transport the ammo to Yorktown. Dunbar here will meet the planes as they arrive."

"Yes, sir."

"I want all officers and Chief Petty Officers to muster here at 0500. Have plenty of coffee on hand."

Perkins and Dunbar started for the door. Perkins stopped and pointed into his office. "Jenkins, bring me my coffee thermos.

It's in that tall green thing on the table behind my desk."

Jenkins went inside and returned with Perkins' thermos.

"We'll be back in less than an hour."

* * *

A makeshift artillery range was set up along the eastern end of Little Creek Amphibious Base. Mounds of sand were piled up in front of the beachhead to keep stray rounds from causing problems.

Dunbar buzzed the range spotter to signal when the area behind the beach area was clear.

Perkins retrieved his thermos case from the front seat of the truck, flipped the catch on the lid, dumped the bottle into his hand and unscrewed the cup. Dunbar watched with concerted interest.

"Care for a cup?" Perkins offered.

"No, sir. What's that made out of?"

"What's what made out of?"

Dunbar pointed to the empty, green thermos cylinder. "Your thermos container. Mind if I look?"

Perkins tossed him the case. "Knock yourself out."

Dunbar opened the lid and looked inside, then tested the leather flap. Next, he walked over to the ammo box, opened the lid and carefully lifted out a long, cylindrical popcorn bag.

"What's in the bag?" Perkins asked.

"Some totally serious pop, sir." Dunbar placed the bag inside the thermos case and closed the top; it was a perfect fit. He carried it over to Perkins.

"Well, I'll be danged. You just solved a problem that's been nagging me for a couple hours."

"Yeah, how's that?"

"The bulk powder for *Constitution's* cannons is stored in the lower powder magazines and filling rooms. That means our powder monkeys have to run it up to the gun decks."

"Powder monkeys? How many of those do we need?"

"Minimum of one per active gun."

"That's fifty-four additional men, for Christ's sake."

"Yes, sir, if you're shooting all fifty-four guns at once. We shouldn't need to do that unless *Queen Anne* can attack us from both sides at once."

Perkins grinned...Dunbar got him on that one.

"Back in the day, powder monkeys carried the stuff in leather buckets because metal ones could cause sparks. As they ran back and forth, a fair amount of powder got spilled on the deck. Next thing you know, a dropped igniter or a stray bullet came in contact with it, and flash, bang, boom. Not the kind of thing you want on a loaded warship."

Perkins followed Dunbar over to the ammo box. "I solved one of our problems this morning at the Exchange."

Dunbar reached into the box and pulled out three empty popcorn bags. "When I helped my old man with Civil War re-enactments, we'd measure powder and dump it in paper bags like these and store them in ammo boxes behind the cannon. *Constitution's* twenty-four-pound guns use a six-pound charge. These extra-large popcorn bags hold about seven and are roughly the same diameter as the gun's bore. All we have to do is fill each bag to within three inches of the top, put them in one of these thermos cases and our monkeys can carry the powder from the magazines to the guns without spilling a flake."

"We'll have to remove the metal clasps," he said, pulling at the closing mechanism. "Reinforce the strap a little bit and we have a tailor-made powder sling."

Dunbar removed the powder bag and handed the thermos case back to Perkins.

"Chief, you're a genius," exclaimed Perkins. "I knew you

had to be smarter than you look." He flashed Dunbar a large grin.

"Now all we have to do is find about a hundred of these," replied Dunbar.

Perkins tossed the case back into the cab. "I'll put Jenkins on it when we get back." He looked down range. The spotter was waving a green flag. "Alright, let's get this show on the road."

Dunbar walked back to the ammo box and pulled out a stick with a piece of rope attached to the length of it. He stepped away from the box, fished a Zippo from his pocket, sparked it, and held the flame to the end of the rope until it glowed cherry-red.

"This is called a slow match," he said. "It's made from hemp rolled in gunpowder and dipped in lime water. Each one lasts about thirty minutes. Our gun captains will use these to light the powder in the cannon's touch pans.

Dunbar reached into the ammo box again and produced two sets of headphones. He handed one to Perkins. "Sir, you'll want to put these on. It's gonna be a bit noisy."

Dunbar cupped the phones around his head. Perkins followed suit, looked back down at the range spotter, then gave Dunbar a nod.

Dunbar stepped to the side of the cannon and tapped the slow match to the touch pan. A thick plume of smoke mushroomed into the air and the cannon thundered. A few moments later, a spray flew up off one of the sand piles.

Perkins removed his phones and slapped Dunbar on the shoulder. "Excellent shot, Chief."

"That's with only three pounds of powder, too," said Dunbar. "With a full charge and low winds, this beauty has a range of 1200 yards."

"Impressive," said Perkins.

Dunbar cocked his head. "We've got about fifty useable rounds here, but will need at least nine hundred to a thousand more.

We got to take a lot of practice once we're aboard ship."

"Where in the hell are we gonna find cannon balls?"

"I think I have that one figured out too, sir," replied Dunbar. "But it's going to take a little doing. A drought last year here in the eastern US dropped the level of the James River near Richmond, Virginia to a record low. It exposed a sealed doorway to an abandoned section of an old Civil War munitions factory called Tredegar Ironworks. There was an article on the Internet about it last fall."

"How does that help us?"

"When the Confederate Army was retreating from Richmond to Petersburg, they hid most of their ordinance so the North couldn't find it and use it against them. Appears they stashed a good chunk of it in that lower section of Tredegar. The place was full of cannon balls. All sizes, including bars, preserved in crates with grease-packing. If that ordinance was manufactured for the Confederate Army or Navy, technically it's still the property of the United States government. It's all being stored in a warehouse somewhere until the folks at Tredegar figure out what to do with it. The way I see it, we take a couple trucks to Richmond and collect our belongings. A nice little handling fee to the owners might soften the intrusion."

Perkins grabbed Dunbar by the shoulder and gave him a brisk shaking. "Stellar work, Dunbar. Goddamn it. Before this is over, you just might make an admiral out of me. Do you think the stuff is any good?"

"The rounds pictured in the article looked better than the one we just shot."

Perkins shook Dunbar again. "Let's wrap this up and get back to the office. I'll inform Admiral Hays that we need to organize a working party for Richmond."

* * *

Ritter was hanging up the phone when Perkins and Dunbar returned. When he saw Perkins he sprang from his chair.

"Alright, Commodore. I've got you one hundred seventy-nine rifles, and two hundred and sixteen more pistols. All I need is a couple purchase orders and we're all set."

"How about shot, powder and supplies?" Dunbar asked.

"Six thousand rounds of 50-caliber sabots, ten fifty-pound kegs of Pyrodex, and enough percussion caps and cappers to outfit the Chinese Army."

Dunbar looked at Perkins. "Commodore, we'll need at least a hundred kegs of powder and another five thousand rounds of shot."

Perkins turned to Ritter; Ritter's moustache started twitching again.

"Holy Mother of Jesus, Dunbar!" exclaimed Ritter. "What are you guys planning?"

"We've got about three hundred men to train how to shoot these things," said Perkins. He tested the weight of one of Ritter's pistols. "And Dunbar here will need plenty for his toys as well."

Ritter scratched his head with the butt of his pen. "You guys aren't making this easy."

"Call your people and tell them that we'll take the weapons and any more they can spare," Perkins said.

"The rifles are in the Knight warehouse in Centerville, Iowa," said Ritter. "When I visited two years ago, I flew into an old Navy Flight Training Center near Ottumwa. It's about forty-five minutes from Centerville. The pistols are in Deep River, Connecticut. I've got no clue where that is."

"Jenkins, get a map and find Deep River. Then call Captain Hotard and tell him to round up a couple C-130s. Ritter, instruct

Centerville to get all the stuff together and have it in Ottumwa by nineteen-hundred hours. Then locate me the rest of that shot and powder I need."

"How you planning to pay for all of this?" Ritter asked.

"Hell, I don't know." Perkins yanked out his wallet and flung his platinum card at him. "See if they'll take freakin' American Express!"

Chapter 21
2100: 27 August 2008

Darkness descended and the men aboard *Constitution* were growing anxious. To ease the tension Maynard switched on a small, portable radio.

At nineteen-thirty hours, Maynard received a weather report from Admiral Hays. The night would be cloudy with a good chance of rain.

The refit teams had worked tirelessly on preparations throughout the day. They were only interrupted twice when overzealous tour boat captains steered a little too close to *Constitution's* bow for comfort. Any unusual sounds might draw unwanted attention.

Lieutenant Pasarelli conducted class all day teaching the midshipmen and *Constitution's* regulars the art of setting sails and running rigging at night. At eighteen-hundred hours, he knocked off to give everyone a chance to get some shuteye.

At twenty-fifteen, Maynard received his last call from Admiral Hays. They ran through the plan one last time. Everything was set.

At twenty-forty-five, Maynard mustered his officers, chiefs and leading petty officers in the wardroom. He had to make absolutely certain no detail was overlooked. Somewhere across the inner harbor and up the Mystic River, the ocean-going tug *Saw Grass* was lighting off its engines.

At twenty-two hundred, *Constitution's* shore power was disconnected and all power lines were removed. Gimbaled oil lamps and battery-powered battle lanterns were distributed to illuminate the interior of the ship. Baffles were positioned at the hatchways to prevent the light from spoiling up into the darkness.

At twenty-two fifteen, the lights along both sides of the Charles River suddenly went dark. Silence washed over the port; the moonlight was trapped behind a curtain of dense clouds.

It was so dark Maynard could barely see his fingers wiggle at arm's length; his heart was pumping pure adrenalin.

From the east rose the wailing of distant sirens...everything was clicking along right on schedule.

Maynard glanced over at the Charles Town Bridge. There were no headlights. The bridge was empty—there would be no witnesses from that direction.

It was a straight shot for *Constitution* over the Summer and Callahan tunnels, through the narrow Inner Harbor passage, past Logan Airport and into the mouth of Boston Harbor. From there, *Constitution* would slip through the pinch between the Deer Island Water Treatment Plant and Long Island, then cross Massachusetts Bay into the safety of the Atlantic.

At twenty-three seventeen, Maynard detected a rumbling of engines. It was *Saw Grass*, or so he hoped, inching her way up the river toward *Constitution's* bow. Maynard mustered the line handlers from below so their eyes could adjust to the darkness, and ordered them to slack the mooring lines fore and aft.

A slender Zodiac zipped up to the pier. Six dark-clad figures scaled the pilings and fanned out across the pier and seawall. They retracted the port and starboard brows and hustled over to the bollards, preparing to cast off *Constitution's* lines.

At twenty-three thirty-five, the wake from *Saw Grass'* propellers rippled the water as she came about and eased back into position. She was using no running lights. *Constitution* began to rock from side to side like a child waking from a restful nap.

The tug signaled with two short flashes from a soft blue light, a monkey's paw attached to a heaving line thumped down on the forecastle. The line handlers grabbed it and started hauling in one of the two four-inch hawsers the tug would use to tow *Constitution* to sea. They looped the hawser over the starboard anchor cathead, passed the eye over the anchor bits, and worked out the slack. The second line was rigged to the port cathead. Maynard signaled with his flashlight when *Constitution* was ready.

The tug's captain laid a short burst to his engines. The towlines pulled tight and *Constitution* eased forward slightly. The dark figures pulled *Constitution's* mooring lines from the bollards and dropped them into the water, then climbed back down the pilings and started the Zodiac's engine. The line handlers pulled the lines on deck and quickly faked them into long even coils.

The tug slowly increased her throttle, coaxing *Constitution* seaward. In a matter of seconds, she was free from her slip. The towlines popped and creaked from strain, but the two-hundred-year-old catheads and anchor bits held firm.

Saw Grass headed out into the Charles River and made a wide swing to port, then straightened up and turned to starboard. *Constitution*, with Maynard at the helm, followed like a warrior being led into an arena. Chaser boats loaded with DOD personnel whizzed by to seal off the Charles and Mystic Rivers behind them.

The tug guided *Constitution* over the downtown tunnels and around the bend along Waterfront Park. She straightened out again and slipped down the throat of Boston Inner Harbor. Maynard heard another rumble; a pilot boat joined at the head of the parade.

To the east, blue flashing lights knifed through the darkness at Logan International Airport. Logan had been completely shut down. No traffic in and no traffic out; Maynard was astounded by the precise execution of the plan.

Day Boulevard had been closed to prevent access to the beachhead from Castle Island. Every precaution had been taken to ensure there were no unwanted spectators. To Maynard, it seemed to be taking an eternity.

The procession crawled on through the darkness. More chaser boats joined from Thompson Island to the south. Suddenly, running lights appeared from around the southern tip of Logan International Airport; chaser boats charged over to intercept. Like a pair of startled hearts, two rotating beacons pumped short red pulses of light into the night and the intruder's running lights slowed. A wide spotlight splashed upon the boat to blind its occupants. A few minutes later, the running lights turned around and were escorted by the rotating beacons back into the inlet.

The procession continued on. *Constitution* was guided towards the abandoned tip of Long Island and turned into the mouth of Massachusetts Bay.

With the lights of Boston fading in the background, the pilot boat and tug slowed. Maynard could now hear their captains' voices crackling over the radios. He scanned with binoculars seaward and located the running lights of the *USS Winston Churchill*, *Constitution's* escort south to Virginia.

The tug eased her throttle and made slack her towing lines. The line crews removed the eyes from the anchor bits, twirled them off the catheads and tossed them into the sea. *Constitution* was now totally at the mercy of nature and the skills for her crew.

Maynard could barely contain his excitement. He had just gotten away with stealing one of the greatest warships any nation in the world had ever built. He prayed he'd have the opportunity to

213

put it back.

"Man the sails," Maynard ordered. Additional topmen climbed the shrouds and eased out onto the yards. Each man called out when he was in place.

"Mister Pasarelli, cast off the gaskets and sway the yards. One hand for the sails and one hand for yourselves."

The mainsails were carefully raised into position and secured, the sheets on the mizzen and foremast followed in succession. Surefooted sailors held on tight and belted out cheers as each sail popped to the wind. All the peripheral sails would be set after first light in the morning.

Constitution slowly heaved over, bounded forward and finally settled back into a comfortable starboard list. Maynard gazed around him and, for the moment, allowed tears of joy to well in his eyes. It was the most incredible moment of his entire life. 'Old Ironsides' was under sail on the open sea for the first time in nearly one hundred and twenty years.

Chapter 22
0600: 28 August 2008

Three hundred twenty-nine officers and enlisted men were herded into a field house adjacent to SEAL Team Two Headquarters; the building was vibrating with excitement.

Commodore Perkins peered out across the gathering, wondering how he could possibly mold this mob into a cohesive fighting unit in less than forty-eight hours.

Lieutenant Commander Jenkins addressed the group from a podium at the front of the room. "Gentlemen, may I have your attention."

The mass fell silent.

"I'm Lieutenant Commander Curtis Jenkins, aide to Commodore Perkins of Destroyer Squadron Eight, Mayport, Florida. I know you're all wondering why you've been brought here. So grab a piece of deck and listen up. We don't have much time, let's not waste any repeating ourselves. Hold all questions for now. I assure you they will all be answered in due course.

"I'm going to turn things over to Commodore Perkins." He turned to Perkins who was standing off to the side next to Warrant Officers Dunbar and Huber. "Commodore Perkins."

Perkins stepped over to the podium and cleared his throat

215

while the men got themselves situated. "Alright, gents, I'm Commodore Perkins. As Commander Jenkins just said, everybody listen up and pay close attention.

"You have all been selected by your commanding officers to participate in a mission that is of vital importance to our country's national security." He paused to make rolling eye contact across the room. When he continued, his tone stern and exacting.

"I'm not going to bullshit you or beat around the bush. What lies ahead of us is an extremely dangerous job but one that will, in all likelihood, save the lives of countless men, women and children. Its success depends on each of you working as a team and following orders promptly and without question. There will be no tolerance for pissing and moaning. Pissers and moaners will be immediately removed from the ranks and returned to their original commands.

"All I can say now is that some of you young swinging dicks won't be coming back. Those that do can never say a word about where they have been, or what they have done." Perkins paused again; every man in the room was sitting at attention, eyes glued on him. He pushed the podium aside.

"I emphasize that point because the bastards we are going after have already murdered over forty people. From this point forward, this is going to be a voluntary operation. I only want those who are willing to hang their balls over the edge and give me one-hundred-fifty percent at all times for the next two weeks or so. If for any reason you can't give me that kind of dedication, lay to the rear of the room and report to Mister Jenkins. You will be out-processed and returned to your original command. No questions asked.

"There is no dishonor in pulling out now. Quitting when the rest of the team is counting on you may result in our failure or death to one or more of your shipmates. God help any man that pulls a stunt like that because his hell will be directed by me personally!

"Stay or go. You've got three minutes to make up your mind."

Perkins stepped back and watched the reactions of the men. Three hundred twenty-five sets of eyes roamed the room; only twenty or so passed to the rear. After three minutes, he stepped forward again.

"Very well. I commend each and every one of you on your bravery, your devotion to duty and commitment to the people of the United States of America.

"In a few minutes, we will separate you into two groups— blue and gold—to start your training. The first group will remain here for hand-to-hand combat training with Chief Warrant Officer Huber. The rest will head over to the range and muster with Chief Warrant Officer Dunbar for firearms training.

"You SEALS may think you don't need this type of training. Pay attention anyway, and lend a hand with your shipmates who need help. We are all in this together. When the fecal material hits the rotating equipment, each of you will need to cover your shipmate's posterior. Remember that. Don't let your shipmates down."

A lanky first-class petty officer with large owlish eyes stood up from the group and threw his fists in the air. "AR-HUH!" he shouted. The rest joined in.

"Now that's the kind of enthusiasm I want to see," Perkins said. "If at any time anyone needs help, don't hesitate to yell. Don't be a dickhead and think the guy next to you knows any more about what's going on than you do. Now, before we get started, if anyone has a question, raise your hand."

Perkins scanned the room again. No hands raised. "Very well, I want all officers to come forward. The members of SEAL

Two move to the left side of the room, and the rest of you move to the right. Each of you will be given a blue or a gold arm band. Put it on. The gold team stays here, and blue team musters outside by the cattle cars. Let's do this in an orderly manner so we can get down to work."

As the men were forming their groups, Jenkins hurried over to Perkins. "Commodore, Admiral Hays needs you to call him as soon as possible. Hurricane Drummond is closing on the Florida coastline. The ships in Mayport are preparing to evacuate."

"Goddamn it," Perkins griped. "I may have two legs, but I've only got one ass. And it can't be here and in Mayport at the same time!"

"The admiral, Captain Lee, and a few aides are coming here to take over."

Perkins expression changed from disappointment to anger. "He can't just take this away from me."

"Sir, *Spruance* is going to be running point during *Constitution's* sweep for *Queen Anne*. Admiral Hays wants you to command her." Jenkins cocked his head. "It will give you an opportunity to be in the hunt."

Perkins was not holding any real hopes of sailing with the *Constitution* anyway. An old fart like him would just get in the way. But he liked the idea of being involved in the chase.

"Alright then," he said. "Things here are pretty much up and running anyway, Hays can't screw it up but so much. Make sure to distribute the SEALS out evenly. Dunbar and Huber will take it from there. Have Jeremy Ratliff circulate and help out wherever he can."

"There's one more thing," Jenkins said. "Commander Maynard has requested that HT Chief Hatton head *Constitution's* Damage Control Team. He needs Hatton to rig up a gasoline generator and fire pump that can charge two inch-and-a-half fire hoses. He also asked for two hundred pounds of four-penny nails and twenty cases of Mountain Dew soda in the longneck aluminum bottles. Sounds like he's got a couple more tricks up his sleeve."

"Get Hatton up here on the double" Perkins replied. "And tell him to start designing Maynard's fire pump. When he gets here, help him find whatever he needs." Perkins started to walk toward the office, then turned back to Jenkins. "Make sure every man gives his best damn effort. Officers and enlisted alike."

Perkins concluded his conversation with Admiral Hays and hurried back to the field house. The blue and gold teams had mustered in short order. The gold team officers moved the men to the front of the room.

Chief Warrant Officer Huber pushed a manikin to the center of the floor and positioned himself next to it with his hands folded behind his back. Huber's muscular body was crisply tapered into tailored, olive-drab marine fatigues; on his left hip rested the butt end of a jewel-studded broadsword.

"Gentlemen, I'm Chief Warrant Officer Ted Huber. I'll be your drill instructor for this morning's session." He reached across his body, grabbed the handle of his sword, pulled it from its scabbard, and thrust it out in front of him with the tip a fraction of an inch from the chest of a sailor at the front of the group. The poor kid probably crapped his dungarees.

"This is the weapon I will be teaching you to use, and this is what I'm going to teach you to do with it."

In one fluid motion, he spun around, swinging the sword with both hands high into the air and slammed it down, severing the manikin's right arm. With a circular ax-like motion, he swung the blade around in the other direction and severed the manikin's left arm. Then he leaned back and leveled the blade. Slashing it parallel to the manikin's shoulders, he pruned its neck at the base of the head like it was a blade of dry grass. Huber whirled back around, grabbed the orifice of his scabbard, dipped the tip of the blade and rattled the broadsword home.

Perkins was duly impressed; the men whistled and applauded.

"Looks easy, doesn't it?" Huber asked. "Well, it's not. It has taken me over twenty years to master that move. You men must be able to do it after only a couple hours.

"When I give the order, I want each of you to single file to the crates in the rear of the compartment and get a belt and a length of broomstick. Then form lines across the room—five feet between each row—and strap on the belts. Those of you who are right-handed, tuck the broomstick in the left side of your belt. Those of you who are left-handed, tuck the broomstick on your right. My marines and you guys from SEAL Two get two broomsticks. One long and one short; you're going to be my gladiators. We'll get into it with the real stuff after you show me how well you can handle yourselves.

"Now break, get your gear, form your lines and let's get ready to kick some ass."

* * *

The cattle cars pulled up at the small-arms range located in the center of the base. As the men got off the cars, they were divided into two subgroups. Group One mustered at the left side of the range with Smiling Jack Ritter, and the rest with Dunbar on the right side.

Once his men were assembled, about seventy-five in all, Dunbar instructed them to form a circle around him. Amongst his grouping were fourteen of the United States Army's deadliest snipers; a little insurance policy underwritten by the Joint Chiefs of Staff.

At each station along the firing line there were four black powder rifles and a collection of other equipment: straight-line cappers, decapping tools, bullet starters and a stack of ready-made rapid loads.

"Men," Dunbar shouted. "As you look at each firing station you'll see four or five black powder rifles and other equipment. At close range, black powder weapons are the bad guys' weapon of choice. We are going to teach you how to load, fire, and reload these weapons...quickly. You must become so adept with the procedure that you can perform it standing on your head with your skivvies pulled down over your eyes. A reloading speed of fifteen seconds is what we're working toward."

Dunbar walked over to the first station and picked up a rifle with both hands and held it over his head. "What I have here is a Knight Model 93 stainless steel, in-line muzzle-loading black powder rifle. With open sights, it is accurate with minimal drop in low winds up to a distance of two hundred and fifty yards. For the most part, our targets will be no more than thirty to forty yards away, sometimes even closer. Pinpoint accuracy is not a concern. Just aim at center mass, preferably from the waste to the chest, and make sure to hit something."

Dunbar took one of the red rapid loader tubes and held it out in front of him. "This is a quick load." He popped the cap off one end and dumped the contents into his hand. "We will be using a .50 caliber, lead alloy, sabot round. It is actually a .45 caliber projectile inside a plastic jacket called a sabot. The jacket makes the round easier to load and allows for a significantly higher muzzle velocity. When the round hits its target, it mushrooms into a disk about the size of a nickel. The impact will knock your target flat on his ass. If he stays down, reload your weapon and choose your next objective. If he gets up, cap him again."

"Most of you remember the Civil War movies and soldiers

221

with old flintlocks. Flintlocks were slow and cumbersome; these are light and easy to load. Our enemy will be using flintlocks. We have the advantage."

Dunbar picked up one of the in-line cappers, placed a percussion cap on the musket's fire nipple, pushed the bolt closed, aimed the rifle down range and squeezed off a shot; his bullet pierced the bull's eye. Dunbar turned and faced the group again.

"These things have a tendency to kick like a mule if you over-powder them. For that very reason, you will be using premeasured 110-grain loads. You'll keep about twenty quick loads and all this other gear in a 'possibles bag' around your waist. Later, I'll show you how to pack the bag to keep everything straight."

Ritter fired a shot for his group; several sailors around Dunbar jumped.

"The first order of business, gentlemen, is to relax. When the shit goes down, there will be men shooting around you and men shooting at you. Remain cool, calm, and collected at all times. Once you've fired your weapon, take cover to reload. The calmer you keep yourself, the quicker you can reload. The quicker you can reload, the quicker you can fire your weapon again. Get the picture?"

Several of the men nodded their heads; others answered with a cautious, "Yes, sir."

"I believe Commodore Perkins already covered this this morning. Show a little enthusiasm! Has everyone got that?"

"Yes, Sir!!" shouted the men in unison.

"That's better." Dunbar walked back to the firing station and propped his rifle against it. "I want four men per station, single file and in a straight line. Don't touch anything until I tell you to."

As the men were taking their places, Dunbar walked around behind them. "HIT THE DECK AND COVER," he shouted. They all turned around and looked at him. "I said, hit the deck! Now!" Everyone fell to the ground.

"When we're aboard ship, and you are given the command to hit the deck, everyone will drop face down, tuck his weapon closely to his side, and put his arms over his head like this." Dunbar cradled his head in his arms. "You will stay in this position until you hear the order to recover. Am I clear on that?"

"Yes, sir," the men replied crisply.

"Now use a little common sense with this. If you're working aloft when the order is given, stay put. I don't want anyone jumping off a mast. Now get up, brush off, step up to the firing line and take your weapons."

When everyone had their rifles in hand, Dunbar shouted again, "Hit the deck!!"

Everyone hit the ground and secured their weapons exactly as instructed.

"Outstanding!" Dunbar cheered. "You must be prepared for this command at all times. Make certain you tuck your weapon at your side. If you lose your weapon, you're as good as dead. Now, recover."

Chapter 23
0800: 28 August 2008

With Captain Maynard out of town, Mrs. Maynard had invited Barbara and the grand daughters to spend the night. The girls were watching morning cartoons when a news broadcast interrupted their program:

"This is a News Seven special broadcast. Here is WHTV anchorman, William Parker."

"Good morning, Boston. WHTV News Seven is here to bring you this late-breaking story. The *USS Constitution* has been hijacked from Boston Harbor..."

"Mommy!" cried the youngest daughter. "Daddy's ship is missing."

Barbara came running into the den. "What's that, baby?"

"Daddy's ship is missing. Look." She pointed to the television.

"Navy officials could not be reached for comment but Boston police now believe the pirates took advantage of the bridge and tunnel closings last night to smuggle the *Constitution* from her

224

berth along the Charles River and out to sea. At 10:00 PM last
night, a van rented from an area rental car company was rammed
into the Boston Edison Charles River electrical substation, setting
off a series of transformer failures around the city and severing
power to some seventy thousand riverfront area businesses and
homes. By the time police arrived at the scene, the driver of the
vehicle had fled. The van has since been traced to the Old Bay
Rental Car Company where a man wearing a blue baseball cap and
dark clothing allegedly used a phony driver's license and a stolen
credit card to obtain the vehicle. Later, around 11:25, a bomb threat
was called into Logan International Airport, grinding to a halt all
airport operations until 1:45AM, when it was determined to be a
hoax. Meanwhile, it is assumed *Constitution* was towed out to sea.
Officials from the Boston Port Authority reported seeing no sign of
the ship leaving the harbor, and stated it is unlikely a vessel as old
as *Constitution* would be taken far into open waters. Local law
enforcement agencies are asking if anyone has any information that
might help in the investigation to contact the Boston office of the
Federal Bureau of Investigation at the number listed at the bottom
of your television screen as soon as possible.

Once again, WHTV News Seven reports that the historic
frigate, *USS Constitution*, has been stolen from Boston Harbor.
Please keep your sets tuned to News Seven for more details as they
become available. We now return you to regularly scheduled
programming."

Barbara was shocked. "Why would anyone want to steal the
Constitution?"

"Why, I don't know, dear," Mrs. Maynard replied. "Do you
suppose Robert knows?"

Barbara cocked her head. "Mom, I've got a sneaking
suspicion something's going on. I've felt it ever since the Navy

postponed the *Constitution* change-of-command ceremony. Robert should have called by now. It's not like him. You haven't heard from Dad have you?"

"No. No, I haven't. Not since he left for Florida."

Barbara walked into the kitchen to get her address book from her purse and came back a few seconds later. "I'm going to call Mayport and find out where they are."

Chapter 24
0800: 28 August 2008

In the darkness, the topmen were able to set *Constitution's* main, mizzen and foremast sails. At first light, they rigged the spanker to the mizzen mast and three jibs to the bowsprit. Sailing light, and with all but her studding sails to the wind, *Constitution* pushed south at an incredible nineteen knots. Maynard was impressed at the old girl's speed.

Breakfast consisted of pre-packaged MREs. The men were hungry so no one complained. After all, they were sailing the *USS Constitution*. Hardtack and cold beans would have been received like steak and salad.

Fallon and Pasarelli organized the men into duty sections and sent the off-section to their hammocks. Everything was quiet, and the white song of the ocean rushing past *Constitution's* hull would help lure the men to sleep.

The working parties had completed the berthing and mess arrangements several hours earlier and had started checking the cannons, carriages and restraining tackle.

Maynard was rapidly sinking into the bowels of sheer exhaustion. He turned the helm over to Lieutenant Commander Fallon and went below to try and get some sleep. He opened the shutters around the captain's gallery and gazed out over the water. Images of battle filled his thoughts again. This time, however, he managed to shut them down.

Before turning in, he spent a few minutes studying charts of Ocracoke Inlet. The charts were five months old and Maynard certain there had been some bottom shifting since they were drawn. He searched the labyrinth of lines, circles, and symbols trying to devise a strategy to trap Blackbeard in the shallows. Perhaps the charts the SEALS were making would show what he was searching for.

A few minutes later, there was a knock at the inner hatch leading to his father's stateroom. He leaned back in his chair and rubbed his temples. "It's open."

His father entered. "Is everything alright, Captain?"

Maynard smiled. "Just resting my eyes."

"If you can spare a minute, I'd like for you to come over here. I've got something to show you."

Maynard pulled himself to his feet and went into his dad's quarters. He found him standing next to a table in the center of the compartment. Lying on the table was a square of blue fabric, folded back over two diagonal bulges.

"I've got something for you here." He folded back the top layer of cloth.

Commander Maynard's eyes almost leaped out of his head. On the table before him, lay two shimmering swords; one full-length, the other broken in half just above the hilt.

Maynard's lips could hardly form the words. "Are these what I think they are?"

"Yes. These are the very swords our grandfather used to defeat Blackbeard," replied his father. "They are yours now. And every bit as deadly as the day they were first honed."

Maynard grasped the broken cutlass and held it in front of

his face. He couldn't believe what he was actually holding.

"That one just about cost our grandfather his life. Blackbeard severed it with a single blow with his cutlass. Don't forget that."

Maynard gazed at the severed end and turned it from side to side. *Blackbeard's power must be incredible.* He carefully placed it back on the table and took the other cutlass. With two flicks of his wrist, he slashed it through the air. It felt as weightless as a foil, yet as solid as a broadsword.

"There is but one that may champion mine," he repeated softly.

His father leaned on the table. "That's the one that did it the first time, and it will do it again."

Maynard saw the tension in his father's eyes.

"After Blackbeard's men were hanged in Williamsburg," said Mr. Maynard, "the lieutenant retired these cutlasses. Like the diary, they have been safeguarded by our family, and passed down from generation to generation. When my father gave them to me, I never imagined they'd be put to use. Blackbeard's a master swordsman. If he hadn't been mortally wounded when he was, he would have likely killed our grandfather and defeated the British at Ocracoke.

"Robert, you're well aware that there's more at stake here than just anyone's career. God has developed in you the skills you need to defeat Blackbeard, but he can't win the battle for you. Only you can do that. To be successful, your mind and your heart must be joined as one. Lead with your intelligence. Your abilities and your men will follow.

"If you don't stop him, there's no telling what he's planning to do. When you abandon the cannons and go hand-to-hand, you must show no mercy. These are not men you will be killing. They are demons, and they will fight to the last breath until Blackbeard

229

is dead. The sooner you can kill Blackbeard, the more of your men you will bring home alive. The moment you make contact, have your marksmen start burning holes in him. Then cross over, single him out, and cut him down. I know you can do it.

"Watch out for when he starts to windmill his cutlass. Fall back and shoot him with pistols. Don't let him get a hard stroke against your sword, or he'll snap it like he did the lieutenant's. Always keep it moving, and strike at angles. Attack him in groups whenever you can. Once you've worn him down, go for his throat and cut off his head.

"Once that's done, you must kill all his men, whether they attempt to defend themselves or not. When this is over, no pirate can be left alive." He looked Maynard in the face. "That includes Jeremy Ratliff."

Maynard started to object but knew his father was right.

There was a soft rustling sound in Maynard's stateroom. Maynard turned his head to listen, and it stopped.

"After you've finished, get all your men off *Queen Anne* and rig her powder magazines for detonation. Put as much distance between her and *Constitution* as you can before she goes...it's going to be one ungodly explosion."

He reached over and put his hand on Maynard's shoulder. "I've raised you to be a just and honorable man. Put all that aside for now and remember just one thing. This is not a battle between ships and men. It's a battle between good and evil. Place your faith in God, but fight like hell."

His father tried to lighten the mood. "Now, don't worry one millisecond about that load of bullshit Secretary Turnbul gave you yesterday. When this is over, he'll need an extension ladder to climb high enough to kiss your Maynard ass."

Maynard and his father talked for a couple more minutes, then Maynard returned to his cabin. He placed his grandfather's cutlass on the chart table and closed the shutters on the gallery windows.

Constitution gently rolled from side to side. Somewhere amidst the creaks and groans, he finally drifted off to sleep. His last thoughts were of his wife and daughters. He missed them and prayed he would have the opportunity to hug them again.

* * *

Angela climbed the ladder onto *Queen Anne's* main deck. She was wearing a pair of tight-fitting white Capri's and an oversized beige canvas shirt with Blackbeard's bandana tied around her neck. If she was going to be a pirate, she might as well look like one.

The deck was deserted except for the ever-vigilant, and totally spooky, helmsman. She scanned toward the bow and spotted her captain standing next to the foremast. His face was tilted toward the gray clouds overhead. She decided to sneak over and catch him by surprise.

She slinked around to the foremast and silently eased up behind him. As she was about to reach out and tickle the back of his neck, he whirled around, grabbed her by the wrists and pulled her into his arms. Angela wrapped her arms around him and kissed his burly chest—she didn't know exactly why. It just felt like the right thing to do.

"Well, now, milady, what puts thou in such splendid spirits this morn?"

She looked up at him. "I'm not sure. Perhaps it's all this fresh air, or this beautiful old ship. But I feel wonderful."

"Perhaps I may add to your delight then. 'Tis time we broke free of these clouds to collect my belongings. But there is one small matter I have yet to resolve."

231

Another smile radiated across Angela's face. "And what, my dear Captain, is the nature of this dilemma?"

"Aye, your folly does me much good. 'Tis the treasure, of course."

Angela relaxed her embrace.

"There are those who scheme to keep it from us. A man-of-war—much like our *Queen*—loaded with gutless ruffians shall fetch to thwart our passage and collect it for themselves. They have nettled me for all these years." He gritted his teeth. "But I shan't let them have their way again."

"Are these the men you told me about?" Angela asked.

"Aye. The very son of Maynard."

Angela's joy faded away. "So, by fight, you mean with guns?"

"Aye, with cannons, muskets and blades of steel. But fear not my Angel, you shall be safer in mine quarters than the harbor of yer mother's pouch. Nary a single coward shall harm you there."

"Why don't you just let them have it? No treasure is worth risking your life."

"Aye, but therein lies our true dilemma. You see, they don't know where it is. They need me to show them."

Angela got a queasy feeling. Blackbeard tried to comfort her with another embrace.

"Ahh now, I don't mean to worry your pretty little head. Teach and his men t'will be protected by the powers of our age. No harm shall come of us."

Angela didn't know what to say. This was all pretend, but it felt so real. She was finding it increasingly difficult to keep the two sides separate.

"Just think of it, soon you'll be showered in riches beyond imagination. Life is grand when taken in select doses, is it not? We must enjoy each sunrise as though it were to be our last. So let us rejoice onto the day and worry not of the morrow."

Blackbeard rubbed his hand across her back then dropped his arms to his sides. Angela wasn't ready to let him go. She wanted more reassurance of his safety.

"Perhaps your wisdom is best, my dear. Your affections could soften the heart of a raging lion. To appease any hostilities, perhaps I shall offer Maynard a share of the treasure. I promise I shall think on it." He put his hands on her shoulders and gently pushed her away. "Release me now and I shall join you again later."

Angela watched him walk away. Regardless of what else was happening, the emotion she was feeling for her captain was not fiction.

* * *

By 0900-hours, Perkins was on a plane headed for Mayport. When he arrived at DESRON Twenty-four Headquarters, Lieutenant Commander Wright was waiting in his office.

"Good morning, Commander. I understand things have been a little hectic around here. What's the word?"

"Hectic would be putting it mildly, sir. It appears the father of that missing Killian girl's been stirring up trouble. He claims we're not telling everything we know about his daughter's disappearance and has gone to the press, the governor of South Carolina, and all the local television stations. Someone obtained the telephone number to *Spruance's* quarterdeck; we weren't prepared for the barrage of calls we received. A member of the watch inadvertently disclosed the ship's name when he answered the phone. We've since disconnected all shore lines. All communications are being routed through radio.

"Yesterday afternoon a news helicopter flew over and took

a video of the ship. It was aired on the evening news before we could stop them. We had to restrain a group of reporters, and a pack of irate wives. Admiral Godsey's people have stepped up base security. Only active duty personnel with signed orders are being permitted leave. Now that ships have started getting underway, everyone is demanding to know what's really going on."

Perkins pointed to the door. "Close it and have a seat."

Wright closed the door as directed and sat down in the chair next to Perkins' desk.

Perkins folded his hands on his stomach and looked at him. "Does the name Blackbeard mean anything to you?"

Wright leaned back in his chair. "Until a couple days ago, I'd have said 'no'."

Perkins picked up a pencil and started drumming on his desk. "By Executive Order from the President, Admiral Hays has taken the *USS Constitution* out of moth balls and put her to sea. The plan is to go after Blackbeard and blow his ass out of the water with *Constitution's* cannons. Nothing else so far has worked. We're preparing a fighting crew in Little Creek as we speak. That's where Jenkins and I have been.

"At around twenty-three hundred hours last night, some friends of the DOD staged several diversions in Boston so *Constitution* could be smuggled to sea. Only a handful of people understand what's happening. Hell, Maynard's crew doesn't even know."

Perkins got up from his desk and walked over to a nautical chart hanging on the wall. He pointed to an area just off the coast of Maryland. "*Constitution* is to link up with the amphibious dock-landing ship *Anchorage* to transfer the men and munitions. *Anchorage* is currently in Norfolk taking on stores. In fact," he said looking at his watch, "they should be just about ready to get underway for Yorktown.

234

"We've had Hawkeyes up around the clock searching for *Queen Anne's Revenge*. They get a blip off the transponder every now and then but nothing concrete. Our best guess is that her captain somehow managed to maneuver into the center of the hurricane. Looks like we'll just have to wait until they are willing to show themselves."

"How about escorts?" Wright asked.

"That's where we come in. Perkins pointed to the chart again. "The aircraft carrier *Washington* and a task force from Norfolk will fan out to the east and seal off traffic to the north and east. Ships from Mayport will come in behind the hurricane and fill in south. Effectively, we will have Blackbeard hemmed in.

"*Spruance* will push ahead of the hurricane, and *Fitch* will ride the eastern flank. It's going to be a rough sail so rig for heavy seas. Once *Queen Anne* is spotted, *Constitution* will be vectored in and the rest will be up to Commander Maynard."

Perkins walked over and opened his office door. "Set for sea and anchor detail at 1100-hours. I'll be aboard by eleven-fifteen."

Wright took his cue and departed.

Perkins yelled after him. "Make sure there's plenty of cherry bug juice in the wardroom. The wife says all this damn coffee I'm drinking is making me irritable."

Chapter 25
1100: 28 August 2008

The blue and gold teams swapped training venues. At eleven-thirty, bag lunches and canned sodas were brought from the Little Creek mess hall. Half of each team munched on ham sandwiches while the other half continued training.

Admiral Hays watched the men practice with the cutlasses. Their progress was encouraging.

"Everyone stop," barked Huber. "Those of you not comfortable with a cutlass, try using a dirk." He held up a sword with a short, wide blade. "It's lighter than a cutlass and is easier to use in close combat. It was a favored weapon of early marines and pirate boarding parties. Those of you who want to carry two swords, I suggest a dirk as your second."

Lieutenant Clements jogged over to the admiral. "Sir, there's a call for you in the office. It's Captain Stuckey from the Pentagon. He said it's urgent."

Hays followed the lieutenant back to the office and picked up the phone. "Hays speaking."

His mood darkened. "I understand, Captain. Tell Admiral Hawthorne we will be ready to move out by nineteen-hundred hours. Any news on the location of *Queen Anne*? Okay...let me know the moment you have something."

Hays hung up the phone and motioned for Clements to close the door. "Hightail it to the range and tell Captain Lee to adjust his training schedule. We're shipping out at nineteen-hundred hours tonight. All groups will muster back here at eighteen-hundred. Tell Warrant Officer Dunbar to assemble his core gunnery crews and commence drilling. On your way out, send in Jenkins and Huber."

Jenkins and Huber immediately reported to the admiral's office.

"Gentlemen, *Constitution* is making the transit to Norfolk quicker than expected. A new storm front is moving in from the northwest and is going to bring rain and chop. The CNO wants us to complete the personnel transfer before things get too rough. If we wait for it to pass, we'll have the hurricane to contend with. We've got no choice. We're rolling out of here at nineteen-hundred hours."

"Mister Huber, muster the marines and SEALS and start intense combat training. Do the best you can with the time you've got. I'll tell you when to break."

"Yes, sir," Huber replied and he headed out.

"Jenkins, I know you've been working your tail off the past few days. I want to thank you personally for an exceptional effort. Your dedication will not go unrewarded."

"Thank you, sir," Jenkins replied.

"Contact Captain Hotard and tell him to have ten fully-fueled 46-Alpha helicopters sitting outside this command center by eighteen-hundred hours. We'll start ferrying the men and equipment out as soon as *Anchorage* clears the mouth of the York River. Each man will be responsible for his own equipment. Pack as many men on each bird as you can. The fewer trips we make, the quicker *Anchorage* can come to full-steam and rendezvous with

Constitution. You'll be the last to leave so make sure nothing's left behind. Once the men are all aboard have them grab some chow. Afterward, muster them on the flight deck or in the boat well and continue drilling.

"As soon as Dunbar secures from gunnery practice, contact the Sea Bees so they can get the cannons loaded for transport to Ocracoke. Lieutenant Kadleb is due to report in at any minute." He checked his watch. "His men should be about finished mapping the Pamlico Sound shipping channels. Have him e-mail the charts as soon as they're completed."

* * *

Dunbar watched the black sedan drive up, and saw Lieutenant Clements get out and run over to Captain Lee. Something was up.

Lee hurried over to Dunbar.

"Chief, Lee said. "We have been ordered to ship out at nineteen-hundred hours. Muster your gun crews and start gunnery exercises immediately. Everyone is to report back at SEAL Two by eighteen-hundred hours and get ready for transport to the *Anchorage.*"

"Yes, sir," Dunbar said. He waved his hand in the air to get Ritter's attention, then motioned with his finger across his throat.

The two shooting teams were brought together and divided into their groups. The SEALS and marines departed for the field house. Dunbar loaded his men into the cattle cars for the artillery range. Ritter and Petty Officer Mottley stayed at the small-arms range to continue drilling the marksmen and snipers.

Once all his men were on the ground, Dunbar ordered them to count off in teams of eight.

"Alright, guys, things just keep getting better. You're now

going to learn how to load and fire twenty-four and thirty-two pound, black powder cannons. Basically they work just like the rifles, except they pack a little more punch.

"Instead of measuring powder in grains, we measure it here in pounds. The twenty-four pounders hold a six-pound charge, and the thirty-two pounders use two and one-half pounds. Unlike the three and a half and five inch turrets you're used to, you have to prime, load, fire and clear each of these by hand.

"For you carrier types accustomed to stringing bombs on airplane wings, turrets are the big guns found on real Navy ships." His joke brought a round of laughs and snide remarks from the tin-can sailors.

"Does anyone know the true definition of a gunner's mate?" A couple of the older guys raised their hands. "He's a boatswain's mate with a hunting license." Several men booed. "You'll soon understand exactly what that means.

"The work ahead of you is backbreaking, hot and dirty. Uniform of the day will be coveralls skivvy shirts and steel-toed boondockers. Bandanas are optional. There will be absolutely no belt buckles, watches, rings or any other metallic objects that can cause a spark and blow us all to smithereens. From this point on, the smoking lamp is out. If any of you have cigarette lighters or matches, deposit them in the trash cans next to the cattle cars.

"Some of you will be working in the powder magazine filling charges for the cannons and measuring quick loads for the rifles. Those assignments will be made tomorrow.

"Now, most of you are graduates from gunner's mate A-school. During the first couple days of your training, you studied the history of naval gunnery." Dunbar pointed to the row of cannons tackled to buried railroad ties. "If you look across the range here, you'll see six vintage, heavy cannons. These are the real thing, guys. I have ultra-sounded, bore-sighted and test fired each of them. They are rock solid and, believe me, they'll make you want to kiss the man who invented ear plugs because you won't be wearing any. You can't respond to orders if you have your ears plugged. So when the gun captains light the powder in the touch pans, each of you had better have your hands over your ears. Am I clear on that?"

"Yes, sir!" yelled the men.

"Outstanding. Balls of steel and sex appeal; United States Navy gunner's mates. Now let's get to work."

Dunbar walked over to the cannon nearest to him, opened the ammo box and pulled out a powder sling. On each side of the cannon there was a stack of ten cannon balls and a rack with a bore brush and a rammer.

"This gun's called a twenty-four pounder. That means it fires a twenty-four pound ball. Those two on the far end over there are thirty-two pounders. The twenty-four pounders have an effective range of 1200 yards. They fire a high-velocity penetrating ball that is used to blow holes through an enemy ship. The cannons themselves weigh a little over fifty-seven-hundred pounds each, and take a crew of eight to ten men to prepare and fire. We will experiment with crew size tomorrow.

"The thirty-two pounders over on the end there are much lighter. They weigh just a little over a ton and have an effective range of approximately 400 yards. They are used for close warfare or, in our case, when two ships are side by side. When loaded with grape shot and chain, they are used like scatter-guns to slaughter an advancing boarding force. We will be shooting both."

The remnants of humor in the men's faces quickly faded. Dunbar immediately detected the change in attitude.

"Gentlemen, Commodore Perkins told you this morning that the mission ahead of us is dangerous. It is apparent from some of your expressions that his meaning is beginning to hit home.

"I probably shouldn't be telling you this," Dunbar shot a quick look over at Captain Lee who had driven up and was standing behind the men; Lee gave him a nod. "The bad guys we will be fighting a few days from now are experienced and ruthless. We have to be just as ruthless as they are. Maybe even more so. However, we have two aces up our sleeve. One is our CO, Commander Robert Maynard. I would follow him straight into the fires of hell if he led me there. He will make the right decisions at the right times. All we have to do is execute his orders quickly and without reservation. The second? Well, in a couple hours I will let you judge that for yourself. But I will tell you this much...you are going to cream your dungarees. In the end, we will be victorious and the bad guys will learn what it feels like to be on the receiving end of some ass-kicking U.S. Naval gunnery!"

Dunbar looked out across his men; nobody said a word. "Now, gentlemen, we have some cannons to fire. So repeat after me: Run, Sponge, Powder, Ram, Shot, Wad, Ram, Run, Fuse, Step Back, Cover, Fire."

"Again." Captain Lee ran up to the front and joined the chant. "Run, Sponge, Powder, Ram, Shot, Wad, Ram, Run, Fuse, Step Back, Cover, Fire."

"One more time!" exclaimed Lee.

The whole mass shouted at the top of their lungs. "Run, Sponge, Powder, Ram, Shot, Wad, Ram, Run, Fuse, Step Back, Cover, Fire."

"Let me show you what that means," Dunbar added. He took a lighter from his pocket, lit one of the slow matches and handed it to Captain Lee. "You may have the honors, sir."

Chapter 26
1800: 28 August 2008

At eighteen-hundred hours, everyone returned to the Little Creek field house. Admiral Hays watched as the crew collected their weapons and packed their bags.

Each of *Constitution's* men was issued a musket, a possibles bag, a cutlass and a dirk. The swords were attached to green-webbed gun belts so that they could be easily slung over their shoulders.

The SEALS loaded their packs with their own selection of personal goodies. An additional assortment of daggers and knives had been placed on tables at the rear of the room. The Little Creek gymnasium looked like a Soldier of Fortune flea market.

Captain Hotard's helicopters began touching down on the parade ground. In less than ten minutes, the first one was loaded and airborne. Admiral Hays and Chief Warrant Officer Dunbar were aboard.

The ride out to *USS Anchorage* took thirty minutes. After Hays' bird landed, Captain Sorrel—*Anchorage's* commanding officer—ducked his head and hurried out to greet him.

"Welcome to *Anchorage*," Sorrel said and guided the admiral clear of the helicopter downwash.

"Sir, less than a minute ago, radio received a priority message for you. If you'll come this way, I'll escort you up."

A second helicopter landed. Hays gave Sorrel a quick nod, and the two departed.

"Attention on deck!" ordered a chief as Admiral Hays entered radio.

"As you were," Hays said.

Sorrel handed him the message. Hays pulled a pair of glasses from his shirt pocket and read it:

"Commander Surface Forces Atlantic:

Aerial units have established solid contact with the target; the pigeon has flown the coop. All sheets to the wind and pointed north. *Spruance* and *Fitch* engaged in high speed transit: time to shake, rattle and roll! Awaiting further orders.

Regards,

Commodore Basil L. Perkins"

"Outstanding." Hays turned to Sorrel. "Get a message to *Spruance*. Instruct Commodore Perkins to flank and maintain his distance. Under no circumstances is anything to come within 10,000 yards of that ship. Prepare *Anchorage* to commence a full-speed run just as soon as my men and equipment are secure."

* * *

Jenkins was completing his final rounds. Ritter spotted him and rushed over.

"Commander Jenkins, I don't pretend to know what you guys are up against," Ritter exclaimed. "But it looks like it's one hell of a fight. I wish you the best of luck." He extended Jenkins his hand. "Been a pleasure working with you, sir."

Jenkins shook hands. "Mr. Ritter, on behalf of Admiral Hays and Commodore Perkins, I'd like to express the Navy's sincere appreciation for all your help. We could not have pulled this together without you." Jenkins knew what Ritter was thinking. "Sorry we can't ask you to join us. We could certainly use your talents."

Ritter's expression told of his disappointment." I figured as much," he said. Ritter handed Jenkins an authentic Colt Navy 1851 black powder revolver, holster, and a bag of ball shot and wads. "Would you mind giving this to Dunbar for me? Tell him I expect to get it back from him in person."

Jenkins' and Ritter's eyes met. "I'll see that he gets it. Do you have transportation back to Boon?"

"It's waiting around front."

Jenkins gave him a nod. "I've got to get going. Hope your wife enjoys that new minivan."

Chapter 27
2200: 28 August 2008

Anchorage secured from flight quarters and Admiral Hays ordered two Sea King helicopters to remain aboard until the personnel transfer with *Constitution* was complete. Both were refueled and standing-by on the helo deck.

After clearing the Chesapeake Bay Bridge Tunnel, *Anchorage* turned north toward the rendezvous point with *Constitution*.

Hays, Captain Sorrel, and Jenkins were walking the boat deck, checking on preparations for the transfer to *Constitution*.

"Are you certain those cargo nets will hold our men?" asked Hays.

"Yes, sir," replied Sorrel. "We've inspected every inch of them. We had to make a few repairs but, overall, they're in excellent condition."

"How about your boat coxswains?"

"Hand-picked, sir; all E-6 or above," Sorrel said. "Two of them have over twenty year's experience. We'll load each Mike boat with as much as it will safely hold. That will make them more stable in choppy seas and require us to make fewer trips. Each load will consist of men, munitions and stores. No sense putting all our eggs in one basket."

Hays gave a nod and examined one of the Mike's lighting booms.

"Six double-insulated, two-thousand watt Halogen lights per boom. Two booms per Mike. Any more than that and the Mike's generator could not power them. Each Mike has a thirty-minute battery back-up in case there's an electrical problem. Additional lighting can be provided overhead by the Sea Kings if needed."

Hays grimaced. "I'm nervous as hell about this. It's never been done before, let alone at night. That storm front will to be licking our heels every inch of the way. Wrap things up as soon as you can, and get these men some rest. Everyone must be as fresh as possible. We'll hold reveille an hour before rendezvous. Make sure each man observes every possible safety precaution. Drill that into their heads. We can't afford any mishaps during the exchange."

* * *

"Hands. Fetch me another bucket 'o water," Blackbeard ordered. "And batten that hatch to the draft."

With Angela dining with the crew, Blackbeard decided to reacquaint with his cabin for a few moments and take a hot bath.

The portholes and gallery windows were streaked in tiny rivulets of condensed steam; smoke from his whalebone pipe lazed in stagnant layers above his head. There was a fresh, ruffled shirt and a pair of black pants neatly folded on the chair next to his tub; a bolster of pistols lay on top of them.

He leaned back in the large wooden tub and rested his head against the rim. He closed his eyes and tried to relax. There was mounting dissension amongst his crew and he needed to devise an effective strategy to put an end to it.

246

There was a knock at the door. Richards entered.

"Can't you scoundrels leave me one moment's peace?" Blackbeard shouted.

"I apologize for disturbing you, Captain, but I must have a word with you."

"Be quick about it, and don't bother me again."

Richards walked to the foot of the tub. "The men have been talking. They're disgruntled at not being permitted to loot that large vessel the other day. They claim lady Angela has made you soft, and demand she be set ashore at once."

"They do, do they?" Blackbeard replied.

"Aye, Captain. 'Tis their entitlement to obtain a fair share for their efforts. Thus far, they have received nary a penny. They're beginning to wonder if there's any treasure to be had at all."

"Is it not enough that they are free to take breath once more?" Blackbeard pounded his fist on his knee. "Must they require constant reminding? Perhaps they are too stupid to remember."

"Why, no, Captain. But an equal say and an equal share. 'Tis the way it's always been."

"Did I not welcome challenge to my command? Yet, did one of them possess the guts to step forward? No! There isn't enough manhood amongst the lot of them to equal an ounce of bravery. Cowards! Nothing but a pack of cowardly children. And just what are you? The nanny's tit?"

Richards backed away from the tub.

"I guess children must be properly disciplined if ever to stand on their own. I shall see they receive what they require." He pointed at Richards. "Once the lady's asleep, round up these mutineers of yours and bring them before the mast. We shall see then who makes demands of whom."

* * *

Angela was returning to her cabin and spotted Hands down the passageway ahead of her, carrying a bucket. She hurried to catch up.

"Either you've got sore feet or a big thirst," she said.

Hands stopped and turned around. "'Tis not for me, milady. 'Tis for the captain's bath."

"So, he's got you playing cabin boy for both of us."

"Aye. Whatever the captain desires, the captain shall have. It matters not who labors for it."

"Then you wouldn't mind if I gave it to him?"

Hands rolled his eyes across her bosom and grinned. "I'd rather you give it to me."

"In your dreams, buddy."

A despondent look crossed Hands' face; the smile disappeared. "'T'was my dream, dear lady," he said softly, "we'd not be here at all." He placed the bucket on the deck.

As he limped away, Angela suddenly felt sad. Of all the characters she had met since coming aboard the *Queen Anne*, Hands was by far the most mysterious. He was gentle and compassionate but in a very dejected, distant sort of way.

He stopped at the ladder and glanced back at her. It seemed as though he was being forced to do something against his will. He turned and labored up the ladder.

Very sad, she thought.

Angela looked down at the bucket, and her thoughts shifted to the Captain. Was he in for a surprise?

She grabbed the bucket and continued aft. Richards rushed by her as if she wasn't even there.

When she reached Blackbeard's outer stateroom, she opened the door and peered inside. It was empty. She entered and closed the door behind her. She placed the bucket by the door to his inner chambers and lifted the latch and peeked inside; there he was, all laid back in the tub with his eyes closed.

She closed the door and carefully returned the latch. Reaching down, she pulled off her sandals—one at a time—and placed them next to the bulkhead. She unbuttoned her shorts and let them drop to the floor, picked them up, folded and put them on top of her shoes. She next unbuttoned all but the bottom two buttons of her shirt, reached inside and slid her bra straps off her shoulders; pulled her arms through, twisted the clasp around to the front, and undid the hooks, freeing her breasts. Lastly, she slid her panties down over her hips, stepped out, and tucked them and her bra under her shorts.

She took a deep breath and fluffed her hair around her shoulders. This was one of the craziest things she had ever done. But the desire within her was much too strong to ignore any longer and there was only one way to reconcile it.

She retrieved the bucket and carefully opened the door, stepped into Blackbeard's cabin, and eased the door closed behind her. She tiptoed over to the foot of the tub and slowly poured the water into the captain's bath.

Blackbeard's eyes popped open. He cleared his throat and sat up. "Aye, come to scrub me back, have ya?"

Angela gazed down at him; her heart was racing. She placed the bucket on the deck, unbuttoned the last two buttons of her shirt, shivered out of it and stood naked before him for several moments. His eyes drank in every ounce of her body.

She stepped into the tub and carefully slid her body down on top of his. "No, I rather you scrubbed mine." She kissed him fully on the mouth.

Blackbeard's muscles flexed beneath her, his heart pounded against the firmness of her breast. His powerful hands roamed her back and buttocks; mapping her every curve and valley; careful that his calloused hide didn't rasp her more sensitive areas. The warmth of his touch ignited a new genre of passion inside her.

"After all that has been spoken, milady," said Blackbeard, "do you think this wise?"

"Why, my dear captain. You'd not find my comforts to your liking?"

"No, no. Quite the contrary. It's just..."

"Then relax," she whispered. "And do exactly as I command."

Blackbeard lifted her from the water and carried her to the bunk and gently lay her down. He pressed his lips against the side of her moist neck and kissed down across her breast and abdomen. His long hair and beard passed across her skin with the tickle-soft sensation of a Peacock feather: She inhaled in quick uneven bursts. Their lips came together once again. She held him tightly, guiding each of his advances until their bodies were finally joined.

* * *

Blackbeard rested in Angela's arms. He listened to her breathing retreat until it was as faint as the whisper of a butterfly's wings. She was fast asleep.

He eased himself off the bunk and quietly got dressed. He exited his cabin and proceeded topside, anger enveloped him like a stagnant fog. With each step he took, his aggravation multiplied. By the time he reached the quarterdeck, he was seething.

He stomped across to the bow and glared up into the moonless sky. "Speak to me, you lecherous bastard! I demand it!" He waited.

"Dare you use my own capacities against me? She was powerless to stop it, said I. Yet, I have proved the helpless one.

Through mine own weakness of flesh I have been made a fool once more. Though the years have passed, betrayal remains the fulcrum of the wretched. Betrayal!" he shouted.

"Shall I next be dragged from my sleep and hanged? Is that the way it has been scripted once again? And just who shall accomplish this task for you? What Judas have you enlisted from the ambitious of my crew?" He glared across the deck. "Aye, perhaps you already have made your selection."

Blackbeard stormed toward the ladder. "Maynard is but one to blame for this." He stopped and gazed into the sky again. "So be it. I have delivered to my portion of our agreement and, now, you must hold to yours. Deliver the son of Maynard to me by the second rising sun or with mine own hands I shall undo all that I have done."

He hollered down into the gun deck. "Richards! Hoist those mutinous bastards before me and bind their hides to the mast. Garrat, fetch my whip! I will show you all how soft I have become. I shall show the whole bloody lot of you!"

Chapter 28
2200: 28 August 2008

Maynard poured himself into the charts again, reexamining his strategy for Ocracoke. There was a knock at his cabin door. "Enter," he said.

The door opened and a young Coast Guard midshipman took two steps in, popped to attention, and shot his right hand up in an enthusiastic salute.

"Son, this isn't the Coast Guard Academy," Maynard said. "You're with the Navy now." He pointed to the overhead. "We don't salute when covered."

The midshipman blushed and lowered his hand. "I beg the captain's pardon, sir."

"What's on your mind, son?"

"Sir, the Officer of the Deck wishes to report flashing lights off the starboard bow. The duty signalman has identified the vessel as the *USS Anchorage*."

"Very well, midshipman..." Maynard searched his uniform for his name.

"Wood, sir. Midshipman Wood. But everyone calls me Woody."

"Very well, Midshipman Woody. Inform the Officer of the

Deck that I will be up promptly. You can breathe now if you find it more comfortable."

"Thank you, sir." Wood started to render another salute, awkwardly halting himself.

"You're dismissed, Mister Wood."

"Thank you, sir." Wood turned to leave and tried to jump through the hatch before he fully opened it. The leading edge smacked him right in the middle of the forehead. He looked back to see if his captain had noticed, grinned, and then eased himself out.

Maynard chuckled. Being a cadet was an extremely difficult part of every officer's career, at best. It was also one of the most memorable.

Maynard rose from the chart table and went to the sideboard to retrieve a signalman's blinker gun, and proceeded topside via the rear ammo scuttle to join Lt Commander Fallon. The ship's beacons had advanced to three points off the starboard bow.

Maynard aimed the blinker gun and triggered the letter K, the international procedure signal for invitation to transmit. Signaled dash-dot-dash, the dots and dashes were achieved by alternating short and long pulses of light.

The other vessel immediately responded with dot-dash-dot; the letter R, the signal for received. It was the *Anchorage*.

Maynard handed the blinker gun to Signalman First Class Olson. "Okay SM1, do your thing."

Olson took the gun and began signaling approach instructions.

Maynard maneuvered *Constitution* around *Anchorage's* starboard side. All sails were brought in and secured.

Lighting was a critical issue. With no means to generate electrical power, *Constitution's* deck force had to rely on battery-powered halogen lights. The Sea Kings' spotlights helped, but the pilots were struggling against gusting winds. A helo from *USS Churchill* was circling, as well.

Maynard watched as *Anchorage's* rear gate lowered. "Away the landing craft, away," was passed over her 1MC. The first Mike tested the waters like a fledgling cetacean being cast from its mother's womb. The batten of darkness devoured the glow from the floodlights. Maynard held his breath as the flat-bottom boat pitched atop the ragged swells.

Fallon was in charge of things topside. The Mike's cargo decks would be approximately fifteen feet below the top of *Constitution's* raised bulwarks. He ordered the small boats brought in so the boat davits could be used to hoist up the supplies.

The first Mike came along the port davit. Her crew tied fenders to the gunwales to act as shock absorbers. *Constitution's* line handlers lowered the mooring lines; the eyes were looped over the Mike's mooring cleats and secured to *Constitution's* bits.

Heaving lines were tossed up. Fallon's men began hauling up the large cargo nets that would serve as ladders. Once in place, Admiral Hays, Jenkins, Dunbar and Lt. Clements—bundled in cumbersome KAPOK life vests—started up.

When Hays reached the top, Maynard and Fallon helped him aboard. He stripped off his vest and dropped it back into the Mike. The other three climbed aboard and followed suit.

The rest of the men began to negotiate the nets. As they crawled aboard, a chief petty officer directed them to the berthing deck to sign a muster sheet, deposit their gear, and then hightail it back topside. Every available hand was needed to help transfer stores and ammunition.

A threefold purchase was rigged to each arm of the davit so the loads would be easier to haul up, and the running block was rigged with a smaller cargo net. The nets were lowered and filled with supplies, and the line handlers hoisted them aboard.

After the first Mike was in place, *Anchorage* sent a second, then a third. The second Mike splashed astern and bumped alongside *Constitution's* starboard davit. Another set of cargo nets was raised and the next wave of men started up weighted down with packs, cutlasses and firearms.

Maynard escorted Admiral Hays and Jenkins back to his cabin.

"Wish I could offer you some coffee," he said. "But it seems we forgot to pack a pot."

"I've had enough in the past two days to last six months," Hays said. "Commander, *Queen Anne's Revenge* has pushed ahead of the hurricane and is currently sailing up the coast of South Carolina."

He unfolded a chart and placed it on the chart table. "Our last reporting placed her here, just south of Charleston. At her current course and speed, she's expected to be off the Outer Banks by midafternoon tomorrow. Our best guess is she'll put into Ocracoke to lay and wait. The ground forces have prepared a welcoming party should Teach decide to come ashore."

Hays drew a large circle from Miami to Nantucket. "This entire area is free of traffic. Hurricane Drummond has things bottled up to the south, and we've formed a naval blockade to the north and east. *Spruance* and *Fitch* are currently closing in on *Queen Anne*, and we have two Hawkeyes overhead monitoring the weather and the ship's movements. As long as the transponder holds out, we will keep you posted on her progress until you make contact yourself. From there, it's all up to you."

"How about charts of the inlet?" Maynard asked.

Jenkins stepped forward and handed Hays a manila envelope.

"It looks like you'll have at least two solid channels to maneuver in." Hays laid the chart on the table. "The storm surge will cause some coastal flooding. So you'll probably have more water to work with than indicated."

Maynard examined at the collection of symbols and numbers to get his bearings.

"They're not perfect, but it's the best we could do on short notice." The admiral put his finger on the mouth of Ocracoke Inlet. "The deepest passage is the shipping channel cut by the Corps of Engineers last spring. It runs from the mouth of the inlet through the Blair Channel, out into the sound, then turns south and runs into the Neuse River. Its depth varies from twenty-four to thirty-two feet. You should have no problem maneuvering in it. But from there things get tricky."

He pointed next to a fork in the Blair Channel. "At this juncture, the Blair splits off and joins the Nine Foot and Big Foot Channels. At high tide, Nine Foot's depth will be about twelve feet. Stay clear of it. There's no point deep enough for *Constitution* to pass. If you need to, steer right into the Big Foot Channel.

"Big Foot Channel runs east and west. The western fork leads to a dead end. To the east, it connects with Teaches Hole Channel and completes a circle back to the mouth of the inlet. Depths vary from fifteen to twenty-five feet. You'll just have to feel your way along. Keep a sounding crew on standby. If you stray outside one of these channels, you're certain to run aground. There are numerous sandbars littering the bottom the charts don't show. Jenkins has brought along a tidal chart. High tide tomorrow is at zero-six-thirty-nine and then again around seventeen-hundred hours. With the storm at your back door, the tides will come in fast and leave slow. We are also expecting eight or nine feet of storm surge. Use that to your advantage.

"As we approached, I noticed your draft markings indicated between eighteen and nineteen feet. With the additional men and supplies, figure your bow at twenty-one and the stern at twenty-three. You have a total complement of three hundred ninety-eight men, including thirteen officers counting the marine commander and his first lieutenant. Commander Jenkins and Lieutenant J.G. Clements have volunteered to remain aboard and assist." Hays looked at Jenkins. "I think you'll find them quite helpful.

"Gunnery practice is set for 0700 tomorrow morning. Jenkins has the coordinates of the target drop sight. Get in as much practice as you can. At sixteen-hundred, you'll break off and head south. *Anchorage* and *Churchill* will escort you to Ocracoke. From there, you will link up with *Spruance* and *Fitch*. You can reach us at any time over the link."

The Admiral took a deep breath and exhaled it slowly. "Gentlemen. If you have any questions, now is the time to ask."

Maynard was engrossed in the chart. There was a spot in Teaches Hole Channel wide enough for two ships to pass; it was a good tactical point to make a stand and force a fight.

"Is there anything we left out?" Hays asked.

Maynard caught his father's eye; there was no response from anyone.

"Alright, let's get this replenishment completed and send everyone to their racks.

Hays turned to Commander Maynard. "Commander, you have a monumental task ahead of you." He rendered a salute. "Go out there and annihilate those bastards." He looked at Maynard's father. "Captain, we've got a boat to catch."

Mr. Maynard reached over and took Robert by the hand, placing his other hand on top. They held each other tightly. "See you in a couple days, son."

Constitution took a sudden sharp dip to port, followed by a hard return to starboard. There were two shuddering collisions along *Constitution's* port side, followed by a scraping sound and several loud crashes above. Men started shouting.

Maynard dropped his father's hand and rushed out the cabin. He got to the hatch leading to the main deck; cannon balls were plummeting through the opening. He jumped back to dodge them, then bolted up on deck.

A large group of seamen was crowded along the port bulwark, several shining battle lanterns toward the water. Huber was helping a soaking wet sailor to the deck. Maynard rushed over to Lieutenant Commander Fallon.

"We've got at least fifteen men in the water," Fallon said. "We took a rogue swell and must have caught the Mike boat's chine. When we righted, she pitched sideways, foundered and went down. Four SEALS jumped over to attempt a rescue."

Maynard grabbed a battle lantern and climbed out onto the mizzen rigging channel; the halogen lamps from the sinking Mike were still visible. He heard men in the water shouting but the wind and darkness made it difficult to locate them.

"Mister Fallon!" Maynard shouted. "When you find one, keep a light on him so the rescuers can get to them."

Maynard's light fell upon the back of a life vest about twenty yards astern. The sailor's head was slumped forward. "Back here!" Maynard shouted.

Churchill's LAMPS was passing down the port side. Fallon shined his battle lantern on the cockpit and directed the pilot aft.

The tide was rapidly washing the life vest out of reach of Maynard's light. The LAMPS crew found him with their spotlight and lowered a man on a tether; the wind and rotor downwash spun the rescuer in circles. On the second attempt, the rescuer plunged into the water almost directly on top of the floater but somehow managed to get a line around the sailor, and the LAMPS winched the two of them from the sea.

Maynard climbed back down. Fallon came over.

"Six men are still unaccounted for," he said.

258

"The current's got them by now," Maynard replied. "The helicopters will keep searching. Get the swimmers back aboard and continue with the replenishment."

Men and supplies continued aboard in waves. The munitions were passed hand to hand down the ammo scuttles and into the powder holds; food stores were directed into holds on the Orlop deck. Additional communication equipment was hefted aboard and Maynard directed the technicians to set it up in his cabin. Each crewman was giving 110% effort.

As the replenishment wound to a close, the men were stowing the last of the gunnery and messing supplies. The final Mike was waiting for the admiral and Captain Maynard. Maynard helped his father strap on a life vest.

"I'm afraid these six are just the first of many," said Hays. "They will not die in vain."

"Not if we can help it," Maynard replied.

Hays climbed the bulwark and started over the side. "E-mail your muster sheets so we can determine the names of the missing men."

Maynard's father took a hold of the netting. "I wish I was thirty years younger."

"Then I'd have to worry about you," Maynard said. He clipped a safety line to the back of his father's life vest and helped him over the bulwark.

When both men were safely aboard the Mike, the cargo nets were cut loose, the mooring lines were cast off, and the coxswain reversed his engine.

Maynard yelled, "Man the sails!" The men took to the shrouds again. "Cast off the gaskets and set the main course."

Rain began to fall. Dunbar started covering his topside cannons with canvas. Maynard grabbed him by the sleeve as he passed. "Gunnery practice tomorrow at zero-seven-hundred hours."

"We'll be ready, Captain," answered Dunbar. "If I still have any dry powder."

Dunbar whistled at a group of sailors standing by the mizzen pinrail. "You men. Grab some canvas and help cover these guns."

Constitution's lower sails were set in place and she headed back out to sea.

Chapter 29
0500: 29 August 2008

The messenger of the watch awakened Maynard at zero-five-hundred hours sharp. At zero-five-thirty, reveille was held on the crew.

Breakfast—consisting of boiled eggs, fresh fruit, juice and bagels—were eaten in shifts across the berthing compartment and spar deck. Most men ate standing; many elected to form traditional twelve-man messes. As they finished, the gunner's mates mustered on the after-gun deck and the SEALS mustered in the junior officer's wardroom. Jenkins was collecting the names of those who were left.

"Alright, men, now listen up," Dunbar said. "We will be taking live gunnery practice again this morning. Guess what shipmates? You are now standing on the main gun deck of the historic *USS Constitution*. There are thirty twenty-four pound guns here, fifteen to port and fifteen to starboard. You will notice each has been stenciled with a number, such as 2P1 or 2S1. The first number represents the deck. One stands for the spar deck, or topside, and the number two stands for the main gun deck, where you are now. The letters P and S indicate port or starboard, and the last number represents the gun position. For example, 2P1 means the gun is located on the main gun deck, port side, forward most position.

"On this deck, the position numbers run fore and aft from one to fifteen. The thirty-two pound guns above on the spar are numbered 1P1 or 1S1 through 1P11 and 1S11. There are also two twenty-four pound guns located aft at the taffrail. They are numbered 1T1 and 1T2. The one-ten and one-eleven gun crews will also be responsible for firing these guns. Those of you quick with math, that should equal a total of fifty-four cannons. You may be asking yourselves, how can twenty-eight gun teams possibly fire fifty-four cannons? The answer is simple. They can't."

Jenkins and a group of thirty or more sailors joined Dunbar. "You men gather around and listen up," said Dunbar. "We'll get you assigned in a couple minutes. Like I was saying, twenty-eight gun crews can't fire fifty-four guns. At least, not at the same time.

"As you will learn when the captain addresses you later this morning, we will be fighting one enemy ship. That means *Constitution* will only be firing from one side at a time, port or starboard. As the ship maneuvers from port to starboard, you will need to shift sides of the ship and shift guns. This may be tricky for some crews that need to negotiate obstacles. We'll be practicing this so that you can make the shifts in an organized fashion. So, if you're assigned to mount 2P1—when we shift—you will man 2S1. Get the picture?"

"Yes, sir!" roared the men.

"Outstanding. In a moment, I want you to fall out and organize your gun teams like we did yesterday. For the time being, I want crews one through thirteen at cannons 2P1 through 2P13. Crews fourteen and fifteen will alternate between guns 2P5 and 2P6. This is only until the captain gives us access to the guns in his stateroom and we can work in these other men. Crews sixteen through twenty-seven to go topside and man guns 1P1 through

1P11, and crew twenty-eight muster at gun 1T1. When all is said and done, we will be forming a total of thirty-one gun crews—fifteen twenty-four pounders, twelve thirty-two pounders. We'll also form powder crews to work in the magazines and loading room, and four reserve gun crews.

"To start with, the twenty-four pound crews will have ten gunners and one powder monkey. The thirty-two pound crews will have six and a monkey. More men will be worked in as needed."

Dunbar stopped to clear his throat. He was getting hoarse after two days of continuous yelling.

"Now, what are the magic words I taught you yesterday? Everyone, all together now: Run, Sponge, Powder, Ram, Shot, Wad, Ram, Run, Fuse, Step Back, Cover, Fire!" The men responded in unison.

"Outstanding. Let's break, and everyone assume their positions."

Jenkins came over, and he and Dunbar went over the gun crew rosters. They reorganized the teams combining the new men with the one-day veterans, forming the thirty-one crews needed. Ten men were sent to the fore and aft powder magazines to prepare the powder charges. Since the Coast Guard midshipmen were the youngest—and generally in better physical condition—they were selected as powder monkeys.

By zero-seven-hundred, the gun crews and magazines teams were set. GMG2 Mottley mustered the sharpshooters on the forecastle. Several of them had not even touched the weapons. He pulled them aside and ran through the loading and firing procedures. The others threw empty Pyrodex kegs over the bulwarks and started taking target practice.

Down on the berthing deck, Maynard was going over the battle plan with Huber, the SEALS and the Marine Corps officer and leading NCOs.

"You gentlemen have been chosen because of your proficiency with close combat. Our hostiles are all expert swordsmen. They will continue fighting until their captain has been eliminated. Our mission is not complete until we have killed every single one of them. There will be no prisoners.

"Those of you carrying conventional firearms will throw them over the side now and free yourself of the temptation. They will do you no good. We have already shot these people with M-60s and fifty-caliber machine guns. To my knowledge, we have yet to kill a single one."

Maynard walked over to the table and picked up a manila envelope, pulled out a photograph, and walked back to the front of the compartment. "This is their captain. His name is Edward Teach." Maynard watched for reaction; the name was not unfamiliar to most of them.

"He's also known as Blackbeard, the most unpredictable pirate captain to tread the planks of a ship. You can shoot him, you can cut him, and you can run him through with a cutlass. Don't be surprised if he doesn't fall dead at your feet. Because he won't. So, if you must fight him, attack him in groups and from all sides. Do not engage him alone. Watch out for when he starts to windmill his cutlass. When he does, fall back and use your pistols. Let me warn you now, if you challenge him head on, you will be butchered in your tracks."

Maynard walked back to the table and handed the envelope to Huber.

"These are all the intelligence photographs we have of Blackbeard's ship. We'll be taking the fight directly to the *Queen Anne*. Get familiar with the territory. Remember this, no hostile has ever stepped foot aboard the *USS Constitution* and that's the way I intend for it stay. Is that clear?"

The men roared back, "Yes, sir!!"

264

"That's all I have. Except for this. When this mission is complete, I intend to buy every one of you a hunk of grilled cow and as much ice-cold beer as you can drink. And I mean each and every one of you. Got that?"

"Yes, sir!!"

"Be careful, and fight smart."

There were no whoops or shouts. These guys were the ultimate military machines and the gray sheen in their eyes told Maynard they were more than prepared for the challenge.

* * *

At seven-thirty hours, a C-131 Samaritan cargo plane lumbered low along the horizon and jettisoned a series of large, floating gunnery targets; they splashed into the ocean, righted themselves and fanned out on the current.

"Ninety degrees to port," ordered Maynard.

"Ninety degrees, aye," the helmsman echoed.

"Mister Pasarelli, man the sails."

"Man the sails," Pasarelli shouted.

Lines of seamen climbed the riggings aloft. When everyone was in place, the lead man on each mast reported manned and ready.

"All sails manned and ready, Captain," Pasarelli said.

"Furl to the course, Mr. Pasarelli."

Pasarelli looked aloft. "Furl to the course."

The yardmen began taking in bottoms of the lower sets of sails and swaging them like giant curtains to the yards. Posting less sail would reduce *Constitution's* maneuverability and speed, but it would also help her gunners' accuracy. Confidence was a key element to their success.

Constitution maneuvered starboard to within twenty yards

of the first target and matched its drift. "Mister Jenkins," Maynard said. "You may target when ready."

Jenkins shouted down into the gun deck. "Target when ready, Mister Dunbar."

* * *

Dunbar selected cannon 2S7—named Bouncing Billy by her crew during the War of 1812—for the targeting shots. He turned to the gun captain. "Fire and reload."

The gun captain barked the orders to his crew. "Step back. Cover."

The men took a step backwards from the cannon and placed their hands over their ears. The gun captain held a slow match to the touch pan and shouted, "FIRE!"

Sparks and smoke from the pan leapt into the air and the cannon thundered; the force from the blast rolled it backward into the restraining tackle. The projectile sailed high and wide to the right of the target, kicking up a towering plume of seawater a hundred yards behind it.

The gun captain shouted, "Run!" The men lay back on the riggings to fully retract the cannon and prepare it for reloading.

"Sponge!" he shouted again. A wet brush attached to the end of a long handle was forced down the cannon's muzzle to extinguish any remaining burning particles and dislodge debris.

"Powder!" The powder monkey handed a canister to the crewman at the muzzle who removed the cartridge and stuffed it in.

"Ram!" Another sailor armed with a rammer—a device similar to the sponge but with a hard, flat end—thrust it down the bore to pack the powder snugly against the plug end of the cannon.

"Shot!" A twenty-four ball was handed to the powder man. He hefted it up gently and rolled it into the muzzle.

"Wad!" A mass of cloth rags was inserted into the barrel.

"Ram!" The rammer was pushed down the barrel a second time to pack the wadding and ball against the powder charge, a gap between the ball and the powder creating a gas pocket that could cause the cannon to explode when fired.

"Run!." The men pulled back on the rigging lines again and rolled the cannon out through the gun port.

"Fuse!" The gun captain produced a thin, short-bristled brush approximately the length of a new pencil from his possibles bag. He inserted it through a small round fuse vent on the top rear of the barrel and rotated the brush in a circular motion several times to ensure the tool ripped through the bag and into the powder inside. Then he removed the brush and inserted a length of fuse, making certain it extended all the way into the powder charge. Lastly, he took a powder horn from around his neck and dumped a small slug into the touch pan. Satisfied the cannon was properly primed, he stood straight.

"Step Back!" The men stepped away from the cannon.

Dunbar put his hand on the gun captain's shoulder. "Outstanding, gentlemen," he said looking at a stopwatch. "Just under three minutes."

The men began to high-five one another.

"There's only one problem." The celebration halted. "We missed the target."

Dunbar squatted down and made a mark on the quoin, a wedge-shaped device used to elevate the cannon even with the plug. He took a tape measure from his pocket and measured the distance from the mark to the butt of the quoin...it was six inches.

"Everyone measure six inches from the handle end on their quoins and make a mark. This mark will indicate a targeting range of one-hundred yards." He pushed the wedge in another inch and made a second mark. He stood up and waved to Jenkins. Jenkins

267

informed the captain of a second shot.

"Alright, gun captain," Dunbar said. "Proceed."

"Step Back! Cover! Fire!"

The cannon thundered a second time and, this time, the shot hit the water in front of the target. The men quickly reloaded and prepared for a third. Dunbar eased the quoin back a half inch and made a third mark.

"Gentlemen, you must time your shots with the swells," Dunbar barked. "Gun captains, do not report your guns when you are on a crest or a trough of a wave. Remember, fire when rolling up to ruin the rigging and fire when rolling down to hit the hull. Now tend your guns."

The gun captain watched through the gun port until the ship was approaching the proper angle. "Fire!" he commanded and lit the fuse.

The cannon promptly reported. Seconds later, a round of cheers resounded from the sailors topside. It wasn't a perfect hit, but a hit none the less.

The other gun crews marked and adjusted their quoins, and prepared to fire.

Cannon after cannon thundered in succession. In short order, the first target was thoroughly destroyed. The ship sailed onto the second and then to the third, maneuvering from port to starboard allowing the gunners to practice shifting guns.

As the wind and swells increased in magnitude from the approaching storm, the gunners' accuracy diminished. Dunbar showed them how to fire their guns by sensing pitch as well as roll.

Finally, it was time to practice with the topside carronades. Since the thirty-two pound guns were used for close combat, Maynard maneuvered back to within twenty yards of the target.

The *Constitution* made running passes at the target, effectively raking the enemy with shot and ball by firing the forward guns first and the rest in succession. The idea was not so much to score a direct hit on the target, but to come within twenty feet on either side of it—close enough to score reasonable hits on a one-hundred foot ship.

On the first pass, the gunnery was all over the place. The gunners had failed to take into account the ship's forward velocity and the delay between lighting the powder in the pan and the actual reporting of the gun. On subsequent passes, several gun teams scored acceptable hits and the results were encouraging.

Maynard was standing amidships with Fallon when Midshipman Woody climbed up through a hatch in front of them and hurried over. "Captain, there is a call for you on the link, sir. It's Admiral Hays."

Maynard turned to Fallon. "Continue with the port and starboard tack until I return."

"Aye, aye, sir," answered Fallon.

Maynard proceeded down the ladder to his stateroom and picked up the link handset. The muscles in his jaws contracted.

"Yes, sir, I understand. We will secure from gunnery practice immediately and set sail...with Godspeed, sir. *Constitution* out." Maynard turned to Woody.

"Mister Wood, double-time up to the helm and direct Commander Fallon to secure from gunnery practice immediately, then set a course due south. All officers muster in my quarters in five minutes. Instruct Mister Dunbar to have his guns cleaned, reloaded and ready for battle. Now go."

"Yes, sir." Woody bounded for the hatch.

Five minutes later, Maynard was addressing his wardroom. "Gentlemen, *Queen Anne* has not sailed to Ocracoke as expected. She's continued north and is currently rounding the lower tip of Hatteras Island."

The pulse of the room doubled.

"We've been ordered by Admiral Hays to proceed south and intercept her. That gives us approximately two hours to prepare this ship for battle. Lieutenant Pasarelli, have your men double-check every inch of rigging. Start with the blocks and stays. We must be able to raise and lower all sails without interference. Then inspect the canvas, yards and halyards. We must have optimal maneuverability. At least two men at the wheel at all times. Am I clear?"

"Yes, sir," Pasarelli answered.

"Keep all your men focused on the task at hand. You're dismissed.

"Mister Dunbar and Commander Jenkins, maintain no less than three powder charges at each gun at all times. Have three port and three starboard twenty-four pounders ready to fire targeting rounds on my command. Once we have the range, adjust all guns and prepare for full broadsides. Direct your initial gunnery high with bar shot to impair *Queen Anne's* sails and rigging. When I order broadsides half, fire half broadsides in close order until we get within thirty yards. This will help keep *Queen Anne's* gunners off balance. Inside thirty yards, all main guns are to fire at will. Concentrate on the topside elements and main batteries. Make your elevation changes quickly and listen up for shifts. Spar gun crews are to remain in the berthing area and close to the ladders. They are not to come on deck until I give the order. Once in position, I will command the first broadside. After that, they are to fire at will. When *Queen Anne's* boarding party is on deck, all guns are to be loaded with grape shot and chain. Fire each gun as quickly as possible until I order our boarding party across. Are we clear?"

"Yes, sir," Dunbar said.

"Dismissed." Jenkins and Dunbar hustled out the door.

"Mister Clements. Muster the marksmen and snipers in the junior officers' wardroom. Have their weapons loaded with safeties engaged. Make sure every man has all his equipment and a minimum of twenty shots in his bag. When we are within one hundred yards, I want four men on each masthead with extra rifles and supplies for the rigging crews. Have the rest of your men take cover between the carronades. Make certain all marksmen aloft are clear of the riggings when I give orders to shift sail. And tell them to pour on the lead. That will keep the pirates from crossing the gunnels first. Remember, no pirates aboard *Constitution*. Got it?"

"Yes, sir," snapped Clements.

"Dismissed."

"Mister Huber. Muster your men on the berthing deck behind the gun crews. You will be the last on deck. When the topside gunners are called up, fall into position at the ladders. When I order you up, heave over grappling hooks and board across the fore and main rigging channels. Every available man will follow after we have secured from gunnery. Dismissed."

After everyone had their orders, Maynard gave the aft gunners access to his stateroom to ready the cannons. He grabbed his binoculars and headed topside.

Men were climbing the masts, testing riggings, securing lines and loading cannons. Extra lookouts were posted on each mast. While Maynard was amidships inspecting the blocks on the main and main top mast stays, Midshipman Wood approached him again.

"Sir, *Anchorage* reports the target is bearing one-seven-five. Range, fifteen miles." The whites of Woody's eyes were the size of golf balls.

"Very well, Mister Woody. Hey, you're getting good at this."

"Thank you, sir."

"Relax and assume your post."

Woody saluted him and ran off.

271

Maynard called up to the foremast lookouts. "The port bow at ten miles."

"Port bow aye, Captain," the lead forward lookout replied. He passed the word to the seamen on the main who in turn relayed it to the mizzen. All binoculars focused on the horizon ahead.

Maynard continued spot-checking the ship. All the cannons were loaded and primed, the decks were cleared of all obstacles, and everything was secured and battened down tight.

Twenty minutes later, the main lookout sounded off. "SAIL HO! TWENTY DEGREES TO PORT. SAIL HO! TWENTY DEGREES TO PORT."

Maynard turned to Fallon and ordered, "BATTLE STATIONS, PORT SIDE!"

The ship's bell struck out in quick, even clangs. Men raced to their battle stations, up the riggings and down the ladders. The gun crews assembled and counted off. Once all guns were accounted for, Dunbar reported to the helm. "Gun deck manned and ready."

Jenkins yelled out, "Topside gun crews in position and awaiting orders."

In rapid succession, all battle stations reported to the quarterdeck manned and ready. The *USS Constitution* was now fully prepared for battle.

* * *

"Sail Ho, Captain!" sang *Queen Anne's* topsail lookout. He pointed at the horizon. "Three masts, rigged square for speed."

Blackbeard raised his binoculars, focused where the man was pointing, and grinned. "Aye, a frigate man-o-war. A battle of men it shall be at last.

"Morton," he shouted, "ready the cannons!" He turned to

Hands. "See the lady is latched in my cabin and cover the portholes.

"Helmsman, hold your sprit dead to her bow and come about as I command."

* * *

Maynard raised his binoculars and peered across the sea. *Queen Anne* was somewhat smaller than the *Constitution* and didn't carry nearly as much sail. He would have to maneuver in close to give his heavy gunners a fighting chance, making *Constitution* an easy target for Blackbeard's gunners in return.

As the two ships drew head on, Maynard recognized the need to adjust his strategy. It appeared Blackbeard was going to test him with a direct assault, so he ordered the carronades manned and all guns quoined for level fire.

Queen Anne continued to close. Maynard focused on her bow. He wanted to know the instant she committed to a turn as Blackbeard's maneuvers would dictate his own.

Inside fifty yards, Blackbeard showed his hand. Sending his Jolly Roger up the mast, *Queen Anne* rolled to starboard, exposing her port guns.

Blackbeard was being conservative. A straight-on attack against *Constitution's* inexperienced crew would have been much more effective, Maynard thought. Blackbeard was simply testing him. "Okay, old man. Let's play ball."

"Thirty degrees to starboard!" Maynard shouted. Under full canvas, *Constitution* proved to be the more nimble of the two ships, coming about almost as if suspended on a needle. When the ships were nearly even, Maynard ordered, "FIRE ALL GUNS!"

With an ethereal roar, all twenty-six of *Constitution's* port cannons burst forth flames. The recoil from the blasts shuddered the planking, heeling her several degrees to starboard. The salvo was perfectly aimed and perfectly timed, tearing through *Queen Anne's* port bulwarks before she was in position to fire. Splinters and chunks of wood shot skyward, almost half the height of her masts.

* * *

Blackbeard scanned the deck to estimate the damages. Next to one of the cannons lay Miller, motionless. A bloody length of splintered railing jutted from his chest. Blackbeard lashed out at his gunners with a whip.

"Damnation seize your souls!" he roared. "Get off your backsides and ready those cannons!"

His gunners scurried to recover their cannons, retaliating with a sporadic volley of six of *Queen Anne's* sixteen-pounders. All shots landed miserably wide, as Maynard's ship continued to starboard leaving only the width of his stern as a target.

Maynard's guns fired once again and—this time—it was a pair of guns on the taffrail. Bar-shot ripped through the *Queen's* sails and riggings.

Blackbeard was amazed by his opponents speed and agility. He glanced down at his feet as a charred thirty-two pound ball rolled across the deck. He ordered his mains backed and skidded the *Queen* around to port, bringing his starboard guns to bear. The maneuver caught Maynard off guard as he was attempting to circle about to broadside the *Queen's* port quarter. This time, Blackbeard unleashed a full twenty-cannon broadside.

A volley of steel balls rained down upon *Constitution*. Several impacted her hull and bounced off like softballs; one smashed through her bulwarks. The most serious damage ensued aloft. One shot struck the main mast just above the lower cap, toppling the main topgallant and the main upper top and skysail. The broken mast jackknifed into the foremast, ripping the lower topsail from its yards and leaving a tangle of the riggings. Other balls tore holes through the lower canvas.

As the broken mast fell, two men aloft got tangled in the riggings and were yanked from the masthead platform. Plummeting to their deaths on the deck right before Maynard's eyes, the sound of crushing bones caused Maynard to recoil. Medical teams responded and carried them below.

One of the remaining topmen climbed out on the yard, pulled a knife and cut the severed mast from its riggings. Lieutenant Pasarelli collected five men on his way over to the topgallant backstay halyard and struck the broken mast to the deck.

Maynard returned his focus to the battle. Before the damaged mast was cleared, he ordered the ship hard to starboard again. With Blackbeard committed to another starboard turn, the maneuver—though not as crisp as before—would bring *Constitution* even with *Queen Anne* again.

Blackbeard had critically underestimated Maynard's abilities. With his starboard guns still loading, Blackbeard was fully exposed. Maynard commanded another broadside. *Constitution's* guns hammered *Queen Anne's* starboard bow and amidships.

* * *

Blackbeard took cover behind the main mast until the shots had passed, then stepped out for another survey of the damage, immediately realizing he was in serious trouble. There would be no rain this time to wash away the damage. His little test of Maynard's resolve had completely backfired. With half of his cannons out of commission, he was handed a stunning defeat.

He would not underestimate Maynard again.

Blackbeard raced back to the helm, pushed the helmsman aside, and grabbed the wheel himself. He continued a hard turn to starboard and waited for Maynard to react, then spun the wheel full to port.

Maynard bought the trick. In order to prevent *Queen Anne* from ramming his bow, he maneuvered hard to starboard again. But with half his mainsails destroyed, *Constitution* was slow to respond.

Waving his cutlass above his head and shouting profanities at the top of his lungs, Blackbeard headed out to sea.

Chapter 30
1400: 29 August 2008

"Huzza, Old Ironsides!" Maynard shouted and thrust his fist into the air.

"Huzza, Old Ironsides!" resounded the crew. "Huzza, Old ironsides!"

For *Constitution's* crew, it was a decisive victory. In a span of less than twenty minutes, they had delivered Blackbeard something he'd never before experienced: a defeat on the open seas. There was precious little time for celebration. The men had to make repairs quickly and set out after *Queen Anne* again.

The fouled sails would not be difficult to replace. Chief Hatton, Jeremy Ratliff, and the damage control team were assessing repairs to the mast and bulwarks. Lieutenant Pasarelli's men were sorting through the tangled riggings. Maynard joined Hatton and Ratliff.

"It's a clean break, Captain," Hatton said. "We can take a chain saw and clean off the two ends without much loss in length. If you can taxi me to the HT shop aboard *Anchorage*, I can fabricate a collar and splice the two halves together. She'll be as good as new. All I need is the testicular fortitude to climb up there and take measurements."

277

Hatton's fear of heights was a frequent source of entertainment for *Spruance* sailors...all except Hatton, that is.

Maynard looked at Jeremy. "I think we can fix that. Mister Pasarelli, if you please!"

"Aye, Captain," Pasarelli replied from the foremast shroud.

"Rig a block and tackle to the masthead and strap Chief Petty Officer Hatton here into a safety harness. I think it's time we gave this old crow a flying lesson."

"Aye, aye, Captain."

"Oh shit," Hatton muttered. "I was afraid you'd say something like that."

Maynard ducked below to contact Admiral Hays. Hays was relieved to learn *Constitution* had survived the first round with only minor damages. *Anchorage* would be alongside in thirty-five minutes and would dispatch a Mike to pick up Chief Hatton. Naturally, Hays would be coming aboard during the exchange. He instructed Maynard to prepare the two dead sailors for transport over with the chief.

When Maynard returned topside, Chief Hatton was strapped into his harness and trying to psyche himself up for the ascent. He went over and slapped him on the shoulder. "Break a leg, Chief," he said and waved his hand toward the main shrouds.

"Yeah, well, as long as it's me leg and not me friggin' neck," replied Hatton.

Jeremy gave him a wink. "I'd not worry myself none 'bout fallin' mate. 'Tis only tha' last wee bit 'er two that gets ya."

Hatton gave Jeremy a sour look. "Should these riggings fail, perhaps your wee parts would be kind enough to dampen me blow." Everyone chuckled except Hatton.

Hatton meandered over to the shroud and tested the ratlines with his foot. He sucked in a deep breath and stepped up. Three sailors drew in the slack from the safety line as he picked his way the masthead.

When he reached the platform, he started taking measurements of the lower mast, the mast cap, and the stump of the topmast. He drew a sketch of the timber arrangement and then started back down.

Jenkins joined the fray when Chief Hatton was back on deck and free of the harness.

"Mister Jenkins," Maynard said. "I believe the good chief has finally earned his wings."

Jenkins handed the Maynard a piece of paper folded into a crude pair of wings. Maynard took the wings and taped them to Hatton's left shirt pocket. "Congratulations, Chief, you're an official Airedale. Now fix my mast."

Hatton took the spoof in stride. He saluted Maynard. "Thank you, sir," he replied with a drunken, Cockney accent. "I shall honor this recognition with every fartling of appreciation it so dubiously deserves."

Jenkins and Pasarelli burst out laughing.

Maynard returned the salute with a straight face. "Carry on then."

"Yes, sir. I shall proceed with haste." Hatton performed an about face and marched off.

Maynard turned to the other men with a smile. "Alright, gentlemen, the party's over. Let's get back to work."

* * *

Blackbeard raged across *Queen Anne's* deck like a scalded beast, kicking and hurling bloodied sailors from his path as he fumed. "Serves you pitiful bastards right, damn yer hides! Lending yourselves throttled by a lot of pollywogs!"

He glared at his carpenters who were beginning to salvage

the wasted planking from the freeboard and bulwarks. Not a single man met his eyes.

He spotted Garrat and Richards standing on the quarterdeck surveying the damage. Garrat tried to duck from his sight.

"Garrat, don't run from me like a pelted cur. Lay your back ta hauling up pitch and timbers like the rest. I'll have this ship patched from waterline to rail before we make landfall. If I see as much as one drop of seawater squeeze through a crack, it shall cost two of ya your heads.

"You too, Richards. I want you blottin' sweat from your brow, as well. Every one of you sons-of-a-whore shall turn their hand. Any goldbrickers and those too afflicted shall be gutted an' pitched over the rail."

Swinging around, he caught sight of Hands and pointed to him. "You, take ta mending those sails and riggins."

"But, Captain, the lady demands attention. Shall I..."

"Let me fallow to the lady," Blackbeard roared. "You render as I command, rot your soul, or I'll fetch your bleeding carcass to the eels."

Hands leaped onto the main shroud and climbed skyward.

"Helmsmen, make course for Ocracoke and spare no sail. I must have the last sun to prepare my schemes for the morrow."

Blackbeard stormed around topside to make certain everyone was following his commands. Satisfied, he went below to check on Angela..

He unlocked Angela's door and rapped on it with his knuckles. Angela pulled it open and jumped in his arms.

"It is over? Thank God, you're safe," she exclaimed.

Blackbeard forced a pensive smile. "The spirits tend only those who can't tend themselves, my dear. And, as you see, I fare well."

Angela backed away, holding onto his hands like a child.

"Did we win?"

Blackbeard cast his eyes at her feet. "Aye, t'was a narrow victory, my love. And not without consequence. Poor Miller is dead. When I knelt by his side to tend his wounds, the cowards took advantage of the lull and fled to our lee. In such misery as I was, I could muster not the heart to pursue."

Angela embraced him again.

"We shall put ashore and provide for his leave. I've ordered the helm to make sail for Ocracoke. It was his home as a child. We'll make a final resting place for him there."

Angela's eyes welled up.

"I fear we have not witnessed the last smoke of those villain's cannons. We shall need to defend ourselves once more. But fear not, no harm will come to you as long as I am alive."

He pulled away from her. "As for now, the devils have done great harm to our *Queen* and there's much work to be had in repair."

Angela bounded for the door.

"'Tis not safe above. You'd best remain below while we see to our tasks."

Though he'd been able to restrain his anger, he couldn't dampen the burning he knew showed in his eyes. Fortunately, for the second time in as many days, Angela observed his request.

"I shall call for you later once the inlet of anguish is close at hand."

* * *

The Mike boat carrying Chief Hatton plodded through choppy waters back toward *Constitution*. Maynard studied the sky. Pronged clouds provided unmistakable notice that Hurricane Drummond was drawing ever closer.

Maynard stood beside Admiral Hays on the starboard quarterdeck and watched Hatton's Mike moor alongside.

"Is there anything else we can get for you, Commander?"

"I think we're good, Admiral. Unless you can pipe over a hot shower."

Hays glanced skyward. "Looks like you might get your wish. The real soup's still 160 miles south. I'd rather it all pass before we sent you in."

Maynard looked to the south. "I don't think it matters."

The two exchanged a somber look. It wasn't the wind or the dark clouds that bothered Maynard; it was the smell of death. Both of them sensed it.

The admiral puffed down onto the Mike's deck and the bowhook cast them off.

Hatton's mast collar looked like a four-foot length of laterally hinged stovepipe. It took three sailors to hoist it up and another two to guide it onto the platform.

Hatton strapped into his harness again and started aloft. He and his men stood the collar on end, attaching it to the topmast stump and the upper portion of the masthead and loosely bolted the two halves together. The length of severed mast was raised into place, inserted into the top of the collar, plumbed, and the collar bolts securely tightened. Hatton drove long, oak wedges into the space between the collar and the mast for reinforcement.

Once finished, Hatton pushed against it several times. One of the riggers attached a heavy line to the top of the mast and a column of men below applied a slow, steady pressure. The mast held firm.

Hatton stood and shouted down to Maynard. "She's good as new, Skipper."

Pasarelli's men set about reinstalling the shrouds and riggings, and lashed the mended sails to the yards.

Maynard turned to him and said, "Mister Pasarelli, prepare to make sail."

Pasarelli looked aloft. "Cast off the gaskets."

Maynard took the wheel and gave Pasarelli a nod.

"Hoist sail," Pasarelli ordered.

Chapter 31
1400: 29 August 2008

Blackbeard navigated toward Ocracoke Inlet as though he was taking a stroll through his own back yard. But as *Queen Anne* drew closer, it became apparent the years had changed his former refuge. Though the expanse of rugged beaches was the same, the isle itself appeared narrower and more elongated than he recalled. The inlet itself was farther to the south; the shoals were completely different.

He brought in all but his main course and lower topsails and eased into the channel. Two whaleboats were lowered and proceeded ahead to take soundings.

From the bow of the first whaleboat, the leadsman threw a line with a weight tied to it into the water. He waited for the weight to hit bottom, then pulled in the slack. Colored strips of cloth were tied off at six-foot intervals to indicate the depth.

"By the deep four," sounded the first reading.

Blackbeard was surprised to discover a depth of four fathoms. At this tide, he was accustomed to three at most. Perhaps the years had been more generous than first thought.

"A half four," came the next reading—four and one-half fathoms. The whaleboats began to crisscross in front of the ship to determine the width of the channel. When the depth increased to mark five, Blackbeard hoisted the mizzen course to increased *Queen Anne's* forward velocity.

Soon *Queen Anne* was safely inside the breakwaters of the sound and maneuvered for anchorage in the channel parallel to the island. Blackbeard chose a spot that would give him shelter from the wind and a clear view of both sides of the inlet. He would know the instant Maynard arrived.

With Angela by his side—her long, chestnut hair tasseled upon the wind—he ordered all four of *Queen's* small boats into the water to begin charting the channels and sandbars. The rest of the crew was diligently finishing *Queen Anne's* repairs.

Blackbeard raised his binoculars and searched the island. Though he could not see them, he felt the eyes of many staring back at him. He noticed the stubby apex of a lighthouse jutting above the dunes and island juniper, and a narrow mast-like structure threading up into the sky adjacent to a white building and rows of houses. All welcomed navigational aids. He also took note of the shoreline and tidal zone to help estimate water depths with the morning's tide.

✶ ✶ ✶

Lieutenant Kadleb, commander of the Seabee detachment assigned to chart the inlet, contacted Admiral Hays to report Angela Killian had been spotted. Hays received the news with mixed emotion. He was relieved to learn she was alive yet her presence created a host of new tactical problems.

He recalled the Secretary's directive. "If you can find her, rescue her. If you can't, she was never there."

He had his orders. Hopefully, Ratliff could assist in some way. Hays relayed the sighting to Commander Maynard.

Chapter 32
1900: 29 August 2008

A few hours before dusk, *Constitution* had made her way around the southern tip of Cape Hatteras. In an hour or so, the Ocracoke and Hatteras lighthouses would begin their lonely journeys through the darkness. But, for now, there was plenty of daylight left to navigate to the spot where Maynard planned to anchor for the night.

As *Constitution* neared the lower stretch of Ocracoke Island, *Queen Anne's* dark masts became visible against the gray contrast of the retreating light. Her bow was pointed towards the influx of the shipping channel. Positioned such, there was little chance Blackbeard would fire upon them as they entered. Dunbar prepared his starboard cannons just as a precaution.

Maynard had memorized every mark on the charts the Seabees had prepared for him but, as the admiral had requested, he mustered a sounding crew on the forecastle.

"By the deep four," called out the leadsman. A few minutes, later he called out, "By the mark five."

Maynard decided to cross Blackbeard's bow and continue into the deeper waters of Blair Channel in order to give himself a safer margin for maneuvering in the morning.

286

Queen Anne's top deck was deserted, save for one hulking figure standing at her bow, bearing his cutlass to the sky.

Blackbeard.

Maynard glanced at his chart to reference a navigational buoy. When he looked back, Blackbeard was gone.

The leadsman called out, 'a half five.' Maynard checked the wind and piloted the ship to the left side of the channel. He ordered the Bower anchor cast over into the sea. When the anchor struck, the wind blew *Constitution* around to starboard, leaving her bow pointing seaward. Placing fifteen-hundred yards between her and *Queen Anne;* out of cannon range of her cannon and separated by an impassable sand bar.

The topmen made the sails to the yards, and Maynard secured the sea and anchor detail. Fallon posted an anchor watch and ordered additional lookouts to each top.

The men had put in an exhausting day and deserved a hot meal and a chance to relax. Admiral Godsey had arranged for five hundred sixteen-ounce rib eye steaks to be freezer-packed and delivered to *Anchorage* along with canned soda, fresh vegetables, salad and peach cobbler. The HT's converted the galley spit into a grill, and the cooks amassed a feast—the husky aroma of grilled beef permeated every area of the ship.

The whole crew—officers and enlisted—ate together on the berthing deck. Maynard broke out the radio again and tuned to an oldies channel out of Jacksonville, North Carolina: KOOL 98.7.

The men were laughing, telling jokes, and reliving the day's excitement. Suddenly, there was a sharp change in the wind. *Constitution* heeled to port and skidded sideways; bulkhead lanterns rattled against their gimbals.

Maynard bolted to his feet. "Sea and anchor detail! On the double!"

The sea and anchor detail charged up the ladders and out on

deck. The ship's wheel windmilled furiously until it hammered to a stop. Near gale force winds tossed white hats and ball caps over the side. Maynard, Fallon, and Pasarelli shouted orders to ears muted by the howl of the wind.

Fallon mustered enough men to drop another anchor, but it failed grab. With the Bower windlass at 120-feet, *Constitution* crossed over the anchor and careened uncontrolled. The stern passed the bow. There was so much slack in the chain that the wind blew her completely out of the channel.

"Brace for impact!!" shouted Maynard.

'Brace for impact' was repeated; the deck forces latched onto any fixed object within arm's reach and the lookouts pasted themselves to the masts and yards.

Constitution struck bottom and plowed across the sandbar, coming to rest with her stern sitting high above the water line and her bow pitched downward into the channel.

Maynard shot an angry stare at *Queen Anne*. She remained nestled against the wind break of the island, completely unaffected.

Lieutenant Commander Fallon pushed gently at the wheel, trying to coax it to turn. Maynard had a good idea what that meant.

"Mister Fallon," he ordered. "Raise both anchors as quickly as possible. Then I want all non-line handling personnel off this deck.

"Pasarelli, I'm going over the side to inspect the damage. Rig a chair to the after-davit and bring me a vest and flashlight." Pointing aloft he shouted. "Get those men down from the masts!"

The winds subsided. Pasarelli rigged the boatswain's chair as ordered and brought Maynard a life jacket and flashlight. Maynard strapped on the vest and climbed out onto the mizzen rigging channel. Pasarelli attached a safety line to the D-ring on the back of the vest and lowered the chair.

Maynard yanked at his safety line. "Two tugs means stop

feeding line. Three tugs brings me back up."

Maynard swept his flashlight up and down the after-peak and from side to side. It didn't take him long to confirm his suspicions. The rudder stock was bent. He gave three tugs on the line and contemplated his options on the way up.

The first order of business was to get *Constitution* off the sandbar. He decided to try kedging the anchor—a trick used by Captain Isaac Hull to outdistance British warships during a slack wind encounter in The War of 1812.

Back on deck, Maynard had Pasarelli splice together as much spare heavy mooring line as he could find. Next he ordered *Constitution's* thirty-six foot pinnace lowered over the side. When the line was completed, he ordered one end attached to the eleven-hundred-pound stream anchor and the other threaded up through the port anchor windlass and onto the main deck. Chief Hatton fitted a pair of wooden shoes to the anchor flukes so they would better catch and hold the bottom.

Lieutenant Gray and twelve SEALS volunteered to man the pinnace. The stream anchor was lowered down and the SEALS lay their backs on the oars.

Dusk had given way to a murky darkness, and the wind and choppy inlet waters consigned no mercy. A coxswain held a battle lantern at the bow of the pinnace and barked cadence as the SEALS powered out into the channel. It took over twenty minutes for them to reach the end of the line.

Maynard gave two flashes with his light; the coxswain responded back with two. The SEALS hoisted the anchor upward and dropped it over the gunwale.

Maynard allowed several moments for the anchor to settle. "Lay back on the stream," he ordered.

Fallon had two hundred sailors strung out across the spar, positioned on each side of the line. The rest of the men were herded into the forward part of the ship on the decks below.

The line handlers drew back on the line.

At first, *Constitution* didn't budge. The men leveraged every available deck structure and laid into the line harder. Chief Warrant Officer Huber raced up and down the line shouting 'HEAVE, HEAVE, HEAVE'. He ran astern, grabbed the end of the line, and reared back himself.

The stream anchor began to drag bottom and the column shifted backwards. Suddenly, it took a firm hold and *Constitution* inched forward.

Everyone shouted 'HEAVE' in unison. Movement increased. As it grew, the men at the end dropped the line, ran forward, grabbed ahold and threw back on it again. When the ship's bulk inched over the edge of the sandbar, the extra weight of the men in the bow drove her forward and she tobogganed back into the channel.

"Drop the sheet!" commanded Maynard. The sheet anchor was returned seaward. "Drop the Bower!" When both anchors caught, *Constitution* nudged to a stop.

Fallon hustled back to the wheel and gave it a turn. It wouldn't move. He worked it from side to side until it broke free then turned it as far as it would go one way and back the other. The rudder had full range to port but only forty-percent to starboard.

The SEALS rowed alongside; Maynard, Fallon, and Chief Hatton climbed down into the boat to take a closer look at the damage.

"Captain, have them cycle it again," Hatton said.

Maynard looked up to the taffrail. "Mister Pasarelli, cycle the rudder. Slowly." He watched as the rudder pivoted from side to side.

Hatton shone his light around the peak and spat a wad of tobacco juice into the water. "Sir, there's no place to leverage back here. If we apply direct force to the shaft, we're liable to wrench it completely from the sternpost." He ran his light down the length of the rudder again. "We can re-attach the guide chains, but I'm afraid it's going to take professionals to fix this one. Soon as we're back aboard, I'll inspect the steerage gear and quadrant for any signs of damage. That's about all we can do."

Maynard took a deep breath. "Alright, we'll work with what we have. Let's get this boat hoisted up and get the men to their hammocks."

Lines were lowered and the pinnace was hoisted up. Maynard climbed over the taffrail and the deck forces secured from anchor detail. The day was finally over.

Maynard was extremely proud of the way *Constitution* and her crew had responded to all the challenges the day placed upon them. He ducked down the ladder onto the main gun deck and headed back to his stateroom; shaking hand and patting the back of his men along the way. Once inside, he closed the door, took off his shirt and sat down at the chart table.

"Having difficulty, are we Maynard, my old chum? Shall I bring the *Queen* about to lend you some assistance?"

Maynard whirled around and stared at the commercial-band radio. "Blackbeard," he muttered. *Where did he get his hands on a working radio?*

"Stay calm," he told himself. He gathered his thoughts and picked up the handset. "Come if you wish. I will have a sharp cutlass waiting for you. I believe the two of you have met once before." He smiled and released the transmitter key.

"Oh, the terrible images that must be playing inside your head," Blackbeard replied. "Perhaps thoughts of me pinching your head from yer neck and dangling it from the *Queen's* bowsprit? I can feel the tendrils of it in my hands now, young Maynard, as I slowly choke the wind from your lungs. The journals of history shall be written once again and, this time, victory shall be mine."

"I've got you out-vesseled and out-gunned, old man," Maynard replied coolly. "Surrender while you still have the chance. If you don't I will be pissing in a pool of your blood before the sun reaches the nine o'clock sky."

He switched off the radio before Blackbeard could reply.

* * *

"Prepare to taste the blood of your ancestors, you pious coward!" Blackbeard roared. "And with it so shall depart the last of your miserable ilk from this world." He grabbed the radio and threw it to the deck and crushed it with his foot. "I shall pot and boil what is left of you and dine upon it for my midday meal."

He scooped up a tankard of rum and drank it to the bottom. "Blackbeard shall live forever!"

Though angered, he was no fool. What Maynard said was true. He could not afford to battle it out with cannons; his losses had already been too great. He must attack swiftly and fight it out man-to-man...and that advantage would be his.

For the remainder of the night, his men splintered the darkness with harassment cannon fire. Hell had no need for sleep, though the living most certainly did.

* * *

Maynard calmed himself by focusing his energies on his charts once again. He heard a shuffling noise behind him.

"Ya'd 'ave 'im fiercely angered now fer sure, Capt'n. 'Tis when he's most dangerous."

Maynard faced him. "Jeremy? Where did you come from?"

"Been that way ever since I knowed 'im, he 'as." Jeremy

walked over and took a seat at the table. "He 'as 'is good side too, ya know. He'd be a tough skipper for sure, but he always saw to it we had plenty 'o grub to eat. An' good grub too, it was. An' 'eh never tried cheatin' a crew out of 'is share like so many of them others."

Jeremy removed his garrison cap and placed it in his lap. "Bein' a hand in Blackbeard's crew made a man special. We was treated with respect. Even a little imp like me." He searched Maynard's eyes and then gazed down at the table. "After this is over, I'd not suppose there'd be a small space fer a man like me in this world, now. Would there?"

"So that was you in my stateroom yesterday?" Maynard asked.

"Aye. That it was, yer Lordship."

"I wish there was some other way."

"Aye, it's for the best. Yer father is right. Dead is where my kind belongs. It ain't so terrible once yer there."

He reached over and patted Maynard on the shoulder. "In truth, I should be a thankin' you. Why, in jest a few short days, lookie all I've done. I'd flied the skies like a bird, got me the best suit of clothes I'd ever knowed, an' made a whole shipload of new mates.

Ratliff rose to his feet and started for the door. "An' Capt'n, regardless of what happens on the morrow, Jeremy Ratliff will not be letting ya down. You have my word on that. I just ask this one small favor."

"Anything you want, Jeremy," Maynard replied.

"Make certain the lady Angela gets home safe 'n sound. She'll need refuge of the hearts which love her dearest."

Maynard felt his own heart tumble. "I promise you the name Jeremy Ratliff will never be forgotten."

Jeremy gave him a faint smile and nodded. "I shall take my

leave, then. Good night, Captain," he said, and left.

Maynard returned to his charts for a few more minutes, then switched off the lantern and went to his bunk. He closed his eyes and tried to relax but the arms of sleep would not embrace him. An image of Captain Lawrence lying on the stretcher bubbled into his consciousness; a video of the dream raced back and forth across the backs of his eyelids.

It was all crystal clear to him now. The battle, the blood, the death...it all made perfect sense. Each link in the chain was intended to prepare him for what awaited him and his crew with the light of the coming day.

He sat up and started to pray. He prayed for his men, and he prayed for his wife and daughters. He ended with a brief prayer for Jeremy Ratliff.

Chapter 33
0430: 30 August 2008

Though Maynard changed position in his bunk, his eyes remained fixed on the same spot on the overhead. Actually, he was staring through it; the images from the dream permitted him precious few moments of rest.

His cabin door opened and Midshipman Wood entered holding a flashlight which produced a pale blue light; time for his wake-up call. Maynard rolled onto his side and closed his eyes.

Woody eased over to his bunk. When he was standing right next to it, Maynard shot his hand out like a striking cobra, grabbing Wood's leg.

"Shit!" Wood shrieked, practically leaping out of his boondockers.

Maynard lit the lantern on his nightstand. "Remember, Woody, be prepared for everything. Instruct the officer of the deck to reveille the crew. All hands will muster on battle stations at zero-five-hundred."

Woody hesitated and his eyes searched Maynard's face. "Am I going to die today, sir?"

His words carried the sting of innocence though not the slightest suggestion of fear.

295

"No, Mister Wood, you are not going to die today," said Maynard. "Today will be the most important practical exercise of your life. Today, you will receive an education in courage. You will witness it, and you will demonstrate it. You will learn the importance of following orders and understand the consequences of leadership. The real challenge is how you apply what you learn today throughout the rest of your life. Now go reveille the crew, and get ready to work."

Wood popped him a salute. "Cover or no cover, sir."

Maynard returned the salute. "Cover or no cover, Mister Wood."

Woody rushed out.

As Maynard got dressed, his father's words filtered back to him. He repeated them out loud. "Lead with your intelligence. Your abilities and your men will follow."

Maynard strapped on his grandfather's cutlass and inspected himself in the mirror. "Captain Lawrence, today we fight once again!" He turned out the lantern and headed up on deck.

The winds were not overpowering, but still gusting. No captain in his right mind would attempt to navigate shallow waters in these conditions.

The sun had not yet brightened the horizon yet Maynard was already sweating. He tried using the long flashes from the fixed beacon of Ocracoke lighthouse to locate *Queen Anne*, but the darkness was still too thick to permit it.

The men were served a breakfast of bagels and juice, and hustled out to their battle stations. The cannons were readied and everyone was in place. Maynard counted down the seconds to first light...slowly, the darkness released its grip. The day had begun.

"Bandits, dead ahead!" shouted the foremast lookout.

"Hoist the anchors and raise the topsails," Maynard ordered.

As expected, Blackbeard had gotten the jump on him and was closing on *Constitution* through the main shipping channel.

Maynard raised his binoculars and scanned *Queen Anne's* deck. The pirates had heavily fortified her bow, freeboards, and bulwarks with additional timbers; Maynard quickly calculated his options. He could attempt to turn about, sail further up the channel and cut over to Big Foot. Or he could maneuver to block the channel here and force a fight. He chose the latter and called up the topside gun crews.

Queen Anne continued to close. It seemed to take forever to weigh anchor. As soon the anchors were up, Maynard ordered the helm full to starboard. As *Constitution* started the turn, he ordered the rudder amidships and then full to port. Aided by strong winds, the ship came about crisply and stopped perpendicular to the channel.

"Fire guns at will!" Maynard ordered. All twenty-six of *Constitution's* starboard side guns responded. Splinters exploded from the *Queen's* bow and freeboard.

The carronades fired intermittently along the spar, soon followed by a second salvo from the twenty-four pounders below; snapping *Queen Anne's* foremast about five feet up. As the mast toppled downward, it tore through the riggings of the main and ripped the main topgallant. With her foremast skewed athwart ships, she looked like a knight struggling to control his joust. But she kept coming. It was obvious Blackbeard intended to ram *Constitution*.

"Cease fire, reload and stand by," Maynard ordered. He climbed out onto the port rigging channel to get a better look. "Helm, full to starboard."

With a damaged rudder *Constitution* was sluggish to respond. As the two ships converged, *Constitution* was still perilously angled. For an instant, Maynard and Blackbeard locked eyes.

Blackbeard stood poised like a bronze statue, his eyes were the color of molten fire. His beard was set in an array of thick braids running from his jawbones down to his chin, pulled away from his head like the outstretched wings of a raven. Each braid was tied off in a bright red ribbon. In his right hand, he held his massive cutlass; his left arm was clinched in a fist at his side.

Across his shaggy chest rested three braces of pistols, hammers drawn and ready to fire. Slow matches were tucked under a flat hat atop his head, the burning ends left to dangle about his neck and shoulders; the wind to drove spiraling vortices of smoke across his face and beard.

He looked more frightening than Maynard could possibly have imagined.

The crackling of muskets erupted as snipers from both ships opened fire. Blackbeard swayed slightly as a bullet bored into his chest, but he continued his hypnotic stare.

"Brace for impact!" Maynard hollered "Fire all cannons!"

Instantaneously, the big guns on both ships blistered the air and torrents of acrid smoke filled around them. *Queen Anne* collided with *Constitution's* after port quarter, crushing the captain's gallery with her bow. Her severed mast hooked *Constitution's* mizzen shroud and ricocheted back into her own rail, smashing into her bulwarks and loosing cannons upon her deck. *Queen Anne* caromed off and shuddered ahead.

Maynard looked across his deck in horror. Blackbeard had loaded his topside cannons with grape, blowing holes through *Constitution's* tall bulwarks around the gun ports. Two gun crews, staying their posts, were slaughtered where they stood. Others were dismembered and bleeding. He turned to Jenkins standing in the hatchway. "Medical teams on the double."

Chief Warrant Officer Dunbar charged from the hold. He

organized a pair gun crews at the taffrail and fired the two twenty-four pounders. The rounds smashed through *Queen Anne's* stern, leaving large, jagged holes.

* * *

Blackbeard shouted at Hands. "Grab the girl and haul her down the secret passage!"

Hands limp-ran across the deck, down the ladder and back to Angela's cabin. He slapped the bolt aside and kicked open the door.

"Lady Angela," he called. "Where are you?"

"Get me out of here!" Angela screamed from under the bed. He ran over and groped beneath it; Angela grabbed his hand and he dragged her out.

She was crying hysterically; her dark hair was matted to her face and her knees were bleeding. Hands wrapped his arms around her and hurried over to the wardrobe. He flung open the doors and grabbed the leather thong at the bottom exposing the hidden passage.

"We must hurry." Hands ducked into the wardrobe and started climbing down the ladder.

* * *

Blackbeard examined the damage from the initial pass. *Constitution's* pointblank cannon fire had destroyed the *Queen's* prow; the bowsprit was shattered, her foremast was gone, and the main mast was clinging to remnants of a whittled trunk.

He scanned the port rail. Only three cannons still claimed to their riggings; the rest were scattered. The tether on the port anchor was severed and the anchor was hanging precariously from its cradle. Fearing the consequences, Blackbeard pointed to it and shouted, "Unshackle and cast that anchor seaward!

"Back the main course and come about," he hollered again. "Prepare to furl to all remaining sails. Garrat, break out the grappling hooks."

* * *

Maynard watched *Queen Anne* turn into Big Foot Channel. He maneuvered *Constitution* into the mouth of the shipping channel and made a turn to port to enter Teach's Hole. There was a spot roughly two-thousand yards ahead where the channel was extremely narrow. He would block *Queen Anne's* passage again, and finish the fight there.

"Man the port cannons and stand by," he ordered. "Mister Dunbar, load the carronades with shot."

Dunbar brought up the reserve gun crews and got another from the main gun deck. All the carronades were loaded with cut chain and rolled back into place.

Blackbeard sailed back around to Teach's Hole Channel and brought in the last of the main course and main lower topsails.

Maynard called down through the main hatch. "Ready the boarding party." He turned to Dunbar. "Post the gun captains and fire on my command. Send the rest below to get their weapons."

Chief Hatton and his damage control crew came on deck lugging a ten-horsepower gasoline engine, a bulky red fire pump, and two fifty-foot lengths of inch-and-one-half hose.

"Charge the hoses and take cover!" Maynard shouted. "I'll tell you when to spray."

"Aye, Captain." Hatton coupled the hoses to the pump, tossed the suction line over the starboard side and fired up the motor. The hoses inflated like a pair of serpentine balloons.

Maynard stripped off his khaki shirt and called back to Lieutenant Clements, pointing to his chest. "Don't shoot the white shirts."

Warrant Officer Huber was shouting last minute instructions to his SEALS and marines. "If your cutlass becomes too cumbersome, throw it aside. Use a dirk or anything else you have. A tired soldier is a dead soldier. Now let's go kick some pirate ass!"

When *Queen Anne* was within seventy-five yards, Maynard ordered the upper topsails reefed. The wind against *Constitution's* hull and topgallants would be enough to take them the rest of the way. With the sails secure, he ordered the snipers to the nests and tops. Petty Officer Mottley was the first man up.

The two ships converged. Maynard ordered the gun captains to stay low in case Blackbeard fired another round of shot. He raised his binoculars and scanned *Queen Anne's* deck. Only Blackbeard and a handful of men were topside. He heard Blackbeard call for the grapples.

The grappling hooks latched onto *Constitution's* raised bulwarks. The lines pulled tight, and the two ships drew together. The top of *Constitution's* bulwarks was about two feet above *Queen Anne's* rail.

Blackbeard's men prepared bottle grenades. When they were set to hurl them over, Maynard shouted, "Hit the deck!"

The gun captains dropped and covered. The bottles exploded, showering the deck with shrapnel and a blanket of smoke.

Maynard climbed back on the rigging channel. "Man your cannons!" he shouted. The men jumped up and returned to their guns.

Blackbeard hoisted his cutlass into the air and roared, "Charge!!"

A sea of pirates swarmed upward from below decks, whooping and shouting war cries. The ones up front threw across boarding ladders and tied them off.

Maynard called back to Jenkins. "Away the grenades."

Seventy-five sailors rushed from *Constitution's* hatchways, carrying a longneck Mountain Dew bottle in each hand. Each bottle was filled with a mixture of gunpowder and nails, fitted with a fire nipple and percussion cap in the bottom. The bottles were hurled over, striking solid objects and exploding in waves across *Queen Anne's* deck

Maynard leaned forward and with all his might ordered, "FIRE!"

Constitution's port cannons fired their final bloody salvo. The carronades cut eleven swaths through Blackbeard's boarding party; the twenty-four pounders below hammered *Queen Anne's* main gun deck.

Mottley's snipers leveled the first wave of boarders off the ladders with their muskets.

Maynard gave Hatton the signal and his teams climbed the rigging channels, blasting Blackbeard's boarding parties back with the fire hoses. Several pirates fell over the side and *Constitution's* snipers shot them dead in the water.

The nozzle men began sweeping their streams of water across *Queen Anne's* deck and masts, thoroughly soaking everything.

A sharpshooter on the pirate's main top drew a bead on Hatton and fired. The chief collapsed, struggling to keep the fire hose from whipping out of his hands. Two sailors rushed out to help him; one grabbed the hose and climbed back onto the rigging channel and the other dragged Hatton below.

Mottley leveled his rifle and shot the chief's assailant as three more pirates made their way up the shrouds. With his hands a blur, Mottley picked one off the shroud and got the second as he was pulling himself onto the top. As he started to reload again to get the last of them, his rammer got tangled in a rigging line and flipped from his hand.

The third pirate made it to the top, stood and gathered his sights on Maynard.

A voice boomed skyward from *Queen Anne's* deck. "Their captain shall be left to me!" Blackbeard ripped a pistol from his brace and shot his own man. The pirate's body plummeted from the mast into the crowd below.

Blackbeard looked up at Mottley and grinned. "As the Good Book says, an eye for an eye, and a tooth for a tooth." He pulled a second pistol, aimed it at Mottley, and fired.

The impacting bullet sent Mottley somersaulting backward and he disappeared into the chop of the Pamlico Sound.

Blackbeard looked at Maynard and laughed. "Aye, and such a fine lad, too." He grabbed his cutlass and started shouting at his men.

"Away the marksmen!" Maynard ordered.

Constitution's riflemen filed on deck and formed three lines along the port bulwarks. The first group moved forward, stepped up on the firing blocks constructed for them and fired, another wave of pirates tumbled to the deck. The first group retreated behind the third line to reload, and the second line took up position and fired. They in turn retreated to the rear to reload and were closely followed by the third line. Precisely the way Maynard had choreographed it.

Each time Blackbeard's men tried to advance, they were greeted by a wall of lead. Those that made it to the boarding ladders were dropped by the snipers. *Queen Anne's* deck quickly became a sea of bodies.

Another wave of Blackbeard's sharpshooters took to the

shrouds, seeking a clear field of fire at *Constitution's* deck. But as they leveled their sights to fire, not a single musket discharged.

Maynard smiled. His fire hose scheme had soaked their flints and powder precisely as planned. The pirate's long guns and, hopefully, most of their pistols were now useless. He watched Blackbeard's men ready another round of grenades. The moment they released them, he shouted the order to hit the deck again. When he gave the order to recover, all but a handful got up and continued to report their weapons.

Maynard jumped down from the rigging channel. "Mister Jenkins, away the boarding party. Put twenty more snipers aloft. Have the rest of the men prepared to cross on my command." Jenkins snapped him a salute.

The boarding party was immeasurably pumped and came roaring on deck, Warrant Officer Huber leading the charge. Maynard slid his cutlass from its scabbard and waved the men forward. He climbed the boarding ladder and led his force across. With one eye on Blackbeard, he took his cutlass in both hands and laid into the first pirate he came to. The cutlass sliced through him as though he was made of clay; it felt as weightless as a foil yet as solid as a broadsword.

An army of white shirts flooded over behind him, driving the pirates back once again.

Blackbeard thrust his cutlass into the air. "The fires of hell shall grant you strength! Let's thrash these scoundrels to ribbons!" He brought the cutlass down in front of him like a silvery baton and hacked his way into the crowd.

The bloody battle was on.

Huber worked his way through the crowd, wielding his broadsword with the accuracy of a surgeon. Maynard knew exactly where he was heading but was too far away to do anything about it.

Huber and three marines converged on Blackbeard.

Blackbeard pulled a pistol and shot one of them in the face. The other two laid into him while his sword was idle, burying dirks deep into his midsection. Blackbeard let out a roar and raised his cutlass to hack them to pieces. As he swung his blade downward, Huber lunged forward with his sword and stopped his motion in mid-sweep. The marines retracted their swords.

Blackbeard groped for another pistol, but Huber lashed out with his dirk and slashed it from his hand.

"Not this time, big boy," Huber taunted.

Like a medieval gentleman-at-arms, Huber swung his broadsword around in a salute and lowered his dirk, giving Blackbeard a chance to recover.

"Blackbeard the Pirate, the master swordsman," Huber hissed. "I say it's time for the United States Marine Corps to put your old shit to rest for good."

A smile crept across Blackbeard's face and the two titan's swords clashed overhead in a shower of sparks, Huber's two swords to Blackbeard's one. All fighting around them came to a halt.

Across the deck and toward the foremast pinrails they battled, each wielding his heavy steel only to be equaled by the other. Blackbeard swung his cutlass above his head, attempting to slam it down on Huber's right shoulder.

Huber hefted his broadsword perpendicular to his body, stopping Blackbeard's movement again. With his left hand, he slashed the dirk across Blackbeard's chest. Blood gushed from the wound. Blackbeard ignored the punishment. Swinging his cutlass around with a smile, he aimed for Huber's neck. Huber ducked and the blade passed over his head, severing the foremast rigging lines and sending belaying pins sailing into the air.

The momentum from Blackbeard's missed swing caused him to lose his balance. Huber scolded him a second time across the midsection with the dirk. Blackbeard regained his footing and slashed back again. Huber raised his dirk to intercept the stroke but Blackbeard's power was too much, and his cutlass sheared the stubby blade in half. Blackbeard snatched a pistol from his brace and thrust it in Huber's face.

Maynard aimed one of his pistols at Blackbeard and fired but the mighty pirate didn't even acknowledge the projectile that ripped into his flesh.

There was no time for Huber to cover. He pushed himself upward with his legs and twisted his upper torso just as Blackbeard fired his weapon, the bullet struck the right side of Huber's chest. Blackbeard reached back to finish him off with his cutlass, and a foursome of marines jumped at him. Blackbeard spun around with his sword perpendicular to his body and three of his men filled in around him. Inspired by their captain's victory, the pirates let out a round of cheer and the fighting resumed.

Several of Maynard's boarding party threw down their swords and attacked with daggers and long knives. Maynard signaled to Jenkins and another wave of white shirts poured across the boarding ladders.

Hurricane winds howled around the battle in swirling gusts; waves smashed over *Queen Anne's* deck and railings.

Maynard stepped across a sea of bodies to Jenkins. "I'm going to search for the girl. If I'm not back in ten minutes, load the men and get out of here."

Jenkins handed him two more pistols. Maynard tucked one in his belt and headed down onto *Queen Anne's* gun deck. An incredible stench was the first thing that struck him. Wet and caustic, it was the same as the smell in his dream.

Constitution's punishing cannon fire had left the space in shambles. Jagged holes, some the size of basketballs, lined both sides of the outer bulkheads. Bodies were everywhere, many only in parts. The corpses were displaying signs of advanced decomposition, the flesh was literally rotting off their bones before his eyes.

One of *Queen Anne's* cannons had exploded, blowing a hole through to the deck below, disintegrating whatever stood near it. Blood and bile were dripping from the overhead and sagging down the bulkheads.

Maynard pulled his tee shirt over his nose and mouth, filled his lungs, and fixed his eyes on the rear of the compartment.

Just like *Constitution,* the captain's quarters were the furthest compartment aft on the main gun deck. He ran to the rear bulkhead, jogged right and followed the short passageway back to the wardroom and kicked the hatch aside.

It was abandoned, but one of the inner stateroom doors was wide open. Holding his pistol in front of him, Maynard peered into Blackbeard's cabin. It was empty, too. As he started to leave, he noticed all the clothes in the wardrobe had been pushed to one side. He ran over and discovered the trap door.

He called Angela's name; there was no answer. No time for caution. He stepped into the wardrobe and started down the ladder.

After a few steps, he twisted and peered into the hold. Movement caught his eye. There was a female scream followed a shot. A bullet grazed his right shoulder. Maynard recoiled, lost his balance and fell to the bottom, the pistol bounced from his hand.

Someone was on top of him in an instant. The pirate pulled a knife and raised it above his head; Maynard reached for his wrists to stop him. Another shot rang out and the pirate slumped forward.

"Hands!" shouted the female voice again.

Maynard rolled the pirate's body off him and jumped to his feet. Before him stood Jeremy Ratliff holding Maynard's pistol, a thin trail of smoke rising from its muzzle.

Angela came out from her hiding place. "Jeremy, why?"

she shrieked.

Maynard reached for his second weapon. Jeremy lowered his arms and closed his eyes.

Angela jumped in front of Ratliff with arms spread. "NO!!"

Maynard lowered his pistol. "I'm Commander Robert Maynard, United States Navy. Now let's get you out of here."

Angela put her hands to her face and started to cry. "Please. someone. Tell me what is going on!"

Hand's body moved and a match flared in his right fist. Trails of sparks shot off in all directions.

"She's gonna blow!" shouted Jeremy. He grabbed Angela by the arm and pulled her toward the ladder. "Come quickly." He started up, dragging Angela behind him. Maynard followed Angela out of the wardrobe and through Blackbeard's cabin.

"This way." Jeremy pushed Angela toward the after-ammunition scuttle.

Angela climbed the narrow stairway, up through the hatch and onto the top deck. She helped Maynard out behind her, and then looked back down the scuttle. "Jeremy, where are you?" she called. Maynard searched, too, but Jeremy was not there.

"Let's move!" Maynard exclaimed. He pulled Angela to her feet and rushed her in the direction of *Constitution.* At the top of his lungs he yelled, "*Queen Anne's* rigged to blow!"

The men closest to him repeated the warning and word spread across the deck. Seamen grabbed their wounded shipmates and hurried toward *Constitution.*

Maynard hoisted Angela onto one of the boarding ladders and shouted, "GO!"

He pulled his cutlass and began cutting grappling lines. His only thoughts now were of protecting his ship and crew. After the explosion, they could come back and finish off any survivors. He ran forward, cutting lines as he went.

Blackbeard leaped out from behind the main mast. "Leaving in such a hurry? Why, we've not yet had a chance to get acquainted. I insist you remain." He lashed out with his cutlass.

Maynard sidestepped and gripped his grandfather's sword with both hands. Using every shred of leverage he could gather, he swung it in an upward arching motion and gashed Blackbeard from the right side of his stomach up through his left shoulder.

Wrought by bullet holes and numerous cutlass wounds, Blackbeard's chest and midsection were glazed in blood. But with his tenacity firmly intact, he recovered and pursued Maynard aft.

Maynard circled around the mizzen to an open expanse of deck. He whirled around, planted his feet wide, and raised his sword at a forty-five degree angle.

A large wave broke over the taffrail behind him, washing his legs out from under him. Maynard fell backwards to the deck; he had to release his cutlass in order to catch himself as he landed. He searched to his right and found his cutlass standing on end— point down in the deck—two arm-lengths away.

Aboard *Constitution,* men were shouting at him. Maynard felt a crushing pressure in the center of his chest, pinning him to the deck. He looked up and standing above him was Blackbeard, grinding a booted foot into his breastbone.

"Surrender while you have the chance or else I will be pissing in a pool of your blood before the sun reaches the nine o'clock sky. Well spoken, young Maynard. Though, on this day, the piss is mine." He raised his cutlass above his head with both hands.

From somewhere behind Blackbeard came a piercing scream, a sound beyond anything Maynard could have believed humanly possible. Maynard caught sight of Chief Warrant Officer Dunbar leaping off *Constitution's* mizzen channel. He wrenched his black powder Colt revolver from its holster, pinched the trigger and fanned the hammer with his left hand. Six bright pulses of white light flashed from the muzzle, all six balls buried into Blackbeard's back.

Dunbar landed on the deck, twirled the Colt back into its holster and reached for his sword.

Blackbeard's mouth gaped open and he staggered to his right. Maynard rolled out from under his foot and dove for his grandfather's cutlass.

"Not this time!" Blackbeard roared. He drew the last pistol from his brace, aimed it at Dunbar, and fired. Dunbar pitched backward onto the deck.

Maynard jumped to his feet and rushed Blackbeard. "Nooooo!!" he shouted.

With both hands firmly on the grip, he slashed the cutlass down with all his might, severing Blackbeard's outstretched arm. He looped the cutlass back around to his right and, with every ounce of strength he could muster, pulled the sword level with his shoulders and aimed at a spot an inch below the base of Blackbeard's lower jaw. The blade met no resistance as it sliced through both flesh and bone.

Blackbeard's mouth drooped open and his detached tongue slithered out across his lower set of teeth, landing with a plop on the deck. His head angled slightly, then slowly slipped from its perch upon his neck. His knees buckled...but before they hit the deck, both head and body vanished in a whooshing vortex of particles and smoke.

Maynard turned to *Constitution* and shouted, "SAIL!"

Constitution's furled sails dropped into place. She separated from *Queen Anne*, heeled over and heaved forward. Maynard rushed to Dunbar, hefted his weight onto his shoulders and sprinted aft, hurtling over the remains of bodies littering his way. With his strength all but exhausted, he continued on sheer determination.

He came to a break in the *Queen Anne's* railing and propelled himself over the side. His momentum was barely enough to bridge the expanding gap between the parting ships. With one arm hooked around Dunbar's leg, he grabbed onto the top of *Constitution's* bulwarks and held on; waves lapped at the soles of his boots.

Just when his hold was about to fail, he felt Dunbar's bulk lifted from his shoulders. The next moment he was in the grasp of a pair of powerful hands. He looked up expecting to see the face of God. What he discovered was the tortured eyes of Chief Warrant Officer Theodore Huber.

Huber hoisted Maynard aboard and then collapsed to the deck, pulling Maynard down on top of him. Maynard attempted to get to his feet but was still trapped in Huber's powerful grasp. He reached out with his hand and patted Huber's chest. His fingers recoiled when they encountered a patch of gristly flesh and warm, sticky blood.

Huber's hold softened. Maynard pushed himself up with his hands and looked his friend in the face. Huber smiled faintly; his eyelids fluttered several times then gently drew closed.

With barely twenty yards separating the two ships, a series of powerful explosions ripped through the belly of the *Queen Anne's* holds. Flames vaulted skyward, timbers splintered in every conceivable direction, burning chunks of wood hailed down upon *Constitution* like a swarm of burning locusts.

Almost instantaneously, the winds ceased. Damage control teams raced to the fire hoses and started spraying *Constitution's* deck and sails to extinguish the flames.

* * *

Midshipman Wood, bloodied and burned, hurried below to

get blankets for the wounded. He heard a stream of profanities pouring from the captain's stateroom.

"Will somebody answer the goddamn phone over there?"

Wood hurried over and snatched the handset. "*USS Constitution*, Midshipman Wood."

"What in the name of thunder is going on over there?" Perkins shouted. "It looks like a goddamn holocaust. Get me whoever is left in command!"

* * *

Amidst all the rubble that was once the flagship of the most notorious marauder in the history of the Atlantic Ocean, nobody seemed to notice the one piece of debris that slowly piloted itself toward the shoreline. When it reached the beach, a little figure scurried from alongside it and sought refuge under a clump of pouting juniper.

He sat on the sand for several moments panting to catch his breath, then reached inside his shirt and produced a zippered plastic bag. Inside was a black, cloth pouch which he opened and pulled out a piece of rolled parchment bound with a strip of bright, red ribbon. He slipped off the ribbon and unfurled the document: a crude map of the Virginia-Carolina coastline. Toward the bottom, on the southeastern tip of Ocracoke Island, lay a jut of land labeled Springer's Point. On Springer's Point, next to a symbol representing a pile of rocks—intermingled with gold, coin-shaped objects—was a pair of cutlasses crossed in an X. Above the X, neatly printed in Blackbeard's own handwriting, resided the words "EDWARD'S POCKETBOOK".

The little figure rolled the treasure map, replaced the ribbon, and carefully returned the parchment to the pouch. He fished around inside the pouch again and pulled out a small brass plate and gazed down at the engraving:

Angela J. Killian
20 South Battery
Charleston, SC

He peered out across the water and smiled a little rat-like grin.

Chapter 34
1000: 28 February 2009

A chilling breeze meandered about the gathering assembled along the docks of Charleston Naval Yard as the change-of-command ceremony wound to a close. The ship's bell rang four times welcoming Commander Curtis Jenkins as the new Commanding Officer of the *USS Constitution*. Jenkins saluted Commander Maynard, saluted the flag, and limped down from the platform.

Old Ironsides graced the waterfront in full dress, her crew standing tall and proud along the pier and atop her rails. A young man, dressed in a midshipman's uniform of the United States Coast Guard, stepped forward and popped Maynard a crisp salute. Maynard smiled and returned the honor.

But before Maynard could walk away, he had to take one last look. Behind him, a Navy band was playing the closing bars of *Anchors Aweigh*. He lingered beside the podium and gazed outward at *Constitution's* regal masts and timbers. The breeze gently rolled across her two open sails as if to bid him farewell.

But he could never really leave, not fully. The two of them now were eternally bound. He was heralded as a national hero; the commander of a crack Navy SEAL boarding party who wrestled

Constitution away from a band of Middle Eastern thugs. But *Constitution* was the real hero; she was the one that made victory possible.

Rumors surfaced about a fierce battle between two large sailing vessels at Ocracoke Inlet, North Carolina and the press was furious about not being allowed to take part in *Constitution's* capture or even provided access to the bandits before they were deported back to Syria. But, as always, in time, that all faded away.

All in all, the Pentagon did an excellent job containing the whole affair. Even the incident with the cruise ship—for which the Navy hired a motion picture crew—was reenacted and passed off as a Hollywood venture. Life always moves on.

Maynard reached up and touched the gold medallion around his neck. By special executive order, he had received the Congressional Medal of Honor.

"You know a place where a guy can get a beer around here?" said someone behind him. "I understand the Navy's buying."

Maynard immediately recognized the Tennessee drawl. He turned and found Chief Warrant Officer Dunbar standing at full attention, dressed in his ceremonial uniform and rendering a salute.

"Cowboy!" Maynard grinned. "I thought they'd shipped you to the Mediterranean."

"Yeah, well." He lifted the Congressional Medal of Honor hanging around his neck. "I got me a three-day pass."

Maynard returned the salute, jumped down off the platform and clasped Dunbar's hand.

"Say, there are a couple scoundrels over there that want to say hello." Dunbar pointed to the rear door of the *Constitution* museum. Assembled there were Maynard's father, Lieutenant Commander Fallon, Jenkins, Senior Chief Petty Officer Hatton and Rear Admiral Perkins. All in their ceremonial dress uniforms.

"You didn't think we could let you say good-bye to the old girl without us, did you?"

Maynard took his wife Barbara by the hand and rushed over to join his friends.

"Careful there, mate," Hatton slurred. "Can't have ya damaging the goodies. What's it gonna' be this time missy, a little bloke or a blokette?"

Barbara gently rested her hand upon her engorged abdomen. "Twins, actually. One of each."

"And a lively pair they shall be too, milady."

Perkins turned to Maynard. "Well now, you're looking rested. Don't tell me one of the Navy's most celebrated superstars has suddenly developed a taste for shore duty. There's a freshly-painted destroyer in Mayport, Florida with your name on it. And when you're finished there, I understand Admiral Hays has a little project you may find of interest."

Maynard looked at Barbara and smiled. "You married a sailor, sweetheart."

"They've got tea and crumpets in the lobby," Perkins said. "But I've got something with a little more horsepower to it back in the office. How about we go inside and knock the chill off? I'll see if Jenkins can find a sarsaparilla for the missis here."

Perkins held the door and everyone filed inside. As he was about to step inside himself, he overheard a comment passed between a pair of officers standing a few feet away.

"What was that, mister?" Perkins demanded.

"I meant no disrespect, Admiral," the officer replied, somewhat embarrassed. "I was just wondering why that uniformed officer walking in front of you is wearing an earring." The officer glanced around. "Why are all these uniformed sailors wearing earrings?"

Perkins grinned, craned his head to the right, and pointed to the small gold hoop piercing his own left earlobe. "Piratus Americana, baby." He laughed out loud. As he turned to enter the museum, he shouted, "HUZZA, OLD IRONSIDES!"

A chorus of Huzzas echoed back and the door closed behind him.

* * *

Roger Killian sat at the kitchen table in his home on South Battery, folded over a cup of forgotten coffee he had taken such pains to prepare. All he could really think about these days was Angela.

She had been restless ever since returning home. During the first month or so she had always looked so tired, rarely sleeping more than a couple hours at a time. Her cultured tan faded, and her flowing hair often strayed in reckless tangles. From time to time, she would lapse into fits of consuming depression. At one point, he and Angela's mother feared she was contemplating taking her life.

After several weeks of steady coaxing, her friends managed to convince her to start going out again. She even returned to the office for an hour or so each day. Life seemed to be returning to normal.

Then gradually, the sexy outfits disappeared again, replaced by faded Levi's and shapeless button-down shirts. Even her beautiful, green eyes seemed to have changed, becoming pale so very distant.

What could have possibly happened to her out on the sea all those days, adrift by herself?

* * *

Angela preferred spending most of her free time alone in her room at her parent's house where she passed the hours lying on her bed or gazing out the windows.

After the Navy's investigation had concluded, she spoke little about her experiences. Her father was urging her to seek professional help.

God knows, she had certainly been through an amazing ordeal. But she didn't need a doctor; at least not yet. Everything was fine. All she really needed was just a little more time.

She often thought of Marc. His case was ruled a disappearance with no signs of foul play. Wherever he was, she hoped that he was happy.

Today she found herself drawn to a park bench down by the Battery, overlooking Charleston Harbor and Fort Sumter. She relaxed and let the salty breeze waft across her face, her thoughts wandered out upon the sea.

Once or twice she had the feeling she was being watched but, each time she looked around, there was nobody there. By now, everybody in Charleston knew who she was; she had grown accustomed to the whispers as she passed. If people wanted to gawk, let them.

The sun slowly sought companionship of the ground in the distance behind her and Angela began to smile. Night would be coming soon...how she loved the nights.

She returned home in time to catch a late dinner with her parents; there was little conversation, as usual. Her father watched as she meticulously ate every bit of her food—he always made it a point to be home now and have dinner with her.

After she finished, Angela excused herself and withdrew back to the sanctity of her room. She closed and locked the door, and quickly got dressed for bed. The dreams would be coming soon.

Her head started gently rolling from side to side and the images began to focus. He was there! She could feel his hot breath upon her skin, kissing the ridgeline of her breast and up the side of her neck.

She caressed his back and shoulders; the warmth of his body sent a wave of euphoria rippling through her once again.

Then, abruptly, he disappeared and a frightening coldness enveloped her. Her thoughts began to spin. *Where did he go?* This had never happened before.

A series of violent images raced through her mind. Swords lunged at her from the darkness. Bursts of cannon fire thundered inside her skull and a booming voice accosted her from behind the shadows:

"I've come to claim that which is mine."

"The nest I forge in blood and guts, shall nurture..."

"Such delightful treasure."

"I'd never do such things to a creature as lovely as you."

"Blackbeard shall live forever."

"Must pay the devil's tax."

"A rare brew of spirit and compassion."

"The nest I forge. Revenge! The nest I forge. Revenge! The nest I forge...THE NEST SHALL NURTURE SATAN'S SEED!"

The decapitated head of Blackbeard appeared before her, masked in blood and sweat. There was a loud clap of thunder. Angela gasped as his lifeless body crashed to the ground. A scream escaped her lips and she flailed upright in bed.

Her father came running down the hall and started pounding on her bedroom door.

"Angela!" he exclaimed. "Is everything alright in there?

319

Unlock this door and let me in!"

"I'm okay, Daddy," Angela said, her heart pounding in her throat. "I'm sorry. It was just a bad dream." She lay back holding her head.

"Are you sure, baby?" asked her father. "Let me sit with you for a few minutes."

"Thanks, Daddy. I'm alright. It was only a bad dream."

"Okay, sweetheart. You call me if you need anything. Won't you?"

"I will, Daddy," she replied. "Please, tell Mom everything's fine. Goodnight."

"Goodnight, sweetheart."

Angela reached over and opened the top drawer on her nightstand, and felt around in the back of it until she came across what she was searching for. She retreated to her pillows, unclenched her fist, and stared at Blackbeard's ruby ring. She slipped it on her thumb and kissed it.

The ruby began to glow like an evil red eye; the gold inlay of a ram's head turned dark and ominous. Slowly, its horns began to straighten and tilt inward. The head transformed into the face of something manlike.

But the shape of the inlay didn't matter, and the glow from the ring quickly faded.

Angela lifted herself out of bed and walked carefully to the bathroom. She pushed open the door and reached for the light switch. Golden rays flooded into the bedroom, stretching an elongated shadow of her pregnant body across the floor.

She bellied up to the sink and gazed at her reflection in the mirror. Her skin no longer possessed that motherly hue it held only hours earlier; the whites of her eyes were rough-sawn and veiny.

"It won't be long now," she told herself softly.

Angela wet a washcloth and gently patted her face, folding

320

it neatly into quarters and placing it on the counter to the right of the sink.

A smiled extended from the corners of her mouth as the warmth ebbed back into the recesses of her abdomen like rivulets of soothing oil. She placed both hands upon her stomach.

"Soon the world will know the real truth of Blackbeard's buried treasure."

-END-

Thank you for perusing the pages of *Operation Darksail*. Our extended *Darksail* family and I hope you found it to be an entertaining read. I would very much welcome your thoughts and comments in a written review on the *Darksail* book page at Amazon.com. Also feel free to also drop me a line at:

www.kphayden.com
Darksail@comcast.net.
On Facebook at
http://www.facebook.com/Darksail.The.Adventure
Smooth seas and following winds...
Kevin P. Hayden

Also look for:
CHEAT MOUNTAIN
By K.P. Hayden
Available now at Amazon.com

Author: Kevin P. Hayden (Gonzo) served aboard *USS Spruance* DD-963 (The Silent Warrior) from July 5, 1979 through September 12, 1982. He and his shipmates, many of whom you have now met—Ivan Dunbar, Jeff Huber, Jimmy Wright, Jack Lawrence, James "Perky" Perks, Tom Wolf, Jeff Olson, Steve Lee—scratched the mighty blue together from the Caribbean to the Indian Ocean projecting the superiority of the United States Navy. *Spruance* was the first in class of a new breed of swift, marine gas turbine warship, and one of the last of her class to be decommissioned (March 23, 2005) providing the people of the United States of America nearly thirty years of dedicated naval service. Though her name lives on in a magnificent new *USS Spruance* DDG-111, the original *USS Spruance* now lay at the bottom of the Atlantic Ocean, approximately 300-miles off the Virginia Capes, sunk in December of 2006 by a battery of US Navy Harpoon missiles during Operation Sinkex. Yet, to those of us who still harbor fondness in our hearts for the old girl, The *USS Raymond A. Spruance DD-963* shall forever remain *haze gray and underway.*

The heavens exploded in a spectacular display of twisting blue and white tridents of lightning, spawning towering walls of water; releasing the full power of a hellish fury returned from days long past...a hellish fury bent on revenge. Commander Robert Maynard and a select crew of US Navy and Marine Corps warriors must find and destroy it before it accomplishes what it was sent to do. DARKSAIL: a contemporary swashbuckling adventure.

*Rear Cover: Starboard side gunnery of the **USS Constitution** pier side at the Charlestown Navy Yards Boston, MA (Darksail Media 2012)*

www.ingramcontent.com/pod-product-compliance
Lightning Source LLC
Chambersburg PA
CBHW062028170626
46813CB00001B/327